Stephen Ridenour was still having nightmares...

The road home stretched endlessly. Stephen's knees shook. His eyes blurred.

He was going to be late. Mama would be mad...

A loud honk. He stumbled up the rattled bank. A car slowed and stopped.

"You look very tired. What's your name?"

"Zivon Stefano—" he had to pause for a breath "—vich Ryevanishov, sir."

The man turned to the others in the car. Laughter. Zivon frowned, wishing they would leave.

"You're a long way from home, Zivon Stefanovich. Would you like a ride?"

He climed into the backseat. The man beside him laughed—a nice laugh—and he was smiling. Zivon smiled back and ducked his head as they left the road and whooshed across the field. The laughter from the back took a different note. The man beside him said something to the driver and the car stopped.

Outside were bushes and tall grass. He didn't know where they were, but he knew it wasn't home.

"What's the matter, Zivon Stefanovich?"

Stephen felt the man's hot breath on his neck...

ALSO BY JANE S. FANCHER

GROUNDTIES
UPLINK

Published by
WARNER BOOKS

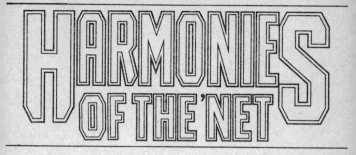

HARMONIES
OF THE 'NET

BY JANE S. FANCHER

WARNER BOOKS

A Time Warner Company

WARNER BOOKS EDITION

Copyright © 1992 by Jane S. Fancher
All rights reserved.

Questar is a registered trademark of Warner Books, Inc.

Cover design by Don Puckey
Cover illustration by Barclay Shaw
Cover lettering by Ron Zinn

Warner Books, Inc.
1271 Avenue of the Americas
New York, NY 10020

W A Time Warner Company

Printed in the United States of America

First Printing: November, 1992

10 9 8 7 6 5 4 3 2 1

Ever since my first attempt at plotting turned from a simple adventure story into *Groundties*, *UpLink*, and *Harmonies of the 'Net*, it seemed to be tempting fate to dedicate it before all three parts were done. Well, here's the last, and it even ended up basically where I intended—just 250,000 words later than anticipated—so I guess it's safe now to thank those who made it possible.

To Brian, for giving me the time I needed to learn.

To Barclay, for working so hard to give me the Look I wanted.

And especially to Carolyn, for suggesting I try writing in the first place, then asking enough questions to get me out alive . . .

. . . and to the Bannik in the upstairs shower for having all the right answers.

I

i

"Stephen? Stephen Ridenour, is that you?"

Wesley dodged the long strands whipping water drops in his face, swore, grabbed a slippery fistful, and yanked.

"Siddown," he grumbled, his irritation vacillating between her indecent display of energy and the annoying object of her query. "It's *not* Stephen. *Can't* be. Shuttle's not even due in for another hour."

Anevai Tyeewapi, on the root end of those strands, ignored him (as usual), her intent scan of the steam-enshrouded shoreline pulling the offending locks slowly from his fingers. Beyond the sweep of hair, her bare rump described a tempting, just-within-reach curve.

With a firm reminder to his glands exactly who that curve belonged to, Wesley said: "*Relax*, I tell you."

"I *am* relaxed." That, as the muscles in her rump tightened and her back stretched, seeking a one-inch-greater perspective on the hotspring's forested border.

Within Jonathan Wesley Smith's own exquisitely unique

morality, Anevai Tyeewapi's ass might be off limits in one sense. In another...

He swatted the curve. Hard. "Siddown!"

She squawked something indelicate, and sat.

It was entirely possible the mysteries of fluid dynamics would forever elude him. Certainly what empowered a slender, female-type body to displace such a huge volume of water was beyond today's comprehension. But the scowling visage facing him as the tidal wave retreated suggested the laws of thermodynamics entered the equation somewhere.

"What the hell's *your* problem?" he demanded.

The scowl faded. She sighed and settled into the embrace of water-polished rock. "I'm just worried about him," she said, a candor which forced him to admit reluctantly:

"Yeah, brat, so am—"

A second wave: her flattened hand slapping the water aimlessly. He swore again, and grabbed her wrist, while blinking his eyes clear of water.

A third flooding, as her captured hand fist-squirted—

"Gotcha," she pointed out.

—not so aimlessly this time.

He caught a drip on his tongue. "So you did." He released her and brushed hair, slick with water and sweat, back from his face. "But Stephen Ridenour's a big boy. Cantrell said he put in for leave just like one of her crew." He slouched lower, finding a conveniently placed jet for the persistent ache between his shoulder blades. Too little sleep. Too damn many hours at the keyboard. Too damn much worry about a thankless—"Todacious scum sent me a lousy message. All we've been through and ever since he left—a whole goddamn *week*—silence. Then, a lousy message on a lousy computer with a lousy ETA... Well, I had other plans, didn't I?"

She snorted. "Like soaking your rear end in a hot spring, 1000k from SciComp? Not exactly unalterable, Smith."

"Promised you I'd visit." He closed his eyes on the mist-covered pool—and her accusing glare. "Keep my promises, I do."

"I *meant* after Stephen arrived, as you damnwell know. —Can't fool me, Smith. You're pissed because he arranged his return trip all by his lonesome—didn't have to ask your help once."

He glared back at her. "And you 'damnwell know' he didn't 'arrange' anything. I had Cantrell convinced to send him back down *before* he left. Had it all planned, didn't I? Operated on three hours a night for days getting the shit cleared out of my queue so we could party once *Dr.* McKenna released him from hospital. But did he bother to ask? *No–o–o.* Did he even bother to ask could I get time off? Ditto. I rest my case." He shrugged. "I left a message in his rooms at the 'Condos. Let him contact me—if he's so inclined."

"Left a message—a *handwritten* note to a CodeHead, for the gods' sakes—in a room he's been in a handful of times. A room he might not consider available to him, now he's no longer a registered transferee. A room for which he no longer has a keycard. Real friendly, Smith."

Conscience twinged.

"Of course, he might not be coming to see you at all," Anevai continued airily. "He knows so many people on HuteNamid, after all."

"He knows you," Wesley pointed out in self-defense. "And *you're* his official watchdog."

"Was, Smith. And *I* didn't know he was coming! Besides, Dad's leaving for *Cetacean* today and didn't want me home alone."

"Why not? You're a big girl."

She flipped a careless hand through the water. "I haven't been feeling real terrific lately. He thought I should be near the grans, with both him and Mom upstairs. Anyway, I *assumed* that when Stephen *did* arrive, you would want some time alone with him to do guy-things, or parade him around your programming buddies in SciComp and do 'NetHead-things. I certainly didn't expect you'd be here, three hours' express from anywhere."

"He can find me."

"You *should* have met him at the spaceport." Sinking to her ears in the bubbling water, she cast a searching look up at him. "I don't understand why you're acting like this. I thought at first it was a joke—that you'd go back to get him. But you're not going, are you? Why? I thought you liked Stephen."

He shrugged, unable to give her the easy reassurance she sought. Anevai was a good kid, and damned bright. But she was Recon—an Ethnic Reconstructionist in the purest sense— planet-bound and thoroughly infected with all her AmerInd ancestors' poetic philosophies and openhanded lifestyles. She couldn't possibly understand how every time he laid eyes on Stephen Ridenour, he was fighting memories of spacer-academy life, and of colleagues he'd lost to a gilded trap he himself had—narrowly—escaped.

To her eyes, Stephen Ridenour was an exceedingly attractive young man of near-heroic stature. A fellow Reconstructionist (never mind he hailed from a totally different planet and ethnic background) who had defied the Separatist bigots and graduated from a spacer academy in that most esoteric of spacer disciplines: NSpace Communication Network Programming Technologies. And in proper heroic style, defying the evil machinations of those same bigoted slime, he'd exited that experience at the head of his class, with the attention of all the Important People...

...and (even the little witch blowing bubbles next to him would have to admit) more than a little insane.

Of course some people (like said bubble-blowing witch) would insist it went with the territory—that *all* 'NetTechs were crazy. Not far from the truth, he supposed, if sanity required a mind stuck in RealTime and RealSpace logic. NSpace was *so* much more interesting.

Crazy, sure. Certifiable—that was something else.

Last time downworld, the academy-trained bit-brain had

practically killed himself several times over, him and his damned drugs. Ran himself on the edge, kept himself going with drugs that caused him to make dangerously crackpot decisions . . .

Pity. Ridenour was a clever lad, even so. What he might have been . . .

But Stephen was doing his best to dry up—so he said. Stephen had also had a job to do which required Wesley Smith's cooperation. He'd believed that job, for all intents and purposes, complete, but if Ridenour believed differently . . . if that promise had been given simply to mollify him, and if the child-like appeal the kid could project seemingly at will had cut through his better sense . . .

All he'd wanted was a break before having to deal with any of it.

He shook his head, which cleared nothing except the water from his ears. "He is, without question, the schitziest thing I've ever run across."

"Would you like him half so much if he weren't?" she asked seriously.

"That's why it bothers me," he replied, matching her tone for tone, and slipped down into the water, where ingenious plumbing invisibly enhanced the hot spring's natural therapeutic ability, swirling tension downstream.

Tension he damnwell didn't deserve. Exhaustion, sore muscles— those he'd earned fair and square. The tension—that was Ridenour's doing.

Wesley Smith was thinking clearly for the first time since he'd met the elegant academy-clone, and a return to that confused mental state was not on his agenda. Tonight he'd reserved for Metzky—she'd been inhumanly patient for days— and a thorough, no-holds-barred debauch. Now, because of Ridenour's sudden, unalterable decision, she'd probably dump him permanently.

Make that semipermanently, he mentally revised his self-pity. Metzky liked presents too much for any permanent rift.

Black hair drifted in front of his nose. He poked a finger up through the middle, and the long strands swirled and twisted in the current like living creatures, victims of those elusive mysteries of fluid mechanics. Fascinating.

Maybe that was his problem. Maybe he liked things that eluded him . . . "You said you and Stephen made love—"

"I didn't say that."

"Did so."

"We didn't make love, Wes. We had sex."

"Picky, picky. Just because *you* had to do a little work—"

"You've got it all wrong, Wes. It was *all* for me. Stephen treats it like—currency. He thought he owed me. But if you want my advice—"

"I don't. Owed you for what?"

"Being nice. Listening to him—about the academy—his folks—and . . . other stuff."

"Was it good? Was *he* good?"

"Wesley!"

"Well, was he?"

"You're awful! What difference could it possibly make?"

"Want to know what I have to look forward to. You did nothing but chat; think what he owes *me* after all I've—"

Hot water filled his nose and mouth as an avenging water sprite pushed him under.

Clouds.

Clouds, clouds, and more clouds.

Admiral Cantrell said: GravityWell physics—think about it.

Wesley said: Planet fart, and yawned.

Anevai said: Rainbow fell to the earth to nourish the crops, and Earth Mother breathed his essence back to the sky, making the clouds, completing his Cycle.

Rain happened out of clouds, therefore they must contain water, perhaps similar to the 'clouds' in the gym steamrooms;

but steamrooms were *hot*, and it should be cold out there, colder than on the surface, he understood that much of planetary physics. Certainly colder than the steamrooms. Beyond that, the logic became...

...irrelevant, Stephen decided, leaning his cheek against the shuttle's cool window and focusing on nothing-in-particular within that wealth of plush whiteness.

Perhaps all the cause and effect which had ruled every thought for years became irrelevant to someone on vaction. He didn't know, never having had a vacation before, but Dr. McKenna had said: Rest. Heal. No work. No worry. R&R.

Sounded like a vacation to him.

The shuttle dropped between cloud layers and he leaned eagerly toward his first overview of the planet below.

Not, he thought wryly, that it was his first *chance* at the sight, but the first time down, the perspectives had incited severe inner-ear...disagreements, and the second...between storm-tossed darkness and dodging lightning, he'd somehow overlooked a landmark or two. This time—

Anticipation dissolved.

—he didn't recognize a thing. It was all...flat.

"Dr. Ridenour?" A man leaned over the forward seat, teal-blue *Cetacean* uniform, tanned face, a cup in one hand, a plate of sandwiches in the other. "Captain says smooth as silk to touchdown, so food's happening. Tea-drinker, right? Party's on in the rear. Welcome to join us."

Stephen accepted the tea with gratitude, but passed on the sandwich, declining also the invitation to the rowdiness developing in the rear of the cabin. While the crowd of *Cetacean* crewmembers on leave and HuteNamid colonials returning home from a visit to the orbiting ship was friendlier than most crushes he'd endured, he preferred to party with people whose names he knew.

He sipped the tea and turned back to the window.

Flat, indeed. Flat, green, and (he dialed up the viewport

magnification) grassy: except for the color, far more 'homelike' for him than the mountains he so eagerly awaited.

Rostov might have looked like that in certain seasons. He remembered brief periods when the hills rolled green, in between bouts of freezing sleet and drought; Rostov's terraformed weather patterns had been uncertain at best. But in his final memory, an overview through a similar viewport, his receding homeworld had been brown and withered, like some dying weed, an ecosystem altered to compromise with human needs . . .

Vastly different from this HuteNamid, whose blue, oxy-rich skies and ready-to-eat vegetation welcomed humanity.

Those sometimes nightmarish Rostov memories had receded to haunting dreams in his academy years. Coming here had resurrected them in full, but the two most responsible for that resurrection, Anevai Tyeewapi and Wesley Smith, had also helped lay them to rest.

Perhaps that was the reason for this unaccustomed contentment—

—that and the promising dark irregularity on the hazy horizon.

"Bingo." Chet Hamilton grinned at his computer monitor. "I've got you now." He transferred the grin to his commanding officer, who was leaning over his shoulder, resting her elbows on the back of his chair. "Does this mean I get to keep my job?"

"Your chances just increased," Loren Cantrell responded absently, her dark eyes narrowing, taking in the energy readings and probability profiles of the system disturbance which had forced him to roust her out of bed three hours early. Beyond her, in the security communications' small lounge, the handful of advisors she'd called in hovered over a large plateful of donuts. "Noisy sucker, isn't it?" Her narrow-eyed gaze flickered to him and back to the screen. "You've ID'd the profile?"

His nod caught her chin. "Sorry, boss-lady. —Yeah. Comp

finally sorted the probability flux. It's one of those experimental SWI Stingrays.''

"*Stingray?*" Dora Partain joined them at the boards, gulping coffee, and licking icing off her fingers. *Cetacean's* ordinarily tongue-tied chief pilot sighed, and in a voice of sheer lust: "I got to fly one of those in the sims during the Vandereaux layover. I thought I'd died and gone to heaven."

Cantrell chuckled. "Nice machine, is it?"

A second, deeper sigh. "There's almost room to sit—the rest is engine, and oh, can they move." She studied the screens, and chuckled. "Conservative suckers: only to SH7, if they're on standard decel."

Laughter from TJ Briggs' self-appointed guard station (he was, after all, Cantrell's Security chief) beside the donut box. "Wouldn't you overshoot a tad if you hadn't comped a free-crossing since basic? My guess is their navigator is still in shock."

"With that sweet thing," Partain said, "they'd damnwell *better* comp. Highly experimental *and* hot. I sure wouldn't trust it to a standard beam."

So, (Chet smiled at his boards) Cantrell had infected another with her own peculiar brand of adrenaline rush. Time was, Dora Partain wouldn't have taken that stance. But Cantrell had learned navigation from the Old-timers, rocket jockeys who'd never heard of the 'Net until they were retirement age, and never did learn to trust its auto-cross guidance beams. Her own crew never knew which to log with the system controller—the 'Net signal or their own crossing coordinates—until the last minute.

Cantrell's word on it was, *she* trusted the 'Net, she just didn't trust a navigator who did. Besides, (so she said) signal crossings were boring.

TJ's point was well taken, however. The Etu system's ComNet Link had been shut down for over two weeks, making a beamed crossing physically impossible. Regardless how the

Stingray had begun its crossing, it had finished under the crew's instruction.

Bad enough entering crossover knowing you were on your own, another to discover it after you'd committed. Then, you'd better pray those coordinates you might have remembered to log and properly copy into your ship's databank were right. If not, you'd be NSpaced for a hell of a long time.

If that ship had been in-transit when Cantrell ordered the local shutdown, the crew might very well be sincerely pissed. Could be the reason for their bordering-on-illegal com silence.

Cantrell asked: "Whose is it?"

"That baby?" Partain's answer held a hint of regret: "One of the big three. There're only a handful. *Way* too energy hungry for mere mortal use."

Big three: Council, Security, or 'NetAT.

"Out of Vandereaux?"

"Have to be."

"How many stages?"

"From Vandereaux? —Two. Maybe even one."

One shot crossing? Made the mind a shade uneasy.

But Cantrell evidenced no such astonishment. Cantrell asked simply:

"Docking capabilities?"

"Main deck disconnect. No AG—they'll be walking funny when they come aboard."

No artificial gravity—too small to spin. Another potentially mood-altering circumstance. One Chet could personally understand. His stomach did not take kindly to floating.

"Orbit to ground?"

"Glorified emergency pods."

"Comfy. —Crew?"

"Solo, if need be: top-o'-th'-line comp interface. Dozen will handle manuals easy—two, if they're sincerely into redundancy. Carries thirty, max. Made for speed, admiral."

"Lot of energy to get a handful of people here. —They still silent, Chet?"

He nodded.

"Let's send them a wake-up call. They may be official with a capital O, but the least they can be is polite."

"Will do, admiral."

"What's the delay?"

He shrugged. "Fourteen, give or take—if they're doing a standard decel. Can comp you an exact, once comp's completes its analysis."

"Close enough. I think we have time for a cuppa."

"What the hell, splurge: have breakfast."

"We'll mail you a flapjack."

"Now *that's* a commanding officer."

"For that, we'll include OJ. —Teej, let's go eat."

ii

Time was, the jagged crags had terrified him, as had the deep rift gouging the heavily forested terrain below. But Stephen understood them now. Understood them by a means he didn't pretend to comprehend, and to a depth he was reluctant to admit to anyone.

He'd shared his mind once, with the help of an alien machine buried in the mountains below. Shared it with something (or some*one*) who knew this planet to its—soul. Real experience or imaginary, neither held the power to frighten him any longer. Not the machine-entity. Not the planet.

And not Nayati Hatawa, for all the Recon indigene had nearly killed him trying to force that linkage. Nayati, too, he understood, and empathized with in a way which might confuse certain people.

And those same people might not appreciate knowing that his primary purpose in returning to HuteNamid was *not* to see them.

The shuttle swooped lower. Landmarks took shape: natural rock bridges, some of which spanned the rift itself, animal-shaped outcrops . . . and beyond them, the Recon capital city, Tunica, emerged from the riverside landscape, expanded into the towers of the Indigene Corps administrative offices. Somewhere within those elegant highrises, Sakiimagan Tyeewapi, the Recon governor (and Anevai's father), had a suite of offices. Offices he'd never seen. His downworld contacts had limited him to . . .

Judging direction from those towers, he searched the rift-rim for the Science Complex, which housed Wesley's office and Paul Corlaney's labs; the researcher condominiums, whose bevelled-glass atrium dome sparkled rainbow colors even at this distance; and beyond that, across a grassy meadow and abutting dense forest—

Cloud-shadow darkened the window, and for an instant, his own face gazed back at him.

—the barn. Anevai had taken him there, the day they'd met. Their friendship had started (and nearly ended) in that dust-filled building. Nayati Hatawa's first attack had come there. His second had come . . .

Like a beacon, Stephen could point to the spot deep within the snow-covered volcanic peak to the north, where the Cocheta machine lay buried. He had no conscious recollection of the Library's geographic position—had travelled to and from the cavelike entrances at night, walked unlit tunnels to the massive Library Vault itself—but part of the Other's legacy was that internal knowledge of what was.

He shivered the feeling away and deBooted the memory. A sane explanation for what he'd experienced in the tunnels—and reexperienced nightly ever since—existed; and vacations meant free time to explore *his* interests—and *his* interests included what that sane explanation was.

Nayati Hatawa had forced that interface with the Cocheta Other. Nayati Hatawa also knew those tunnels, had experienced the Other—or something similar—himself, and Nayati Hatawa was going to help him learn to control the dreams—or make them go away altogether.

As soon as Stephen Ridenour could find his outlawed, unwilling guide.

The shuttle slid onto the runway, smooth as an interstation bubblecar into a decel track, and a purposeful flurry erupted throughout the cabin as the other passengers, with total disregard of the standard *Please remain seated* signs, prepared to disembark. By the time they coasted to a stop beside the terminal, the center section was vacant, the passengers crowding to one of the two exits.

Stephen experienced no such sense of urgency. Lethargic contentment had enveloped him again, and he waited for the press to clear, searching the packed tarmac below for Wesley's sun-bleached mop—or, if Wesley couldn't make it, Anevai's sleek black braid. But as the wave of exiting passengers intercepted the mass, and individual identity was lost in a sea of grins and wild gesticulations, contentment vanished. Suddenly, nothing seemed quite as important as one of those welcomes aimed at him. He grabbed his duffel from the overhead and slipped into the human stream.

Outside the filter of the shuttle's protective shields, sunlight reflected off the tarmac and made blinding glares of the terminal windows. Stephen paused at the top of the steps, letting the other passengers brush past, while his pupils sought relief in the gentle greys and greens of the mountains beyond.

And more than relief. For that moment, it was as if the alien Other stirred a different sense within him: warmth, security, a homecoming like a lost child seeing his parents.

Planetary progwuzzles, he silently chided himself, and searched the rapidly dispersing crowd for any—unclaimed personages.

Nothing. No one. No Wesley. No Anevai. Only a handful of maintenance crew hustling about the shuttle, prepping for the return flight.

Disappointment threatened, but he denied it any validity. After all, he hadn't been able to give them much warning. Dr. McKenna had given him an early release, and he'd escaped before she could change her mind, or think of another test to run, his own needs urging him back to the planet ASAP.

He shrugged the duffel's shoulder strap into place and skimmed down the steps to follow the crowd through the terminal doors, up an escalator to the main corridor, down which and to the right, as he remembered it, was a bubblecar transport system. He'd go to the Science Complex. See if the secretary there had any messages, and if not—

"Ridenour! Hey, man, wait up!"

Who? . . . Almost-familiar voice, long-limbed, rather gawky figure running toward him across the terrazzo floor: "Nigan?"

Nigan Wakiza skidded to a halt beside him, grabbed his hand and started pumping.

"What are you doing here?" he asked, half-hoping this friend of Anevai's was there to meet him. Then, beyond Nigan's shoulder, he saw Governor Tyeewapi and realized: "You're going back to *Cetacean* with the shuttle?" He laughed at Nigan's brain-jostling nod, reclaimed his hand to extend it to Anevai's father. "Hello, sir."

"Dr. Ridenour." The fingers that closed around his were, like the man himself, lean and large-boned: impressive in sheer size, intimidating in their obviously controlled strength. "We had no idea you were coming down. I'm surprised Anevai failed to mention it. Is someone meeting you? Dr. Smith, perhaps?"

Stephen glanced down the corridor, still half-expecting Wesley to show. "Evidently not."

"Don't worry," Nigan assured him. "He'll get here, once he's upheld his image." Then, to Sakiimagan: "C'mon, sir. Don't want them to go without us."

Sakiimagan Tyeewapi's black eyes crinkled at the corners. "Forgive Nigan, doctor. He's—excited. This is his first trip up. He's convinced his services would prove useful to Hononomii's recovery."

The governor's reference triggered an unexpected chill. He'd never met the man whose incendiary actions and subsequent arrest had mandated his own initial downworld venture, but Hononomii Tyeewapi's fate had grown increasingly linked to his own. Another victim of Nayati's Cocheta—albeit a willing one—as an indirect result of that linkage, the governor's son now lay semicomatose in the *Cetacean* sickbay.

He controlled a shiver. "How is your son doing, sir? —if I'm allowed to ask."

"Who has more right, Dr. Ridenour?—To my knowledge, Hono's condition is still improving. My wife has requested I join her aboard the ship. They're simulating Nayati's voice through the ship's computer. Cholena indicated they were having some success, but I suspect she needs my help with the translations. Nayati speaks Athabascan as if he were born to it. My wife . . ." Patient, gentle humor touched his deep tones. ". . . is hardly fluent."

"Hononomii isn't much better," Nigan muttered, criticism that triggered a frown from the governor, who said, in a voice from which any hint of gentleness or humor had vanished:

"Nigan *thought* he might prove useful, since he was often present at the sessions and claims to know specific terminology Nayati used." The frown deepened. "But that *usefulness* is subject to reconsideration at any given moment."

Nigan shifted his weight and set his jaw firmly, his eyes dropping to the floor. Stephen felt some sympathy. Nigan was not, after all, responsible for Hononomii Tyeewapi's condition. Neither had Nigan personally experienced Nayati's Cocheta linkage.

He, on the other hand . . . "I hadn't considered that possibility. Perhaps I ought to return with you—"

"Not at all," Tyeewapi said. "Anevai and Nigan consulted. Evidently, Nayati's tactics with you were . . . unique."

"Of course. —She was there . . ." A dizzying shift from smooth walls and marble floors to high-ceilinged caves, couches, rusalka-lit, gravity-defying stone formations, and Nayati's voice ordering him to *Fly with his Cocheta* . . . as the helmet eclipsed the stone. "B–besides . . ." He forced his way past the blackness, back to airport-terminal normalcy. "His goals were d–dif—"

"Dr. Ridenour," Tyeewapi interrupted him, "if I could undo what my nephew did . . ."

Stephen stilled the humiliating tremors with the reminder that he'd experienced nothing more threatening than those memory flashes—so far—and said, with determined sincerity: "Don't even think about it, governor. No lasting harm done. And potentially a great deal of good."

"I wish we could be certain of that."

"It got you and the admiral working together, didn't it? Just get your son well and home, sir. That's the best—for everyone."

The shuttle pilot's amplified voice announced the final boarding call for *Cetacean*-bound passengers. Tyeewapi extended his hand again. "Goodbye, doctor. If Wesley doesn't arrive soon, ring Paul Corlaney. He should know where his people are. Failing that, Anevai has gone to stay with her grandparents in my absence. Go to her."

"Thank you, sir, but I'll be fine." Stephen grasped the strong hand for an instant before Tyeewapi released him and clasped him higher, wrist to wrist.

"Be patient" Tyeewapi urged. "Wesley will come . . ."

"Don't count on it, Ridenour," Nigan said, urging Tyeewapi toward the escalator. "This is the Wesser you're talking about. Time and appointments . . . he doesn't deal well with them. —C'mon, Gov. Let's *go*."

Tyeewapi laughed at Nigan's eager irreverence, and let himself be pushed onto the escalator. Stephen waved until they disappeared down the stairwell, then, having no set time to *be* anywhere, settled into a chair near the window to watch the liftoff from this new vantage.

Before long, the sleek vehicle swept down the runway and off the ground in a near-vertical climb. The down-pattern ground-beam caught the rear shield and within seconds, the shuttle had accelerated beyond the clouds and out of sight.

Amazing. No wonder that secondary boost had the kick of a mistimed highbar release.

Which reminded him of something else this vacation must include. Rest was one thing; atrophy was something else entirely. SciCorps' extensive complex *must* contain a gym somewhere. But first things . . .

A trip to the freight desk to ID his luggage and fill out a delivery release form—he'd notify them where to send it when *he* knew—a fruitless call to Wesley's office, and an equally nonproductive check of the SciCorps Bulletin Board.

He should call Paul Corlaney right now, as the governor had suggested. Paul Corlaney *was* the head of the local Science Corps research units, so it *was* technically Corlaney's responsibility to see to visiting researchers . . .

He'd rather die first.

Besides, he could afford to wait for Wesley—for a while. And if Wesley didn't show—well, he'd deal with that when the time came.

His focus drifted groundward to the mountains, experiencing for the third time that inner sense of . . .

. . . homecoming. How thoroughly silly. He'd been born on a planet, yes, but not this one; his only 'home' for years had been a station floating among rarely seen stars.

He slumped into the seat, resting his head against the padded back and letting his eyes drift shut. As Nigan had pointed out, Wesley's sense of time was—existential, at best. He could appreciate that. Might even choose to emulate it . . . while on this vacation. You could do that on a world where the whims of nature rather than the vibrations of a string regulated time.

Warmth on his face coming and going with the light varying behind closed lids. On the inside: images of clouds.

Clouds, clouds, and more . . .

"What do you mean, he was on the early shuttle?" Lexi Fonteccio stared across the breakfast table at her superior,

unable to believe she'd heard correctly. "Dammitall, I *told* her—"

"*You* don't *tell* Cantrell anything," TJ said, in rare reprimand. "You're an advisor. —A junior one at that."

A reprimand she damnwell didn't deserve. "Her *Recon* advisor, and last time I looked, Stephen was still Recon. If she's not going to listen, why the hell should I—"

TJ frowned. "That's enough, Fonteccio!"

She bit her tongue.

TJ's watch beeped.

"Damn," he said, "I've got to go—meeting with Cantrell and Hamilton. Finish your breakfast and get your head together. We'll discuss this later."

He stood to leave.

"One more thing—the *reason* I mentioned the shuttle in the first place. Cantrell's ordered a fast turnaround. Tyeewapi will be here—" He consulted his watch again. "—in a little over an hour. You're to meet him and show him to his son's therapy session. Cantrell and I will go directly from this meeting to the observation room."

Abrupt dismissal. Cool and impersonal. Not a word about the subject of said meeting. Not a word about an informal debriefing on said meeting later. No mention either of the implied insult to a local dignitary. After all, Sakiimagan Tyeewapi was only Recon.

"Yessir," she acknowledged, rigidly proper, control TJ ignored, if he even noticed it. He hurried from the messhall, leaving her alone with coffee gone tepid and eggs gone petrified. She pushed the coffee away, and smashed the eggs into the plate with her fork, wondering where everything could have gone so wrong.

Alexis Fonteccio had grown accustomed to a position of some trust in Admiral Cantrell's service. Seven years ago, chance had thrown her (a Venezia Recon and involved to her eyeballs in the reactionary movement Cantrell had come insystem to rout) into that service; her admiration for Cantrell, her hard work and an instinctual knack for Recon psychology had kept her there; and now, in a matter of days, *some*thing—some action of hers, an unconscious statement or opinion—or some*one* . . . had compromised that trust.

Or perhaps not so unconscious.

She remembered gemstone eyes glowing desperation in the hand-held spotlights, an exhausted plea, soft-spoken, yet echoing eerily in the alien tunnels . . . *Admiral, I must go back with you* . . .

Cantrell had ignored Stephen's petition; had ordered Lexi to put him in restraints if necessary and haul him back to SciComp. Lexi had defied those direct orders and let him follow them back into the Library tunnels, an act of independence, which, she now suspected, had cost her that hard-earned trust.

But—dammitall—Cantrell claimed to value autonomous action. Claimed she wanted thinkers, not blind followers, under her command. There'd been no overt chastisement—how could there have been when Stephen had saved everyone's hide? —only a . . . chill when she entered the room. A cessation of conversation, an exclusion she'd not felt before—not on this ship, at any rate.

She wished she could believe it was her own hypersensitivity, but this—

Cantrell had asked her opinion on Stephen's leave request; Lexi had strongly advised against it, based on her observations of Stephen with the downworld IndiCorps and the researchers— Smith in particular. Cantrell had professed understanding, had *expressed* agreement. But this morning, according to TJ, Stephen had slipped out on the red-eye shuttle a full day before his scheduled release from sickbay, a feat he could only have accomplished with Cantrell's express permission.

Which meant Lexi Fonteccio's opinion no longer meant a thing to Loren Cantrell.

And now, TJ left for a meeting with Cantrell and Chet without a word to his so-called partner regarding the subject of said meeting, without a word of explanation why she'd been shut out.

Lexi swept up the dishes, tossed them in the recycler, and headed for her quarters. Since her—services—were evidently no longer required, maybe she could get some long-overdue study in: there was still a great deal about the ComNet Alliance she didn't know. . . .

Even more she didn't understand . . .

And maybe she'd just take a nap.

The tray rolled smoothly into the incubator, the clear door slid shut, the green light blinked, indicating a successful seal, and Paul Corlaney moved on to the next section, taking notes as he went.

If he lived a thousand years, the stubborn tenacity of life would never cease to amaze him. Nothing should *live* at these temperatures, let alone thrive.

The cultures were (thank all Anevai's gods plus a few he'd picked up elsewhere) developing nicely, despite the neglect of recent (damn Wesley's disruptive delusions of deityhood) interruptions.

Humbling, really, to know how replaceable a father's TLC was. A few gears, a refrigeration unit, an AI monitor—hell, old Pop could just go on an extended coffee break, if he were so inclined.

Which he wasn't—*especially* after all the 'recent interruptions.'

Of course, some interruptions (he smiled into the facemask at the thought of Loren Cantrell and long-overdue reconciliations) had been welcome. Others (he swallowed the smile, warming and rehydrating frozen teeth as Stephen Ridenour's too-pretty features displaced Cantrell's mature elegance in his mind's eye) had been less so.

The outer phone rang: a call from Someone too Significant for Thiery to put off. Paul swore softly, and hurried from the incubator, shedding gloves and mask as warm air and amplified voices flooded the airlock.

"Ya'at'eeh, Paul."

"Sakiimagan?" he answered into the air. "I thought you were headed upstairs."

"I'm calling from the shuttle."

Paul grunted, listening with half an ear, expanding his notes before he lost the logic train completely. A name registered. Combined with other bits. "What about Ridenour?" he asked, interrupting the governor.

"You haven't been listening, have you, Paul?" Said with a full complement of patient-AmerInd resignation.

"Can you blame me?" One hated to sound self-pitying, but *dammitall*— "First solid working day I've had in weeks . . . hell, the only reason *your* call got through was because I hadn't the sense to take you off the exemption list. I thought you were safely occupied with Hono. So what about Ridenour?"

"He was at the spaceport," Sakiimagan repeated patiently. *"He was waiting for Wesley Smith to meet him."*

"Fat chance of that."

"Obviously. I got the impression he was somewhat at a loss, so I advised him to contact you if he found himself stranded."

"Gee, thanks. Damned kid makes me feel like a—"

"Paul, he's a very polite young man, who holds you in great esteem. I don't find his reluctance to impose at all unusual and certainly no reason to make him feel unwanted."

"You're saying it's better he should disrupt *my* life than those who would welcome him with open arms? What about Anevai?"

"Ridenour is SciCorps."

"Which makes him *my* responsibility. I know. I—"

"Only if Wesley doesn't show."

He swallowed a retort. Sometimes Sakiimagan forgot he'd come to HuteNamid to escape the admin duties awaiting him elsewhere—

"You might contact Anevai. I don't believe she's aware he's coming. She said nothing. But she's gone to Acoma—and that's

a long ride from the spaceport, Paul, and she's still not well, so don't you ask her to make it, hear me?''

"Yeah, yeah, I hear you." He just didn't like what he was hearing. "Is Anevai any better?"

"Worse, if anything. Three spells in one night . . ."

Sakiimagan sounded worried. Hononomii. Now Anevai. Thank God he had no children of his own. He had worries enough sharing Sakiimagan's.

"Have they figured what's wrong with her yet?"

"Inyabi thinks she knows. That's why I've sent Anevai there."

"I'll keep in contact."

"Thank you, Paul. Seriously."

"Yeah, well. So I'll see you when. Say hi to Lena and tell Hono to quit fooling around, I need him back in the lab."

He hung up and buzzed Wesley's office. No answer, no forwarding message. Predictable. Why the Wesser's co-workers hadn't poisoned him years ago . . .

He auto-dialed the Tyeewapi clinic.

"Ya'at'eeh." A distracted female voice answered, putting the listing in doubt. Unusual greeting for the clinic, which catered (partially due to its local hot spring) to Recon and spacer-scientists alike.

"Hello?" he said cautiously. "This is Paul Corlaney calling for Inyabi or Matowakan Tyeewapi . . ."

A chuckle, warm and friendly, reassured him. *"Hi, Paul. Sorry. This is Inyabi. There's a big game today, so I'm sans secretary and clients—they'll wait to die until the game's over. Catching up on paperwork. —What can I do for you?''*

"Actually, I'm looking for your granddaughter. Is she around?"

"In the house. I'll transfer you, but I warn you in advance, we just put in a new system, so if I lose you . . ." Her voice faded off, distraction and the new system equal possibilities. He waited, hoping she'd remembered him.

"Hi, guy." Anevai's voice bubbled from the speaker. *"What's up?''*

"Ridenour's here." Frustration made him abrupt. "Any chance I can sweet-talk you into babysitting?"

"*Unkind, Dr. Paul.*" The bubble popped, reminding him an eighteen-year-old female might view Stephen Ridenour slightly differently than might a well-seasoned male.

"Joke, darlin'. It's just I'm busy, and Wesley—"

An audible sigh cut him off. "*Is he there?*"

"That's the problem. Wesley—"

"*Not Wesley. Stephen.*"

"Oh. Not yet." He explained the situation as briefly as possible, then: "So, how 'bout I head him your direction—"

"*No!*"

"What d'you mean, no?"

"*You need a translation? I just—*"

A pause. A muffled *Shush! I'm trying!*

Paul swore softly. She wasn't alone. Probably had a hot date beginning to take exception to conversation about another man. "Anevai, listen. I've interrupted you. Never mind, I'll handle it. Who knows, maybe a miracle's happened and the Wesser had an attack of Responsibility."

"*But he's . . .*" Now *she* sounded distracted. Hopefully, it was a localized plague. . . .

"Forget it, missy. Go have fun."

"*I . . . Thanks. Bye, doc.*"

"Yeah, yeah, yeah . . ."

He left a message with his secretary to accept calls from Ridenour, rounded up a fresh cup of coffee, exchanged a few updates and insults in the lounge, and wandered back to his office.

Still no call. Please, God, let Wesley make himself useful. Just this once.

Ordinarily, he didn't mind the supervisory position Sakiimagan had thrust upon him all those years ago. On some occasions, he even (secretly) enjoyed it. The HuteNamid researchers were an elite, independent lot, and in general 'overseeing' them meant making sure the coffee never ran out and enjoying the unquestionable right to sit in on *any* brainstorming session, regardless of the disciplines in question.

Life could be harder.

Witness the last two weeks.

He wondered if he should be angry at Sakiima for thrusting Ridenour into his lap, examined the options and decided not. To Sakiimagan Tyeewapi, Stephen Ridenour was a guest and, as such, not to be casually directed to a generic secretary for a key to a generic room. But he was a SciCorps problem, and therefore Paul's problem.

This time, at least, he could trust his feelings. Maybe someday he'd be able to trust them all the time.

A flash of resentment; justified, he decided, so he fanned the flash to a healthy glow.

He understood Sakiimagan's desire to protect the magnificent—and potentially dangerous—discovery his people had made on their planet. Noncontrolled influx of alien technologies throughout Alliance would have brought SciCorps Central personnel to monopolize site investigations—and assume control of any resultant patents.

But Sakiimagan's motivations were only marginally economic. Some of the early contacts with the Cocheta (as Sakiimagan's people called them) technology had proven disastrous. On one planet—Ridenour's home planet, Rostov—the influence of the Cocheta machines had apparently driven an entire IndiCorps—Ridenour's parents included—homicidally insane. Until he understood more, Sakiimagan had wanted to control the infoflow out of their region of space.

Not an easy task in the ComNet Alliance, where knowledge was allegedly available to all interested parties.

That inflexibility of their own system had practically forced Nayati to mess with Hononomii's head so that (as had happened) should he come under Alliance interrogation, he would . . . time out . . . perhaps permanently. And Nayati had learned those mind-bending techniques from his uncle; Sakiimagan had felt similarly compelled to . . . adjust . . . Paul's head—as well as most of the HuteNamid SciCorps. Not as cavalierly as Nayati, but enough to carefully manipulate their loyalties. Enough to make them never inclined to leave HuteNamid.

And he'd done it without asking permission.

In retrospect, Paul understood and even respected Sakiimagan's actions. He'd reviewed (along with Loren Cantrell, herself a fully licensed Deprivil interrogator) the meticulous recordings Sakiimagan had kept of his sessions with the researchers, and the suggestions were basically innocuous—quite thoroughly in line with his own natural inclinations in coming to HuteNamid in the first place.

But—dammitall—the man claimed to be his friend. He *could* have asked.

The only really good part of Ridenour's visit to HuteNamid, as far as he could tell, was getting that small fact out in the open. At least it had given him the peace of mind that he wasn't going mad: that the uncharacteristic fits of anger he'd experienced were actually an unforunate by-product of the 'adjustment.'

But Sakiimagan *could* have asked.

Resentment having run its course, Paul took refuge in his notes, transferring them into the SciComp database for eventual inclusion into the 'Net report—adding bits and pieces, disregarding some speculations he didn't want on any official base. Illegal as hell, but if SciCorps Central, the Council, or the 'NetAT itself decided to take exception to the practice, they'd have to incarcerate ninety percent of SciCorps researchers. Laws were one thing; public humiliation was another.

He had plenty of data to create a growth sim. Maybe with the 'Net down, he could con Wesley into writing it. They had five RealSpace programmers on staff—good people, too, just not Smith's caliber, though he'd never admit that to the 'Netter. Wesley's head was already too internally pressurized. But he'd have to wait until Ridenour was gone for good—

—A state of affairs that couldn't happen too soon for his peace of mind. The boy was a menace to the tranquillity he'd found here, from his ties to people Paul had once known to the local disruption his investigation of Wesley's paper had caused. Even his open idolatry of Paul himself.

Idolatry? Shit, the kid was petrified of him—couldn't complete a sentence to him without stuttering or blushing.

Once upon a long time ago, Paul Corlaney had sought that kind of recognition. Now he had it, it was a damned—

The phone rang. He jumped, jamming the keyboard. The computer beeped a protest and instituted auto-save; he reached for the phone.

"Dr. Corlaney? This is Stephen Ridenour."

iii

"Hononomii? Ya'at'eeh, sik'is?"

Deep firm voice speaking the HuteNamid Recon language over the speakers.

Hononomii. Are you well, my brother?

Pale-blue letters spelling out the translation on a darker band across the screen.

Behind that band, a young man lying motionless, eyes closed, a beatific smile sitting strangely on his strong features, his contour couch the only piece of furniture in the darkened room.

On the far side of a sound-damping window, Cholena Tyeewapi, the young man's mother, and a licensed psychotherapist, assembled those AmerInd phrases, conferring hastily with *Cetacean* psych staff before instructing the simcomp, which in turn created these deep tones.

A supposedly routine Records Clarification mission, an equally routine questioning of a local firebrand, and of a sudden *Cetacean*'s crew had found itself in the middle of a situation the repercussions of which were destined to echo to the heart of Alliance and beyond. Her primary job, as she read it now, and in lieu of input from her superiors, had become the control of those reverberations—to make them a progressive breeze, rather than a destructive whirlwind.

And that control began with a cure for Hononomii Tyeewapi's bizarre affliction.

Minimize sensory input, Nayati Hatawa's other brainwashing victims had recommended. *Let Nayati's voice create his reality.*

And at that point, with *Cetacean* machinery maintaining Hononomii's physical existence, and Nayati's alien tapes controlling his neural activity, Loren Cantrell had been willing to try anything to restore the vitality she'd glimpsed three weeks ago.

Nayati? Is that you?

Hononomii's answer: likewise in the translation bar.

'Anything' appeared to be paying off, 'appeared' being the operative word. Cholena was leading Hononomii slowly down a familiar path. Routine. Every session began the same way. Every session took Hononomii a handful of steps farther down the pathway. They kept waiting for the time he'd break free of the forest.

Cholena had hoped to wait for Sakiimagan Tyeewapi's arrival for this morning session, but the Stingray's system entry had eliminated that option. If there was any chance of getting Hononomii pulled out of his private reality—better still to have him, his mother, and all other distracting Unusuals back downworld—before the authorities on that incoming ship arrived, they had to take it.

"So, how much do you plan to tell them?" TJ Briggs stirred a fifth spoonful of sugar into his coffee, licked the spoon, and looked expectantly at her over the handle.

"Them?" She cocked her head rimward.

TJ nodded.

"All depends, doesn't it?" she answered, willingly distracted from the on-screen ritual of waking Hononomii up. "I don't even know whose they are yet, do I?"

Frustratingly slow, RealSpace transmissions. Theoretically, a war could be engaged and won or lost before they had identification verification, let alone negotiation. Fortunately, neither she nor anyone else in human history had ever had to test that theory.

"I'm betting they're Security," TJ said. "Old man Morley getting nervous about the shutdown."

"Into optimism today, are we?" she asked. "Security isn't the only entity likely to object to a localized silence, and with the 'Net out of operation, that Stingray is the fastest means of communication available."

"You think Morley's the least of your worries?"

"I'd rather Security than 'NetAT. Certainly rather than Shapoorian's mental-midget thugs."

"Could be Kurt Eckersley's."

"I'd almost rather Shapoorianites," she said dryly. "Them I could fry with a clear conscience."

"Admiral?" Chet's voice, barely detectable past TJ's choked laughter, whispered in her head. Unusual choice of communication; the personal beeper added a level of security rarely required aboard ship. She tappped an acknowledgment on the implant behind her left ear, holding up a finger to stave off TJ's curiosity.

"Message back from that hot shit ship. It's faster than we thought. Be here in three hours—maybe four."

Wonderful.

"ID?" she queried aloud, and TJ nodded acknowledgement: he'd guessed the nature of the exchange.

"'NetAT. Three of them. Eighteen crewmembers. Got their numbers; Comp's pulling up background on them even as we speak.—Be waiting for you in your office when you get there."

"Thanks, Chet. Keep me posted." And to TJ: "'NetAT. They're going to want to know about the shutdown."

"So tell them," Briggs said, then grinned: "Hell, give 'em Smith; he'll keep them occupied."

"Admiral?" A more conventional page, this time: over ship's com and in Alexis Fonteccio's voice.

"Yes, Lexi. Shuttle in?"

"Yessir. Governor Tyeewapi and Nigan Wakiza are with me now. Should I bring them out?"

"ASAP. Cantrell out."

"Well, at least she's talking to you," TJ commented.

She grimaced. "Barely."

TJ's mouth twitched, his nose wrinkled.

"Don't just sit there imitating a rabbit," she said. "Out with it, Mr. Briggs."

"You could've asked her opinion. She didn't even know Ridenour had put in the request."

"Is that what she told you?"

"Not in so many words, but she was mad as hell when she discovered he was on that early shuttle. I haven't seen that attitude since her first year aboard."

"Startled, maybe. So was I. Mo had indicated another day, at least, before she'd turn him loose. But Lexi knew I was considering it, though she counselled against it."

"So why'd you okay his leave? Her judgement's been pretty sound where he's concerned."

"No argument. But technically, I had no right to deny it. He's a free agent, now his job's done. Give credit, the fact he put in the request at all shows more sensitivity to the local situation than we've given him points for."

"Probably didn't know he could just take off—probably so damned used to following orders and asking permission to pick his nose, he doesn't know *how* to operate on his own jets."

"He knows. He specifically said he wanted to make certain his presence wouldn't compromise our search operations or anything we might have going he wasn't aware of."

"Pumping you for information, was he?"

"What a suspicious mind you have, Teej."

"That's what they pay me for. —What were Lexi's objections to getting him out of our hair for a few days' R&R?"

"She didn't really explain, she's been appallingly tight-lipped the past few days, but I suspect it's to who's sharing that R&R."

"She doesn't trust Smith."

"Smith promised he'll just talk politics and relax. Wise the kid up a bit and let him have some fun for once in his life—sounded like a good deal all around."

"Lexi thinks Smith is a bad influence."

"Of course he is. He's also a canny SOB. Knows Vandereaux politics from the inside, though he tries to hide the fact. Has RealTime common sense that Stephen woefully lacks. Lexi, too. *She* could do worse than take a few lessons from Smith." She shrugged. "Let Stephen have his fun while he's got a chance. A couple of days won't hurt."

"Long as he keeps out of trouble."

"On the other hand, Ridenour's proven he can take pretty good care of himself."

"He's also proven he's damn good at getting himself *into* trouble in the first place."

"Smith promised to keep an eye on him—keep him from anything disastrous."

TJ just looked at her.

She laughed and focussed her attention on the screen, where Hononomii was finally sitting, blinking into the darkness. She'd hoped to have a whole son waiting to surprise Sakiimagan, but this increasingly animated Hononomii would suffice.

Moments later, the door slid open, and she rose to greet the indigene governor, taking no offense when his eyes slid past her to the screen. After three weeks' separation from his son with only her word for the boy's condition, she would hardly begrudge him the reassurance. She gestured toward her vacated seat.

"Sit down and watch, governor. Plenty of time for formalities later."

Nigan Wakiza nodded to her, his eyes lowered in deference to her authority. But manners exhibited, those dark eyes abandoned his moccasined feet to dart about the room as if trying to absorb all the monitors and dials at once. Sakiimagan had said he'd begged to be included in the invitation, and seeing this unabashed curiosity, she no longer wondered why. *Hang in there, kid,* she promised him silently.

"It's so like Nayati's voice," Sakiimagan commented quietly. A short time later, he chuckled softly. "For somone who stumbles over the simplest phrases, Cholena is doing quite well. I must remember to compliment her."

"Actually," Cantrell explained, matching his low tone, "your wife is supplying the substance. The translation is computer generated, based primarily on the sample recordings you provided us. The young man's style is—distinctive. Would you like to join her?"

Sakiimagan shook his head without taking his eyes from the screen. "Better not to interrupt whatever she's doing. If I could listen to the entire process . . . ?"

"Of course. —Here." She flicked a switch, handed him earphones. "I had my doubts, but Dr. Liu insisted Athabascan was the only way to reach him, and it seems to be working. It's certainly the most interactive he's been since the initial collapse."

He nodded absently. "If, as Nigan insists, Nayati made the suggestion in that language and always used it when Hononomii was on the Cocheta machine, it would be . . ."

He seemed unaware he'd left the sentence hanging, concentrating on the exchanges between his spouse and son. Cantrell let him alone and motioned the others into the adjacent room.

"Lexi," she said, carefully casual, "I think our young friend here would enjoy a tour of the ship."

Nigan nodded eagerly.

Cantrell smiled indulgently, and asked Lexi: "Think we can accommodate him?"

"Is that an order, admiral?"

Cold formality. Not quite insubordination, but—

"Excuse us a moment, admiral," TJ interjected and motioned Lexi to follow him to a corner of the room. Cantrell deliberately blocked the interface to TJ's personal beeper to give them privacy. She was aware of Lexi's tension, though not the cause, and Lexi was more inclined to open up to TJ if Lexi knew she wasn't listening in.

"Admiral Cantrell," Nigan said nervously, "I'm fine. Honestly. I'm supposed to be here to help the governor. Sgt. Fonteccio doesn't—"

She forced a smile. "None of your doing, lad. She'll enjoy showing you around." His worried look remained, and with considered confidentiality, she explained, "She's Recon herself, you know, and sometimes gets a bit overformal aboard the ship."

Fortunately, when Lexi and TJ rejoined them, Lexi's normal friendly self was restored—at least toward Nigan Wakiza. To her commanding officer, she retained the formal exactitude.

But that formality was tempered, and as the door slid shut behind her, TJ asked: "What if Ridenour decides to stay?"

"He can't do that—God, I hate to think of the red tape it would cause. But come back someday? Why not? If he really wants to ruin his career, who am I to stop him?"

"And if something happens to him down there this time? He's not got a sterling record, Cantrell."

"It's not my concern any longer, Teej. Can't be. Not legally. If something happens, he either goes back in a body bag or to hospital. Either way, the red tape becomes simple—it was his responsibility. Neither can I morally put his welfare ahead of the crew and our own commitments here. His job's completed, the report filed with Chet. We've got his depo on everything he can tell us about Rostov. Enough to suggest important linkages to this planet and its alien artifacts . . ."

"Meaning, his usefulness is ended?" TJ made no attempt to mask his disapproval.

"Say, rather, diminished in priority. I almost hope these 'Netters *are* after Ridenour and not Chet. Chet's finally beginning to find some order in those damned interference patterns disrupting the scans. I promised the governor this would be a Combined Council matter. I need proof to justify that status.—I *need* more Libraries—solid artifacts I can take back."

"You have me," TJ said. "The Cocheta devices didn't destroy *my* ability to record."

"You *really* want to get into that?"

He shook his head emphatically.

"Thought not. Besides, Sakiimagan has promised to give us all he knows, which is far more than Stephen, who was only a child when he left Rostov—"

"Don't underestimate that child."

"I won't. But we're onto the Cocheta now. I'd like to keep him out of any further involvement. He's 'NetTech—maybe 'NetAT one of these days. He doesn't need political entanglements. Chet has been devouring that report of his. Says the kid's done a brilliant job explaining Smith's theory and outlined a potential operating system we'd better keep out of casual hands, it's so obvious. If necessary, Chet can give the report."

"So Stephen *could* stay here."

"Only if you want to fill out the paperwork. —Let's run that crossover when we come to it. Right now," she jerked her head toward the observation-room door, "I'd like Hononomii healthy and out of here, thanks."

Sakiimagan acknowledged their return with a polite lift of the chin, and sat back with a sigh, freeing one ear of the headphones.

"Can they hear us?" he asked.

"Not a word."

"Good. Cholena's holding her own quite well, but she can't hope to imitate Nayati. He has a speaking style the ancient singers would envy. She's gotten away with it so far only because she's kept the statements simple and because Hononomii himself has very little natural talent with the language. But Nayati insisted he practice, and he's improved. If Lena tries to..." His brows knit. He adjusted the headset and muttered under his breath, and with a trace of wry humor, "Cholena, no... for the gods' sake, even you know better than..."

A sudden warning beep from the windowed monitor display. The quiet conversation faltered.

"*Nayati?*" Hononomii wavered to his feet, his eyes searching the shadows, his bios racing wildly. "*Doo shil aanii da.*"

Sakiimagan's head dropped, all sign of humor vanished. His quiet curse overlapped his son's cry: a protest perfectly understandable to all the listeners:

"*Nayati? Where'd you go?—Nayati, it's not you! No! —No!*"

iv

Ping. Ping: pleasant, light chime from the speakers.

Acoma station—five minutes: HUD against the bubblecar's clear dome.

Stephen blinked, yawned and checked his watch. Three hours plus a bit. That was the longest contiguous real sleep he'd had in weeks. McKenna should be happy.

Happier than Paul Corlaney.

He rubbed his eyes clear, wishing he could rub out the memory of that ill-advised call as easily. He should have followed his instincts: it hadn't required a vidfone to sense Corlaney's forced amicability. He'd ended the conversation quickly, assuring Corlaney he'd manage.

And manage he would. Even if it took reprogramming the automated bubblecar to accept his locally offLine ID. Even if it took thrusting himself on people who pointedly didn't want his company any more than Corlaney had.

But Corlaney hadn't practically ordered him to come back downworld. Corlaney hadn't promised him wild parties and endless debauchery HuteNamid-style. Corlaney had never gone to great effort to make him feel warm and welcome.

Damn Wesley, anyway. The man *had* received his message, he knew that from the verification tag returned to his own terminal aboard *Cetacean*. Late, he understood.

Two hours could have been, as Nigan Wakiza had suggested, Wesley validating his reputation.

Four, without so much as a message, was a stand-up.

Maybe Wesley *didn't* want to see him. Maybe Anevai didn't. Something might well have occurred to change their opinion of him. It wouldn't be the first time—he had a talent for unwittingly alienating people—but if that was the case, they could damnwell tell him to his face and leave him karmically free to pursue his *important* downworld goals.

It didn't make a spit of difference to him one way or the other, he informed the disappointed twinge in his gut. Their seemingly friendly interest had been . . . pleasant diversion . . . while it lasted. Once he left the HuteNamid system, they'd likely never meet again. A couple of pleasure-filled days one way or the other would have marginal significance on the rest of his life.

But they could have the decency to tell him to go to hell to his face.

Besides, fair was fair: Wesley and Anevai were, after all, the ones who'd taught him he had the *right* to such explanations.

Governor Tyeewapi had said Anevai was at her grandparents'. He'd been there before; Anevai, herself, had taken him there his last trip downworld. He knew Anevai's grandparents, Matowakan and Inyabi. Even remembered the name of the Recon village where they lived.

So he'd commandeered a private bubblecar—forcing his way into the local system through the repair override, transferring charges to his *Cetacean* account—and headed for Anevai's retreat. Let *her* find Wesley.

The bubblecar pulled into a very normal-looking terminal, the top half lifting smoothly while a bodiless voice announced, *Acoma station. Please watch your step.*

For an instant, Stephen thought he'd mistaken the name: it looked like every other 'Tube terminal. Acoma had been— different. Very *unlike* anywhere he'd been.

In deference to those waiting for the vehicle, Dr. Ridenour, please exit quickly. If you wish to continue to an alternate destination, please enter the code now.

He murmured an apology, and had stepped from the bobbing vehicle before realizing he'd made that apology to a program.

CodeHead indeed, Ridenour, he chided himself. *Making manners to a robot.*

The hood closed automatically and the bubble accelerated, faster than human comfort levels, down the track to answer another hail. This better be the right place; three hours back to a night landing on Paul Corlaney's 'Condo doorstep would really fry his credibility with the researcher.

Fortunately, once outside, his sense of 'place' returned. Not the Cocheta trace this time, but very real personal experience.

Circle of buildings, primarily single-family shopfronts, roads leading away from a central roundabout like spokes of a fueling station. Shops he remembered from his previous visit . . .

Across the central plaza, he recognized the shop, closed up and dark now, where he'd found the fur-lined robe. If the shop was there, the hot spring should be—sparkle of falling water . . . a few degrees left—there, which put the Tyeewapi clinic—there.

Sure now of his direction, he slung his duffel over his shoulder, energy renewed, now his goal was in sight.

But as he swung toward the distant clinic, enthusiasm waned. Something was wrong. It was too quiet. There should be children all over, their laughter as much a part of this place as the whispering trees. Not only the children were missing: there wasn't a single adult in sight. As the clinic's familiar wooded drive came into view, he slowed to a halt and, pivoting a careful step at a time, searched every shadow.

Nothing.

Nerves.

But those same nerves had survived too many ambushes in the past for him to dismiss them utterly now, and slipping into the nearest shadow, he edged cautiously toward that distant wooded lane.

According to Cantrell, rumor held that Nayati hadn't died in the underground explosions he'd set off—that Nayati was very much alive. Rumor held that many of the mountain folk were protecting him. Rumor placed him elsewhere, but rumor had been known to lie. And while Stephen intended to test those rumors, he'd test them on *his* schedule, not Nayati Hatawa's.

He tightened his grip on the duffel and headed down the forested drive, keeping carefully to the center of the road, listening, searching the shadows, denying the images his mind created.

Deep shadows to the left. Movement. Dammit, he was being watched. He *knew* the feeling. He'd swear it was real. He edged to the right of center.

"Nayati?" His voice cracked. He steadied it, and said firmly, "Nayati Hatawa, is that you?"

Flash to darkness, the loom of glowing stalactites, and black pits. The same sense of being watched.

Another step.

"Boo!"

He whirled, used that momentum to fling the duffel into the bulk materializing behind him.

A shouted curse.

A crash of bushes.

Laughter, full and inviting. Definitely *not* Hatawa's. "I warned you, Smith."

Smith?

Stephen straightened from his defensive crouch and pulled his duffel off the collapsed, moaning bulk.

A muddy face glowered at him from the bushes. Behind him, Anevai followed her voice out of the shadows.

"Hi, Wesley," he said, and dodged the foot that swung wildly at his knees.

"Hononomii? Nanina' ya'at'eeh, shiye'?"

"Shizhe'e? Shi'niidli. Kodi iiyisi deesk'aazgo doo shil ya'at'eeh da. Dii doo shagha'at'ee da. Hooghangoo ne'iikaah."

"K'ad neiikah, shiye'. K'ad neiikah."

"Doo shil aanii da. Doo shil aanii da."

"Iilhaash, Hononomii. Iilhaash, shiye'." A note of soothing

finality edged Sakiimagan Tyeewapi's transmitted murmur. He set a hand on his son's shoulder and left it there until the young man's eyes drifted shut.

Following his explosive objection, they'd moved Hononomii back to his sickbay quarters and the change was, at least to Cantrell's eyes, for the better.

Below the imaging screen, healthily active Bios displayed on an array of monitors. Dr. McKenna, *Cetacean's* chief medical officer, was busily transferring and analyzing specifics of that data which were well beyond a mere admiral's capacity to understand.

On the other hand, Cholena Tyeewapi's face, as she sat back in her chair with a sigh, relaxed for the first time in two hours, was explanation enough.

Cantrell nodded toward Hononomii's readings. "Look better, don't they?"

"Anything's better than flatlined," Cholena said dryly.

On the screen, Hononomii stirred again, shifting and muttering, sometimes in response to his father, other times not.

"He says he's cold," Cholena explained, "but as you can see, the adrenaline surge Sakiima's arrival induced is still with him. He doesn't really believe it's Sakiima after I . . . But he wants to believe so badly . . ." Cholena ran her hands up and down her arms as though Hononomii wasn't the only one feeling chilled. "I'm so thankful Sakiima was here. If anyone can get through to Hono, he will. Even so . . ." She shivered. "Even so . . ." Her dark eyes stared vacantly at the screen. "Have you any idea what it feels like to kill your own son?"

Fortunately, the question was clearly rhetorical; Cantrell couldn't have answered, any more than Cholena Tyeewapi could have known the answer was 'yes'. TJ's silent, encoded empathy helped. She acknowledged his efforts with a grateful tap and Cholena's painful guilt with a quiet: "Far from intentional on your part. You couldn't know our machine would try to interpret anything you said, even if there *was* no translation."

"Our success or failure is all based on faith and trust," Cholena said quietly. "We've destroyed Hononomii's faith in Nayati's voice. Now he suspects his father's as well." She shook her head, as though to clear it of the memory. "Sakiimagan always said I'd regret my lack of fluency. . . . At least he was here." Another shake, and she was tracking solidly. "Sooner than I expected, admiral. Why?"

"I thought you'd like him up here, so I had the crew do a fast turnabout." She grinned, seeing the opening to lighten a mother's unwarranted guilt. "They were *not* happy at losing their afternoon in Tunica. Your people are spoiling my staff, Cholena."

"Can you blame them, Adm. Cantrell? *Your* people are so easily amused."

"Touché, Dr. Tyeewapi, touché," she said on a laugh.

Cholena looked steadily at her. "We've got a problem, haven't we?"

Cantrell answered easily. "I collect about three per hour. To which are you referring?"

"Whichever pushed you to that early session with Hononomii—whichever necessitated that too-fast turnaround for the unhappy crew."

"I wanted your son well for his father. . ."

"I don't think so, admiral."

She exchanged a glance with TJ. Took a small chance.

"All right, Dr. Tyeewapi, you've got me. A ship has entered the system. 'NetAT envoy, so they say."

"So they say. Is there reason to distrust their claim?"

"Under the circumstances, I distrust my own mother."

"What do they want?"

"We don't know yet."

"Nayati's meddling on the 'Net brought you and Dr. Ridenour to HuteNamid in the first place. Perhaps more discrepancies have come to light—or perhaps the shutdown itself prompted their coming."

"Possibly. Probably. We won't know for certain until they arrive."

"What about the Cocheta, admiral? Will you tell them?"

"Promised your husband I'd keep quiet, didn't I? And that includes your son's condition. I was hoping to be able to send you and your family home intact before they got here. After yesterday—when we almost had him . . ." She shrugged. "But they're 'NetAT. Their jurisdiction is confined specifically to the NSpace Communication Network. Local politics and archaeological discoveries are none of their concern."

Cholena frowned and tapped her stylus against the notepad. "I hope that promise doesn't get you into trouble, admiral. What would you like us to do?"

"Lie low, for now. Stay out of their way. If they are who they claim, we'll likely ship them downworld—let Ridenour and Smith handle them. If not—" She shrugged a second time. "—they'll have a lot of explaining to do—too much to concern themselves with you and your son. In the meantime, if you should happen to run across them, you're just one of the local visitors."

"I don't plan to leave this area, admiral, but you'd best tell—"

The hauntingly beautiful sound of a Recon flute drifted unannounced over the com: somewhere aboard the ship, an impromptu concert was in session, and someone had cleared a universal channel to share the treat.

Cholena glanced around the room and smiled. "That didn't take long," she murmured cryptically.

"Admiral?"

McKenna's hand on her arm drew Cantrell's attention to the monitors. Hononomii's stress-filled readouts had begun to . . . pulse in time with that melody, and with each pulse to relax a degree, until he shifted onto his side, tucked a hand under and burrowed into his pillow.

And over the speakers, a clear, sighing murmur:

"*Ya'at'eeh, Nigan Wakiza.*"

* * *

"Your quarters, Dr. Ridenour, sir." Anevai pushed the door open and swept a low bow. "Top drawer and left-hand closet are all yours."

Stephen tipped his head, returning ostentation for ostentation. "Thank you, m'lady. But such generosity is—" He raised his duffel bag. "—hardly neces . . ."

Confusion puckered his forehead as he looked past her into the room . . .

. . . where his luggage awaited him.

She held her breath, anticipating. Stephen Ridenour had a boundless quota of question marks, and when this thoroughly justified query popped, *she'd* relay it right where it belonged: into the lap of the—todacious scum—smirking in the hallway behind them.

But Stephen failed her. Without so much as a backward glance, he tossed his duffel on the bed and neatly stored its contents, tucked the duffel itself on a closet shelf; and (still sans comment) flung the large suitcase onto the bed, cleared the bio-lock and emptied it with similar dispatch.

The suitcase collapsed and stowed under the bed, he asked easily, "What now?"

"I . . ." She paused—checked, if not mated—wondering if she'd been set up. Neither Wesley's you-won't-get-an-answer-out-of-me face nor Stephen's polite, expectant innocence gave her a clue. She sucked in her lower lip, then announced: "Dinner."

Wesley's face glowed.

Feeling deliciously wicked, she continued: "I think we should help fix it." Horror replaced the light. "Grandmother's treating us to an old-fashioned spread, which is a hell of a lot of work and *she's* been doing the books all day, while *we* goofed off."

"I wouldn't call flat on your back in bed goofing off, brat," Wesley said, serious now.

"I would," she answered shortly and flicked a glance toward

Stephen. Wesley knew better. That problem was not Stephen's concern. She winked a grin at Stephen's worried look, and—herded them both downstairs.

But once in the kitchen, there was the *pii'chum* litter to admire, their growth rate to be exclaimed over, and all their kittenish tricks to show off—until Wesley's imitations nearly cost her grandmother a finger, and Inyabi ordered them out in no uncertain terms, filling Stephen's arms with kittens, and Wesley's with niblets, and chasing them from the kitchen. When Anevai protested, she simply laughed. "I've been cooking for ten times as many since before you were born. I love you. I love your friends. Right now, the lot of you are driving me crazy. Besides, it's not every day I get to show off my cooking talents *and* my granddaughter to a guest from the Capitol Station. Go. Go watch the sunset with your charming—if rather energetic—young friends."

"*You're* going to show off?" Anevai exclaimed in mock horror. "My waistline's in big trouble."

"And my fingers are if you don't get those friends of yours out of here." Inyabi laughed again, and hugged her. "Just take care of it, child. Remember today's lesson in common sense."

"That was just plain stupid on my part, grams," Anevai said. "Too much wrestling in the hot spring. But I promise, I'll be careful—no walking the cliff faces until the spells stop. Deal?"

"Deal, *shitsoi*." Her grandmother touched her face with a flour-covered hand, laughed and tried to brush the powder away, which only made it worse.

Outside, Anevai led her two charges through the unseasonably warm twilight to a gently sloping hillside and a moss-covered box-seat view of the sun setting over the mountains.

"Just let them down," she advised Stephen, regarding the struggling armful of fur and pinlike claws. "They won't go far."

Stephen knelt and released the kits carefully, then settled beside her on the log, leaning forward to rest elbows on knees, shoulders hunched slightly forward, remaining close but not quite touching. Reserved and a little shy, that was their Stephen, and she'd take him however she could get him.

Besides, for cuddles, Wesley, whose arm wrapped her shoulders, whose thigh brushed hers as he settled on her other side, was invariably available. She leaned her head into his perfectly positioned shoulder-pillow, and that hold tightened ever-so-slightly.

Watching a sunset, sitting on a moss-covered log, sandwiched between two good-looking male-types . . . Person could grow to like this line of work.

Wesley's arm tightened again, calling her attention to Stephen. He'd slipped off the log and was holding a sliver of boiled meat out to a tiny drooling mouth. Needlelike teeth snapped, caught fingertips instead. Stephen, do him credit, didn't flinch, but held the piece steady. A second, more cautious, attempt elicited mewling appreciation, which announcement brought a horde of sibs bounding and tumbling through spring grass for their share. Stephen shifted about to sit cross-legged on the damp grass and soon the munchie supply had transformed into a purring pile of stuffed fuzz curled in Stephen's lap and draped over Stephen's knees.

A silent chuckle vibrated through Wesley's arm. A shiver which could have been hers as Stephen's long-fingered hands moved delicately over the furry mass. Stephen Ridenour did have a way about him.

Unkind, the trick Wesley had pulled. She wondered if Stephen had had the sense to realize he'd been set up—if it wasn't a setup to get her rather than Stephen.

As if his thoughts had been following the same path, Stephen said suddenly: "How'd you know I was coming?"

"Ha!" Wesley gloated. "Knew you'd ask sooner or later."

On the chance she hadn't been set up, Anevai explained minimally: "Dad called Paul from the shuttle. Said he'd met you at the terminal. Paul called us here."

A remote silence Stephen-ward; an abrupt: "When?"

"You're up, Smith," she said.

"Why me?"

She didn't answer. Knowing he knew, and that he knew that she knew that he knew.

Heaving a sigh, he grumbled, "I told them to deliver your shit here. What more do you want?"

Another, slightly further removed, silence. "I suppose the port authorities forgot to pass on your message."

"Hell, kid, I didn't want to embarrass you in front of the hired help."

The hunched shoulders twitched. Stephen's oddly reflective eyes glinted sunset orange as they stared up at them. Another twitch and the stiff reserve vanished. Stephen leaned over, sweeping a careless, graceful bow. "My humblest apologies, sir. Of course, I am forever in your—"

"Stuff it, brat."

Silent chuckles Stephen-ward, a wordless bend to pick up a stirring kitten—the same blue-furred one that first accepted food from him—and soothe it back to sleep. A low-key exchange, overall, as all their interactions had been low-key since Stephen had knocked Wesley into the bushes.

Laughter. A few brief hugs. Rather more formal greetings to her grandparents, which Inyabi had quickly brushed aside, chasing them off to settle Stephen into the guest room with her typical *Of course you'll stay with us.*

It was all quite strange. So . . . normal.

Somehow, she'd never perceived the possibility of 'normal' where Stephen Ridenour was involved.

And as evening shadows closed in, other normalities: a child's laughter drifting on the wind, an elder sib's frustrated threat to have him for dinner if he didn't come home *right now.*

"Where were they this afternoon?" Stephen asked.

"They?"

"The children. The adults, for that matter. Place was deserted."

"Local shops were closed down for the *natsi'taawet* games."

"What's that?"

"Sorta like Bracketball," Wesley answered. "Only easier."

Anevai snorted. "How would you know?"

"He should, Anevai," Stephen stepped in. "He used to play on the varsity team."

"So what?" she persisted. "He's never played *natsi' taawet*—at least, not so you'd recognize."

A choking sound from Wesley's side, laughter from Stephen's, and she lost all control. Taking a thoroughly unchivalrous advantage of her helplessness, Wesley harrumphed and pontificated:

"Never mind her, brat. *She* has no appreciation of the obvious superiority of spacer athletic endeavors."

"Why'd you quit, then, if you were so good and it was such a superior game?" Anevai squeezed out between gasps.

"An attack of sanity while I still had ten fingers and a whole skull."

"But was *everyone* at the game?" Stephen persisted in his original line of thought, making her wonder what he was edging toward.

"Well, some people were at work." She grinned at him. "Some people have to do that, you know."

"Everybody, evidently, except you and Wesley."

"I resent that," Wesley drawled. "'Net's down, isn't it? Can't do anything, can I?"

She twisted her head, letting the fall of hair hide the exchange from Stephen, and looked a question at Wesley. He answered with a raised eyebrow. But if that was the way he wanted to play it, she'd follow his lead:

"Nothing except help out Renee and Gayle and—"

"RealSpace programming?" Indignation incarnate: the Wesser, in full bloom. "You must be joking. Waste of talent, that would be."

"Never mind it's what you're supposed to be doing here," she said, reminding him of the fact Stephen politely overlooked: a transgression for which Stephen had every legal right to fry him, his accesses and the terminal he'd keyed in on.

"Poof, brat. Good ol' Chet says that's all irrelevant now.

That I did what I had to do. Didn't have anyone else to do the RealTime 'Netting, did we, once Suze passed away?''

And never mind he'd been RealTiming long before that.

Stephen buried his face into the kit's fur as if he wasn't listening, but she could imagine the uncertainty running through him. She reached over his shoulder for a hand and closed the subject. ''Like Chet said, all irrelevant.''

His hand squeezed hers, then fingers quietly interlaced, though she wouldn't swear who clasped whom.

Chill fingers; and through them, an occasional, quickly squelched shiver. The sun had dipped below the mountain ridge, leaving a decided chill in its wake. Gathering the stirring kits, they headed for the warmth of the garden and cookfire.

They intercepted Inyabi on her way from the house. Stephen thrust the sleepy-eyed kits into Wesley's hands and rushed forward, taking the heavy pot from her. Inyabi thanked him with a smile, then explained an emergency call had delayed Matowakan at the clinic, and dinner would be delayed.

Wesley groaned and complained and groaned some more.

Inyabi, accustomed to Wesley, dismissed him with a pat on his cheek and a calm, You'll live, dear, and led Stephen toward the fire, while Anevai and Wesley returned to the kitchen to deposit the kittens in their corner basket.

''Why didn't you tell him?'' Anevai asked as she knelt to release her armload.

''Tell him what, brat?''

''You know. That you've been working your butt off.'' She reached up for his kitten.

''*Ouch!*'' Wesley yelled, jerked his hand, yelled again as the startled kitten held tight with four tiny paws full of pins. Do him credit, the Wesser didn't throw the tiny creature into the wall, but stood there bravely silent while she prized it loose, only then muttering, ''Little bastard bit me.''

Anevai giggled and tucked the blue furball into its mass of

sibs. "One thing he's not is a bastard, Wes. Only one other *pii'chum* on this planet's that color."

"Touché."

"Now—" She stood up and handed him a bowl of fruit from the sideboard. "You going to answer my question?"

"I just didn't want him to know, that's all. Give him ideas."

"Like staying? I thought you wanted that."

"No. —And maybe I do, maybe I don't. —Like he should be down at SciComp now, helping out. Like he should feel *guilty* for not. He's pretty dumb that way. He's here to party. Let's make him do it."

"You worked yourself cross-eyed so *he* can take a vacation."

"Something like that."

"Pretty nice, Smith."

"Shit. —Don't tell anybody."

She giggled and kissed him lightly. "Secret's safe with me, Wesser."

"What secret?" Stephen's curly head popped inside the open door.

Anevai shoved a bowl in his direction. "If I told, it wouldn't be a secret, now, would it?"

V

At the cookfire, Stephen shadowed Inyabi's every move, inadvertently getting in the way while asking What that ingredient was, and Why that shaped pot rather than this one, and How could you tell if it was done. Her grandmother, with tact gleaned from three generations of inquisitive children, dispatched him to fetch the backrests from the portico.

He left, all eagerness to help.

When she was certain he'd be out of earshot, Anevai said, "Sorry, Grans."

Inyabi smiled. "I don't mind, Anevai. Not in the least. He's a sweet boy."

"Sweet?" Wesley squawked in protest. "Deadly dull, more like."

The Wesser was bored.

"Sweet." Inyabi repeated. *"And* charming. —Thank you, child." That last to Stephen as he arrived with the seats.

And the Wesser positively hated being bored. Worse: being upstaged.

Anevai watched with some misgiving as Wesley plopped into the first of the rests. Stephen's head tipped in seeming confusion and definite disapproval, and he quickly adjusted a second rest, silently offering it to her. Anevai thanked him and murmured, *Don't mind him,* before wriggling down into the padded leather comfort. Stephen placed three others carefully around the common bowls, settling on the last one to watch Inyabi, wide-eyed and silent for a blessed moment. Then:

"But if some of these spices are native and some—"

Wesley leaned over and placed a muffling hand across Stephen's mouth. Stephen brushed him away almost absentmindedly.

"—are imported from other worlds—even space, how do you know how they'll taste, or even if they're safe . . ."

Frowning darkly, Wesley hauled himself ostentatiously to his feet—

". . . to . . ."

—and disappeared into the shadows.

". . . com . . ." Stephen watched him leave, his question evidently forgotten. Anevai answered his puzzled glance with a slight shake of her head, a murmured *Don't let him get to you.*

Inyabi, accustomed as she was to Wesley's snits, drew Stephen's attention smoothly back to his question. Anevai sneaked a piece of dewberry-gel and tucked it in her cheek to quiet her stomach's increasingly audible complaints . . . and waited.

A Wesley-shadow coalesced in the bushes beyond Stephen.

For one idle instant, Anevai considered drawing his attention to the fact, then decided it entailed too much effort—besides,

Stephen needed to learn basic self-preservation—which did not include ignoring the Wesser.

A sudden leaning look into a bubbling pot thwarted the Wesser's initial assault; the five-fingered extension retracted into the bulk, and the bulk sank back into its plant-shadow camouflage.

Sweetness spread through Anevai's mouth and laughter through her gut as Stephen, at Inyabi's ostensibly innocent invitation (her grandmother couldn't *not* notice that shadow), made a round of all the dishes, tasting their contents and solemnly comparing flavors.

From the shadows, a sound suspiciously like a jealously growling stomach.

She swallowed the last of the gel and stifled the laughter, then aided in thwarting Wesley's dire purposes, slightly repositioning Stephen's backrest before he settled.

A sigh not totally wind generated. Stephen, still chattering enthusiastically around the gel, appeared oblivious . . .

. . . until the shadow burst out and clamped a very *non*shadowy hand over Stephen's mouth, pulling him to the ground, backrest and all. But Stephen rolled over Wesley, twisting free and to his feet, crouched and ready for Wesley's tackle, a wide grin on his face.

Funny, she'd never thought of Stephen as particularly physical; but he *had* been a gymnast, and that trained flexibility and strength proved a fair counterbalance to Wesley's greater reach and weight—until Stephen started laughing.

Nipping another bit of gel, Anevai advised the writhing mass: "Give it up, Stevie-lad. You've blown it."

Wasted breath. She avoided a flying foot and sat back on her heels, awaiting the inevitable. Within moments, Stephen was flat on his back, hands pinned above his head, and Wesley sitting on his heaving belly.

Anevai got up, ready to play referee and call a truce, but before she reached them, a sudden, supple twist, a startled howl of protest, and Stephen had Wesley pinned facedown, his hand slithering under and around in an effective, if somewhat naively achieved, half nelson.

"Stevie's shoulder's feeling better," Anevai commented, squatting in front of Wesley and resting her elbows on the ground, her chin in cupped palms. "Admit it, Smith," she said, between puffs of dusty air exploding in her face. "He's got you."

"Yeah." Agreement on a veritable cloud of dirt. "Give the old man some slack, brat. You're breaking my neck."

Stephen released him, all solicitous. *Seriously* solicitous.

Anevai was appalled—even before she caught the wicked glitter in Wesley's eyes before he tucked his head and began groaning.

"Wesley?" Stephen said uncertainly.

She tucked a hand in Stephen's elbow and pulled him away from the moaning blob. "Stevie-lad, let me explain: he starts it, he takes the consequences." The moans increased their pitiful quotient; she sensed resistance in the elbow and hissed: "Don't you *dare*, Ridenour."

A muttered, *Spoilsport*, interrupted the groans, and the tension in Stephen's elbow wavered.

"Cheer up, Wesser," she said, as beyond the fireglow a familiar form materialized beside her grandmother. "—Soup's on!"

The moaning lump hopped to its feet. Stephen stared at him, at the spot he'd occupied and back, accusation in every poker-faced gesture.

"What can I say?" Wesley threw up his hands. "It's a miracle!"

Stephen laughed—aloud this time, a delightful sound that prevailed over several attempts to smother it. Stephen rarely laughed, but when he did . . .

She poked Wesley in the ribs. "Take that smug look off your face. You weren't *that* funny. —You found the *on* button. Find the *off* or starve."

Wesley's eyes widened in alarm, and he grabbed Stephen's ears, forcing his attention.

Which naturally set Stephen off again. Wesley looked him straight in the eyes, nose to nose, and said firmly:

"You listen to me brat."

Stephen held his breath. And hiccupped.

"I'm starving. Shut up, or be eaten."

Stephen hiccupped again, and in a tiny, cautious voice: "O—*hic*—kay."

Several *hics* and only two threats later, Stephen finally managed to hold on to a plate, and fall into line behind her.

Her grandmother must have prepared everything she could lay her hands on. In addition to the common bowls set out in the middle of the dinner circle, she had a dozen bowls of sampler dishes laid out spacer-cafeteria style.

Anevai piled her plate, years of experience giving her an artist's touch for space utilization, thankful the annoying dizzy spells hadn't affected her appetite. Stephen matched her spoonful for spoonful, meticulously copying her placement pattern.

"Aren't you worried you'll go all purple or something?" she asked finally.

He grinned. "Dr. McKenna gave me a shot and some pills. Said, eat all I want. I'm taking her at her—"

A dirty hand seized his arm, spun him around to face full-blown Wesley-anger. "She did *what?*"

Stephen pulled free, his jaw clenching spasmodically, his free hand forming a respectable fist. But the fist relaxed; he responded calmly, "Settle down, Wes. She said the stomach problems are allergies. Says that academy meds should have diagnosed it years ago."

"Dammit, I *told* her —"

"*She's* my doctor, Wes. Not you. —Anevai, do you mind?" He handed her his plate; took Wesley's arm. "Let's get cleaned up, shall we?" And, promising to return shortly, pulled him protesting into the shadows toward the house.

"Wesley needn't worry," Matowakan said, starting to eat as

though such disturbances were nothing. "Dr. Ridenour is looking quite well."

"Wesley *ought* to mind his own business," Anevai muttered and plopped down beside him. "And Stephen *ought* to have decked him."

"Gently, *shitsoi*. Surely Wesley's concern for his friend is an admirable quality? And not entirely unjustified, considering Dr. Ridenour's drug-induced collapse the last time he visited us—"

"That breakdown wasn't from any stomach prescription. Wesley knows that as well as I do."

"And how do you know what he took?"

"I don't, exactly. But it was the same stuff he took in the cave before we—" She swallowed hard. Embarrassed. Not easy to talk about one's sex life with one's exceedingly dignified grandfather—not even when that grandfather was a doctor.

From her grandfather's far side, Inyabi said calmly, "It's all right, Anevai, I explained your concerns to him. Also, that your blood tests were clean of any...unusual...chemical substances."

"Hours after the fact." Hard to keep bitterness from her voice. For all Stephen was a friend, that betrayal still rankled.

"Never mind, granddaughter. The boy didn't mean to give you the drug. How does that morning reflect upon his later breakdown?"

"That first night he spent with you—before he locked himself into the bedroom for three days translating that diary of his—I'd been out walking. When I came in, he was sitting beside the fire, all excited, babbling about how he could read it now—"

"It?"

"His diary. And then he kissed me, and that time I *tasted* it. It was awful. Bitter. Then sickly sweet. —But that doesn't matter. Point is, he had to take *that* in order to read his diary. Wesley calls them sudsies, and they're definitely *not* for digestion."

"Sudsies?" Her grandfather looked puzzled. "You say he

took these 'sudsies' prior to making love and that they helped him read his diary?''

"I don't see the relationship either. I think they're sort of like stay-awake pills."

"But that's not how they affected you."

She blushed and shook her head, just the memory of that morning in the cave igniting a flame in her gut. "Why are you asking? *You* know what he took; Wesley got all those vials out of his room, and you and gram ran tests..."

He smiled. "Of course we did. And Sud'orsofan—Wesley's 'sudsies'—was certainly among them. You're absolutely correct: Dr. McKenna said—"

"Cantrell's Dr. McKenna? When did you talk to her?"

"Manners, *shitsoi*," he chastised gently. "When do you suppose?"

Following a few moments' thought: "The 'emergency' in the clinic?"

He nodded, a single lift of his square chin. "McKenna says he has a sensitivity to—among other things—a growth stimulator commonly used in station greenhouses. Quite interesting, actually. As Cantrell's chief medical officer, McKenna has had ample opportunity to study the matter. Suspects tolerance begins in the womb; that if mothers don't ingest the substance, the child can't. But no one really knows. Few spacer doctors deign to recognize the condition, preferring to attribute it to Recon space-hysteria."

Which would account for Stephen's condition. After ten years of trying to digest the stuff... "But Stephen said McKenna fixed him up. So why'd she call?"

"She didn't trust him to explain to us—wanted me to know the full extent of the condition. She ran tests. She's accounted for those known problems in the shot. The pills she's given him are for allergic reactions to new foods—he's liable to be prone to them now, so she says, though she figures when she has time to monitor him over a period of time, she might cure the problem permanently—depends on how resilient his body is after this much time—and she just wanted me to know. I must admit.'' He glanced at Stephen's loaded plate. ''It appears wise. The boy doesn't know moderation.''

''In anything,'' she acknowledged quickly, hearing footsteps crunching toward them.

Wesley was clean and resigned, if not particularly happy. Stephen was—subdued. Anevai held out Wesley's plate in silent invitation, patted the seat on her other side for Stephen.

Wesley threw himself down and began shovelling food in his mouth; Stephen folded gracefully into the backrest and began picking slowly at his plate. Wesley, his temper as transient as flash paper, grew increasingly cheerful; Stephen withdrew, speaking only to compliment the various dishes.

Anevai controlled the urge to bash them both. Matowakan, more practical than she, simply asked, in a voice expecting an answer, ''So, Dr. Ridenour, did you have a smooth flight down?''

''P–please, sir, call me S–Stephen.''

His stutter was back. He *was* upset.

Matowakan nodded. ''Of course. And the flight?''

''B–beautiful, sir.''

''Did you come in from the North? or East?''

''I—'' Stephen blinked. Startled. ''I d–don't—'' His head cocked quizzically. ''I'm not sure. I believe . . . we came down the rift . . .''

''From the East, then.''

But Stephen was staring into the fire, brow puckered.

''Dr. Ridenour?''

Stephen's eyes flickered up. ''What made it?''

''Made what?''

''The rift. How did it get so—large?''

''Oh, oh,'' Wesley muttered under his breath.

Matowakan laughed. ''Geologically? or philosophically?''

Following another careful, head-cocked consideration: ''Geologically.''

And Stephen was off, question marks in full flower, having

discovered a new, and equally patient, victim in Matowakan. Her grandparents glowed in his interest.

Wesley glowered.

Finally, in an undertone meant only for her: "It's that fucking computer, you know."

"Watch the language, Smith," she admonished, absent-minded reminder whose territory they were in. Then: "What *are* you talking about?"

"That fancy fucking mentor program. Taught him to ask questions, it did. Nothing but questions."

"Nothing?"

He glanced through his lashes at her.

She chuckled, and leaned to hug him. He shoved her off: a joking push, but it jerked her head, bringing a sudden wave of dizziness. She fell over into Stephen, caught at the arm he raised to steady her. She held there a moment, eyes closed, fighting to keep dinner down, the buzz in her ears muffling his startled query.

The spell was over in seconds. She squeezed Stephen's arm thankfully and pushed herself upright, taking her own weight. Once freed, Stephen rubbed absently at his shoulder. Not overtly or overlong, but enough. She hadn't spent several days entertaining him in sickbay not to recognize the symptoms. She brushed his concern for her aside and said: "If that shoulder's still bothering you, why'd you take on the Wesser, idjit?"

"It *wasn't*," he said disgustedly. "Besides, as I recall, it was *him* doing the taking."

"You earned it, brat," Wesley said, all pious innocence.

Stephen leaned forward to glare at him. Wesley raised an eyebrow, and the glare melted into a slow, shy grin. "Yeah," he said softly, "I suppose I did. —Always with the questions?"

Wesley looked at her. She looked at Wesley. They both looked at Stephen and nodded.

Stephen's grin faltered, his eyes dropped, and he set his half-eaten dinner aside. "Sorry. Didn't mean to be a —"

"Nor have you been, Dr. Ridenour," Inyabi interjected

smoothly. "Don't mind these two. I get the impression you've not felt able to question freely before."

"I—" Stephen's eyes flickered up. "Of course I have, ma'am, it's just . . ." He spread his hands: a graceful apology more eloquent than any words. "This is all very new. Honestly, I will *try* to keep my—vulgar curiosity—under control."

"I, for one, do not find you the least bit vulgar," her grandfather said, "and shall be greatly disappointed if you succeed in your efforts. However, my rude granddaughter's question has some value, *shitsoi*. How *is* your shoulder?"

Shitsoi.

A twinge of jealousy stiffened Anevai's spine. *She* was a rude GD. *Stephen* was *shitsoi*.

Stephen dipped his head, and with eyes respectfully lowered, said, "Better, sir, thank you. But I did jerk a few tendons in directions they'd rather not go before her repair job had fully healed."

Jealousy faded; she recalled a room deep in the mountain, and Stephen strapped to a Cocheta couch. Helpless, or so she'd thought, until he warped his whole body into a pretzel and slithered free. "You're lucky you didn't pull it right out of its socket."

"Again." Quiet, self-conscious laughter. "Dr. McKenna was *not* pleased. She insisted on going back in—minor stuff, but she said to rest it—or else." More self-conscious laughter. "I think I'd rather attend another of Nayati's parties than face McKenna's 'or else.'"

That hint of laughter, and the total lack of condemnation of Nayati's 'party' scattered her jealousy to the wind.

"What you need," she said, rolling to her knees at Stephen's back, and putting her hands on his shoulders, "is good old-fashioned therapy."

He tensed.

She whispered *relax* in his ear and started rubbing his neck gently, pausing occasionally to fingercomb his curly hair and lightly work the scalp. Muscle softened and she pressed the massage deeper; deeper still as his head started swaying with the motion.

Wesley rolled his shoulders suggestively. "He's not the one who had the neck-lock on him."

"My heart bleeds," she said, moving Stephen's newly relaxed shoulder gently in circles.

A full-blown Wes-sulk aborted in mid-sniff. "Swimming is good therapy."

"Wesley, I don't—" Stephen began, and Wesley interrupted: "I'll teach you."

Muscle solidified under her fingers. She gave a gentle shove between the shoulder blades. "Relax! Silly tode, —you don't have to swim if you don't want to." And when he'd acquiesced: "But much as one hates to endorse the Wesser, he's got a point—marginally. Water *is* good therapy. Remember the spring, CodeHead?"

"Spring?" His head fell back, and his eyes, glistening firelight gold, crossed slightly as he searched for her face, frown lines forming between his well-defined brows.

She smoothed the pucker with a fingertip and grinned. "Hot springs? Steam?"

He still looked confused.

She gave a curl a gentle tug. "Bubbles?"

A slow downside-up smile. "Oh . . . yeah." He sat up, all heavy-eyed eagerness. "Now?"

"You'd fall asleep and drown." She tapped him between the eyes and slipped back to her unfinished dinner. "Tomorrow. Lots of time, Ridenour."

"Gotta learn to swim, first," Wesley said smugly.

"Full of shit, Smith," Anevai said, despite her grandparents' disapproval of Wesser-ese. Sometimes, you just had to transmit in the frequency the antenna received. "Spring's waist deep, max. I think he'll survive."

vi

"Here they come!" Barry, their Designated Lookout, announced Cantrell's imminent arrival, and sped into place in the hastily assembling Security line. Across the reception foyer, lounging engineers and navigators likewise scrambled for position.

Communications was conspicuous in its absence.

Lexi pulled at the dress uniform's stiff collar for the fourth time and resignedly loosened her belt another notch. No doubt about it, she'd grown since the last time she'd had the thing on. TJ called it maturation; *she* called it putting on weight. Damned Recon fry bread. More dangerous than mama's pasta. And now (heaven help her uniform seams) ship's kitchen had imported it.

Dress unis. Formal reception. Last time Cantrell had pulled out all the stops was Councillor Eckersley's official inspection tour of *Cetacean* at Vandereaux. At that time, Lexi's Special Advisory Staff Sergeant position at the head of the security line had been a matter of pride; today, it left nothing but a sour taste in her mouth.

The Stingray's maindeck was in *Cetacean* core-dock, her highly classified transit thrusters parked in sync-orbit, 2.5k aft, properly shrouded in a field of sensor disrupters *Cetacean's* equally classified instruments could easily pierce if the thruster's specs weren't already in her onboard SecOneDB, which all her senior officers could access at will.

Politics. Who could figure?

Chet had been in contact with the SWI crew and their passengers. Lexi knew that. Knew also that he and TJ had been cloistered with Cantrell much—though not all—of the time since. She *didn't* know who they waited to greet in this highly formal fashion, or what, if anything, she'd be expected to do or say to him, her, it, or them.

For the first time in recent memory, she knew precisely what every other regular recruit knew and no more.

Worse, she didn't know why she'd been kept ignorant. When Cantrell had shunted her off to nursemaid Nigan Wakiza, she'd understood the Stingray to be hours away. Her call to ship's com to open-channel Nigan's little concert had intercepted the skuttle regarding the intruder's imminent arrival. She'd settled Nigan with a bunch of off-duty personnel, and returned to her quarters, expecting—at the very least—some message from TJ, corroborative or otherwise.

But there'd been no message, not even of the 'Meet me in my quarters' persuasion. Nothing until the general call to formal muster had echoed in her head—along with every other head currently in this reception hall. Technically, she had no right to complain.

Operationally, her unusual status made the whole situation damned uncomfortable.

Briggs and Cantrell entered, deep in conversation. Of Chet Hamilton, there was still no sign. Curiouser and curiouser. Shipboard rumor held the visitors hailed from one of the Big Three; 'NetAT should be represented. She sensed the stirring in the line, the glances to her for enlightenment she couldn't give.

A final private word and TJ joined them, leaving Cantrell with the engineers on the far side of the assembly room.

TJ's critical gaze scanned her, head to polished toe, nodded approval, checked out the rest of his personnel in the same way, then returned to her, brows raised expectantly.

She kept her eyes forward, chin up, and said nothing. She could feel the stirring from the rest of the line, all of them waiting for her to ask, all of them aware of the special relationship she had with the ship's upper echelons. They'd been noisy enough about her lack of knowledge when she'd arrived. Had made her the receiving end of no few kindly intentioned gibes.

Well, let them wonder. Let them all wonder. Including TJ. Time he decided was she a confidant or a mere recruit.

TJ's brow tightened. He took a backward step, and faced the line in more formality than he was wont to use.

"As you all know, the ship now in core-dock entered the Etu system early this morning without transmitting regulation ID codes. We issued a standard query, they returned an answer."

"Printable?" Someone downline asked, and the general tension eased in a ripple of laughter and ribald speculation.

"My response was less so," TJ responded.

More laughter. And Cantrell looked up, chance-met Lexi's gaze. Lexi ticked her chin up another notch and deliberately turned away.

"Soon as we get back to Vandereaux," TJ was saying, "Old Man Morley's going to get an earful. We know *who* they are, but not much else. They're from the 'NetAT. Two senior PR operators, Richard Herzog and Clarissa Naghavian. An aide, name of Daoud Ali. The rest aboard are SWI crew. They had the proper clearance, and the 'NetAT had the legal right to maintain com silence. Chet claims he's not surprised; that the 'NetAT prefers doing business face-to-face—which is marginally legal and dangerous as hell, if the locals happen to be nervous and a bit trigger-happy."

'NetAT; and Stephen downworld partying. One more reason to blame Cantrell. Dammit, she shouldn't have let him go down.

"I heard they requested a rim-side dock." Another downline query, voicing shipwide rumor.

TJ nodded. "At least, the passengers did. The Stingray captain nixed that idea before the admiral could even respond—no way he was risking his baby to preserve some stationer's dignity. They'll easylift from the core."

More laughter, amusement at the visitors' expense Lexi couldn't share. As a Recon transplanted into a spacer-filled environment, she'd grown a bit touchy about behind-closed-doors humor. What difference did it make that the 'Net Authority representatives were on their way out on the easylift, making a laboriously slow transition from the null *G* of the core? She'd seen no few of these station-born scoffers led blindly across the negative curvature of a planetary surface.

"How many are coming over?" she asked, now she was one of many.

"Everyone," TJ answered with similar impartiality. "Left the thrusters on baseline auto. Cantrell claims to want security verification on the lot."

She glanced past him to the admiral, who was deep in conversation with the engineers, presumably performing a similar edification. "Claims?"

TJ shrugged carelessly.

"All 'NetAT?" she persisted. "The crew, too?"

"They all collect their paychecks from the AT, but the flight crew is provided by the SWI Corporation. This Stingray is evidently very hot, and very closely guarded."

"So why the bios check?"

"You tell me."

She thought a moment, hazarded a guess: "Keep them close until we know their scam?"

A faint smirk twisted TJ's thin-lipped mouth.

"All 'NetAT," she mused aloud. "Seems strange that energy guzzler would come from Vandereaux and not bring Council reps as well."

TJ grinned outright.

"For all we know," Cantrell said, appearing at TJ's side, "someone aboard *is* Kurt's. Wouldn't be the first time one branch infiltrated another."

"What if they want to see Dr. Ridenour, admiral?" Lexi asked.

Cantrell raised an unruffled eyebrow. "I'm counting on it. He claims he wants to help out, let him keep them distracted. Get them down in the Well and out of our hair while we concentrate on Hononomii."

"And the Cocheta?" she persisted, all those present being privy to the high-security mission *Cetacean* had inherited on this planetary stopover. "The search for the Libraries?"

"No reason for them to know anything about it—it's not ComNet related."

"Stephen says it's his key to Smith's theory. Seems to me that makes it *related*."

"He says. He has yet to substantiate anything."

"And once they find out he knew and didn't say anything? *You* might have the authority to make that level of security override; it means Stephen's career. That's not fair, admiral."

Cantrell frowned. Hard.

Lexi's heart skipped a beat, but she refused to allow concern for her own career to show. Cantrell claimed she wanted candor from her advisors; let her prove it.

"Another reason to keep them close for a while, isn't it?" TJ interrupted. "Give us a chance to prepare Ridenour—so he *doesn't* screw up."

"Meaning a screwup would be his fault, TJ?" Lexi asked. "What *would* you two do without him to play scapegoat on this trip?"

The trapped audience's collective inhalation created—if her light head was any indication—a vacuum in the room.

"Admiral, —" TJ's hand closed on Lexi's arm . . . "Excuse us a moment." . . . and pulled her to the corridor's relative seclusion.

"Dammit, Lexi," he demanded. "What the hell's the matter with you?"

"With me? What about her? Sacrificing Stephen Ridenour for the sake of expediency just doesn't make sense—economic or otherwise. He's—"

"A big boy. And one who's caused enough trouble for all our lifetimes. He's lucky Cantrell doesn't lock him in the brig—"

"And me there with him?"

His head jerked as though she'd struck him. "Why would you think that?"

"Isn't that what this is all about? I let him go. You know that; I know that—Cantrell certainly does. Never mind he was right, and I was right to trust him—fine mess you all would have been in if he hadn't gone back—but none of that counts, does it? I disobeyed the admiral, no matter I was reading the situation more accurately than she was, and now I'm not to be trusted. Now my opinion means nothing. Well, dammit, TJ, if that's the case, *put* me in the brig. I'd rather—''

"Freeze your jets right there, Sgt. Fonteccio," TJ snapped. "I don't know what your problem is, but you're way out of line. Cantrell's got enough to handle without childish histrionics out of her own people. She worried too fucking much about Stephen Ridenour for too fucking long. She's finally exorcised him from her system and I suggest you manage the same. She couldn't deny him downworld visitation rights—that was out of her jurisdiction—''

"Wasn't out of her jurisdiction to force him down there in the first place."

"That order was necessary for him to accomplish his mission. But that mission is done; therefore Cantrell's power over his actions is dissolved. Get it through your head: He's an unassigned civilian. Chet's 'NetAT DProg cert and could, if necessary, competently replace Stephen Ridenour at a moment's notice. Could legally usurp him if he considered Ridenour the least bit incompetent to carry the information to the 'NetAT. Dammitall, anyway, what's your *problem* with him going back down?''

Finally, someone had asked the Question. Relief displaced anger, and she said, giving it every ounce of sincerity she had, "I'm afraid he'll stay, in spirit if not body."

"Would that be so bad? Chet's got that report of his. He can take it back to Vandereaux."

"And Stephen? What about his life? His career? What he personally can accomplish?''

"Lord, Lexi, you, too? Can't you and Loren get it figured? Stephen Ridenour doesn't *want* to represent Recons to the rest of our politically fucked up society."

"I don't care about that. I care about what he personally will lose if he's trapped here. I don't know *what* Cantrell cares about.''

''Don't push me, Lexi. —It's hardly a prison down there. Ridenour's a researcher. What he wants to do, he can accomplish from here. Better—he can work with Smith, a feat no one else apparently can accomplish.''

''Not if Smith and Anevai Tyeewapi continue to plug his holes, he can't.''

TJ's mouth gaped. ''His *what?*''

She tried desperately to explain, to take advantage of the rare confusion her accidental word choice had created. ''Everybody has psychological niches that friends—and enemies—fill. Stephen has black holes. He desperately needs affection and, even more, a place to belong. Smith and Anevai—''

''Fill his niches, do they?''

She nodded. ''I'm honestly afraid he'll create ties to this system nothing will break. And he can't stay here. In a way, where Stephen Ridenour is concerned, Recon contamination might be quite real. Kid's so damned lonely—''

''Smith's not Recon.''

''Anevai is, and I suspect *she's* the reason those two haven't killed each other.''

''You'd know.''

''Why do you say that?'' she asked, taken aback.

''Stephen talks to you.''

''Not since that last trip down.'' She twisted the ring on her right index finger, slipping it up and down over the knuckle. A ring that had belonged to another young man who'd suddenly grown silent and distant. ''I *don't* know . . . maybe that's why . . .''

His hand touched her arm; he'd known Tony, knew what that ring meant to her. ''You worry too much. He'll be fine. He's more spacer than not. And these *aren't* his people.''

''You know that. I do. But does Stephen? It's no good, Teej. He needs to eliminate the—'' She pulled the term up from her morning studies. ''—singularity from inside before he'll accomplish a damn thing—personally or professionally.''

TJ's pale eyes stared through her and she held her breath. TJ Briggs affected cool detachment, but she'd seen changes in Cantrell's treatment of people—suspected his hard-nosed justice behind it. Cantrell could use people, Lexi had seen her; TJ couldn't, and Lexi counted on that innate fairness now.

Above his head, the light signalling the corelift's arrival flashed. Lexi reluctantly called the fact to his attention, and TJ snapped back into RealTime.

"C'mon, kid. One problem at a time."

"TJ, wait." Lexi grabbed at his retreating arm. "What do I tell these people? What am I?"

Another stare, this time focussed on her soul, and a warm smile. "Use your judgement."

He led the way back into the room, but stopped just inside the door to whisper, "Cantrell was listening." He tapped the personal beeper implanted behind his ear, and when she opened her mouth to protest: "I made her, Lex. She tried to cut it and I wouldn't let her. I'll talk to her, Lex. It'll be okay. Promise you."

She dared not answer. Not here. Not now. Not with Cantrell's eyes on them. She moved back to her place in the security line; TJ fell in behind Cantrell.

The lift door remained stubbornly closed. Not terribly surprising: one never knew how practiced stationers were at shipboard gymnastics. Could be a lot of ruffled feathers needing preening.

The doors slid open at last on five people. Two, in 'NetAT fleet black, nodded briefly to Cantrell and fell in with the *Cetacean*'s engineers, who would take them to a secured area—making certain no one slipped them valuable information, inadvertently or otherwise.

The other three paused in the lift doorway as if—Lexi had the sudden impression—they were waiting to make sure all eyes were on them before making their entrance. A woman: tall, blond, excessively elegant; a man: her stylistic match, though dark; another man, noticeably younger in every way, clutching a briefcase and more than a little green about the gills. Likely the cause of the delay.

"Remind you of somebody?" TJ whispered from the corner of his mouth.

"Unkind. I was never *that* bad."

"I was thinking of Ridenour's first time downstairs."

She swallowed the first laughter she'd felt inclined toward in days. He was right, Stephen had assumed that precise shade of bilious on the short walk between shuttle and terminal: his first planetside walk since his childhood transfer to space. For Daoud Ali, the sudden reinstatement of gravity after days—perhaps weeks—of nullG, must have created a similar dislocation of Reality.

Not so for his superiors.

Power. Money and power. They reeked of it. It was in their clothes, their perfect features (doubtless under constant modification according to the latest published Standard of Beauty), but mostly it was in their expression, the assured confidence surrounding every gesture.

The Nexus Space ComNet was the unifying core of the Alliance, and the 'Net Authority the arbiters of justice in all matters regarding that device and the DataBase it controlled. 'NetAT personnel had to be well paid. Their decisions had to be what was best for the 'Net, now and forever. Unlike political parties and platforms, those decisions could not be revoked: a narrow-focussed mistake would be with the unalterable DataBase forever.

If it was unalterable.

The *Cetacean* crew had learned to question that universally accepted concept on this trip. If, as Stephen's research and their own experience here suggested, the 'NetDB *could* be modified, the resultant . . . mortalization . . . of the 'Net could adjust the entire balance of power within the ComNet Alliance. Make these three fight for raises, and they'd be as purchaseable as ordinary citizens.

Flawless features; precision responses to ritual phrases. Lexi wondered whether Stephen Ridenour would feel compelled to fall into this particular mold once the 'NetAT snatched him up permanently.

However, little as she understood the underlying structure at the 'NetAT, she rather doubted that Stephen would end up working for them in quite this capacity. He enjoyed anonymity, preferred keeping his pretty profile out of the public eye. What made his eyes sparkle was Design Programming. Lexi didn't know what that was exactly, but she'd watched Stephen with Chet and later with Smith. Commonplace power and money would hold no sway over him.

Unlike the poor sod standing puppylike at his superiors' heels.

Daoud Ali was, Naghavian was explaining, along to take notes for them and obtain field experience. Dark-haired, olive-skinned, with a large nose and eyes rather too closely situated, he seemed sad and a bit harried in this elite company.

"And this must be Sgt. Fonteccio, your Reconstructionist advisor I've read so much about. Most impressive." Herzog's perfect smile on his perfect face turned toward her. *"Quella vita brava, quando breva, bravissima."*

Hiding her surprised tingle, Lexi replied smoothly, "Not that brief, sir, but your recognition honors me, as does your command of Italian."

The smile twitched. "It's my job. But, I admit, more pleasant at some times than others." His sensual gaze shifted, scanned the room, settled on Cantrell. "And where is Dr. Ridenour? In bed, perhaps, at this—forgive me—unconscionable hour?"

"Downworld," Cantrell responded in similar tones.

"Downworld?" Surprise touched the smooth voice, the slightest of frown lines marred the smooth skin between his dark brows. "Victor Danislav indicated you'd agreed to bring Smith aboard the ship. That you understood the unusual circumstances of the boy's background. That you acknowledged the potential dangers . . . ''

Cantrell's backbone stiffened a degree, but she responded evenly, ''Better, perhaps, than Dr. Danislav. However, circumstances dictated otherwise. And he seems to have survived the experience quite—unaffected. He's doing a good job.''

''Ah, admiral, in your opinion, I'm certain he is.''

''Not mine, Mr. Herzog. I defer in 'Net related matters to DProg Hamilton.''

''No doubt. But I'm sure you'll understand that we must reserve judgement until we've spoken with Dr. Ridenour—and Security Communications Chief Hamilton. I am surprised he, at least, is not here.''

''Which? Stephen? or Chet?''

''SecCom Hamilton, obviously, since Dr. Ridenour is, as you just stated, not readily available,'' Naghavian broke in impatiently.

''Chet has his own schedule to keep. Your arrival was rather—precipitous, you must admit. You'll meet him soon enough.''

''At this—identity verification, I presume. Really, admiral, this is the height of—''

Cantrell frowned. ''And *this* is hardly the time or place to discuss the matter. The balance of the SWI crewmembers will be arriving shortly. I suggest we retire to my offices and continue there.''

She headed for the exit.

''At this hour?'' Naghavian's shocked query triggered a pause, a polite: ''Is there a problem?'' from Cantrell.

''Admiral, it seems to me that having ordered us from our beds, forcing us en masse over to your ship for an unprecedented inquisition into our veracity, the least you could do is provide us quarters to sleep out the rest of the night before *beginning* said inquisition.''

''Night? —Oh, yes. Forgive me.'' Cantrell's smile never warmed her eyes. ''I forgot. You're on 'Net standard. We've synced ship-time with Tunica—the Indigene capital. Of course, morning—your morning, whenever that may fall—will be soon enough.''

Naghavian's response was equally cool. "If you please, admiral, we shall require temporary quarters internally secured, separate sleeping facilities and connecting offices.''

"Of course.''

Lexi controlled her surprise at Cantrell's tacit acceptance of the visitor's decree, swallowed dismay as Cantrell continued:

"Lexi will see to it. However, it will, you understand, take some time to prepare such a suite.''

Herzog, obviously the more accomplished diplomat, intervened. "No rush, admiral. Give us an opportunity to get to know each other—perhaps even for a cup of coffee. You will understand, I'm sure, when I ask that Daoud accompany Sgt. Fonteccio to monitor the arrangements?''

"Of course,'' Cantrell said, and Daoud looked eagerly across the room at her.

Lexi's heart sank. Relegated to housekeeper and babysitter in one fell swoop. No forgiveness, then, regardless the admiral knew her reasons, but preferable—marginally—to the brig.

vii

"What about Nayati, Anevai?''

The light banter around him died. Stephen looked up to find all eyes on him.

"What do you want to know?'' Carefully noncommittal, the aura of easy confidence vanishing on the gusting breezes that set fireshadows to dancing in the forest.

"Have you . . . heard anything from him?'' Stephen returned his attention to the bowl of berries and cream resting in his lap, wondering absently where it was going to fit, imagining the glances being exchanged over his head.

They all thought he was crazy. Likely he was.

Nonetheless, he'd come here to find him—had to know:

"Is he . . . all right?"

"For God's sake, bit-brain—" Wesley, not Anevai. "—the man tried to use you for fertilizer; failing that, he tried to fry your brain. . . . 'Course, his mistake there was in assuming you had one."

Wesley, who had escaped clear to Acoma rather than meet Stephen Ridenour at the airport.

Berries bumped and jostled for new positions; Stephen forced his hands steady. "Well, he didn't succeed in either case, did he?" And in a more emphatic undertone meant only for Smith: "Ease off, Wesley, this *is* his family."

"That changeling doesn't have a—"

"Dammit, shut up!" he hissed in sudden anger. He'd had the term thrown at himself all too often to find Wesley's use of it now amusing.

Wesley held up his hands. "Hey, fool, I'm out of it. —Annie-girl, see if you can talk sense into him." And tossing plate aside in favor of coffee mug, he slumped deep into the backrest.

"Recognizing the inherent danger of reinforcing any Wesserism . . ." Anevai's scowl negated any implied humor. "Why do you want to know?"

"It's difficult to . . . Cantrell couldn't—" Or *wouldn't.* "—tell me much—not about him, anyway. Only that he survived the cave-in. I just—wondered how he's doing."

"Why?"

"I'm—worried, I suppose."

"Why?"

"It's just . . . I feel like we have something in common. Something . . . signifi—"

Anevai choked.

Wesley swore and slapped her sharply on the back. "You're crazy, Ridenour."

"Forget it," he said, and pretending it didn't matter, floated a berry into his spoon. This wasn't going to work. If there were any way to do it without insulting his hosts, he'd return to the Science Complex tonight. He'd found Nayati on his own before; he could do so again. 'Changeling,' Wesley had called him. Well, maybe Nayati was. Maybe *he* was as well. And maybe that similarity would...

"Perhaps," Matowakan's deep voice invaded his thoughts, "you will indulge *my* curiosity, Dr. Ridenour. What is this...commonality you feel exists between you and my nephew?"

Stephen set his jaw. Kind as Matowakan and his wife were, he barely knew them, and he was not particularly anxious to make a fool of himself. Increasingly uncertain of his motives, he preferred to drop the whole subject.

A hand pressed his shoulder. "Please, Dr. Ridenour. Trust your own spirit's advice above that of your well-meaning, but possibly naive, friends."

"Sir, I—" Stephen looked up into Matowakan's dark-brown eyes, and the rest faded in his throat. Something lay behind those eyes. Something warm...something safe...something— familiar.

He barely remembered his own grandfather—Ylaine Rye-vanishov's father; Papa's had refused even to look at him—but Mama and Papa would leave him in Granther's care when they went to church, and those vague memories roused something... warm and...safe...

He'd told Granther all his deepest feelings on those long, lonely mornings, and Granther had never laughed at him. And on the day Mama sent him away forever, Granther had hugged him and made Mama tell him the truth.

Matowakan, large-boned, square-jawed, his long grey hair held back from his face with red cloth, bore no physical similarity to that wraith from the past, but Matowakan Tyeewapi *felt* like Granther, and with that realization, his reticence faltered.

"I— It's hard to explain. That's why I want to talk with Nayati."

"Stephen, are you worried that what happened to Hononomii

will happen to you?'' Anevai asked. ''Is that why you want to find Nayati? Have him undo what he did?''

''No. . . . At least, not really. . . .''

''Succinct, clone,'' Wesley sneered.

Stephen swallowed a retort, said defiantly: ''He tried to make me unable to discuss the Cocheta. Obviously, he failed.''

''Obviously? How, obviously?''

''I answered all the admiral's questions, told her everything I know—''

''Under Deprivil?'' Wesley swore, long and loud. ''What *is* it with you? After Hononomii's—''

''I insisted, Wesley. But not under Dep, I can't take the stuff under the best of circumstances. She used hypnosis—also at my insistence.''

He didn't add that he'd *had* to know. Couldn't stand not knowing if he was doomed to become like Hononomii, possibly in the middle of his 'NetAT report. Reassurance he *still* didn't have. . . .

Stephen, let's talk about the tunnels, Cantrell had said as he lay on the Quiet Room couch. *After you escaped Nayati, how did you find your way out? How did you find us?*

And the answer had frozen in his throat—even under hypnosis. All that came out was the same half-truth he'd given Anevai . . . *Luck, admiral. Sheer, unadulterated, for once in my life, luck.*

But it hadn't been luck. Not totally. . .

He didn't want to lie, not then, not now. But he was no more able to tell Anevai and her grandfather than Cantrell. ''I told her about the Cocheta Library, the tapes, and Nayati's suggestion—I could remember it word for word. But that suggestion didn't work, did it? I mean, he told me not to tell, and I have and I'm not . . . how did he say it?'' Such false nonchalance: as if those words would ever haze in his memory: '' 'Flying with my Cocheta' at all. —No, that's not . . . I want to know . . .'' He swallowed hard. ''Anevai, what happened to

Nayati's father? Was he one of your people who disappeared—like my folks did on Rostov?''

"I don't know, Stephen. —Grandfather? Do you?''

The old man's face was unreadable in the flickering firelight. "What is the significance of the question?''

"Governor Tyeewapi said he'd used the Cocheta machines like—like Nayati did,'' Stephen explained. "I—I want to know if that's why Nayati disappeared, a—and why. I—I want to know—'' He laughed, slightly hysterical, and shrugged broadly. "Where I live, impromptu walks in the outback are a bit more . . . problematic. I thought maybe he and I could just talk, like we're doing now. I'm—off the clock now. I'd like to know *how* he experienced the Cocheta tapes. If he—feels different than—before. Who else am I going to ask?''

"Me,'' Anevai said abruptly. "Paul. The grans. We've all experienced the Cocheta tapes.''

"Not the same, Anevai. Not unless you lied to me.''

"You mean the suit? How much difference—''

"Zero to infinity. I've had it both ways, Anevai. Remember?''

"But—''

"Not the same,'' he maintained stubbornly.

After a long, suspicious stare, Anevai asked, with seeming irrelevance, "How did you find your way out of the mountain?''

He squirmed uneasily, the relevance obvious to him, and shrugged again, as meaningful an answer as he had to give.

"What are you driving at, Anevai?'' Wesley asked.

"I want to know how he found his way to Cantrell, that night in the Cocheta tunnels. —He'd never been there before, and you know how absolute the black is.''

"Nayati set him a light trail.''

"No, he didn't. Remember, I was there. Nayati was testing him. He wouldn't—''

"He *said* he was testing him,'' Wesley said, the two of them discussing him as though he wasn't there—or his recollection was of no importance. But Stephen said nothing, letting Wesley's rational explanations lead the conversation out of dangerous territory.

"Maybe he just didn't want Stephen to die. Nayati's a lot of things, but he's no murderer."

"Stephen called it luck . . ."

"Which, if Nayati didn't set a trail, it was. Our Stevie couldn't find his way out of a bathroom without help."

Stephen forced a laugh, swallowed it when no one joined him.

"Well, Stephen?" Anevai asked.

Avoiding all the curious faces, he stared into the fire, his face hot, while night chill touched his back. "Like I told you before, Anevai. Luck."

A long silence. The chill spread.

"You and I both know differently, Ridenour."

He shuddered, pressed his arms against a stomach gone inside out. "I don't know how to explain. I—I'm hoping Nayati does."

"And is that experience the brotherhood you suspect?" Matowakan asked, an honest-seeming curiosity, which chased the chill into remission.

Stephen nodded.

Wesley lurched to his feet, muttering an obscenity and sending his coffee dregs hissing into the fire. Stephen reached for him, drew back at the harsh scowl Wesley turned on him. "He . . ." But Stephen found the very breath frozen in his throat. Found himself physically unable to voice what he'd experienced in the darkness. Felt sickness rising to engulf him.

"Stephen?" Wesley's hand on his arm sent a startled shiver through him. . . . "You're serious, aren't you? What's this all about, really?"

. . . But a shiver of released tension, not emotion, and of a sudden, he found the words flowing quite freely. "I knew where to go because I could *feel* the mountain. I knew, when I . . . listened, exactly where every molecule was, every drop of water, every pebble—everything."

"Listened?" Wesley's touch deserted him; the words faltered.

He grabbed at Wesley's hand, soliciting that voice-steadying reassurance. "I could *hear* where Cantrell was, just —knew—how to find her, the way I know where my hand is, how to open the Cocheta doorway, and how to close it, the way I know how to open and close my eyes. When we were escaping, I knew when the tunnel was going to collapse, and when it was safe: the flaw in the tunnel structure was like a —a blister ready to pop. And Nayati *knew* I knew. *That's* what he challenged me to admit at the last. He *knew* I'd listened. And he knew what I'd heard. But I *couldn't* tell Anevai. Couldn't tell Cantrell. Couldn't until—"

—*until now.* He finished silently, wondering why, and subtly terrified of discovering the reason. He shivered, and dropped Wesley's arm.

"Listening to the mountain," Wesley parroted, increasingly sarcastic. "Good ears, Ridenour."

"Not—not just with ears. Everything. Like *you* know your own heartbeat, or the pressure in a vein—"

"What I *know* is you're nuts, AC."

AC. As in Academy Clone—Wesley's favorite derogatory term for him. He'd thought he'd never hear it again—not from Wesley, at least.

"Do you hear me arguing?" he asked quietly, and looking to Anevai for comprehension, if not sympathy: "That's what I'm afraid of. That's why I need Nayati. Why I need to know what *he* feels. I need to know if I'm c–cracking for good or . . ."

Anevai said reflectively, "Nayati did say you had the power, if only you'd *listen* . . ."

"Those were his exact words, *shitsoi*?" Matowakan's intense regard shifted to Anevai. She met that look, frowned hard as if considering her answer carefully, then nodded emphatically.

"Was there anything else?"

"He speaks of the Cocheta as gods. Of Cantrell and her people as demons."

"Not entirely unusual: Nayati has a melodramatic bent. . . ."

For the first time since that night in the mountain tunnels, Stephen allowed himself a glimmer of real hope. That he might not have to conduct the search for his sanity alone. He clamped his jaw on the question echoing in his head, slowed his heartrate, measured the time in breaths slow and deep, while Anevai and her grandfather lapsed into their own language.

Finally, as hyperventilation threatened, Matowakan said, "Forgive us. Some things are best expressed in their own terms. Tell me, Stephen, —*shitsoi*, —what do you understand about the Cocheta and their Libraries?"

"Understand? I *understand* nothing. I know they are—leftovers. Artifacts from some nonhuman species. I know you found them here. I know my father and his people found them on Rostov. Other than that—"

"You ask what Nayati experienced. Have you attempted yet to describe what *you* experienced?"

"I told you—"

"Before that. From the time you awoke in the Library, and later, during the session itself. What did you experience? How did you *feel*?"

"I—I remember being cold, and—surprised."

"Surprised?"

"That I was so clearheaded. Usually, when I've been anesthetized I'm...sick." An understatement, if ever he'd made one. Cold. Surprise. That odd cessation of his sense of touch when Nayati put the Cocheta suit on him. Even more strange, the lack of any real fear—

—until he recognized the machine, and older memories intruded. Memories of Papa and pain and the overwhelming need for silence. *Forgive me, Papa...*

He was shivering. Chill or fear, real or remembered—somehow the distinctions seemed irrelevant. Matowakan asked a question. It was important that he answer. He tried, but those ancient memories objected.

Warmth on his shoulders. A blanket. Wesley's arm settling on top. He pressed into that unexpected support and suddenly found the emotionally charged memories defused into simple, plain-language events. Nayati had put the suit on him, strapped him onto the couch, and then . . .

"There was sensory—input. First Nayati's. Then, the Other . . ."

"What 'other,' Stephen?"

Perhaps the voice was Wesley's. Perhaps Matowakan's. He no longer sensed who asked the questions, only an overwhelming need to answer. "The Cocheta—the entity Nayati's machine . . . introduced me to. I thought at first the Other was only in my mind. . . ."

Programmed sensations interfacing with his own nerve endings: the alien machine sending impulses through that suit, like a virtual reality TA without the tank. He remembered thinking at first that the 'invisibles' of Zivon Ryevanishov's memory were nothing more than a child's interpretation of those same sensations. That Stefan Ryevanishov's manipulations, first to force his son onto the Rostov machines and later using those same machines to silence him, were nothing more cruel than the act of a dedicated scientist using all the tools at hand to understand and protect the discovery of the century—perhaps of all time. He remembered thinking Nayati was similarly motivated.

And in thinking that, he had given Nayati and the Other the opening they needed. . . .

He faltered again, this time from very real embarrassment. He hadn't anticipated—had actually suppressed the memory. . . .

"Stephen?" Wesley's arm tightened, as Stephen shifted self-consciously out of his hold.

"The stimuli . . . the Other's motivational responses were . . . reproductive."

"That's a new euphemism for it," Anevai said dryly.

"N–not euphemism. I d–don't *mean* sexual. The input was *not* sexual—"

"For god's sake, Ridenour, I was there, remember? I saw—"

"It *wasn't*—" He paused, burning now, and not from the fire. He *hadn't* remembered. He should never have opened the subject, but since he had, some masochistic stubbornness forced him to continue: "My b—body may have reacted—as you saw, but the Other was—I'm telling you, the stimuli were—different, the responses were protection of the young, continuation of the species—"

"I've got news for you, Ridenour." Anevai jerked to her feet and retreated to the far side of the fire. "That's what it's frequently used for." She threw herself down beside Inyabi, who shushed her tenderly, but firmly.

"And 'hearing' the mountain?" Matowakan prompted, his scrutiny never wavering.

"I—" Stephen, embarrassed and confused, found welcome refuge in Matowakan's clinical detachment. "It first happened when I was on the machine. I thought then it was like Vandereaux's virtual reality trainers: programmed input that just feels real, but later—"

Wesley snorted, protested loudly about coffee and 'wrong throats,' and Stephen, tired of providing comic relief, clamped his jaw on the rest.

But Matowakan persisted:

"Later. You mean when you 'sensed' your way to Cantrell? You were not on the machine then, were you?"

His resolution wavered.

Before arriving in this system, he'd never, not in all his years at the academy, talked about himself and his feelings. Possibly because no one had ever asked, but neither had he ever sought an audience. From the first, Anevai Tyeewapi had gotten under, around, or through his comfortable privacy screen, and now this quiet, kindly man was realizing similar success.

Perhaps it was just that he needed answers—enough to ignore his embarrassment. Certainly enough to risk these ephemeral friendships.

Time folded. "I couldn't see anything." Memory took hold . . . "I was exhausted. Dizzy. Lack of food, I suppose—or maybe it was the Cocheta drug after all—and there was no light at all. I—I remember leaning against the wall. That's how I felt it the first time—through my hand. I was hopelessly lost—desperate for *any* answer. Anevai. Wesley. Nayati had threatened them both..."

He recalled how that strange throb that *was* the mountain had hit his gut. How he'd torn the Cocheta suit to press his heart against the mountain stone, and beyond that...

Nothing. Not an absence of words as before. He simply couldn't remember.

"Dammit, Ridenour," Wesley broke in, "can't you see it? You were right in the first place. That Cocheta thing's nothing but a fancy sim. Nayati planted the tunnel layout in your wetware 'banks and waited for you to get the sense to boot them up."

"No, Wesley," Anevai answered for him, "Nayati said—"

"Nayati *says* a hell of a lot. Nayati doesn't *know* a damn thing."

"And you do?"

"I know Stephen Ridenour didn't *hear* any fucking mountain!"

"Anything that doesn't fit into the Universe According to Smith can't possibly be, can it?"

"Anevai, —Wesley, —please..." Stephen murmured, their growing animosity making his gut churn...

"I know there's a logical explanation for Stephen's presence in that tunnel at the same instant the Door disappeared, and that fucking bit-brain, Nayati, is behind it."

...and getting them nowhere. "Wesley, *dammit*—" he yelled, and grabbed Wesley's arm; and Anevai yelled from across the fire: "If you know so damn much, what's *your* explanation?"

Wesley shook him off. "And if *you* know so damn much, why aren't you up on *Cetacean* helping your brother, instead of down here soaking your butt and stuffing your face?"

"I *couldn't.*"

"Why the hell *not?*"

"Because I'm *pregnant.*"

Instant silence.

"Pre—" Wesley began, then faltered.

"Yeah, Smith, pregnant." She jerked to her feet. "I've had

enough for one day. You two are on your own. See you don't kill each other—damned if I want to explain to Cantrell.''

She turned on her heel and left the circle of fireglow.

Anevai stormed off into the night shadows. Inyabi, with quiet reassurances to Matowakan, followed her.

Wesley found himself caught between concern for his young friend and the stimulated afterglow of one of their better arguments. Arguments that got the adrenaline flowing and the mind working at top efficiency.

Harmonies had been the result of one of their loudest.

''For God's sake, Wesley,'' Stephen said, his voice shaking with controlled emotion. ''How could you talk to her like that?''

Obviously adrenaline inducement was not a technique a prim AC like Ridenour understood. And Wesley, figuring it was time *this* AC discovered the fine art, shrugged indifferently. ''You're the one who started it, Ridenour.''

''Gently, Wesley,'' Matowakan intervened, old hand at reading and defusing that he was, *''Dr.* Ridenour doesn't realize this is perfectly ordinary for you and my granddaughter.'' And to Stephen: ''Normally, *shitsoi*, my loquacious granddaughter holds her own quite well. Right now, she's just a bit . . . hormonally imbalanced. Once she adjusts to her body's condition, Dr. Smith will not prevail so easily.''

Wesley met Stephen's under-the-brows glower with a superior smile. ''See?''

The glower darkened. ''Just remember, Smith, she's—unarmed right now. Lay off until it's a fair match.''

''Unarmed? *Fair?''* Wesley laughed. ''This is my first chance in *history* at a fair match.'' Stephen opened his mouth to protest, and Wesley grabbed his shoulder and squeezed. ''All right, kid, all right. I'll give her a reprieve.'' And far more seriously to Matowakan: ''How is she, really, sir? She said something this morning about not feeling well—had to lie down this afternoon. . . .''

''Early times, yet,'' Matowakan said calmly. ''Mostly, I

suspect she's upset because Nigan got to go up to *Cetacean* instead of her. She spent hours on the phone with him last night, telling him to check this, that, and the other that *she* never got to do, being under 'house arrest' as 'twere.''

"H–how early, sir?" Stephen asked quietly, staring into the glowing coals.

Matowakan shrugged noncommittally. "Early."

"A–and I took her from the sh–ship. P–practically *forced* her to go—she wanted to stay with her brother. And the crash—Nayati and the tunnels. My God—" He was shaking now, quite thoroughly horrified. "He *hit* her. And I—No w–wonder she's—" Stephen's eyes, glowing with reflected firelight, darted from him to Matowakan and back. "What did I *do* to her?"

viii

Finding the room configuration Naghavian had ordered proved easier than Lexi had anticipated. There was a suite on CDeck that Daoud declared adequate, and for internal security, a call to Chet assured her he'd heard Naghavian's pronouncement and would—quote—take care of it.

Somehow, she doubted they really expected an isolation scrambler. *Cetacean* was a SecOne Cruiser. Let Naghavian watch her tongue if she didn't want Loren Cantrell to know her business.

Daoud, sent to ensure the security of the accommodations, evinced concern only for his briefcase, which seemed reasonable, especially since he agreed to a security check without hesitation, once Chet's crew arrived. The check turned up nothing but notebooks, and a simple enhancement on the standard vector-shift lock on a single drawer in his personal quarters had the smile back on Daoud's face.

Daoud registered his Bio-print and relinquished the briefcase with a relieved sigh, grinned at her—flash of large, very white teeth—and asked, "Where now?"

"According to your boss, you're exhausted. Figured you'd want to crash."

"Oh, no. Huh-uh." He took a little hop. "I'm back in solid up and down. I've gotta stay awake until my brain believes it."

She smiled, less resentful of her babysitting assignment by the minute. "You didn't care for floating about, then?"

"The floating's not so bad. It's the bumping into walls and floors I found—disconcerting."

"You and Chet. He hates ZG with a passion."

"DProg Hamilton?"

She nodded.

Another gleeful hop. "Wonderful! Maybe that means it's in the genes."

"What genes?"

" 'Netter genes. Maybe I *can* make DProg."

She felt laughter bubbling again and jerked her head toward the door. "Let's get out of here and let the techs do their thing." As they sauntered along the corridor to the lifts: "Do your bosses hate ZG, too?"

"Them? Nothing fazes them."

"There goes your theory."

"Not at all. *They* aren't 'Netters—not really."

Interesting distinction. Lexi ticked it into memory to mention to TJ, but didn't press for more. Daoud apparently considered it usual enough, and chances were it was another 'of course' of 'NetAT dynamics she simply wasn't privy to.

She touched the call button for the lift and faced him. "What about Stephen?"

"Stephen who?"

"Ridenour. *He's* pretty good on the 'Net and he *loves* ZG."

"Hm-m-m." Dark brows made a solid straight line above his nose, and she couldn't tell if he was angry or just thinking. She'd meant to probe his feeling about the young 'NetTech, not start an argument.

"Hey, forget it. I was just—"

"I've got it!" Teeth gleamed again in his dark face "He's Recon. *Must* make a difference."

The lift arrived, and feeling at once frustrated at this old, old argument and nervous as hell that he so easily dropped SecThree information into a SecFive ear, Lexi hauled him into the lift and jabbed the EDeck code, snapping, "According to Shapoorian, a *big* one."

Daoud looked crookedly at her until the lift slowed and the door opened. He prevented her exiting with a lifted hand, stuck his head out to check carefully both ways, stepped stealthily into the corridor, and pulled her with him to the wall.

"Yeah," he whispered, "but *she* claims it should be the other way 'round. Us *spacers* should be more comfy in ZG, right? Looks like maybe the old bat has her ass on backwards again." He winked and let her go. "Remember, sergeant, the 'NetAT isn't Vandereaux. We don't adhere to its politics or social idiosyncrasies." He grinned and patted his stomach. "So—what's for dinner?"

She was growing to like this homely fellow, who seemed to find her laughter button with ease, and was oddly pleased when, given a choice between mess hall—which would be virtually empty at this hour—and sandwiches from the off-hours rec, he chose the latter.

As they wandered downrim, she probed cautiously, "You do realize, don't you, that *that* is not generally known?"

"You mean about Ridenour?"

She nodded.

He waved a dismissive hand. "You're Cantrell's Recon advisor. He's Recon. Makes sense, doesn't it? Your knowing, I mean."

"Yeah," she tried to keep the sour from her voice, "makes sense."

"Besides—" He grinned. "It's hardly a secret around the 'NetAT. Subject of some damn fine discussions, now his scores have circulated."

"Wonderful. He'll get there and it'll be the academy all over again."

"What do you mean?"

"Just that they knew there, too," she said cautiously. She figured Stephen could use a friend on the inside. Maybe . . .

"Knew which? His scores? or his parents?"

"You think his scores would matter to that lot?"

"Shit," he muttered. "Poor sod."

"You've got that right." She let the matter rest there. Let Daoud Ali draw his own conclusions regarding the results of their knowing.

Just maybe, that friend could be this increasingly charming Daoud.

A party was in full swing in the rec hall, and Nigan Wakiza was square in the middle of it. Word had filtered throughout the ship, and every onboard musician and wannabe who could get off had gathered for an impromptu jam. The result was an odd blend of the inspired and the positively painful.

They got drinks from the bar—Lexi gave Janna the high-sign and got a secret virgin—ordered sandwiches and wormed their way to an unoccupied pair of seats, Lexi making generic intros in the process. TJ had said use her instincts and those instincts said don't offer unasked-for information. She knew her fellow crewmates and they'd keep their distance.

The 'song' ended amidst a roar of applause and shouted requests.

"What's a Recon doing here?" Daoud yelled right in her ear.

"Which one?"

"The one on the—" The furor settled and he lowered his voice. "—flute, of course."

"There are three flutes—"

He glared at her.

She asked innocently: "You mean the one with the fringed jacket and moccasins?"

His nose twitched. "No, the one with Navigator's stars."

When she'd caught her breath and shooed all those who

wanted in on the joke out of their vicinity, she explained: "Half of those up there are Recon recruits. But the one you're asking about is Nigan Wakiza. He's from downworld."

"And maybe the next recruit?"

"I doubt it. Nigan is only one of several visitors. The admiral encourages it. Cultural exchange and all. That's how *I* came to be with her."

"Then you really *are*—that—Alexis Fonteccio?" Daoud's voice held a charming hint of awe.

"I'm not certain." Lexi half-smiled. "Do I want to be? Which?"

"Were you *really* involved in the Julian rebellion?"

She laughed outright. "Yes. Though it's nothing I'm particularly proud of."

"Still, it must have been exciting. I've seen the vid records and he seemed such a compelling..."

She frowned, and his comment trailed off. "Trust me, Mr. Ali, you'd not have enjoyed the experience."

He tipped his head apologetically, and said, "Forgive me. I open old wounds. So, what shall we talk about?"

"How about yourself? Where do you call home, Mr. Ali? And how do you come to be in such august company?"

"Hmm–m–m." He eyed her speculatively. "Only if you drop the 'Mr. Ali.' Makes me nervous. Daoud or Dave, *please*."

"Fair enough. So, where *do* you call home, Daoud?"

"Ptolemy Station Beta. They've got a small 'NetTech academy there run—or I should say, ruled over—by a retired DProg. She's a tough old broad, but she noticed me and recommended me to Sect. Beaubien, and he got me this far. Now, if I can just get someone to 'notice me' into the DProg track..."

"Listen, Daoud." Lexi laid a hand on his arm, withdrew it immediately as worshipful dark eyes met hers. "Let me clue you in. You want an organization like the 'NetAT to let you into its inner circles, you don't tell your life's history and ambition to a room full of strangers.''

"Have I?" His bright gaze flashed about their small niche. Every local ear was solidly attuned to the duet taking place on the improvised stage of tables. "Besides—" As the duet drifted to its conclusion and applause erupted around them. "How can you know I've been telling the truth?"

His brilliant grin split his lower face. He winked and then twisted around to join in the accolade.

Nigan caught her watching and waved, folded his flute into a beaded carrier and stuck it into his back pocket, complaining to the crowd of collapsed lungs, and jumped down. Another quartet immediately leapt up, taking his place amidst heckles and thrown napkins.

A moment later, Nigan joined them, breathless and obviously bursting with news. He nodded to Daoud, then said in Lexi's ear, "Did you hear about Hononomii? He recognized my music over the 'com. Cantrell thinks—"

Lexi hissed at him to shut up, flicking a glance toward Daoud. The 'Netter appeared to be watching the foursome onstage, which had settled into a fairly respectable comedy routine. But Lexi didn't trust that seeming obliviousness.

Nigan swallowed what sounded like a curse, muttered: "Sorry, Lexi," and : "I'll see you later," and disappeared into the crowd.

The room was well into party mode, and Daoud starting on his fifth (stiff) martini, when Lexi lamented her own need to retire. "I have to be up at the crack of, regardless what time Cantrell and TJ finally crash and burn."

Daoud laughed and said his bosses would sleep forever and quite certainly mess around for hours after, but seemed ready enough to follow her back to his room, and sober enough to remember to take his drink with him. He made it sound as if they made a habit of making their own rules.

"I thought they wanted to go after Dr. Ridenour immediately," she probed carefully while they waited for the lift.

"Hell," he said, slurring badly, "those two don't really plan on going downworld unless nec—es—es'ry. Give time to convince Rid—nour 'n' S—Smith t' c'm up."

Another interesting. She added it to the list of Things to pass on to TJ. The lift arrived, delivered them to his corridor, but as he had before, he drew her to the wall as if that would in some way protect them from being overheard and said quite clearly:

"It's not Herzog's business, is it? What the boy said. That's why you're afraid—"

Lexi just looked at him, knowing full well it was to Nigan's comment he referred.

"Don't— Just don't worry, okay? I won't say a thing. —Hey, what do I know, anyway? Just a name. What's in a name, eh, Juliette?"

He winked and disappeared into his room.

"That's it, kid. That's really all I can tell you. Hell, you were flying with it a week ago." Wesley tossed the last handful of bread crumbs into the pond and stood up, the enthusiastic fishy response shattering his ghosty-blue reflection into a thousand rippling pieces.

Tiny mouths sucked Stephen's fingertips, searching for more. He concentrated on that feeling, imprinting it on his memory, one sensation among many he would have to surrender forever soon. So very soon.

Wesley had brought him here to this actinic-lit pond after Matowakan and Inyabi chased them from kitchen and cleanup, assuring them of Anevai's good health and arming them with food scraps for the fish. Wesley had also deliberately led their conversation away from Anevai's—condition—to the far safer topic of his paper and the theory Stephen had come here to investigate.

And coward that he was, Stephen had let him.

And the quiet conversation—that unfamiliar give-and-take of ideas—had carried them back to the mesmeric glow of their first hours together. To a time before politics and subterfuge and personal idiosyncrasies had complicated their relationship.

"Strange," he murmured, half to himself, "it all seems so real now."

"What does, Stephen?" Wesley asked, quiet question from the shadowland of peripheral vision..

"The 'NetAT. My report. I came here knowing it would result in a query, regardless of my findings, but I never—" A slime-slick body caressed his fingers, then flipped away in a flash of blue scales and red-tipped fins. He pulled his hand from the pond and the mirrorlike surface slowly restored itself. "There's still so much I don't know..." he told the blue-scaled fish, "...so many questions they could ask that I have no answers for."

"Then I wouldn't have, either." Wesley's hand pressed his shoulder; and Wesley's eyes, reflecting blue in this artificial twilight, met his at the pool's surface. "We could spend the next fifty years discussing and arguing the fine points and ramifications, son, but we don't have fifty years. You know all you'll need, and a hell of a lot more. There's not a soul in a million out there that will even comprehend the questions you've answered yourself, let alone the ones that still drive you nuts."

"I wish..." But he didn't voice that wish. He had no right to it, and less to impose it on Wesley. He didn't *need* to go back—Chet could accomplish as much alone—but he had to. Had no choice but return to Vandereaux.

"So do I, kid. So do I." The edge of laughter he'd come to associate with Wesley was missing from that murmur. "More than that, I wish I could be there when you tell the 'NetAT the facts of life, just to see their faces." The laughter returned. "Unfortunately, somebody's got to stay here and keep these local-yokels out of trouble. So the report is all yours, sunshine."

Stephen snorted halfheartedly. "I've moved up on the scale of Wesser pronouns. Perhaps if I live long enough, I'll actually grow into my name." He paused, saw his reflection's brow knit for all he wasn't conscious of willing it. "Whatever that is. I don't really know anymore."

"C'mon, kid." Wesley grabbed his elbow and pulled him to his feet. "Bedtime. We're getting maudlin, and you don't need that, nor do I. Now about that self-motivation complex you were babbling about . . . "

They argued their way into the house and up to his room, where Wesley released him at last. He collapsed on the bed, breathless with laughter.

"I give up!" Wesley exclaimed, throwing his hands in the air and heading for the door. "You can't have a serious conversation with a mental midget!"

"Wait a minute!" Stephen hauled himself upright. "Who was it likened the 'Net to a man made of lead—"

"Tin. Learn your mythology, brat. —I don't know." Wesley leaned against the doorframe and examined his manicure, repaired it with a tooth-edged nip. "The 'Net is a system in definite need of a heart. I thought it a brilliant piece of insight, moi."

"You would."

Wesley grinned and said softly, "G'Night, kid. Hahstee manyahnee."

Dinner, wine, and station gossip. On her tab, in her office, and on her time, with her expensive HoloImager providing ambience to appease her *guests'* delicate sensibilities.

For people whose schedules had been so hideously disrupted, these 'NetAT employees certainly hid it well.

And while Cantrell fought heartburn, TJ sat across from her, stuffing his face as if this weren't his fourth meal of the day, and flirting outrageously with Clarissa Naghavian.

"Do you mind telling us what this is all about?" Richard Herzog asked abruptly over coffee.

If he thought to throw her off guard, he'd missed his mark.

"Do you mind explaining your mass overage?" Cantrell countered.

"Our—" Naghavian began, with every appearance of outraged virtue, but Herzog set a restraining hand on her arm.

"No need, Rissa," he said, smiling. "As you have obviously deduced, admiral, we have a few more passengers than we initially admitted to. We were guarding against—possibilities. They are 'NetAT police. You see, it is imperative that Dr. Ridenour return with us."

"Why?" she asked baldly.

"'NetAT override, admiral. ComNet security at stake. Please don't ask me to explain what I shall simply have to refuse to tell you."

'NetAT override. Nothing she could do about that, except to counter with her own diplomatic province:

"And I have operations underway which I likewise cannot allow you to jeopardize."

"Related to the shutdown? If so—"

"Only indirectly. Evidence we've gathered here indicates contamination of the 'NetDB is possible. We shut down to prevent further abuse."

"Then the fallouts on the 'Net *were* deliberately induced?" Naghavian asked, reference to their initial mission, a mission of steadily decreasing significance in the overall scope of their discoveries here, and Cantrell tipped her head, avoiding at once both direct lie and full explanation. "Then the perpetrators must be handed over to us."

"Not much chance of that. It's a big, friendly world down there to someone who knows how to take advantage of it."

"Threaten the populace."

"I already have. They prefer the shutdown to jeopardizing one of their own. Access has been curtailed. There's nothing more they can do to the 'NetDB, and much we can ruin if we press the issue at this time."

"You don't know what you're dealing with—"

"On the contrary. Nor shall *you* know before a combined committee has reviewed the entire situation. Until then, the shutdown remains."

" 'NetAT override—''

"You forget what you're dealing with, Mr. Herzog. *Cetcacean* is a SecOne Council ship. Mr. Briggs, Mr. Hamilton, and myself constitute a full Head. Our agreed-upon decision takes precedence over any single-body preference. Only a combined committee decision can override."

"Stalemate, then."

"Not quite. I'm not at all unreasonable. Your head offices had reason for sending you out here. We'll aid you as we can without jeopardizing our own operation. As for your police: they will stay aboard your ship or ours, as you please. They'll be more comfortable here."

"We'll require them to be with us."

"Not downworld. Under no circumstances will they be allowed contact with either HuteNamid Corps. If you find it necessary to strongarm Smith—or Ridenour—you'll do it through *my* people. We've a rapport with the indigenes I'll not give untrained troops the opportunity to undermine."

"We'll need to see Ridenour."

"We've shuttles going down daily. I'll assign security liaison with downworld clearance to accompany you—once Chet has cleared you."

"You persist in this belief, admiral, that we shall go downworld after this person," Naghavian said. "Quite the contrary. We expect Ridenour to meet with us here. Immediately."

"I—advise against that. Smith will undoubtedly distrust such an abrupt recall . . . perhaps advise him. Would you undermine that association? take that risk?"

"Would you undermine his association with the 'NetAT? Additional review of his records has already assured their interest. We're here to expedite his mission and return him personally to Vandereaux, where he may begin his studies."

"And Smith's cooperation?"

"Smith's cooperation has become—irrelevant, admiral. Recent developments have made Dr. Ridenour's original mission—obsolete."

"I don't understand."

"Forgive me," Herzog said placatingly, "but it's not for you to understand, admiral. This is 'NetAT business, and between Dr. Ridenour and us. I expect him to be here when we awake *tomorrow*."

Cantrell stiffened. "Tomorrow morning will not be possible."

"I'm sorry?"

"Aside from the Security Checks which you have personally delayed, there are planetary constraints. It's evening, planetary local. If would be rude to attempt contact before morning. Even then, it might take some time."

"Why?"

"I told you, Dr. Ridenour has gained Dr. Smith's confidence. Dr. Ridenour is . . . out of pocket. He and Dr. Smith have gone to Smith's personal retreat to review Smith's concept. Communication with them has been—curtailed."

"You mean he's not been informed of our arrival?"

"When you made a silent entry? When you had to be challenged before giving us a baseline ID? Stephen Ridenour is not *Cetacean* personnel, Ms. Naghavian. Had your ship posed a physical threat, I would be remiss to put his life in danger by insisting on his return."

A cool smile slid across Naghavian's face. "You must admit that cessation of NSpace-interface with this system was sufficient motivation for caution on our part."

Point, Naghavian, TJ tapped to her ear.

"Possibly. But then, your deliberate falsification of entry data gives me ample reason now for caution." **And counterpoint.** She allowed the side of her mouth to twitch an answer. "Once you and the crew have passed Bio and Psych scans, we'll have more to talk about."

Naghavian frowned and said, "I thought Dr. Hamilton would be here by now. I assure you, this is not the treatment to which we are accustomed."

As if on cue, Chet's voice paged her over ship's 'com.

"We're still here, Chet."

"Any coffee left?"

"C'mon down. We'll combine the dregs."

"*Offer I can't refuse, boss-lady. Two minutes—shit. Have to wait. Tell them I'll have the boards set for them first thing tomorrow. Gotta go.*"

"Ciao, Ham."

From the exchanged look, the 'Netters failed to appreciate the casual repartee; TJ, silently inhaling a second desert, reached up as if to scratch his head and tapped a silent **tsk tsk** to her inner ear. She returned a rather more explicit phrase via the same code, and his inhalation underwent a sincere disruption.

With an air of polite revulsion, Naghavian rose from the table.

"If you don't mind, admiral, I'm quite exhausted. I assume our quarters have been prepared by now?"

Cantrell smiled tightly. "Let's find out, shall we?"

She tapped the com-connect in the armrest console, and paged Lexi, who answered immediately with a *Go* on the rooms, showed up moments later to accompany the two agents to their rooms.

When they were gone, Cantrell said to TJ:

"They're going down."

"Wish you could stop them, Boss-lady. He's not up to their standards. Not now. Even if he could before—Smith's gotten to him. He's ready to believe in kindness—that makes him dangerously vulnerable."

"Lexi's word on it?"

He nodded. "And mine."

"You're both right. But we can't stop them. Not legally and not morally. The 'NetAT had a reason for sending them. If Chet can't divine it, maybe Stephen can."

"We've got to warn Ridenour. Prepare him."

"Talk to Smith. He knows the game better than any of us possibly could; claims he wants to help the kid. So let him prove he's useful."

"You want to do the talking?"

"Are you kidding? I'm a challenge. Anything I suggest, he'll try to accomplish exactly the opposite while appearing to comply with my every wish."

"Chet, then."

"Wrong."

"Paul?" A woeful-eyed, last-ditch suggestion.

She shook her head. "Way beyond his jurisdiction."

TJ sighed heavily. "I'll put the call through first thing tomorrow."

II

i

Wesley couldn't sleep. Too many short nights; a brain that refused to deBoot.

He tossed. He turned. He battered his pillow.

Which got him covers on the floor and a lumpy pillow.

He rolled off the bed, tossed the covers back up over the mattress, and went to the door that led out onto the balcony. Light from the waxing moons seeped past closed drapes. A slit allowed a temptingly cool trickle of air, heavily laden with night scents, into the room. He pushed the door wide, and the trickle burst into a river that swirled and eddied around his body, drying the sweat and making him tingle all over.

Outside, a figure leaned on the railing. Soft silk molded to rounded muscle on one side, snapped gently in the breeze on the other. The curly head tipped to face the breeze, an idle hand combed through the curls, slipped down the collarbone, lingering to slip a button or two, opening the collar to the wind, and smoothed the fabric over narrow waist and hips.

Wesley swallowed—hard—and eased toward the quiet figure, his bare feet obligingly silent on the wooden balcony.

Moonlight limned a high cheekbone, tipped long eyelashes in silver. Hands braced on the wooden railing, Stephen leaned into the wind, eyes closed, tiny, vaporous whirlpools whipping hair and pajamas where it would. His shoulders lifted, his chest expanded, held a moment, then relaxed into a low chuckle.

"What's the joke, kid?"

Thanks to his amazing reflexes, the kid failed to make a mess on the rocks below: a feat which, from the shocked expression that greeted him, he was incapable of appreciating.

"Good *God,* Wesley," Stephen gasped. "Don't *do* that!"

Definitely incapable. Wesley released his steadying grip and sprawled onto the balcony seat, crossing his legs and resting his arms comfortably along the back, as night breezes played gently across his bare skin.

"Aren't you afraid of catching pneumonia?" Stephen asked dryly, collapsing onto the opposite end of the bench.

"Jealous?" Silver-blue nightlight might disguise color, but he recognized the minute duck of Stephen's curly head.

The kid was blushing.

But a less pronounced duck than might have been, and the white flash of teeth indicated tempering embarrassment. He grinned back and pushed the envelope another degree: "Besides, with me there's no pretense. You think that thing you're sporting does anything other than make a person want to rip it off?"

The flash of white vanished.

Mistake. Definitely high oops-quotient.

He grasped silk-clad shoulders and turned Stephen toward the moonlight to find a face puckered with upset. He leaned forward, examining the worried face at exaggeratedly close range until the worry dissolved into choked laughter.

Never failed, that Look.

"And did you?"

The past tense caught him off guard. "Did I what?"

"Want to rip my clothes off."

"What are you talking about?"

Stephen's moon-silvered eyes avoided him, taking in everything and nothing of the surrounding shadows. "That first day, when we met and you..."

He remembered, all right. Remembered an elegant academy-clone standing in the shadows by the pub door, awaiting, so he'd assumed at the time, *the* perfect moment to make the most dramatic entrance. Remembered his own blatant disregard of Anevai's warning...his hands running uninvited under a tantalizingly draped sweater and over shrinking bare skin...

"You asking why I tried to rape you right there in front of God and everybody?"

Stephen's eyes flickered his way. "I—I wouldn't put it quite that way, but—"

He shrugged. "I would. Hell, kid, that was a test. I never thought that coming out of Vandy-O you could possibly be as modest as Anevai maintained you were—oh, yes, she warned me—I just didn't believe her. A stuffed shirt, yes, but unable to handle a pass—that I didn't look for—particularly in someone with your looks."

"W–why did you—"

"Because I'm a bastard, Stephen. At first, I was testing you to see if you would take it with a sense of humor, or if you were going to be an ass. Later—I just don't know. I haven't been thinking real clearly where you're concerned."

"Then you didn't really want to..."

"Honestly, Stephen?"

A tentative nod.

"Then I'd be lying if I said no. Under some circumstances, I have an appalling lack of discrimination, and you're a very attractive fellow. If you'd been willing, I wouldn't have been sorry—unless you'd turned out to be an ass after all. Probably not even then, if you'd been a well-trained ass."

"But *why* did you think..." Glittering eyes dropped and long fingers plucked self-consciously at a draped shirttail. "Oh."

He'd meant it as a joke: Ridenour wore such outlandishly

sexy clothes, he'd assumed from their first meeting it was a conscious look—

"I—I never thought much about... I never meant... I just choose fabrics that f–feel good. Styles that..."

—He should have known better. He'd told Cantrell to send the kid down here for a confidence boost. So far, he was batting 1.000—for the opposing side.

"Son," he said, with every ounce of sincerity he could pack into his voice, "the day you can't walk around in a garbage bag and make most people want to tear it off, will be the day they send your ashes into some lucky star. That doesn't mean there's anything wrong with you, or with the people who want to do the tearing. It's human, it's healthy and it's honest. Those who say they don't feel such things are lying to themselves."

"Good—God."

"But it's not because they want to rape you, or even to make passionate love with you—though no doubt no few of them would be ready and willing to oblige you—it's because you're damn beautiful."

"Wes, please—"

"Hear me out, child. Your physical beauty is the wonderfully serendipitous sort only genetics and a lifetime of training can achieve. It's the ultimate expression of the magic of nature—not the science of humanity. Looking at that kind of beauty reminds us of the magic."

"Wes, —"

He raised a hand. "Manners, brat. —All that shit that happened to you at Vandereaux was exactly that—shit. Screw them all, I say. If Bijan Shapoorian hadn't been jealous as hell of you—if his *mama* hadn't been a council member—he'd never have gotten away with all those terrible things. And if—"

"Wesley, I *know* that, I'm *not* the fool you—" A sudden, startled look. "What 'terrible things'?"

God save him from adolescent egos. "That you told Anevai about. —And don't worry—" As Stephen swore and retreated to the rail, clutching it with both hands. "—nothing for you to be ashamed of. Hell, kid, that you survived at all is something to be *proud* of. Remember, I *know* Vandereaux. When I think of the fights and petty back-stabbings you must have had to deal with—"

"Yeah, right. Fights."

The sullen murmur triggered memories: a figure huddling in the dark, wide drug-dilated pupils, soundless endurance when escape failed . . . Escape from him. And his accusations. And his blows . . .

"Is it because you didn't fight back, Stephen?" Residual guilt, however warranted his actions may have seemed at the time, made his voice gentle. "No one can blame you for that. You were younger, outnumbered—"

A careless hand cut him off.

"Oh, I fought back, at first. How do you think this—" His left shoulder twitched. "—happened? Eventually—well, I survived."

"That's all that counts."

"Yeah, sure." But it was acquiescence in word only. The sullenness remained, and attractive as the kid's backside was, it wasn't his most revealing view. To know what he was really thinking, you had to see his eyes.

One thing was certain, anyone who had graduated top in his class, with a fourth-echelon rating, and who had the attention of the 'NetAT before his twenty-first birthday, had no business wallowing in self-pity.

"Time to grow up, kid," he said. "You're going back into that world—back to the Bijans and the Victor Danislavs who think you're fair game in a variety of ways."

Stephen swung around to face him.

"Wesley, dammit, I *know* that, I'm not the fool you—"

"But you've got the tools and the power to laugh in their faces. Don't let them frighten you or dictate your life anymore."

Silver eyes slipped past him. Behind the curly head, moon-shadowed, windblown clouds chased one another across the sky.

Eventually: "I'm not stupid, Wes. It's just—" Stephen faced him squarely. "Do you remember the last time someone held you and it didn't hurt?"

His mouth twitched . . . "I sure do, although maybe that doesn't count. Sometimes you did get a little—"

"Dammit, I'm serious. When was the last time someone gave you a just because?"

. . . and laughter bubbled out. "A *what?*"

But Stephen wasn't laughing. Wasn't even close to it. "A just because. Not because they want something, not because it's the politically correct action. Just—because."

He sobered. "Specifically?"

Stephen nodded.

"In that case, I couldn't tell you. We're pretty friendly around here—"

"I can," Stephen said, his voice more whisper than not. "Before I came here, it was Monday, the twelfth of March, 'Net standard."

Monday. March twelfth. Something odd about that. He calculated quickly—finally resorting to his fingers: "But March twelfth wasn't on a—"

The whisper grew stronger, revealing a touch of bitterness . . .

"It was eleven years ago." Stephen sat back down and clasped his hands in his lap, a quiet, self-contained statue. "Three days later, Mama held me for the first time in months— just before I boarded the shuttle. Not that she really cared: that's what mothers are supposed to do, isn't it? —What would *you* do if virtually every touch from a human hand you clearly remembered had brought pain—deliberate, physical pain—and if much of that pain involved what your rational mind knows as physical intimacy, which, according to its hype, is pleasurable?"

"For God's sake, Stephen, let it—"

Bitterness and a hint of desperation:

"What would you do if the only times you'd ever—" A

white edge of teeth clamped the full lower lip, drawing blood.
"If the only reactions you'd ever experienced were . . . If you
knew you were responding to totally outrageous stimuli and
responded anyway?"

Responded? How and to what?

Stephen's words roused memories of another night in this
very house, less-than-gentle caresses, and a hoarse *I suppose I
love you too. —So what?* And later, a whispered *I can't.* And
an escape over the footboard.

But Anevai had said *It was all for me . . . He treats it like
currency. . . .*

Probably a difference in the exchange rate, he thought,
deliberately encouraging the cynic within. Since Ridenour insisted
on confronting, then skirting, this particular issue every time
they met, let it be over and done with.

"Maybe there really *is* something wrong in me." Stephen's
eyes fell to his lap, where hands clasped white-knuckled on
silvered silk. "That what I regard as not only unpleasant but
quite—repulsive—is what others regard as loving and healthy
sexuality. . . ."

Silvery eyes met his. Silver limned with sparkling damp.
The kid was good. He had to give him that. Made a body
wonder where the stutter had gone. It was the only thing
missing from the act.

". . . Wh–what *would* you do, W–Wesley . . . ?"

Ridenour's *revelation* reeked of manipulation, though he
doubted Stephen manipulated for his own sake. In Jonathan
Wesley Smith's experience, there were all too many people
ready to use gems like this boy—and all too many gems ready
and willing to be used—to waste pity on one more.

". . . I–I'd r–really like to kn–know."

"Ah. The stutter. I'd nearly given up hope."

After an appropriate period for the barb to register, the eyes
would widen:

Right on cue. Next came the shiver.

And still he found himself thinking foolishly: *Why, Stephen?*

Why now? Don't you have everything you could possibly want from me?

He challenged that gut-level ache:

"What is this, Ridenour? Some new brand of come-on?"

"God, *no!*" The predicted shiver—

—and a retreat to the shadows inside.

Bait.

He didn't snap. Vulgar curiosity about Ridenour's next move kept him where he was, though the night breeze had turned cold and urged him back to bed. (His own, thanks.) Stubborn pride kept him there long past the time the chill reached bone-deep, and pride clenched his teeth against audible chatters, knowing those silver eyes were watching.

Softness brushed his thigh, drifted into fuzzy folds at his feet; Stephen's silky-smooth voice whispered from the shadows, "You don't need to freeze your ass to prove your superiority. I'll leave in the morning."

"Like hell. You're Anevai's gues—" Teeth chattered, caught his tongue, and his superb gesture disintegrated into a well-rounded, multisyllabic curse.

"Just put on the damn robe." Stephen's whisper cut through the stream, and the shadow disappeared into the deeper shadows of the room.

A creak of springs.

A rustle of quilts.

Silence.

Shit.

Wesley hooked the robe with his foot, shrugged it on without standing, and sat in the warm tent until the shivers evaporated. Fur brushed his chin, unwittingly recalling a childish exclamation and a rush across a crowded market to the open stall just to pet that fur lining, a careless agreement to pay the outrageous marked price—which had so scandalized the shop owner, she'd practically given the garment to the kid. . . .

I just choose fabrics that feel good . . .

No matter what base you added in, Stephen Ridenour made

no rational sum. And that elusive unknown would haunt him forever if he let Stephen escape tomorrow.

"Stephen?" Wesley called from the doorway. "Where do you want the robe?"

For a moment, he thought Stephen was going to pretend to be asleep, but: "Keep it."

"Don't be an—"

"I said, *keep it*. I—don't need it anymore."

"For God's sake, fool—" He stepped inside and dropped down beside the lump on the bed. The lump disappeared and a shadow-Stephen slipped across the room to stand near the hallway door.

Escape route.

Wesley folded his arms and glared at the shadow, momentarily checked.

But far from mated.

He relaxed back against a pillow and, as though Stephen had just asked, said conversationally, "I suppose I'd grow into a resentful, screw-them-before-they-screw-me bastard. Figuratively speaking, of course. There are a number of very creative ways to screw people politically and economically."

From the shadow: "S—sometimes that isn't an option."

He controlled the amused twitch of his mouth. Ridenour was playing the game, dancing lightly over the trap. He set another. "I don't *know* what I'd do, in that case, but I know what I'd advise you to do—find someone who can teach you the difference."

The shadow moved around a dresser and sat down on the edge of the bed pressing against the footboard.

"Who?" it asked, diving headfirst into the noose.

And he found he couldn't reel the prey in. He smiled, not quite believing his own banality: "When the time, and the person, are right, Stephen, you won't even need to ask the question."

A tiny caught breath, like a child who'd cried himself to

sleep: a sound he would forever associate with Stephen Ridenour. A sound that obliterated suspicion—at least for tonight.

"Please, don't go, Stevie-lad."

"I—I can't— H–how can you—"

He held out his arms. "I got one humongoid hug going to waste here, brat. Better come use it, quick."

The shadow shivered. He opened his arms a degree wider, and the shadow launched itself, knocking him to the floor, devolving the hug into a laughing, wrestling tangle of arms and legs, heavy robe and pillows until a thump on the wall and a sleepy protest brought them to panting sensibility.

Wesley gathered the pillows, helped straighten the quilt, pointed a demanding finger at the bed, and drew the covers up to Stephen's chin.

Stephen yawned widely, and murmured, "Thanks, old man."

"Any time, brat." He smoothed the curls back, brushed an exertion-flushed cheek with his finger. "See you tomorrow?" And tried to ignore the warm glow when the kid pressed his cheek into his palm and nodded.

"I need you to do me a favor."

Paul Corlaney held the receiver at arm's length where his sigh wouldn't register. He should have known Loren's late-night call would be for other than an exchange of sweet nothings.

"Anything reasonable, Loro, you know that."

"I need a go-between with Smith."

"I said, anything *reasonable*."

"Paul, this is serious. It's why I'm going through you. I can't afford a clash of egos—Smith and I are too inclined to argue."

"So have TJ handle it."

"He's spent the last half hour convincing me to bring you in just so you could."

The coward. "I don't *need* any more 'ins.' "

"No choice on this one. We've got visitors."

"Visitors? What kind? From where?"

"Vandereaux. They're 'NetAT. Got a callback on Ridenour. Haven't been able to figure why yet, but I've got my suspicions and I don't like the smell of it. Smith said he wanted a chance to wise the kid up. I think he'd better not waste any time doing it."

"Wise him up about what?"

"Politics. Functioning within The System."

"Loro, *Wesley* doesn't function within *any* system. That's why he's here, for God's sake."

"By choice. I've spent too much time with politicos and technocrats, Paul; Smith has the moves. Better than you ever did. So do these two. I fear Stephen's going to need all the help he can get."

"So what do I tell him?"

"He's got one day for sure. Maybe two. I'll stall them, but they seem damned eager."

"I'll call him first thing tomorrow."

"Thanks, old friend. One more thing."

"Yeah?"

"Tell Smith to watch his own ass. If they find out the score, I'm not so sure they won't sweep him in as well."

"I'd be more inclined to warn the agents, considering the state he's in right now, but I'll tell him."

"What 'state'?"

"He's been pushing hard the last few days. Was looking forward to sleeping and eating, swimming and eating, and not much else."

"Call me after. I want to know how he takes it. If he's about to blow, I'll pull Stephen out myself."

"Yeah. G'night, love."

She made a suggestion designed to keep him awake for hours and signed off. He waited for the severance click of orbit to ground com, responded in kind to the security op's pleasant *Good night, Dr. Corlaney,* and hung up.

So, Wesley was going to instruct Ridenour in the pitfalls of life in the fast lanes. He'd like to be a fly on the wall of *that* schoolroom.

As the offspring of two highly political individuals, Jonathan Wesley Smith certainly had the training. He'd lived in Vandereaux station, gone to (and been expelled from) Vandereaux Academy. Beyond that, he didn't talk much—odd for so vociferous and egocentric an individual.

Something had made him hate that selfsame 'system' with a passion. Something had made him thumb his talented nose at the 'NetAT Design program and escape to a minor academy for an undistinguished degree and to HuteNamid for an undistinguished career.

Undistinguished until that paper of his reeled in Stephen Ridenour. And Ridenour's investigation of that paper might just blow Wesley's little personal cover-up wide open.

His story had all the trappings of a bad romance without any apparent love interest, but it certainly hadn't turned him into a monk. While he left (according to his own report) a well-deserved rep behind him everywhere he went, none of the locals who'd been the recipient of his 'favors' had ever complained.

No, somehow Paul doubted a human love had played any part in Wesley's disillusionment. Somehow, he suspected the disillusionment was with the System itself. That very System which Ridenour's arrival was about to thrust him back into.

And Paul Corlaney was the one elected to give the final push.

Thanks, TJ.

ii

Someone had stuck his head in a drum and was beating hell out of it.

Wesley groaned and buried his head under two pillows.

The pounding continued.

The door. Someone was mutilating the door.

"Wesley! Wake up!"

The door opened. He threw the pillow, the only weapon at hand. It bounced two meters off-mark.

"Missed me," Anevai pointed out kindly.

He growled and pulled the quilt over his head. She laughed and yanked it off—all the way. He protested and covered himself with another pillow.

She laughed harder.

He sniffed. "Whaddaya want?"

"Phone, Sleeping Beauty. Dr. Paul. Said to wake you up. Says it's important."

"It'd better be," he growled, and, throwing on Stephen's robe, stalked the phone in the hallway.

Anevai grabbed his sleeve as he passed. "That's Stephen's."

He gave his best Cheshire cat as he picked up the receiver. "Hang up the other, will you? Private, you know."

She sniffed and bounced down the stairs, last night's little pique evidently forgotten. He waited for the click, then growled, "Whaddaya want?"

"Please hold."

Wasted: Paul had put on the auto-recept. He sighed and slumped down on the top stair, waiting. Only so far you could play the game, and only something really vital would have prompted Paul to interrupt—

"Wesley?"

His eyes snapped open.

"Yeah, Paul, I'm here."

"Time to pack up and come home. Party's over."

Stephen stopped, panting heavily, and leaned over, braced hands above the knees and stretched his lower back, arching up . . . and down. Up . . . and down. Hands flat to the ground to attack hamstrings gone metallic. Light bounces. Hands behind the knees, press the chest—

"It's Dr. Stephen!"

Stephen jerked upright. Gravity attacked blood pressure, and he went down in a dizzy tangle as Acoma youngsters swarmed around him, small hands and shrill voices all talking and pulling at once.

"They said you weren't coming back—"

"We found the tapes of you—"

"What's it like, flying in ZG?"

"Will you show us how to—?"

His head finally cleared enough to sort out the faces. Male and female, all prepubescent, all with the dark hair and eyes of the local IndiCorps. Some he'd met in passing his last time here. Others, he didn't know at all. One seemed to have discovered his own checkered past included a stint on the Vandereaux gymnastics team—a concept which apparently held universal fascination—and nothing would do but that he give them a demonstration.

He smiled and held up his hands in tacit defeat, their enthusiasm reviving the best memories of his academy days. Memories not only of his own experiences, but of the joy of working with the beginning students, of reliving his own first flight time after time through theirs.

He stripped off his sweats and running shoes. His sweat-wicking gym suit would keep him warm enough and the sweats could be dangerous working with kids' flailing hands. The shoes would just get in the way.

Besides, the grass felt good between his toes.

The receiver clicked into the cradle. Wesley yawned and pulled the robe closer. Damn Cantrell, anyway, waking a man up from a perfectly good sleep for such disgusting news. 'NetAT agents—the real thing, this time, not a kid drafted as a scum-of-the-universe Del d'Bugger.

And they were after the kid—likely himself as well. He knew that even without Cantrell's suspicions. The puzzle that was Stephen Ridenour mandated it. Now, just when they were getting comfortable, he had to break the news to Stephen that it was finals week.

Shit.

He went back into his room and pulled on his jeans, leaving the robe hanging free.

Least Paul could have done was find out Names. Probably thought it made no difference. Probably bought that second-biggest line of crap ever perpetrated on a populace: that the 'NetAt was apolitical.

Parts were. The true practicing DProgs were too absorbed in theory to care how that theory was used, and too busy figuring elegant ways to clean up the chaff to worry about what caused the chaff in the first place. And the linemen—the 'NetTechs out there chasing down information and writing addenda to rectify erroneous information—were too damn busy keeping their heads above the electromagnetic ocean to be buyable.

But those decision makers—those like the faceless pair out in orbit, or like Sect. Beaubien—they were the dangerous ones. They were the ones who controlled the subtle policymaking precedents. If they were good, they could manipulate that policy one way or the other and implant seeds that could remain dormant for years.

Whoever controlled the 'NetAT controlled knowledge, which was power. That was economics, which was cash flow, which was politics. If these 'visitors' were some of the old school, if they were some of old MDP Phyllis Nelson's crowd, they'd be no trouble. Probably join the party—any party. If they were Beaubien's . . . if they were his, they were Shapoorian's, and that meant trouble.

Even before coming to this off-the-trade-routes planetary paradise, he'd ignored Shapoorian's Separatist movement. The terraforming Indigene Corps as a whole were a segment of society he'd rarely crossed, and the Ethnic Reconstructionist substrata at which Mialla Shapoorian aimed her bigoted barbs little more than artistic curiosities.

But although he'd ignored the movement, he'd not been

oblivious to it. He'd been born into the heart of the ComNet Alliance, to parents on the tail end of their Politically Activistic stage of life. They'd since gotten an attack of sanity and shed those ties, but not quite soon enough. Not before they'd infected their son with Knowledge. And one couldn't forget enough not to recognize the Facts of Life when one confronted them head-on.

Fact one: Councillor Mialla Shapoorian was a bigoted bitch.

Fact two: Politically speaking, Shapoorian and her whole Separatist crowd were economic sharks sensing a sociological wound in the making, and (fact three) the so-called Recons, the Ethnic Reconstructionist planetary colonists, were nothing but humanity's most recent socioeconomic underdogs.

Personally, the only unusual quality he'd noticed in HuteNamid's Reconstructionists was an overall higher common sense quotient.

On the other hand, Rostov's Recons, from his sample of one, hadn't had an ounce of common sense.

One thing was clear, Cantrell didn't like the signals these agents were giving, and while he and the admiral might have their personal differences, the woman had undeniably good instincts.

He'd bet Beaubien.

Oh, joy.

He hitched the robe again, tugged the sash tight and turned to find Anevai waiting anxiously at the door to his bedroom.

"What is it, Wes? What did he want?"

He grimaced. "Looks like Stevie's not going to get his vacation after all. Where is he?"

"Passed him on his way out. Had sweats and running shoes on. Draw your own."

Oh, rapture.

Hoping to flag Stephen down, he pulled her through his room and out onto the balcony, explaining as they went.

Children's laughter floated up to them. In the garden below, Stephen, stripped down to a dark, form-fitting bodysuit, cavorted among a veritable cloud of Recon rug-rats in a bizarre form of tag, leaping, flipping, and rolling past small hands trying to catch him, requiring only face paint to complete the clownlike image.

"Idjit!" Anevai's vehement mutter increased his amusement.

"What's your problem? He's having a—"

"What if he breaks something?"

"Anevai, he's a pro, for—"

"*Was*, Smith. Dammit, *think* what that body's been through the last— Ridenour!"

Stephen, helping a child copy one of his simpler exploits, grinned up at them, and let go a pair of young legs to wave.

"You bit-brain!" Anevai called down to him. "What do you think you're doing?"

Stephen steadied the wavering handstand, then flipped the youngster over his forearm and tossed her into the air, his laughter echoing her giggles as he caught her and flipped her again, touching his shoulder and calling back: "Therapy—" and catching her and setting her on staggering feet: "Remember?"

"You're crazy!"

His grin widened. He murmured something to the kids that earned him a communal hug, then crossed the yard at an easy run, which exploded into a series of flips, twists, and generally inhuman moves, ending in a final bounce just below their balcony, a one-hand of the rail and swing up to perch on top, laughter bursting out on an unforgivably slight gasp after breath.

"Hi, guys," he said, and, swinging his legs over the railing, he hopped down beside them.

"Show-off," Wesley muttered, wasting another insult as Stephen had leaned over the railing to receive a bundle the kids were trying to hand up to him. He stretched another degree, balancing on his stomach, his feet leaving the floor slats, his round-muscled rump tightening as he tried to grip the rail with his stomach. Wesley, in a replay of last night, grabbed Stephen to keep him from falling on his head. Only this time, Anevai's warning fresh in his mind, he felt a twinge of guilt as bony ribs pressed his arm into the rail.

An easy heave had the kid back on solid footing, bundle and all. Stephen unwound the outer layer, a thin towel he draped around his neck, and dropped the rest at his feet. Leaning against the rail, he wiped the sweat from his flushed face and gave them a disarming grin. "Don't be angry with me, Anevai. I was careful, honestly."

"I can vouch for that," Wesley reported. "His left hand never touched the ground."

"I wash *my* hands of you both," Anevai said, crossing her arms, turning her back on them. "If you end up a cripple for life, Ridenour, don't come crying to me."

Stephen gave him an alarmed look.

"She'll get over it. —Here, kid." He slipped the robe off and slung it around Stephen's shoulders. "Let's go have breakfast."

"Wait."

"Hell, no. She deserted me in my hour of need last night. Let her stew."

But Stephen eluded him, leaning over to free a small box from the bundle of sweats. "Anevai?" He removed the lid, touched her arm, held out his hand. "Please, Anevai, don't be mad."

Her shoulders began to shake. Finally, the laughter refused containment and she faced them, propping her hip against the rail. "I'm not mad, bit-brain, you just . . . What have you got there?"

"C—Cantrell's men found it—at the barn. I—I thought you'd like . . . since you've got the others . . ." Stephen blushed and opened his hand. Nestled in a dirty, grass-stained palm, a trembling spark of blue/red/green. "I–it's for y–you, i–if you want it."

"The missing button!" Anevai twirled it between her fingers, sending rainbows across the balcony floor. "But I thought you said they didn't find it."

"I didn't know. . . . She only gave it to me the other day. . . ." His pale eyes took on an anxious look. "You–you don't have to take it. I just thought, since you've got the other two—"

Anevai handed Wesley the button and wrapped her arms around Stephen's waist. "Of course I want it. Good things always come in threes—didn't you know that? Thanks, friend." And rewarded Stephen with a solid—and lengthy—kiss.

ZRS twinkled in the morning sun. Custom-cut crystal. Button from The Coat. Pretty thing. As had been the coat, before Nayati Hatawa had cut it to bits. The man should be arrested for that, if nothing else.

And Anevai had the other two. Now all three.

"Hmph," he grunted, tossing the button carelessly from one hand to the other, making the rainbows dance. "Prezzies. I'm jealous. All I've done for you . . ."

Anevai intercepted the next toss. "Lose that and die, Smith."

"P–prez . . . ?" Stephen shook his head like his ears weren't working. "I—I suppose."

"Presents," he clarified, and sniffed expressively.

"Oh." Stephen laughed, a rather charming sound of dawning comprehension. "Think I'd forget you? Here. Catch."

Something dark sailed over Anevai's shoulder. Something that squished clothily when he intercepted it.

Socks. Thick. Woolly. Rolled. He started to laugh, mock jealousy forgotten.

"What is it?" Anevai leaned on his shoulder. He held the sock ball up, and Anevai's giggle joined his.

She layered the top back. "Shee-it, Smith, they even match."

"Thanks, kid," he said when he could breathe again.

Stephen grinned too, but it was an oddly hesitant grin that trembled around the edges. "Think maybe you should check the toes? Might have holes."

"Unkind, brat." And remembering his Mission: "A man doesn't always want to be reminded of his—idiosyncrasies."

Stephen bit his lip, his brilliant eyes sparkling with some controlled excitement.

Anevai whispered in his ear, "I think you'd better check the toes, Smith."

Taking the unsubtle hint, he flipped them loose. A box spun free; he caught it on the fly, fingers intercepting soft velvet.

Tiepins. Three of them. Vandereaux sun opals nestled in a perfectly graded sapphire swirl. All desire to laugh deserted him. He closed the case slowly and requested quietly: "Anevai, will you leave us alone a minute?"

With her usual good sense, Anevai left without a word. As the door slid closed behind her:

"I—can't accept these, Stephen."

"Why not?" He didn't have to look to know Stephen's disappointment. "Anevai . . ."

"Anevai's buttons are one thing, though I can't believe you wouldn't get that coat replaced. These . . . You must have mortgaged your next ten years for them. I can't let you do that; you must return them."

"But I didn't! I *can't*. Whatever you think they're worth, they're paid for, long since. —Please, Wes. I never wear them. I—I thought I would, but I . . ." His remarkable eyes flickered, searching Wesley's face, and dropped. "All right, Wes, whatever. . . . S—sorry."

Stephen rolled the small fortune carelessly back into the sweats and dropped the bundle inside his room, tossed the shoes on top and turned to lean on the rail, facing outward, the subject ostensibly forgotten.

'Prezzies.' The young AC-wannabe *hadn't* understood, had just meant to please them both—presents in the truest sense of the word and most definitely *not* in the academy clone handbook— and here he was, throwing that gift in the kid's face.

He'd insisted the pins were paid for. His student stipend never would have covered it, and he'd arrived at Vandereaux without a credit to his name, but athletic endorsements at the height of his career, or tax-deductible gifts of unsalable dust magnets—hell, who knew what brand of rabid fans he'd collected on the athletic circuit? Alumni were the worst, and Vandereaux's were certainly a well-heeled lot.

Maybe that was the crux of the problem. Maybe the pins reminded him of that shattered career. . . .

"Stephen?" He joined him at the rail. "Listen, kid, if it means that much to you, I'll keep them."

The curly head ducked, concealing any expression behind a carelessly hunched shoulder. "Doesn't make a spit of difference to me. I thought you'd like them, that's all. Stupid for them to go to waste."

In his experience, outright lying was not high on Stephen Ridenour's list of accomplishments.

Wesley took Stephen's shoulders and forced him to look at him. "Kid, they're beautiful. Unlike any I've seen before. I simply can't believe you don't want to keep them for yourself."

Hope sparked behind cultivated clone-indifference. "I don't, Wes, honestly. I've had them for years and I've never. . ."

"Okay, kid. Okay." He succumbed to the inevitable. "I'll keep them, provided you do me one favor."

"What's that?"

"If you *ever* need money—"

"That's not why I—"

"If it were, I wouldn't offer. And I have every confidence you'll do perfectly well on your own. But just in case—I'm your backup. Promise me? Or if there's ever anything you just *want* and can't afford."

Stephen grinned and pulled free to fumble after the box and press it into his hands. He felt the eager stare as he took another look.

"You really do like them?"

"Lord, brat, what do you want me to—" He met those eager eyes, eyes that refracted color much as the stones in the pins. Probably the reason that unknown fan had felt compelled to give them in the first place. "Plan to haunt me forever, don't you, spook-eyes?"

"Huh?"

He felt his mouth twitch. Stephen never had appreciated the value of those eyes—or anything else. He made a mental note to check into the kid's tax records—and Vandereaux gym-team-related deductions—and square him with the Internal Revs. Probably wind up costing him more than the damn pins.

"Kid, we've got to talk."

"Well, Chet." Rissa Naghavian's looks had changed, but no amount of fine living and etiquette training could destroy her innate abruptness. "What have you got to say for yourself? Are we cleared?"

"Hello to you, too, Rissa," Chet replied pleasantly, and extended his hand to her partner. "Mr. Herzog? Pleasure. I'm Chet Hamilton."

"Forgive her, Dr. Hamilton." Herzog's grip was as firm and perfect as his smile. Harder to tell the natural state of someone you'd never met, but something told him this man, like Rissa, had never lacked confidence. "Short on sleep and the bosses are breathing down our necks."

"Not to worry." Chet grinned at Rissa, who scowled back. "We're old study partners. My going into DProg split up a good chess team, —eh, Ris?"

"I'm surprised you remember, the way you've insisted on—" She waved a hand at his desk and their scattered test results. "—this."

"Oh, you've passed—as you knew you would. —Please, both of you, sit down."

Chet settled on a desk corner—his chair being full of papers,—and waited.

"Neater than ever, aren't you, Ham?" Rissa remarked almost pleasantly.

"No one to pick up after me now. —So. You two going to tell *me* what this is all about?"

"We're here to take Ridenour back," Rissa said simply.

"So you've told Cantrell. Why?"

An exchange of glances; two blank faces turned to him.

"Look, guys. I may seem irresponsible in your eyes, but I take my job seriously. Considering the positions I've been in over the years, if I didn't, I'd have been—eliminated from it a long time ago. If I'm to help you, you'll have to come clean. Cantrell's got a real touchy one of her own going down here. One to legitimately override about anything you could come up with, short of the collapse of the 'Net itself."

Another exchange of glances; slightly less blank faces turned back. Not a bad bit of baiting, if he did say so himself.

"How much do you know about Ridenour's job here?" Rissa asked cautiously.

"I've read Smith's paper. Talked to the kid. I know of the records problems on the 'Net, and the suspicion the two might be connected."

"And do *you* believe the 'NetDataBase can be altered in a controlled fashion?" Herzog's question this time.

"Is this a test? If so, I'll tell you, not according to the Rasmussen equations. If you believe in them, no, it cannot. If you're willing to believe they might not be the perfect mathematical model of NSpace, the possibility exists."

Rissa sipped her coffee, apparently deferring to Herzog, who asked, "And Smith's paper? This *Harmonies of the 'Net*? Does it make sense to you?"

"More now than when I first read it."

"You'll not trick anything out of him, Dick," Rissa interrupted. "He's no fool. —Ham, it appears more errors are showing up in the 'Net records, and the 'Heads back home are beginning to seriously worry. They want to know for certain whether or not Ridenour's chasing VBs. If not, they want him back *now*, and maybe Smith as well."

"That *would* be asking for trouble."

"Orders, Ham. Not a time for jokes."

"I'm not joking. I haven't met the man, but I've talked with him. I'd advise you take matters real slow. Ridenour's got everything under control—getting more out of Smith than anybody back in Central could. As for Smith himself, if you *really* need him, use Stephen to get him up here, then pop the news. But I'd advise you to get better arguments if you want to keep him here. He's highly—independent, if I read him correctly. He might not give a hang if the 'Base crashes, and if he's not cooperative, he'll likely do you more harm than good anyway.''

"And will Ridenour—cooperate?''

"Whatever you want. He's a good kid and wants into the 'NetAT DProg program. —More to the point, they want him, believe me. This kid is good.''

A third glance. "So we've heard. —Regarding arguments: that's all we know—and *you* know that's the truth. They don't let us in on their secrets, big or little.''

"Wise, don't you think?'' Chet pointed out. "You're damned vulnerable. I wouldn't trade you jobs for all the credit on the 'Net.''

"But the 'NetDB collapsing? More than a bit unnerving, to my way of thinking. Can you blame us for trying to sort it out for ourselves?''

"I doubt it's that bad.''

"And yet you endorsed Cantrell's shutdown.''

He nodded. "For my own reasons. Do you know the extent of the so-called damage?''

"Only that it was enough for Beaubien *and* Council to become directly involved in our briefing—for all I know, it goes clear to the 'NetAT BoD. Now, will you help us get Ridenour and get the hell out of here?''

"Not that easy. The boy's had a bit of a rough time and needs some R&R. Give him a day or two, then we'll ask.''

"We haven't got a day or two. We're going down on the next shuttle whether you and Cantrell like it or not. We *can* override, if we must, but, dammitall, help make it easy, will you?''

He couldn't disagree. They didn't know what was happening on the 'Net but he did—or what *had* happened. And after going over Stephen's report, there was one highly probable result.

Cleaning up the DB was going to take a long time of

extremely careful probing. Once the interlacing addendizing routines were eliminated, and one was dealing exclusively with pristine files, Smith's alternate operating system could become universal. However, if Nayati had severed too many files, a local instability could be unravelling threads clear into the foundation files.

The mind boggled.

"I'll do what I can. Tomorrow. The boy's been a trouper. No need to push him past his limits."

Herzog and Rissa again eyed each other. If one didn't know better, one would think they had some special electronically induced rapport. But one knew better. One had seen the bios and knew exactly what these two carried, inside and out.

"All right, Ham," Rissa said. "Tomorrow. No later."

And when the door closed behind them, Chet touched his pocket com and murmured, "You copy that, admiral?"

"Damn right."

"We're talking universal collapse, if I make my guess. We need to close up shop fast."

"Damn right."

"Have to talk with Smith—get him to cooperate."

"Damn right."

"Better coming from me."

"That's a *copy*."

iii

"Wesley, I don't get it. You keep implying I was sent. Of *course* I was. *Harmonies* had no sites. You had to know the 'NetAt would investigate it eventually."

"Of course I did. It's you, Stephen, and who and what the 'NetAT has become. That's what Cantrell—what I—want you to understand *before* you face them. I don't think they had the least notion just how good you are. Sect. Beaubien would never have given me a chance at you—"

"Chance at *me*? But, *I'm* the Del d'—"

"Not that way, Stevie-lad. JP tends to think I'm irresistible—which I am, naturally. I suspect he sent you as a—greeting card. He never considered the scope and viability of *Harmonies*, just saw a way to lure me back."

"Wh–who's JP?"

"Sorry. Jean-Phillippe—Second Secretary Beaubien."

"Wh–Why would he want you back?"

"We were friends, once—before he sold out to the establishment. He knows me pretty well. I suspect he'd like me back where they can control me—keep me from spreading bad religion." He grinned. "Going to surprise them all, we are."

Stephen's eyes dropped to the notes he'd been taking on their meandering conversation. Kid seemed to live to take notes—almost as if he couldn't have a serious talk without such a memory aid. Not that he ever referred to them. Just took them. Kid's memory didn't *seem* defective, but maybe all those years swilling drugs—

"Wesley, I know you said you weren't going to release the patent on the SmitTee.SYS, but what if they insist? We all know what it can do. What if they just decide to implement whether you like it or no?"

"Eyes up, brat. Don't ask your knees; they don't know anything but bend and straighten. —You really think they'll pursue it, don't you?"

"Of course they will. They must! The NSpaceDB is in chaos. Eventually—all too soon—it will be utterly useless."

"You know that. *I* do. But do you think the 'NetAT is going to let Joe Dweeblethorpe know?"

"Why wouldn't they? Why keep the 'Net going as is, if it could be cleaned up—made infinitely more efficient? *Do* what it was designed to do?"

"The word, child, is optimized; but They won't replace a dinosaur until it dies and rots."

"Why not?"

"Too much work. Take too long. Cost too much. But mostly, po-li-tics."

"Politics?"

"Nobody—not the 'NetAT, not the Council, not nobody—wants the peons out in Alliance-land to realize that the very theory upon which the 'Net is based is wrong. The John Dweeblethorpes—"

"I thought his name was Joe."

He looked sharply at Ridenour. "You're kidding, right?"

"I—don't *think* so."

Laughter grew and burst out. Stephen blushed and jerked to his feet, heading for the door. Wesley caught at his arm as he passed.

"Naw, kid, park it. I'm sorry. But sometimes—you just gotta let it out, you know?" Stephen's eyes dropped. "Maybe you don't. Better learn, kiddo. It's healthy."

"Just let me go, will you? I'm tired, and we're not getting anywhere—won't now."

"How come?"

He wrenched his arm free. "Because you're laughing at me."

Wesley bit back an instinctive denial. Opted instead for the truth. "Yeah, kid, I am. D'you want to know why?"

"No."

"Once upon a long time ago, you wanted to know what you did to make me hate you. Aren't you equally curious what you did to amuse me?"

"You're treating me like a bit-brain. When you're ready to talk, let me know."

"Stephen, I'm talking *now*. Will you please sit and talk back?"

Stephen threw himself back down. Not particularly receptive; not leaving either.

"Shit, kid, help me out here."

A long sulky silence, an under-the brows glower, and finally, a reluctant: "All right. What is it the 'NetAT won't want the *Joe* Dweeblethorpes to know?"

He choked, caught himself, then leaned toward Stephen, staring him in the eyes. "Can I laugh now?"

The kid tried hard to keep his self-righteous anger in the face of that challenge—

—and failed miserably. The curly head ducked and nodded.

"Well, I tell you, kid," he continued—several moments later, "old *Joe* doesn't understand unified quantum cosmology real well, and if you start throwing 'Networking and 'Nests at him, he takes a lunch break real fast."

"Meaning he doesn't know shit about the computer he uses every day and prefers to keep it that way."

"You're learning, kid. —Anyway, if Dweeblethorpian confidence in the 'Net is undermined, confidence in the 'NetAT, the Council, Alliance itself is in jeopardy. Ol' Dweeb will only see that he's been screwed. If They wait until the dinosaur dies, then come up with the Big Save while Dweeb's attention is occupied with Sheer Terror, They come out the big heroes instead of the perpetrators of wrong thinking."

"They?"

He shrugged. "Whoever happens to be the current power. SciCorps, the 'NetAT, Council, mein papa. . . . Actually—" He grinned, completely without humor. "—In this case, yours truly. *Harmonies* will have them by their collective balls."

Stephen sobered quickly. "You know, Wes, it *is* frightening. The 'Net has been the one stable thing in my life—perfect, somehow, in its immutability. The thought terrified me in the beginning. Now, of course, that's changed, but—"

"And *you* understand it. What about those who don't? Something else, has it occurred to you yet, to wonder *why* anyone actively promoted the 'Net's inflexibility? Why we have Del d'Buggers?"

Stephen shook his head.

"This whole rotten culture functions on the idea of slow, steady technological growth. No big discoveries—no leaps of logic. Everybody knows everything, each new development is divvied up among its so-called contributors: no one makes economic killings; no abject poverty either.''

A long thoughtful moment, then Stephen said slowly: ''Meaning those with money and power keep their relative importance?''

He grinned. ''You're learning. Steady-state economy, and all the peons happy as ticks.''

''What's a tick?''

''Never mind, child. Economic and political change stays minimal, no one comes out with bombshells to make big money and all of a sudden become a political and economic power with unknown affiliations.''

Stephen was almost funny in his intensely solemn consideration. How anyone could live for ten years in Vandereaux academy and remain so politically and psychologically naive as Stephen . . .

Suddenly the naive kid asked, ''But what about Paul?''

''Corlaney? What about him?''

''*He* discovered the restoration virus.''

''Not alone, he didn't.''

''But—''

''Humanity still needs its heroes. He was part of a team—the most visible and well-known part. But you don't see him rolling in riches, do you? He was a hero SciCorps could control.''

''I don't understand.''

''That's because you like a low profile, child. Some people like the limelight; like the power that limelight gives them even more. Paul has a damned good profile and he likes to see it on the NewsVids.''

Stephen drew back. Wesley knew he risked alienating Stephen forever with this attack on another of his heroes, but Stephen needed to understand about people like Paul Corlaney, or the nest of snakes he was going back to would have him for lunch—wouldn't even have to spit out his tender bones.

''Paul's a good man, Stevie-lad. —One of the best. But time was he wanted nothing more than to make his mark in history.

He was good—damned good—and he knew it. Knew he deserved that mark. The system, as it exists, would never allow it. He was willing to sacrifice one project if that sacrifice meant he'd get that eternal recognition.''

"But he's still a researcher—the virus had problems and—"

"It wasn't money that motivated him, Stephen. That's what you need to understand. And the virus *didn't* have side effects. There *were* no problems. *That's* what he sacrificed in return for even that flawed recognition. SciCorps would have taken him clear out of business, else.''

"No!" Stephen shook his head violently and covered his ears. *"No!"*

Wesley endured this performance with a patience those who knew him might not fathom. But he'd been known to pull a similar snit once or twice. —And meant it. That's what no one understood about sensitive types like Wesley Smith. —And Stephen Ridenour.

He grasped Stephen's wrists and gently urged those hands away.

"Truth, Stephen."

Stephen scowled and tried to pull free.

He didn't let him.

"How do you know? How could you possibly know?"

"I've been on the stuff for five years, son. I know."

Stephen quit pulling. "Truth?"

"No reason to lie, son."

"And the rest?"

"Been his sounding board for a lot of years. He's real sorry now he did it."

"Why?"

"Because History will know. Historians record according to their politically correct viewpoint, but ultimately, History reveals the truth. History will know he lied, and why. He's spent the past twenty years doing things that will really matter. The last few years he's even quit worrying about the history books.''

Another of those periods of intense concentration. Then:

"And you? What about your reasons? If they aren't for the history books, if they aren't for money, why refuse to release your 'NetOS?"

He gave a shout of laughter. "The best of reasons, of course: spite. It's the ultimate I-told-you-so!"

"C'mon, Smith. You're so quick to judge Paul—"

"Okay. *Okay.* How much do you know about the Transition, Stevie-lad?"

"You mean to the Nexus ComNet?" As if there were another. "What everyone knows, I suppose. Adrian Smedlund and Bonneville Taylor proposed the theory, and Seneca Smith— you said she was your great-grandmother?"

Wesley nodded, felt a vague irritation when Stephen looked adulation at *him*—as though GrannieSan's accomplishments were his. But at least the kid didn't dwell on that brush with the past. He'd known Seneca Smith better than anyone. Knew: few people realized she was still alive, and sometimes even he forgot. There'd been so little of his GrannieSan the last time they'd met. She'd given him his first lessons in 'Net theory when he was five—and no teacher had touched her since. He'd learned more from one of the lesson tapes she'd left him than Victor Danislav would ever dream of.

She'd taught him to think. And had it not been for those fabricated reports on Paul's joy juice twenty-five years ago, she might still be teaching and he would never have had to settle here.

But if he hadn't come here, Anevai and *Harmonies* might never have happened either, GrannieSan or no GrannieSan.

"Wesley? Wesley, are you all right?"

The way Ridenour was looking at him, you'd think he'd grown antennae. He asked What about Seneca Smith? rather more harshly than he intended, but he wasn't in a mood to apologize, not even when Stephen blushed and mumbled an apology.

"For *what?* You didn't do anything wrong."

That ready blush deepened, and Ridenour continued softly, as though reciting for some damned classroom report, "Seneca Smith developed the hardware based on that theory which allowed us to access and adjust the energy states. Earth and some of the others refused to abide by the rules of 'Net usage and so—"

"For God's sake, clone, I expected better of you."

The blush vanished and in a no-longer-soft voice, Stephen said, "Well, dammit, Smith, ask a generic question . . ."

"*Much* better, brat. It wasn't generic. You're talking development of the hardware. Ever ask yourself *when* all this wonderful change took place? Under what conditions?"

Stephen shook his head.

"I'm not surprised: not a fact anyone wants advertised. A good twenty years before anyone ever paid attention to it. Granny Smith was old and grey when that patent finally bloomed. But she'd seen it coming—prepared for it. Smedlund and Taylor were dead—left her the whole thing. She knew the mess the existing system was in—hell, anybody who used it must have—and when MultiSidDiskOpSys 2004.01 finally locked—crashed—blooied every goddamned linkage in existence—she was waiting. She never figured the 'NetSys would be as widespread and misused as it is. I've—read her notes. She figured the powers-that-be—what the 'NetAT was *supposed* to be—would vet every entry. Would use it just for the important, need-to-remember-for-future-generations shit—not Dwee-blethorpe's grocery list."

"So you're saying we—that is, humanity—deliberately ignored changing until catastrophe forced change."

"Of course. Always does. And then makes a half-assed, finger-in-the-dike, emergency-dictated mess of what should have been an elegant solution. At the moment, the 'NetAT is operationally apolitical because they *have* all the real power. Undermine that power, and suddenly they have to play the same backscratching, backstabbing games as the rest of us."

Stephen forced a grin: "Can you imagine being the poor sod

who made that final entry? Push a button and shut down the universe."

At least the clone was trying to overcome his limitations. Wesley relaxed and grinned back. "April fool from God himself."

"Herself, Smith." Anevai's voice interrupted them from the study door. "Had to have been a female god. *Man*kind in need of a butt-kick. —Time to break it up, boys. Soup's on."

But he could tell the kid was upset: the clone was fading. It really wasn't fair to throw all this shit at him when he had to go back and ask the 'NetAT not to wield that very real power. He stood up and held out his hand. "C'mon, kid, let's go eat."

Stephen ignored his hand, unfolded from the couch and slipped his moccasins back on, still with that intense look on his face.

When he joined them at the door, Wesley said, "Listen, kid, tell you what. You go back, get the 'NetAt whipped into shape—tell them the facts of Life with *Harmonies*—hell, tell them they can have the thing—then tell them to go to hell and get your butt back here. We'll pack old Anevai here up and haul her into the mountains for a month of dirt and risking your neck and stomach on a daily basis: it'll straighten out your perspective in a hurry."

Stephen looked longingly out the window, but: "Please don't, Wesley, you know that's impossible."

Anevai looked from Stephen to him and back again. "What are you two babbling about?"

He winked at her and said, "Hell, Stevie-lad, invite your Admiral Cantrell along and I guarantee, by the time we come out of the mountains, you'll have it *all* worked out."

"All? All of what?"

Wesley threw his arms around the two confused children. "What's important—what's not. Life. Death. Love. And most important of all . . ."

"Sex," Anevai said dryly.

He drew back, offended. "You wound me."

Anevai just looked at him; Stephen asked, "So what *is* the most important?"

"Hell, kid." He pushed them both out into the hallway and pulled the door closed. "I don't remember now. She blew it right out of my mind."

"Which indicates *she* was right and you were lying."

"Unfair! Libelous! I've been outnumbered." He released them, shoved them both toward the kitchen ahead of him. "Keep your mitts where I can see them, and don't try anything funny."

"And *you*, Smith," Anevai returned, putting her arm around Stephen's waist, "keep *your* mitts in your pockets!"

Wesley leaned against the doorway, watching them disappear down the hallway, replaying the list in his mind, trying to—"Wait!" He ran after them. "I just remembered!" And as he reached the kitchen: "Swimming!"

iv

Zivon ran home all the way from school. Papa was still in the fields. He crawled through the fence yelling, Papa! Papa! *as loud as he could. Papa straightened, stretched hard, then held his arms out for him.*

He dropped his pack and leaped. Papa caught him and threw him high. He twisted and curled and dived straight for the ground. Papa caught him at the last minute and swooped him up, his feet swinging back to brush the grain stubble. He laughed as Papa hugged him and his head swirled and Papa's face fractured into a million pieces.

He hugged Papa's neck, and said, "Papa, I've got a friend. I've got a real friend!"

"*Of course you have a friend, sweetheart. You have lots of friends.*"

He shook his head so hard the world went funny again. "No, *no, no. I mean a* real *friend. Cincy doesn't think I'm ugly. She likes* my *eyes!"*

Papa frowned his Worried, but Zivon hugged him again, then wiggled to get down. "Too old to be carried."

He slung his pack onto one shoulder like the older boys did, (he only staggered a little bit) and tucked his hand in Papa's. Papa told the others to gather the tools and take off early. As they walked, he told Papa about Cincy and how he'd helped her with math at lunchtime, and how she'd smiled and said his eyes weren't ugly at all, no matter what the others said.

Mama was waiting at the front door. She was frowning, too, but it wasn't a worried, it was a mad. He found his excitement going away, sensed a stutter coming, so he quit talking. Mama jerked her head toward the stairs and said: "Homework."

Papa's hand squeezed his then let go, telling him now was probably not the time to tell Mama about Cincy.

Which sounded like a very good probably. He went up to his room and pulled out his books and thought about Cincy.

Stephen yawned and stretched. Blasted dreams were becoming a habit. Too many memories reBooting too fast: the wetware compiler couldn't sort and process fast enough.

He shivered. Shadows had moved in while he slept. He pulled the robe tight, picked up the novel he was supposedly reading, and moved back into the sunlight's warmth settling onto the large rocks rimming the pool.

Balancing the book against his knees, he burrowed into the fur lining, protecting his ears against a chill breeze off the lake. Man could get used to this, he thought.

"Yo! Steeeee-vie!" Wesley's screech even overpowered the roaring splash from the waterfall. Wesley himself followed, diving from some perch halfway up the falls, then leaping through the turbulence like some oversized fish, crossing the pool in long, gliding strokes. Five meters offshore, he disappeared.

Unconcerned at this sudden disappearance, Stephen simply pulled his feet in closer. A moment later, a dripping appendage groped across bare ground, tilted back and twisted as though searching for its prey, then retreated into the water. A blond head popped up in its stead. "C'mon, kid. You've been sitting for too long."

He shook his head, tucked deeper into the robe. Wes laughed and said, "S'okay. It's only cold for the first few seconds."

"I don't know how to swim."

"So I'll teach you. Can't let that new suit go to waste, can we?"

"That's the problem, Wes. Sunburn. Dr. Mo said—"

"Screw her. Shadows, brat. You won't burn. Just a little while . . ."

He didn't regard Wesley's urging: nothing could make him voluntarily take off the robe and get in the water.

Shadows crept around them, making Wesley's hazel eyes darken. . . .

"I wish I had brown eyes."

"Whatever for, kid? Yours are the most exquisitely odd—"

"You can say that, and still ask why?"

"What brought this on, Stephen? You've been watching my eyes for days now—"

With a grunting heave, Wes was out and dripping on the pool's rocky edge. Stephen tossed him a towel, then tucked his head as water splattered from Wesley's thick mane of hair. From the depths of the towel:

"—and never said anything before."

"Do you remember asking me once why I studied at home?" A quick nod, another sprinkling. Stephen grabbed a corner of towel and wiped his face. "I remember now—part of the answer, anyway. The kids at school were scared of me."

Understanding dawned. "The eyes?"

He nodded. "My father had dark, beautiful brown eyes—he was blond, too. I always wanted . . ." He looked off across the water. Papa would have loved this spot, used to talk of the 'swimming pool' at the 'club'. But that pool couldn't have been like this one. Water on Rostov was too precious to let it stand outside. Probably they were like the academy pools. He'd seen those—once. Strange countercurrent tanks, like VRTs filled with water. He preferred to do his floating in nice, *breathable* air, thank you.

A hand on his head dripped a wet trail through his hair and turned him to face Wesley's pout.

"You telling me I remind you of your *father?* Take that one back, kid. Precocious though I might have been, I'm not *that* old."

He chuckled softly. "Hardly, Wes. But in some very nice ways, yes, you do. I wish you could have..." He couldn't quite bring himself to finish that. Papa was a long time ago—a lifetime ago, a universe away.

The pout disappeared, the hand on his head slid to his shoulder and pulled gently. "Don't think about it, Stephen. Come on into the pool. It's fairly shallow here...."

"All *right*, Wesley, all right." To please Wesley, he relented, and slipped the robe off as Wesley dove back in. He was chest deep in water chill enough to set his teeth chattering and shorten his breath before Wesley's head surfaced.

"H–hi."

"Good boy." Wesley grinned— "Now relax. Think of ZG." —and dived again, a final flipping foot sending a wave of icy wet into his face. He shook the water from his eyes and the movement of his head, the chill in his knees, the pressure waves pulling and pushing at his body combined to confound up and down.

And here, unlike ZeroG, *up* mattered.

He felt his way a few cautious steps from the rocks on the edge.

"Wes?"

His vision cleared, but Wesley had disappeared.

Another few.

"Wes?"

And suddenly, Wesley was back, cavorting around his legs, threatening to pull him under.

"Wes!" Chattering teeth snapped on his tongue. He swore softly and tried to kick Wesley away. "Cut it out!"

He staggered for the edge, but Wesley got in the way. He turned toward what he thought to be a shallower area. Again, the blond roadblock. He could no longer feel his feet. An injudicious toehold slipped, water closed over his head, and Wesley's undulating course dragged at him. He kicked free, flailing wildly for what he hoped was the surface.

Water sprayed everywhere. Wesley trod water in the midst of his all-time-best fountain, laughing and gasping for breath. He blinked his eyes clear while his fountain settled, then stroked lazily for the shore, still laughing.

"Well, kid," he called, "what'cha think now? Not so ba—"

Stephen wasn't there.

"Stephen?" He trod water a second time, searching the shadows in the trees. *"Stephen!"* he shouted, and shouted again, useless though he knew it to be. Something brushed his foot, something soft and human; he gulped air and dived toward the source, found an arm and pulled for the surface, hauling Stephen's limp body after him.

One hand gripped stone, the other wrapped Stephen's waist, boosting him up and half over his shoulder. Gasping breath exploded behind his ear. He squeezed hard, felt Stephen's heave and expelled water running down his back. Another gasping breath, and a third. He relaxed his arm and straightened, controlling Stephen's slide down to the rocky lake bottom, keeping his arm around him for stability. He leaned back and looked into those eyes the boy claimed to hate and he increasingly adored. "You okay?"

A convulsive nod, an abortive attempt to answer past chattering teeth. Damn, damn, damn-damn-damn: he should never have insisted.

"Hang on," he ordered grimly and guided Stephen's shaking hands to the rock, heaved himself onto the bank, then hauled the boy out, wrapping the robe around the shivering huddle and holding it there with his arms. "C'mon, kid, we've got to get you home."

Without answering, Stephen staggered to his feet and along the trail toward the clinic. Wesley swore, grabbed up the kid's novel and his towel and hurried in Stephen's wake. He'd caught up and was steadying none-too-certain steps, when Stephen let out a choked cry and fell with a convulsive wrench that carried them both to the ground.

He'd forgotten uncallused, stationer feet. Thinking of the moccasins back beside the lake: "Wait here, kid, I'll go get—"

It required only a moment to overtake Stephen's limping strides, a few more to realize the stubborn brat was refusing further help, never mind he was leaving blood on the trail, so he shrugged and matched pace—content to be there when the kid finally collapsed.

But Stephen didn't collapse. His face assumed an odd intensity, eyes focused solidly on the trail, the limp a precise, though syncopated, regularity. Once inside the house, a murmured personal reminder: *Mustn't bleed on the carpet,* and only his toes touched down. At the door to his room, a similar absent-minded murmur: *I'll see you later, Wes.*

And the door shut in his face.

Wesley sat outside and waited, concern increasing as an occasional smothered cough interrupted rustlings and bumps within. Stephen had had a rough time the past two weeks. What if the boy took seriously ill, all because of *his* foolishness and right before this oh-so-vital meeting?

He tapped lightly on the door. "Stephen?"

A pause, then: "I'll be all right, Wes." Faintly. Another coughed interruption. "J–just go away. Please. I'll be out in a bit. I—I need a few minutes to warm up is all."

"Stephen, for God's sake—"

"Please, Wes."

He didn't like it, but could think of no way to insist. He

fetched dry clothes and settled with Stephen's book near Stephen's door, listening for sounds of distress from within.

Nothing.

Damned overprotective CodeHead, he chided himself, and stood to leave before someone caught him in his stupidity. Suddenly, a single gasping cry escaped the room. He dropped the unopened book and pressed his ear to the door. A barely audible whimper, then nothing.

He didn't stop to ask. Didn't give the boy another chance to send him away. He twisted the handle—

—Locked.

Dammit.

Keys.

He knew where they were kept, but didn't take the time. He'd pay Matowakan for the damn door.

Later.

V

He'd thought Stephen Ridenour had run out of the ability to surprise him.

He was wrong.

The meticulous AC's room was in shambles: drawer contents strewn across the floor from the dresser to the bed where Stephen lay, wrists and ankles (the one bare foot still seeping blood) tied to the posters, a confusion of fur-lined robe, wool blankets, and bare skin.

For the briefest instant, he thought someone, somehow had done this, but no who, why, or how made any sense. An instant later, a choked *Get the hell out*— dispelled any notion of third-party involvement. A liquidy cough, then: "I said, *Get out!*"

"Hell if," he muttered, and stalked over to the bed. "I've known some sick fetishes in my time . . ." He untied the bloody foot. ". . . But this beats—" A second choking cough; the foot

jerked in his hands, jamming his fingers against the footboard
He swore. "—Well, most of them." The foot jerked again
Disrupted blankets dripped slowly to the floor, leaving bare
skin, fur, and that excuse for a swimsuit in its wake. "Hold
still," he growled, and slapped the foot sharply.

"D–dammit, leave me *alone!*"

He ignored the damp whisper. "Chilled, you idiot."

He freed the other foot, muttering continuously, not making
sense, and knowing it. "Cold as a corpse, damned brain-dead
jackass. —Hot bath—hot toddy—fix you right up."

Why should *he* have to when no one else bothered? The boy
scared him witless, and now this—

More coughing. Stephen's legs jerked up, his knees tucked
in tight against his stomach. The spasm subsided and Ridenour
froze, his arms straining against the self-induced restraints
Weird, that's what it was. Senseless. And damned stupid.

Fear and anger, sweat and tears hazing his vision, Wesley
attacked those wrists next, swearing a steady stream, not caring
what he said or in what language, all of which Stephen
ignored, except to grasp the headboard before his right wrist
was free. Then, eyes closed, face hard, he used that leverage to
straighten his legs slowly, deliberately, his whole body taut and
quivering. Wesley thrust past the knees, leaned across Stephen
to reach his left side, where a leather belt was looped around
the wrist, twisted, then held tight with a death-grip.

"So this is how you—" The death-grip wrenched one way
and another avoiding his touch. He grunted, and swore again
prying at the fingers clamped on the belt, resorting finally to
slapping the hand until it opened. "—Damnfool S&M stunt."

Only one way any of this made sense. Goddam, fucking—
he'd thought the idiot was staying clean. "Where the *hell* did
you hide it?" Damp reddened his fingers: blood. The belt was
slimed with it. He threw the thing across the room and wiped
his hand on the sheets. "If you're into pain, you should have
said, I'd—"

Another cough—

—and Stephen's whole body snapped into a tight ball around Wesley's arm. Damp sprayed everywhere. Blood. Lots of blood. And a frantic gasp after air that only induced another fit.

Anger vanished. He cradled the ball of quivering humanity to his chest, holding it against wracking coughs, the iron strength of the contracting torso cutting the circulation to his hand. On the first partially successful breath:

"W—Wes-s-s. P-please—"

This time, he heard the desperation in that whisper. This time, he understood. This was no act; not for his benefit, certainly not for the boy's. That tourniquet-like power, the counter-force of the coughs, must be ripping him up inside.

He wedged himself into the ball that was Stephen, trying to force him flat, every muscle in both their bodies quivering with exhaustion now. He cursed steadily at the boy to help, seeking some last ounce of fight. The convulsive trembling ended in one final seizure; damp lungs made an enormous effort and held; and ridged muscle slowly straightened. Once flattened, Wesley collapsed over him to keep him that way.

"Hell of a way to get you into bed, kid," he gasped into Stephen's throbbing carotid, then pushed himself up to sit on Stephen's legs, his hands clamped on Stephen's shoulders, and shouted for help. Anevai's. Or Matowakan's. —Inyabi.

Anybody.

Because he couldn't leave, couldn't go for help. Could only hold on, as renewed convulsions threatened the next generation of Smiths, until the choking eased and Stephen's efforts to hold himself flat prevailed, his grip on the bedstead putting new twists in the metal design.

"Please, Wes . . ." Stephen's whisper was barely audible. ". . . t–ties . . ."

"Dammit, no, there has to be another—" But damned if he knew what it was. He was out of his depth. *Way* over his head. The fool kid was going to die and . . .

"Here." A brown-skinned hand set a jar on the side table.

"Rub that into his stomach and chest, and then get him to drink this." A glass appeared beside the jar.

Matowakan. He didn't argue. Didn't waste time asking: damned little happened around Acoma that Matowakan didn't know about—nothing within the clinic and his own home. Keeping Stephen flat with a heavy arm across his chest, he dipped his fingers and sniffed.

The body beneath him quivered. He looked up, found Stephen watching him with terror-filled eyes. Terror. Pinpoint pupils.

Sober eyes.

Whatever was going on, Stephen hadn't willfully induced it.

Bereft of anger, even fear, now Matowakan was in charge, only concern remained. Concern and sympathy for a very sick, very scared youngster.

"Don't worry, son. Just a muscle relaxant. Anevai used it on me once. —Hell of a cramp that was. —Won't hurt. Might help. Okay?"

Lips pressed tight, controlling a quivering lower lip. Opal eyes squeezed shut, as the blood-spattered stomach contracted in smothered coughs.

Without opening his eyes, Stephen nodded.

"Good lad." Wesley rubbed the ointment over Stephen's rock-hard stomach, felt the muscle relax and grow pliable as his own hand began to glow with soothing warmth. He ran the stuff up Stephen's arms until, with a shuddering sigh, Stephen released his death-grip on the headboard, his hands falling to lie limp at either side of the pillow.

Several convulsion-free minutes later, he lifted Stephen up, urged him to drink Matowakan's potion, and soon after that, the boy fell asleep, curling around a pillow with none of his earlier frantic tension, not even stirring when Matowakan helped Wesley change the bloodstained sheets around him.

"So what are you saying, Mo? *Is* the boy an addict or isn't he?"

Cantrell sipped her coffee and thumbed through the printed report her chief surgeon had brought—*brought,* not sent—to her as soon as she'd registered into her office.

"I don't know what he is, other than a mess inside. I cleaned up what I dared while I had him under for that shoulder, had planned to build his strength up a bit and get him to sit still for some more on the way home. But from that last batch of tests—Lord, he's back to square one. Between the Eudoxin and that Smith person absconding with his medications . . . The fool should have just shot Stephen; it would've been kinder."

"What's his word on it?"

"Haven't asked him. —First I've said to *anyone* about it. Not illegal—not at his age. Just very, very stupid. Was going to psych him a bit on the way back."

"Why come to me now?"

"That call from Matowakan has me worried, for one."

"You think it's connected?"

McKenna nodded. "No question. I don't think he's got any more—we've been through his quarters—but I'm certain it's what he'd been taking down there, when Smith caught him. Matowakan's suggestion confirmed it."

"Eudoxin. Where would a kid like Stephen have gotten that designer poison?"

"Popular among academy types with too much money and too much pressure for normal socializing."

"Too much money? All he had was his student stipend."

"If he had to pay for it."

"What's that mean?"

"How much do you know about Eudoxin? About the so-called 'Doxies who take it regularly?"

"I know it'll rot your insides out. Some terminal sod might not mind the exchange rate for the thrill, but a *kid?*"

"Do you know the effects?"

"All right. Suppose we say, for argument's sake, Stephen's into exotic sex. That stuff's still rare and exceedingly expensive. Where'd he get it? How'd he afford it?"

"With his looks, and considering what the stuff's used for? He could get it. Probably without paying a millicred."

Considering the possibilities, Cantrell wondered, "Could Smith himself have supplied it? Lord knows he's got the money—and the proclivities."

"Man like Smith will screw anything that doesn't move fast enough or object loud enough—and take pride in doing it right. He'd consider Eudoxin an insult to his talents."

"Could Stephen have counterfeited the symptoms? Maybe things were going wrong—had to cover his ass . . ."

"I seriously doubt it. Besides, the internal mess is nothing recent. The boy was involved a long time ago and in a very big way. As to who supplied him, take your pick, but I'd suggest you look closer to home, and consider with whom he attended Vandereaux Academy."

"Stephen? No. I don't—"

"Before you finish that statement, take a look at these." McKenna leaned across Cantrell's desk to pull a photopack from under the report.

"What's this?"

"The rest of the story."

(*"Remember me, pretty 'buster-boy. Remember me when you take them. Remember me when you want more."*

(*Tiny tablets. Blue with a red insignia. Thirteen. Something inside shivers at the Bad Number. Something else thinks: how appropriate.*)

"Stephen? —C'mon, son, time to wake up."

(*One by one, the pills disappear from his hand.*)

Red on blue on red. Hazy vision focussed, registered a face and a room, the red-and-blue-patterned blanket. The rest of his body reported in, and he wished the universe would return to unconscious black.

Hands. He twisted away, gentle as those hands were. But they persevered, bringing soothing dampness that dragged reality back with it.

"God, Wes," he muttered, "Why'd you have to come in?"

"Because I care, kid. C'mon. Time to wake up and tell me what that was all about. I thought for a minute you'd finked on me, had a stash in here. But you didn't, did you?"

"Forget it, Wes. Please, just get out of here." He turned away, ignoring the protests of his body, and burying himself in the red and blue pattern.

"You've got to come up for air sometime, brat, so you might as well do it now."

He burrowed deeper.

"Will you at least tell me if you plan to die in the next ten minutes? I've got to go take a—"

He felt laughter bubble. A bubble that brought spasming pain in its wake. He smothered both, relented and . . . 'came up for air.'

"Well?" Wesley asked. "Should I call the doctor or the coroner?"

He smiled reluctantly. "Neither, Wes. Old problem. I'll be all right now. —Thanks."

"So, what did you take?"

Suddenly he no longer felt like smiling. "I don't know what—"

"Oh, yes you do, kid. You're not the first academy brat to try. What did you take? How much damage did you do to your innards?"

"I didn't—" Wesley's face hardened, and Stephen amended bitterly, "All right, so I did. Long time ago. Nothing I can't handle. This is the first attack in a long time. I think it was the cold, maybe."

Only he *didn't* know what had induced the convulsions, and that not knowing frightened him more than he cared to admit.

An extended silence later, Wesley asked, in a voice rife with reservation:

"And the ties?"

He shrugged, damned if he'd explain how he'd discovered *that* trick.

"Why, kid?" The reservation faded to seeming concern . . . "What drove you to it?"

. . . concern he couldn't afford to believe.

"Does it really make any difference? It's over and done with."

"Help me to know who I'm dealing with. Might—" A white-toothed grin. "—keep me from throttling you prematurely."

"I—" He relented, exhausted and sick of fighting. "A couple of years ago, after my accident in the gym."

"I thought that might be it," Wesley said quietly. "Losing a career as promising as yours must've been quite a blow."

"Yeah?" He closed his fist on the blanket, denying old pains. "How would you know?"

A wounded look—or perhaps it was indignation. "Hey, I used to date a gymnast. She had some of the most amazing moves . . ."

"But were any of them in the gym?"

"Oo—oo, sarcasm. The kid's feeling better. —As a matter of fact, yes. She was pretty good herself—and put me wise on what to look for." Humor faded. "I've seen most of the competition files, kid. You were good —Damned good."

"Yeah, well." He made that fist relax. "No big deal now. Was at the time."

Wesley seemed to be waiting for some further revelation; for some reason, out of the black void of his mind, he remembered:

"Strangest thing . . . only Bijan ever cared."

"About what?"

"The accident. The fact I'd never fly again."

"Bullshit."

Stephen couldn't blame Wesley for that incredulous note, but Wesley hadn't been there, facing the harsh-voiced doctors, and Bijan's strange, stolen visit . . .

'Afterward, when I was in hospital, Danislav said maybe now I'd get my mind back on important things; Dev was convinced a star complex had made me irresponsible. . . . Only Bijan said he was sorry." Tears threatened. He pushed them aside and sought Wesley's puzzled stare. "He was crying, Wesley. It was the strangest thing. . . ."

"And what was it you said you took?"

He started back to RealTime. Wesley wasn't talking about the accident. He was talking about after. And he hadn't said. Nor was he about to. Anevai didn't know about things like Eudoxin. Wesley would. Wesley would know what it was and why he'd had it. He shrugged. "Something I had in the cabinet. I've had so many different prescriptions over the years. . . ."

"And you can't remember? Pardon me if I don't buy it, Ridenour."

He shrugged and pulled the blankets up. Strove to keep the catch from his voice. "Doesn't matter what it was. Not any more."

"Dammit, boy!" Wesley grabbed him by the shoulders, making the room dance as he jarred old injuries along with the new.

"Not—boy!" He gasped, tried to pull away, felt sickness rise along with the pain, closed his eyes against the whirling room and concentrated on keeping his stomach on the inside.

Wesley swore again and pulled him roughly into his arms, then held him there . . .

. . . with a tenderness that cut—infinitely deeper.

vi

"Sometimes, Wesley Smith, I hate you."

"What did I do?"

Some days a man just couldn't win. Finally get the kid settled and in comes Anevai, hissing condemnation like an angry *pii'chum*.

"You forced him into the water, didn't you? You knew he was scared, you *knew* you swim like a fish. Had to show him up, didn't you?"

Anevai could pack more hostility into a whisper than anyone he'd ever pissed off. And for once, he didn't even know what he'd done. Exhausted with worry, confused, and he couldn't even yell his frustration because it would wake Stephen up.

"I don't know what you're talking about," he muttered, the only option left him.

"Oh, no? You can't stand the fact he can run rings around you on the 'Net, that without half trying he makes you look like a bum, that he does things physically you can only dream about. So you create a Situation where you can prove your superiority."

"I never forced him to do anything."

"The hell you didn't. Any blind fool can see he worships you, tries to emulate you at the slightest opportunity. Would deny you nothing—"

"—Nothing?"

"Not even that, and you know it. My guess is you haven't pursued it because you figure he'll show you up that way as well."

"That's low, Anevai."

"Yes, it is. Can you deny it?"

"I—" He faltered. "I can't tell you, brat. I'm too close to it right now."

She smiled, then, leaned over and hugged him. "That's my Wesser. You're being honest with yourself now."

Confusing, but it felt good.

Too good.

"So?" He pushed her off, embarrassed as hell.

"That means I can trust you with Stephen. And I have to be able to, Wesley. He's— He won't talk to me anymore. I don't know what's happened, but whatever soul-searching he's been doing has gone beyond anything he can express to me. I think he might to you."

"I don't exactly inspire confidences."

Her fingers pulled gently at his hair. "Been a good ear to me for a lot of years, Smith."

"That's you, brat. You know how to talk. Stephen—" He caught those fingers and squeezed. "He tried to commit suicide, you know."

"Only once?"

"You aren't shocked?"

"Shocked? No. But I'm sad for little Zivon. He was killed so very young. I can only be thankful Stephen Ridenour failed the attempt."

"What are you talking about?"

"Things I've no proof for, Wes. Just remember how very young part of him is, and if you find you can't love the man, try the child."

"That child's the father of that thing in your belly!"

"Shush, Smith, he might hear you. —And don't call my baby a *thing*."

"High time he knew."

"He thinks he can't."

"That what he told you?"

She nodded.

"That why *you* didn't take precautions?"

She shrugged. "Wrong timing—I shouldn't have been fertile. More than that, I wouldn't have minded. He's got brains, looks—good addition to the local pool. And since then . . . Before we had the test results, I found myself hoping I was. I don't want him to leave forever, Wesley. At least this way, a part of him won't."

"That's a dumb-ass way to look at it. He—injected you with a bunch of chemicals, not—*him*."

She shrugged. "If that's how *you* want to look at it."

"That's how it *is*."

"Don't start on me, Wes. I don't want to wake Stephen up, which means I might just have to throttle you where you sit, and I really don't want to do that either."

He reached his arm around her waist and pulled her close in a quick hug, batting his eyelashes at her. A smothered giggle escaped her tightly clamped lips. Resting his head against her side, her flat belly formed a half-frame on his view of Stephen. He rubbed that frame gently with his free hand.

"Why did he think he couldn't?"

"I—don't know, precisely, though the implications were pretty clear. He said someone had decided for him—looked pretty sick when he said it. —I don't know what fantasy he's living in, but he's got to break free of it gently, Wes, and you've got to help him. He's had pills thrown at him all his life as the answer to his physical problems. Is it any wonder he might think they could make him happy, too?"

"Do all I can, kid, you know that."

"Yeah, Wesser, I do. Better than you."

On which crypticity, she kissed his forehead and pulled gently free.

"Do you still plan that dinner at the *Miakoda?*" she asked on a whisper.

"With him like this? How could he possibly enjoy it?"

"Eating's not everything. He's got to face those 'NetAT people tomorrow. Maybe could use some friendly support after."

"I suppose."

"You reserved the whole place, Wesley—including their chief of staff—you can't renege on the arrangement now."

"I don't plan to. Just don't know if I'll use it."

"Everybody's counting on you to convince him to come back."

"Everybody?"

"Not just me."

"Then we're all of us crazy."

She smiled gently. "Us, Wesser?"

"God help me, I don't want him to go away at all."

She hugged him, and whispered in his ear, "Love you, Wesser."

He stood up and shoved her halfheartedly out the door, closed it, turned . . .

. . . to Stephen's opal eyes. . . .

"You awake?" he whispered.

. . . which blinked slowly, and turned back into the pillows. "Guess not."

Papa knocked on his door and came in. Zivon twisted around on his stool, felt his tummy twist further at Papa's frown. Papa sat on his bed, but he didn't pat it with his hand, which meant he didn't want Zivon to sit there. Which meant this was man-to-man stuff.

Zivon slid off his stool and tugged it over to face Papa, climbed back on, and folded his hands in his lap and waited.

"About your new friend—"

"Cincy?" He bounced eagerly; maybe this wasn't Bad News. "Yes, Papa? Can she come and visit? Please, Papa? Can I show her Meesha and the baby and—"

Papa looked worried.

His bounce went away.

"What's wrong, Papa?"

"Cincy's mama called this afternoon, Zivon. Cincy is very upset."

"Why, Papa?"

"Zivon, you said you talked with her down by the lake. Was that all you did?"

He thought of the kiss and blushed. But Papa couldn't mean that. Papa couldn't know about that. So he whispered so maybe God wouldn't hear the lie, "Yes."

Papa looked very disappointed, and he wished he hadn't lied. Papa asked, "Zivon, do you remember when we were out with the obatsi and Meesha and Yonshi were playing and I told you how babies were made?"

He nodded, wondering What did Meesha and Yonshi have to do with Cincy being upset.

"Son, I—" Papa couldn't look at him. Papa was Upset and Mad at him.

"Papa, what's wrong?"

"Son, Cincy says that you . . . did . . . that to her down by the lake today."

He stared at Papa, who still refused to look at him. But it took a long time to understand what Papa was saying. His eyes began to sting. He finally thought to blink. He breathed hard and fast. Shook his head, slow and shaky at first, then faster, til Papa's face blurred.

"No, Papa. No! No, no, no, no, no—"

Stephen stirred, muttering softly.

"Stephen?" Wesley set his novel aside and moved over to the bed. "Can I get you . . ." But the kid turned away to face the wall and buried his head in the pillows.

Wesley shrugged and returned to the book.

Some party. Whole damned place had gone to bed. Supper off a tray beside Sleeping Beauty, here. Even Anevai had deserted him.

There was a word for this state of mind. A word he hated with a passion. A state of mind that left far too many neurons free for useless speculation with no hope for answers.

Boredom.

("Pretty, pretty buster-boy. —Too pretty. Are you sure you're a boy?"

(Hand squeezing his knee, kneading its way up his leg.

("Guess you are. —Too bad. . . .")

"Stephen? C'mon, son, wake up."

"Please, Papa, don' make me go. Please, Papa . . . I'm scared, Papa. The researchers hurt m—hurt M—Mama. Please, Papa."

(Hands. More than one set of hands, pulling him one way and the other, prodding, poking, squeezing.

(Another body pressing his against the wall.)

"No . . ."

They didn't listen. They never listened. The hands pulled at him again.

("C'mon, 'buster-boy. Let's find out what you've got.")
"No—"
("Bijan says your kind like it rough—)
" . . . N–n–noooo . . ."
Clawing fingernails broke on textured wall. A foot twisted as the bed shifted. Fingers found purchase, closed frantically, but the handhold shattered and he crashed downward. And down. And—
"Stephen!"
Hands grabbed him, pulled him down. Pressed him into the floor. Through the floor. Pressure on his chest cutting off his air.
"No! Let me go! Let—me—"
("Warned you, Ridenour. . . .")
(Flash of metal in the darkness. Boyish laughter. A woman's satisfied smile.
("No buster-brats allowed . . .")
He screamed, memory-pain confounding with RealTime as he struggled to escape the weight squeezing him through the wooden floor and into the station conduits below. A knee twisted beneath him. Terror as his hands tangled in heavy cloth folds.
Hands grasped his shoulders and pulled him to a T-shirt-covered chest. Other hands, holding his mouth against screams he can't contain. Collapse as muscles turn to nonresistant water.
"Please . . ." His own voice, pleading, shameful as his body's quiescent acceptance of that capture was shameful. "No . . . m–more. . . . Please . . . let . . . go."
But the arms didn't let go; warm breath whispered in his ear: "Never, kid. Never."
His racing heart slowed—nightmare memories faded to fleeting shadows.
The T-shirt came into focus.
" . . . Wes? . . ."

"Yes, son. It's just the ol' Wesser. I'm not going to hurt you. I'll never—knowingly—hurt you."

That reassurance should have brought relief, but he felt, if he felt anything at all, profound humiliation. He hadn't had an attack that bad in years—had learned to anticipate them—to lie awake, knowing he was watched, and refusing Them the satisfaction.

Little doubt what had triggered this attack. Anevai's revelation, Wesley's condemnation, remained with him even awake. He was drenched. Sweat. Tears. Blood. Possibly other bodily fluids as well. Repulsed, ignoring Wesley, he slipped away and down the hall to the bathroom.

Sir...
Chet,

I don't want to make this an issue now. Please keep it until we are en route. But I must write it now—get it into responsible hands—while my reasoning is sound. It might not be tomorrow. Possibly not even tonight. I just don't know.

Please keep this for me, sir. Even when I return to the ship, do not put it back into my hands, but give it directly to Admiral Cantrell the moment we clear this system.

And should my worst speculations prove justified, I count on you, sir, not only to see the message reaches the 'NetAT, but to protect Wesley Smith. He deserves recognition, not incarceration. Thanks, not condemnation. The problem is, he knows that, and knowing it, will do everything he can to avoid it. I know that doesn't make sense, but it's the essence of the seeming illogic—and the undeniably perverse mind—that realized *Harmonies of the 'Net*.

Thank you, sir, for your help, your support, and your faith.

Sincerely,

Stephen NMI Ridenour.

He didn't include his authorization number, the fourth-echelon rating he'd attained at such enormous cost.

With cold premonition, he paged down.

To whom it may concern:

I, Stephen NMI Ridenour, do, upon this document's lawful submission to the Combined Council, resign all rights and commissions as I may now have or, as a result of the current investigation of the HuteNamid Libraries and Dr. Jonathan Wesley Smith's paper, earn. I make this decision in full freedom and in full possession of my senses. It comes as a result of my decreasing confidence in my own judgement. . . .

"My God," Chet said to his empty office. "Sorry, kid. This can't wait."

He copied the file to Cantrell's personals with a Pry1 desig and added his own note:

>Admiral, you can't let him do this. We can't just leave without knowing what prompted it, and whatever—or whoever—is responsible, is down on that planet.

vii

The sweat-soaked shirt slipped slowly from his shoulders. Stephen swallowed hard and opened his eyes—to skin as flawless as a baby's. The mirrored image fractured and whirled. He closed his eyes again and sank onto the toilet seat, burying his face in his hands.

(*"You heard me, 'buster-boy, —kiss it! Then say 'Excuse me, Mr. Shapoorian!'"*)

(*Hands forcing him to his knees, a bare hip thrust in his face. His teeth closing, and the taste of blood.*)

"My God," he whispered, staring into the emptiness of middle-ground. "Did it ever happen? Did any of it?"

(Hands in the dark, holding him flat, pressing his face into the pillows. The Enemy exacting payment in kind.

(KwikHeal searing his flesh from shoulders to knees, the bitterness on his tongue confounding screams of pain and pleasure.

(Metallic flash in the dark. Sweaty sock forcing his tongue—and his screams—back into his throat.)

"What kind of mind conjures such memories?" he asked the demon-eyed image in the mirror. "Zivon Stefanovich, is it you? or is it the Ridenour?" It couldn't be the elusive Other. The memories had been resident long before the session in the caves with Nayati.

Unlike most crazies, he'd had the opportunity to become intimately acquainted with his other resident selves. But neither of them appeared inclined to answer this particular question.

He couldn't say he blamed them.

His hands were shaking. He wrapped them around his waist, held them quiet with his elbows.

Where did Reality lie in a brain riddled with Eudoxin and that Cocheta drug—and who knew what else by now?

He remembered the pain of ripped skin, greater pain as KwikHeal got him to classes, remembered the looks and snide laughter in the locker room and showers. He'd never had the stomach to examine the source of their amusement—not then. Not in all the years since. But he well remembered the pain of getting scarred tissue flexible enough to compete again. He *remembered* Coach Devon's anger when he refused to explain that stiffness, then threatened to quit the team rather than endure the trainer's massage.

But there was no mention in his medical records: he'd looked, once upon a time. Not of the scars. Not of . . .

Would Anevai lie about so personal an issue?

The mirror here refuted the scars. Anevai's claim challenged the—sterility.

It could all be nothing more than some Eudoxin-released evil in his own sick mind. He'd had the stuff in his belongings, so some of the memories *must* be true. But for three days, he'd kept minor amounts of it in his system constantly. He'd gone comatose under the Cocheta machine with their drugs and mechanically induced reactions pouring unchecked into and through his system.

The 'Net was not infallible, *Harmonies* had proven that. How much less reliable was a fragile human mind?

"I don't know, Loren," TJ said, from the bar in Cantrell's private quarters. "Is it fair to bring up what are possibly old and long-buried issues?"

"Buried? You saw those pictures, TJ. Stephen's lived with scars like that on the outside all these years. What's still inside?"

"McKenna cleaned him up once, she can do it again."

"You know that's not what I meant."

He brought two glasses of wine, handed her one and settled beside her on the couch, crossing his legs.

"No room for doubt it was Eudoxin?"

"None, according to Marlo. She says the side effects are pretty distinctive. Lethal if left untreated."

"He going to be all right now?"

"Marlo says he is."

"You don't agree?"

"Depends on whether he's got any more of that stuff. Depends on how he's dealt with those scars over the years—as well as how he got them."

He sipped the wine, licked his lips appreciatively. "From down there?"

She nodded.

"Good stuff. —Seems to me the kid's put things pretty well together these last few days. It's not as if he used the drug for fun and games. He evidently deduced a real use for it, and considered the payoff worth the risk."

"Doesn't explain why he had it in the first place."

"Smith."

She shook her head. "I agree with Marlo on that one. The man would consider it an insult to his talents."

"Stephen wouldn't know that. He didn't have it the first time down—I checked his personals—but the second time . . . that was on his own. He'd met Smith by then. Would have had some idea what he was up against. Wanted desperately to influence the man—"

"And he's back down there again. With Smith."

"Like you said, Smith wouldn't be interested—not that way. But I sincerely doubt he has any more. We've screened his quarters here, a team downworld can scan his temp in SciComp. But it's not illegal, Loren. He's got every right to own it."

"Now. He sure as hell didn't five or six years ago." She swallowed the last of the wine and went for a refill. "Besides, I'm not particularly concerned about here. It's after we return him to Vandereaux I'm worried about."

"So the kid OD'd on the designer drug of the century. It happens, Loren. You can't run his life. You haven't the time, the moral obligation, or the legal right. And if he happened to get in with a rough crowd of 'Doxies . . ." He glanced at the photos on the coffee table. ". . . Maybe he just got carried away."

"Or they did."

"And maybe, just maybe, it's what *he* wanted: he never issued a complaint, after all. Do you really want to add that to your perception of Stephen Ridenour? For God's sake, Loren, let his bedroom remain private. Has nothing to do with the man we work with. McKenna says it's old. Dead. Let it stay that way."

"Dead? Not her words. —Did you happen to notice the drug company with the patent on Eudoxin?"

He lifted a brow, leaned forward to set his glass on the coffee table and pick up the report lying there.

A glance later: "MylaVan— Oh, my."

"Singular understatement. Ring a bell, does it?"

"One of Councillor Shapoorian's by-blows, isn't it?"

She nodded.

TJ whistled softly.

"If Mialla Shapoorian's son was responsible for the Eudoxin—possibly even for the overdose—and Mialla Shapoorian was responsible for Ridenour's coming here—trusting he would choose to stay—could be Mialla Shapoorian wants him out of the way for good reason. Could make trouble for him when he gets back."

"And his coming back triumphant and standing before the 'NetAT to say *I told you so* would not be the best PR that Separatist party has had in the past half-century. I've got another what-if for you: What if these two 'Netters are Shapoorian's?"

"They checked out 'NetAT."

"Doesn't mean they couldn't be bought—with the right currency. A proven 'Doxie might not get all the respect one could wish."

She drained the second glass. Appalling waste—she'd hardly tasted it, her adrenaline level was so high. "I wish to God we could override their orders—keep them away from Stephen, maybe even leave the boy here until we knew the score back in Capital Station—but without knowing the situation on the 'Net itself . . ."

"Can Smith find that out for us?"

"With the 'NetLink down? Not a chance."

He got up, held his hand out for her glass; she shook her head. "Water, with ice."

"You've got it. —What if you drop the hold on the 'Net? Might be worth it. Hell, Smith could probably get you a direct onLine to Council."

Tempting. Sincerely tempting. But: "Not with Nayati and who knows who else out there waiting to access the minute the system goes back onLine. We've got to get back—get the Combined Council on the entire issue: Smith's theory, the Cocheta, even Hononomii's problem. The potential for disaster until the 'Net itself is protected is too great: we simply dare not delay.''

"And your search for the caves?''

"Might have to drop it. Might be up to you after all—and maybe we'll draft Paul. Take him back after all these years. Make him use that notoriety of his for something worthwhile. Add some high-powered Scientific veracity to our claims.''

"He'll love that. —Do you suppose there's any possibility of Ridenour posting charges against Shapoorian?''

She shook her head. "He wouldn't stand a chance, and Bijan Shapoorian has made sure he knows it. I'm more worried what McKenna will do. She's swearing she'll file a malpractice suit in his name if he doesn't—never mind it could mean her career.''

"And his life. Too bad he doesn't have Smith's connections. Shapoorian couldn't touch him then.''

"If he had Smith's connections, he wouldn't need them.''

"Isn't that the way of things? We could kidnap Smith—take him in the kid's place.''

"I'd like to win this one, thanks. Besides which, this obsession of Stephen's for doing this mission right extends to protecting Smith—''

"You're kidding.''

"Fact is, he's right. If Smith goes back, he's very likely to be arrested. Depends on what shape the 'Net's really in and whether or not he can fix it.''

"Dammit, woman, you can't leave him here, then. Ultimately, it's your responsibility.''

"Unbelievable as it sounds, you're wrong. Stephen is here as the official 'NetAT rep on Smith's paper—and its viability. Theoretically, it's not supposed to be in operation, never mind it is. Consequently, legally, Stephen calls the shots.''

"You're sure of that?''

"Once Chet reminded me of it, I remembered the day the 'NetAT pushed the law through. *They* called it keeping the 'Net nonpartisan.''

"Incredible. —Even beyond Herzog's authority?"

"That could get hazy. Somehow, I doubt it's ever come up. Del d'Bug missions rarely have much significance. The sad thing is, Stephen will accomplish precisely what he wants. He'll keep Smith out of jail—for now—take the responsibility for all that's happened and ruin his career, and I can't talk him out of it."

"Declare him incompetent and override."

"He's not. You've read that journal he kept down there. Considering what's happened to him—what he's done to straighten himself out—TJ, I have to admit, I don't see any way out for him that will leave his pride and confidence intact. He's riding high right now. For once, he's holding all the aces, and while he may not win the game, he'll win this hand. In the long run, Smith may still end up behind bars—"

"If not for this, then for something else."

"—Stephen doesn't care that ultimately he's going to lose— has, in fact, already allowed for that eventuality."

"I don't understand."

She pulled a file folder from the stack on the table. "This was waiting for me on my desk this morning."

She tossed it down in front of him:

I, Stephen NMI Ridenour, do, upon this document's . . .

"You going to tell me what that was all about?" Wesley's question greeted Stephen at the door. Quietly. Reasonably.

His laboriously stabilized heartbeat picked up again.

"No," he answered shortly, and crossed to the window, where he wouldn't have to look into Wesley's face, hoping he'd take the hint and leave it at that, possibly leave altogether.

But Wes didn't leave it at that. "You didn't tell Anevai everything up there on the ship, did you?" Naturally. He was physiologically incapable of leaving it at that.

"Let it drop, Wes." And on a second thought: "Please."

"The attacks came in a whole lot of forms, didn't they, kid?"

He tensed, not wanting to share this with anyone, least of all the self-loving, utterly together Wesley Smith.

"Good-looking youngster—already primed not to go to the authorities—"

Unfortunately for what little dignity remained to him, the memories were too close to the surface tonight. Tension became a shudder, which amplified into wave upon uncontrollable wave, shaking him head to foot, turning his knees to liquid.

He reached blindly for the curtains, but it was Wesley in front of him, grasping his arms, holding him upright. Stifling a sob, he tried to pull away, but Wesley refused to let him go.

"D–dammit, Wes, cut it out! I d–dealt with it—long ago. And I d–didn't need you, or Anevai, or any other goddamned self-proclaimed *expert* to do it!"

"You did, did you? Son, —"

"S–stop calling me that! You've no right. You've . . . no . . . *God, leave me alone!*"

He ripped free and stumbled past Wesley to the glass door, gripped the curtains and stared out into twilight that thickened and flowed into the room, engulfing him in blackness, cutting him off from Wesley and all the safety and goodness this place radiated.

Strobe-pierced blackness. Lights flickering as workmen labored through the academy night to stabilize the vital life-support systems . . .

(*Thunder filling the room. Boyish laughter from the far end of the temporary dormitory. The vent above his cot blowing a steady stream of chilled air directly on his thinly-clad shoulders.*

(*Burrowing into his pillow, drawing the blankets over his head, shuts out the light, the chill, but not the sound. Not the nightmares . . .*)

The jokester who had programmed the light-activated sim had never known the reality behind his prank. Didn't know what real thunder and lightning could do to a body caught in it with nowhere to go. Hadn't seen their cousin turned into a blackened corpse. . . .

(Sobbing into his pillow. Anonymous in his corner. Wishing it were otherwise.)

"Stephen?"

(A touch. A low question. Acknowledgement of existence with arms to end the loneliness.)

"Stephen?"

(Damp chill. The salty taste of blood. Fire burning down his spine.

(Slow separation of one sensation from another, one muddled thought from the next.)

Pain: all too familiar, even then. Images his mind refused to understand, then or any time since. Only the wreck of his bunk had been real. Sandy must have misunderstood. Sandy and Jo-Jo had realized his fear was not a game, and they'd tried to stop.

(More hands. A harsh voice egging them on—threatening when they objected—)

"Stephen!" Hands jerked him around, pressed him to the wall. An arm across his chest held him there. The other hand found his chin and jerked his face up, forcing his attention. "What the hell are you babbling about?"

Babbling? Who was babbling? He wasn't supposed to tell! Mustn't . . . Never tell—

Stephen fought to halt his own stammering betrayal, but: "Don't you see? It was the Board. First Mama—then the Board . . ."

He couldn't stop. Couldn't blink. The encroaching memories, the long-withheld bitterness was too powerful. Wesley's shadowy image grew larger, the untamed mane, short and sleek . . .

("B—Bijan, I . . .")

(Sheets draped over the sink edge. Dripping water that puddled, chilling his bare feet. Traitorous stains that had resisted his most determined efforts.

("That's Mr. Shapoorian, Ridenour. What are you doing up at this hour?")

''Stephen, come—''

The hand fell to his shoulder and pulled gently, unconscious echo of that long-ago night. Stephen flinched away, stumbling to the bed, pulling the warmth of a blanket around him.

Warmth that could never ever ever cure that innermost chill.

''Stephen.'' Wesley's voice only, without the touch that drove him—away. ''I can't help you if I don't know what they did.''

''Did, Wes?'' He twisted around and glared into the shadow that was Wesley. ''They didn't *do* a damn thing! Can't you see? They'd heard the stories. They very kindly didn't even press charges against me—it was my *upbringing* at fault—went straight to the sentencing—''

''What—sentencing?''

He shook his head and looked away, gripping the blanket, pulling it tight, as if that cocoon could protect him from the past as well as Wesley's stare. 'Sensitivity exercises,' They'd called it. 'Payment in kind' was the unspoken academy tradition being upheld. But Wesley would never believe that. No sane person would.

No sane person. He thought of the mirrors and Anevai, controlled a shudder, and clung desperately to that past he remembered. ''Doesn't matter now. It got them what they wanted.''

''What's that?''

Bitterness found relief in choked laughter. ''My head on a platter—signed, sealed, and delivered. No contest.''

''You've got to be kidding me.''

He shrugged, the laughter dying.

Wesley slowly sat down beside him, letting his hands hang between his knees, staring at the floor. ''If what you're implying is the truth, why didn't you demand a full-scale investigation?''

''You've seen my transfer. I'm Danislav's—forever.''

''Huh?''

''Didn't do your homework, Smith. I'm Recon; I couldn't possibly handle the responsibility of full Citizenship. *His* association got me into the academy, *he* controls my destiny until the day I die. He'd have to file in my name, and since he hadn't, he obviously believed me guilty along with the rest. Bijan—reminded me of these facts the night I—''

''Bijan Shapoorian?''

Laughter welled up again: Wesley sounded so surprised. ''Of course Shapoorian! Who else?'' The name set his heart racing again. ''It was *always* Bijan!''

''For the love of—Stephen, I'm beginning to sympathize with Nayati! Getting a straight story out of you is damn near impossible!''

''Well, f—fuck you!'' He jerked away, rolled across the bed and up against the wall, and sat, pressing clenched fists against throbbing temples. ''Fuck *all* of you! You with your smiles and laughter, your *I cares* and . . . I *did* deal with this—haven't been bothered in years. Now the two of you—are you *trying* to drive me crazy? Do you really hate me that much? *Why,* for God's sake? *What did I do?*''

''God, Stephen, I don't—''

''*Don't say it!* Dammit, *shut up!* Shut up and leave me alone! I don't want to hear any more *lies.*''

''Stephen—don't start fighting me again. I'm trying to help.''

''Forget it, Wes! You can't—no one can!''

''Dammit, boy—''

Something snapped. He swung wildly, a blanket-tangled blow Wesley blocked easily. He swung again, and a broad shoulder slammed him against the wall. A heavy arm across his chest held him there. Hard, angry breath exploded in his face.

But he didn't see Wesley. He saw Bijan—in the hallway—in the bathroom—facing the Board—and it was Bijan's voice in the dark, threatening Sandy and JoJo. . . .

And Bijan's mother was the leader of the Separatists . . . had dedicated her whole career to forcing the Recons out of Alliance politics. . . .

''My God,'' he said softly. ''It was Bijan. From the beginning. They didn't dare go against the Councillor's son.

Especially Danislav. Danislav was brand new in administration—to file a protest would have ruined him. . . .''

"Stephen?" Wesley's voice, and a gentle tapping on his face, penetrated his thoughts.

The mattress cradling his knees. The wall's texture, a lump that was the blanket at his back. Wesley's face a frowning, out-of-focus blur. He untangled his hand from the blanket, and grasped Wesley's wrist lightly.

"It's all right, Wesley, I just—figured something out, that's all."

. . . If they'd wanted him out, the charge from Sandy would have been enough. But all along, the goal had been the confession. That last night, when he'd broken down completely and given them the proof they wanted—official, signed and on tape—what sort of weapon had he handed them?

Not Bijan. Not the other students. Beyond Bijan: Bijan's mother, Councillor Shapoorian. Perhaps even Council itself. And now, he was here at Council's request. Council was using him. Council was *always* using him.

Could any political end have been worth what that handful of days had done? Not only to him, but to the students carrying out that 'sentence' as well?

And how long would they have let it continue? Bijan's pills had nearly killed him once; Hospital had cleaned him out and sent him back. Unofficial rumor claimed he'd attempted suicide; officially, he'd never been in hospital.

"Stephen?"

The room stabilized. He was shivering again, and Wesley's frown had become concern. "Never mind, Wes. It's all long gone." He forced the shivers to stop, and Wesley let him go. "Now."

Keeping the wall at his back, he slipped down to sit crosslegged on the mattress. Wesley started to settle beside him, but Stephen raised his hand:

"Please, Wes. No more. Not—not tonight."

"Stephen . . ." Wesley reached for him, and Stephen shrank away, looked up and really met his eyes for the first time since entering the room. Wesley froze, staring into his face, then pulled back his hand. "You going to be all right, son?"

He smiled—as unforced a smile as he'd ever felt on his face—and nodded.

"I'll be fine, Wesley."

And as the door closed, leaving him alone at last:

"Now." He let his head drop onto his crossed arms, welcoming a blackness that, for once, held no specters.

"I'm certain you'll understand my saying, admiral," Herzog said, settling gracefully into the chair opposite her desk, the picture of superior breeding, "that this begins to feel like a runaround. You come here looking for two researchers whose records have disappeared from the 'Net, and suddenly, the researcher sent to investigate those—deletions—is 'unavailable.' Have I sufficient cause for suspicion?"

Cantrell waited while Ali pulled up a second chair and fumbled with his notetaker. Herzog and Ali—no Naghavian. Evidently, the 'NetATs had decided Herzog would deal better with her. Interesting.

When rather anxious dark eyes indicated Ali was ready, she said:

"I didn't say Dr. Ridenour was unavailable. I said he was sick. Some problem with the local food, I believe. His physician recommended a few days' rest. I'm certain, familiar as you must be with his records, you're aware he has a relatively delicate constitution. I would not, if I were you, take the physician's advice lightly."

"But you are not us. I see no reason to believe what we're being told without some form of verification. Considering the stakes, admiral, I'd prefer to make that verification in person. If that means attending a hospital bed, I shall do so. Now, when does the next shuttle leave?"

"S–sir?" Ali interjected hesitantly.

Herzog frowned. "What is it?"

"I—I thought we were going to be conducting the interview h—here, sir. I—I don't *do* planets well, sir. I—I'm afraid I wouldn't be much use. . . ."

"For God's sake, then. Stay here." Superior breeding slipped, recovered quickly. "Enjoy yourself. Consider it a vacation. I assure you, it won't reflect on our report of your services."

"I— Yes, sir. Thank you, sir." Ali looked across at her, rather woebegone, and she shrugged. Lexi had reported to TJ that Ali appeared sympathetic to their problems—and Stephen's. He'd tried. She'd tried.

Nothing more they could do except:

"We've two passenger shuttles. One has just been pressure-docked for routine maintenance; the other is downworld. 1100 hours tomorrow morning is the best we can do." She signalled the security personnel waiting to accompany these two back to their quarters. "I'm sure you understand."

Herzog rose to his feet. "Oh, I understand, admiral. I understand perfectly. Tomorrow, you say?"

"1100 hours. Ship time, Mr. Herzog."

Lexi entered the room, along with TJ and three other Security.

"Ship time, admiral," Herzog confirmed. "—Mr. Ali?"

Cantrell noted with some amusement Ali's rather smitten expression as he fell in beside Lexi.

"Got him hooked, hasn't she?" she said to TJ as the door closed behind the lot.

"I hope so. For her sake and his. From what she tells me, she's let a lot slip."

"Unconscious? Or considered?"

"She knew she did it. Calls him sympathetic and good to have on Stephen's side."

"Gotten much in return?"

He shrugged. "Ali talks a good game."

"Doom and gloom, Teej. She understands on one level. And

if she suspects he's trying to use her to get on the inside, have her turn the tables on him. May come in handy.''

"Dammit, Loren, be careful. Someday you're going to use the wrong person. Push someone too far.''

"If you don't push, you never know what you've got. —Tell Paul to contact Smith. Tell him I tried.''

III

i

The kid's color, while neither matching the speed-blurred trees beyond the bubblecar's dome, nor as white as the clouds above, was not what you would term 'healthy.' He should never have left him alone last night.

"Stephen, I'm sorry," Wesley said.

Brilliant eyes flickered his way and refocussed, holding no trace of condemnation.

"Whatever for?''

Lacking time and inclination to enumerate, Wesley picked his most recent transgression. "I should have told you about these two sooner. I was sure we'd have one more day, at least. And when Hamilton called last night . . .''

"Don't be silly, Wes. I've had two full nights' sleep in a row. That's better than I've managed in years. And I very much appreciate your waiting until *after* breakfast.'' A slow smile stretched tight muscle. "If you'd told me yesterday, I'd have been a basket case today.''

And you're not? Wesley thought, unable to ignore the increasingly frequent shivers passing beneath Stephen's thin sweater.

"Here,'' he said, pulling off his coat. "Put this on.'' And

when Stephen objected: "No way, brat. I'm too hot. Told you I'd be."

"Thanks," Stephen murmured and slipped into it, turning the fur collar up around his neck, carefully adjusting the fringe. Tode made the thing look like he thought it would when he'd ordered it.

"Don't let these Virtual 'Netters get to you," he said firmly. "If they give you a hard time, pass them on to me. I'd enjoy the fight."

"I think I can handle them." Stephen's smile trembled at the corners . . . "I'll think of it as a practice session for the real thing. These two are outriders. They can't know too much." . . . and disappeared altogether. "It's starting, isn't it, Wes?"

"Something always is, brat. Nature of the universe. To which something are you referencing?"

"The deterioration of the 'Net."

His own suspicions given voice. Not the kind of validation he liked. "Think so?"

Stephen nodded slowly. "Why else are they here? I don't think you can keep them from implementing your system. I don't think they can afford to wait."

"Into mind reading now, Ridenour?"

Slower negative. "Just a—feeling."

"Like you felt the mountain, right?" He couldn't quite hide a smile, softened it with a teasing half-wink. "Now you're feeling NSpace."

"Something like." Stephen's subdued conviction was far more unnerving than any of the solid arguments Wesley could have given him for the same conclusion. But he didn't pursue the issue, and Stephen himself abruptly changed the subject: "I hope Anevai's all right."

"Didn't look good this morning, did she? But maybe green is normal."

"Mama never was," Stephen responded quietly—cryptic comment, to which there was no answer—then shrugged and turned back to the landscape speeding past the clear-sided bubblecar, an aura of pensive resignation subtly contradicting his outward composure.

Wesley leaned his head against the cushions, watching that almost-profile through half-lidded eyes, wondering again if Stephen had overheard his conversation with Anevai. Eventually, he had to know—certainly before he inadvertently fathered another child. But Anevai had a point: the kid had some real obsessions regarding Parental Responsibilities, and he'd likely rip himself apart, psychologically, trying to figure the 'right thing' to do, and likely end up sacrificing his entire career in some empty gesture. Never mind Anevai was in no danger of being left to raise the child alone, and never mind no healthier or happier environment existed for a kid to grow up in than the communal nurseries of HuteNamid.

No, now was certainly not the time to tell Stephen, nor had Wesley Smith any desire to be the bearer of such tidings. If any portion of what he'd said last night was true, Stephen Ridenour had a helluva lot of personal problems to deal with before trying to raise a child of his own.

If Stephen had rested well last night, the same could not be said of Wesley Smith. He had far too intimate acquaintance with the idiosyncrasies of Vandereaux Academy to completely dismiss the clone-wannabe's claims. Certainly, whatever had happened to him had left its mark.

The kid needed real help. Help he'd never get in Vandereaux, and the 'NetAT's interest would shatter once they suspected any instability of character.

"Stephen," Wesley said, cautiously reopening last night's issue, "let me contact Pop's lawyers. They can wipe that record and get you free of Danislav. Simple shit. Probably won't even have to grease any palms. Vandereaux Academy has nothing to gain, keeping you under wraps. Once you're free, you can come back."

Without turning, Stephen said, "I can't let you get involved, Wes. You've got your own future to worry about. I think Bijan's actions, the cover-up, all of it, goes much too deep to solve with simple bribery, and best left buried, anyway. I'll be fine. If I keep a low profile, maybe they'll even let me work on the cleanup. That'll keep a dozen techs busy for the rest of their lives.''

"That what you want?"

He did turn at that, an ambiguous half-smile on his face. "Don't tempt the habit of a lifetime, Wes. I don't *want* anything except to be useful enough to the Powers That Be to keep alive. I'll be content, so long as I have some purpose."

"Content." Wesley's stomach churned. Sounded like a lifetime of the B-word to him.

Silence enveloped the small vehicle, there seeming nothing to say. And as the minutes and miles passed, Stephen's color improved, his self-possession asserting itself until, for the first time, Wesley saw the 'NetAT representative he officially was, from carefully coiffed hair—he must have cut it himself: at breakfast, it had been charmingly shaggy—to his polished shoes.

But somehow, even the conservative grey sweater and indigo shirt and slacks assumed a Look as distinctive as the crystal-buttoned jacket.

"You look fine, you know."

Stephen started. Glanced up from hands folded in his lap.

"You said you were worried about not having packed a suit. That's fine. Respectful without appearing like you knew they were coming for you."

His mouth quirked. "Know the games, don't you, Smith?"

Wesley smiled easily. "Damn right. Why do you think I'm here?"

"I'm not really sure." Stephen's answer caught him off guard. "Never any temptation to go back?"

"None," he answered flatly, and without a moment's hesitation.

"You realize, of course, you could name your own price, if the 'Base *is* crashing. Maybe get your own research wing at the 'NetAT."

"Doesn't even tempt me."

"You're a strange man, Wesley Smith."

"Lord, talk about the pot calling the kettle."

Stephen cocked his head like an inquisitive bird, and Wesley laughed. "Never mind, brat."

Stephen chuckled, and said, as if the thought had only just occurred to him, "If you came back to Vandereaux, m—maybe we could . . ." He bit his lip.

"Maybe we could what, Ridenour?" he asked, setting the trap.

"If—if everything went well, maybe we could work together."

And snapping it closed: "I already told you. Set Pop's lawyers on it. I'll have you back here inside the year."

Stephen just looked at him. The control slipped for an instant, and Zivon Ryevanishov looked out through those opalescent eyes, sad and lonely—

—and desperately frightened.

A blink and Zivon was gone.

"I've already answered that, Wesley," Stephen murmured, and turned back to the mountains and trees.

Half an hour later, Stephen shook his head, as though freeing it of progwuzzles, and, slipping off the coat, held it out with a quiet *Thank you.*

Wesley waved a hand. "Keep it. I wanted an excuse to get a new one."

"New?" Stephen brushed a hand over intricate beadwork and soft, tanned leather, justifiably puzzled.

Dammit, he'd waited a bloody year for that coat, but:

"Looks better on you anyway." And for vanity's sake: "Binds me across the shoulders a bit."

He still looked dubious . . . as he petted the fur collar.

"Prezzie, Stevie-lad. Say *Thank you, Uncle Wesser.*"

"Thank you, Uncle Wesser." On a soft chuckle. And for a moment, he was all Stephen. "And thank you, Dr. J. Wesley Smith, for my—prezzie."

They passed the rest of the trip to the Researcher Condos in silence, and took Stephen's luggage to the room he'd occupied before. Wesley having called ahead, the room was open, and the key, preset to Stephen's bios and left on the desk, activated at Stephen's touch.

Simultaneously, the computer monitor came to life, a message light flashing in the corner.

Still without a word, Stephen touched the acknowledgement button.

>SciCorps Conference Room B2.
>Immediately upon arrival.
>Dr. Smith's presence required, as well.
>Richard Herzog/Clarissa Naghavian, ComNet Authority *in situ*.

"Well, well, well," Wesley said, "My 'presence,' eh? Guess this is—Stephen?"

Stephen's pale face had gone stark white, and the wide eyes stared unblinkingly at the computer screen.

"Stephen!" He grabbed the kid's shoulders, forcefully breaking that mesmeric contact. "What the hell's the matter with you?"

The opal eyes stared through him, and Stephen said softly, "I thought you were dead."

"According to his beeper signal, he's on his way to the SciCorps offices, admiral."

Chet's voice murmured in Cantrell's head. She asked aloud:

"You made it clear to Smith we need them delayed as long as possible?"

"Clear as I could. The man was less than happy. Says the kid's pretty shaken up. Sounded serious, admiral. Like there was lots he wasn't saying. I don't like it, sir."

"Neither do I. Not much we can do about it, though. Thanks, Chet. Keep me posted."

"So," TJ said from his chair on the far side of her office desk, "what do we do now?"

"We hope Sakiimagan's plan works. Are they coming?"

TJ glanced at his watch. "Five minutes, give or take."

She settled into her chair and rested laced fingers on her stomach. ''Do you realize, I might have to let those people take Stephen back?''

''Pull rank on them, Loren. You've got the Head behind you.''

''Not that simple. If we *are* talking a general collapse of the 'Base, I have no right to stand in their way.''

''So it's on to plan B. You pull up stakes here and take him back yourself. He's dangerously unbalanced, and you've a rapport with him.''

''And the Cocheta? We still haven't located another Library. Without them, we've no solid proof these ETs exist. I hate to put you through a Voice Recall session, and I thought Paul would have a coronary when I suggested the possibility of his going back.''

''A: it's my job. B: it doesn't surprise me, Paul's an egotistical bastard, and C: Hell, if Council is too stubborn to believe you with the evidence you've already got, let them live with the consequences.''

''You don't mean that.''

''Don't I?''

''But what did we see, Teej? Just a large cavern filled with lots of couches.''

''*And* a matter transformer, *and* the weirdest damned lighting system *I've* ever seen, *and* signals that claim that cavern was solid granite, not to mention something that caused all our recording instruments to whiteout.''

''No proof of any of that. They could always claim holos and unregistered human technology and come after the researchers with a club. Where would that get us?''

''There's Ridenour's VR-with-a-kick.''

''Only his claims. You've said it yourself, he's dangerously unbalanced. After the pressure of the 'NetAT hearings—I don't see him holding together for more from the Council.''

TJ's mouth pursed in thought for a long moment, then, as

the signal above the door announced the Tyeewapis' arrival:
"You've got a problem, Cantrell."

She choked on helpless laughter, and keyed the door open.
"Come in, governor."

ii

Hard to believe this was the same Stephen Ridenour who'd
seen spooks in his computer minutes ago. Here in SciCorps
Conference Room B2, the Clone was in full implementation
mode, blending with these two 'NetAT exquisites as if they
were output from the same program, with variables limited to
coloring, age, and gender. All the awkward shyness and intensely careful manners were gone. All Cantrell's worry—his,
too, for that matter—had been wasted. Stephen Ridenour was
finally in his element.

Introductions made, Wesley sat back, waiting to see who
jumped which way, waiting for this Herzog person, who
seemed determined to run the show, considering his top
billing on the message, to justify his 'invitation' to this
'Net-tie party.

Clone #1 began innocently enough: a simple Q & A on
local conditions, Stephen's journey here and a gentle probe into
the particulars of his coming downworld. Give him credit, the
youngest clone protected Cantrell's interests, answering in
vague terms which sounded convincing enough, avoiding precisely where and when certain—encounters—had taken place.
He'd come here as a 'NetAT Del d'Bugger, to prove or disprove
the legality of Wesley's publication, and over the course of the
past weeks, the normal interactions—review of notes, verification of source material, and the like—had all taken place. The
young graduate had, in fact, accomplished precisely what he'd
been sent here to do.

Wesley slouched in his chair, enjoying said performance in a vague, detached sort of way, verifying (when asked) whatever Stephen had said, otherwise offering no opinions.

"In your judgement, then," Herzog said finally, "is your job here completed?"

Stephen's eyes flickered his way, but didn't stay long enough to count. "Yes, sir. I'd say I've accomplished everything I can. When Admiral Cantrell completes her negotiations here—"

"You won't need to wait for that."

"I'm sorry? I don't—"

Herzog's mouth approximated a smile. "You'll be returning with us."

A second flicker of opal, but Stephen dipped his chin acquiescently. "I'm at the 'NetAT's disposal, of course."

"And what of your original allegations, Dr. Ridenour?" So: Clarissa Naghavian had a voice after all.

"Allegations, ma'am?"

"Of the implications of the theory expounded upon in this paper. Of the possible uses."

Possibly even a brain.

Wesley pricked his ears. And his eyes—then decided she was *too* perfect for his taste.

Stephen replied calmly, "That, ma'am, is in my report, which is in the hands of DProg Hamilton. I haven't the experience nor the expertise to determine its proper disbursement. If you please, pose your question to him."

Well done, clone. Well done.

Herzog's smile tightened. "You've attained wisdom, Zivon Ryevanishov. I'm proud of you. We did well to encourage your—curiosity. —In that case, we'll be leaving in the morning. We'll obtain that report, and be back in Vandereaux within the month—subjectively speaking."

Zivon Ryevanishov? Wesley started, remembering Stephen's hoarse whisper: *I thought you were dead.*

What had the kid walked into—or, more accurately, what

had Wesley Smith *led* him into? Who was this Herzog person? He wasn't one of the Names JP had ever mentioned. But he wouldn't be. He was an outward presence. An adequate programmer—enough to understand the 'Net—but not a great one. This one's talents lay elsewhere.

But whatever Herzog had thought to provoke, he failed. Stephen replied evenly, "I'm not the child I once was, sir. I've come to understand my own—limitations."

"Have you? And do you understand your own value?"

"Better than you, sir." Stephen glanced toward Wesley for the first time. "Do you mind if we continue this in private, sir? Dr. Smith is not of a mind to get involved, and I'd like to respect his wishes in that."

"His own actions are in question—"

"I think not, sir. Master DProg Hamilton has cleared him—a decision Adm. Cantrell and Security Voice Briggs support. I believe the 'NetAT will stand by that decision as well, once the facts are before them. I'd prefer not to compromise his integrity further."

"Now wait a minute, Ridenour," Wesley broke in, resenting this high-handed dismissal of his involvement, resenting being cut out of proceedings just beginning to amuse.

Resentment that dissolved in the face of Stephen's level gaze.

"Trust me, Dr. Smith. I understand the situation. I can handle it."

That strange conversation on the tube—the kid was trying to ensure his freedom, was trying to help. Least he could do was play along; let the kid play the martyr. Didn't have spit to do with him, anyway. He was an idea-man, not a key-tapper.

He grinned, winked and shrugged. "Hell, folks, I'm bored. Remember our date, Ridenour."

Stephen blinked. The level gaze faltered. "D–date?"

"I'm crushed. Dinner. *Tomorrow* night. Party time, remember? Gang's counting on it."

It was the only way he could see to retain any control. He wanted to know what transpired in his wake. He wanted to make sure the kid was all right. He wanted—

"Of course, Dr. Smith," Stephen responded, playing *his* game better with each breath. "I'll be there."

"I'm afraid that won't be possible," Herzog began, and Stephen interrupted smoothly:

"One day, sir. What can it possibly matter? The people here have been exceedingly gracious to me. It's only proper I respond accordingly."

Wesley grinned and thought again, *Well done, brat,* and headed for the door, Cantrell's mission accomplished, his own set in motion.

"Excuse me, Dr. Smith." Naghavian's voice stopped him in midstride. "We asked you to attend for a reason."

Asked. That was humorous. He turned and leaned his shoulders carelessly against the door, looked down his nose at her. "Reason?"

She reached into a briefcase, held out a memcube. "From Sect. Beaubien. His compliments."

Stephen cast a startled glance at him.

A glance Wesley refused to acknowledge. As he'd told Stephen in Acoma, his relationship with Jean-Phillippe was old and dead, and certainly none of Stephen Ridenour's business. Jean-Phillippe was undoubtedly counting on eliciting just such a reaction in Stephen, because Herzog most certainly saw it, and would sense a weakness in Stephen Ridenour where Wesley Smith was concerned.

He swore under his breath, and said: "Tell him to put it—"

"I think not, sir," Naghavian interrupted him. "What *you* do with the message itself is none of my business, however, should you care to send a response, I will most certainly deliver it for you."

She held out the sealed cube. He scowled at her, at it, took in Stephen's growing confusion and snatched the cube from her hand.

"Don't count on it." He jerked the door open. "Stephen, —dinner. Tomorrow. Be there. —Herzog, —Naghavian, —it's been . . . swell. Have a nice trip back to hades."

He slammed the door behind him—

—and wished like hell he could have stayed.

"You want to do *what?*"

Cantrell was tired. She knew that. Knew that she'd been juggling a variety of political realities for years. Knew that her mind could be playing tricks on her. But she'd swear the people sitting in front of her desk, calmly describing their insane plan, were real.

Sakiimagan smiled. "Don't worry, admiral. Your hearing is quite sound. —Nigan would like to play for Hononomii. He thinks it might make a difference, and I'm inclined to agree."

Cantrell addressed Cholena as the (in her experience) most practical individual of the three facing her. "I thought you said he was improving."

"I said he'd stabilized, admiral," Cholena said calmly. "But he's still—suspicious. I believe he needs irrefutable evidence that his senses can be trusted. When Nigan first came aboard, Sgt. Fonteccio had his music transmitted over the ship's com. Hononomii recognized it—responded to it, just before falling asleep. If we can reach him on that same base level—"

Cantrell held up her hand. "Who am I to complain? Why haven't you just tried it? For God's sake, people, this is your son. You don't need my permission."

"I did," Nigan said, and all eyes turned to him. He swallowed visibly, but said defensively, "Why not? I just played to him in his room. That's *why* I want to take him home."

"Wait a minute," Cantrell said, "I lost something here."

"He *thinks* it's me, but he doesn't understand *why* I'm in the ship."

"That's what we wanted to discuss with you, admiral," Cholena explained. "Nigan thought the effect would be better if Hononomii was surrounded by the familiar. The smells, sounds, and sights of home, maybe a sunset, since that's when Nigan usually plays. Considering our experience thus far, it seemed sensible—"

Cantrell shook her head. "I can't countenance it, I'm sorry. Until that boy's health is assured, I want him here where McKenna can treat him."

TJ, who had been listening silently in the corner, grinned suddenly. She raised a brow: tacit invitation for him to speak. "We can't take him to his home," he said, "but what if we bring Home to him?"

"You mean the vids? We've tried that, Teej."

"Not the vids. Your 'Imager."

"The Holo . . ." She thought a moment, remotely amused by the confused looks from Hononomii's parents and friend. "We'd need a larger room—"

"One of the briefing auditoriums."

"It'd have to be adapted—reprogrammed."

"What do we pay Chet that big salary for?"

She grinned back at TJ. "Nigan, I think we've got your sunset."

iii

Wesley was gone and coffee had happened.

Stephen, while not overly fond of the drink, accepted the mug, grateful for something to do with his hands, grateful for something to warm chilled fingers.

"Now, Dr. Ridenour," Richard Herzog smiled easily, the cool smile of one professional to another. "Suppose we begin again. May I speak frankly?"

Grateful, too, for the changes time—and money—had wrought in the man's features, changes which removed that smile a step further from the friendly one of childhood memories, which made it easier to say, without stuttering:

"Of course."

"You say you know your own value. I don't think you do. Circumstances have changed—radically—since your departure."

"Changed, sir?" He refused to let the man's melodrama move him. If his suspicions were true, the answer was already in the proper hands—namely, Chet Hamilton's. "In what way?"

"The 'NetAT has had further opportunity to review your notes, and they're far more interested in those than in Smith's paper. They want *you* back—now."

"'They,' —sir?"

Naghavian glanced up at that deliberate hesitation, deigning to notice him for the first time. He let a slight smile pull the corner of his mouth. Found himself almost enjoying this brush with a ghost from his past. Found himself mildly intoxicated with power such as he'd never held before. They needed him. Needed what he could do. Let them—

"Sect. Beaubien. He wants you as his personal aide—he's arranged a special tutorial for Design Programming."

—God help him: his dream on a platter. His sense of power wavered. He steadied it, recalling Wesley's brief mention of the 'NetAT Secretary. *Beaubien would like me back....*

"In return for—what?" he asked, forcing detachment into his voice.

"Did I mention conditions? On the contrary. We were sent to help you wrap up your mission, and get you back as soon as possible."

"Why? What difference does a few weeks—or a few months— make in an apprenticeship of years?" He sensed amusement from Naghavian, irritation from Herzog, and pressed his advantage, small though it was. "Your candor leaves something to be desired, Mr. Herzog. The dropouts are increasing, aren't they? That's why you're really here. The 'NetAT's snatching at straws—any straw that might prove the right one—and they're willing to pay any price for that straw—until it proves useless. What then, Mr. Herzog?''

Naghavian smiled outright. ''Let me handle this, Dick. —You're right, Dr. Ridenour, though a bit . . . melodramatic. Further disruptions *have* occurred on the 'NetDB. You must also realize, you are not the only person aware of the growing problems on the 'Net, and having yourself drawn attention to Dr. Smith's paper, surely it cannot surprise you that others have realized similar potential in his theories. —Or do you consider yourself—and Dr. Smith, of course—so superior—so special— that others couldn't possibly comprehend—or even have examined similar alternatives?''

''Of course not . . .'' he muttered, feeling the heat rise in his face, knowing these people would have had full access to his school records, knowing she was mocking him.

On the other hand, he *knew* what had been published on 'Net topologies. *Knew* what research was in progress, and nothing touched Wesley's system in elegance or potential. The 'NetAT itself might be working the problem, but if that was the case, why come for him?

Naghavian's smile was warm, inviting, and most of all, he suspected, triumphant. ''No need to blush, Dr. Ridenour. No one is questioning your—abilities. But your being sent here was only a stopgap. The law had to be upheld, and Smith cited no precedents in his paper. Your insight gave you the right to receive the assignment. It wasn't until the 'NetAT BoI examined *your* paper more closely that they began to suspect where the *real* talent lay. They want you back. They want that talent nourished.''

She must think him a total bit-brain. Unless . . .

''And Dr. Smith?'' he asked. ''What about him?''

''That's for the 'NetAT to decide. The 'NetDB has been tampered with. The origin of those disruptions is this system. What do you think they should do?''

''Yet you said nothing to Wesley. My guess is you don't *want* to arrest him immediately. My guess is that you want to use *me* to lure him up to the ship where he *has* no choice. Am I right?''

Naghavian just smiled serenely.

And her serenity terrified him far more than anything Herzog could do.

''Well, I won't do it!''

Her smile widened.

His consent wasn't an issue. They would force him up to the ship, use his safety to coerce Wesley into cooperation...

And Wesley, the idiot, had a history of making grand-stand gestures at the wrong time....

''Dammit, it's not his fault! It was Nayati...'' Horrified, Stephen realized where his attempt to defend Wesley was leading him.

''Nayati?''

''Doesn't matter. He's been—neutralized.''

''And did this...Nayati effect the damage to the 'Net?''

''It doesn't matter.''

''Who else was involved?''

''I tell you, it doesn't *matter*. You don't need them. I can locate all changes. Create a global—''

''Who *else?*''

''Local 'Net access is down. No one can—''

''We'll have to arrest them all.'' Agent to agent. Bypassing him completely.

''You can't!'' he cried desperately. Knowing he was losing everything Cantrell sought to accomplish.

''You have no say in the matter.'' Herzog again: cold, arrogant voice from his past trying to reassert that long-ago power over him. And the bastard was succeeding. Blood pounded in his ears. Sweat threatened his hold on the mug. Stephen steadied his heartbeat and tightened his grip, defying that attempt: ''Don't I?''

Herzog laughed, mocking him. ''You think to hold yourself as ransom? You think you're *that* valuable?''

''I *know* I am. Can you prove otherwise?''

"I don't have to. I can take you *and* the others back. Let the BoI decide. If they have to sift your brains, believe me, they will."

"You'd have to know who they are. You'd have to find them. I won't tell you. Wesley won't. You can take us back, you can't fix the DB. You can't make us tell you how. Not even if you—sift our brains."

Herzog sipped his coffee. And laughed. "You're still naive, Zivon Ryevanishov."

"Think that if you choose, *sir.* But there are things you don't know—can't know—until you're RealTiming. Snap decisions based on situational nuances no interrogation can get out of my head. Once you see the process in action—get the *feel* for it—you can do it. If—" He raised his head and stared down his nose at Herzog, deliberate imitation of Wesley's Grand Style. "If you have the talent for it."

Herzog's perfect eyes narrowed. Not particularly smart, that dig. If the man had the talent, he wouldn't be here. But: "You really think he could be interested in someone like you?"

"Like me?" The flank attack threw him off balance. "Half his friends are Recon—"

Herzog's stare swept over him, pausing deliberately, making Stephen resent the overstuffed chair that forced informality. A slight sneer, more memorable than the man's features, edged Herzog's response: "Did I say anything about Ethnic Reconstructionists?"

"Our relationship's not like that."

"Come now. With his proclivities and your—talents?"

He knew what the man was doing, knew and still couldn't prevent a defensive: "He's my friend! He's just . . . my . . ."

"Of course." Herzog's smirk fed those doubts, giving him yet another reason to hate this man—and giving Herzog one more lever against him. "And will he still be when he learns the truth? The man has a well-documented chivalrous streak. What will he think of your record?"

"He knows," he said sullenly.

"Your version? Or the truth?"

"Truth. Is that what you call it?"

"A court did. And what will Smith think when he finds you lied on that as well?"

"I *didn't* lie."

"To Smith? Or to the academy Board of Conduct?"

"I—" He was losing, had robbed himself of supporting arguments long ago. Gravity failed. The world evaporated from under his feet. "What is it you want?"

"What's best for you, Zivon Ryevanishov. Always. And what's best for Alliance."

"What's best for me is whatever keeps Wesley free and here," he muttered, a perverse stubborn streak still hoping to succeed.

Herzog shook his head in ostentatious bewilderment. "I don't understand your persistent protection of this man. Do you think to gain money? Power? He's a worthless, spoiled prankster. You don't really think he'll want anything to do with you once he knows what you are, do you?"

"What do you mean?"

"With his money and family? Come, pretty buster-boy, you know what I'm talking about. You might have provided momentary entertainment, but a man like him, with his connections, doesn't need to settle for whores."

"I'm not . . ."

"No? I've got a present for you, Stephen Ridenour." Herzog reached in his pocket and pulled out a cut-crystal vial. An expensive trifle, but a throw-away compared to its contents. Herzog held it out, and when Stephen refused to take it: "Stand up, Zivon Ryevanishov."

"Go to hell."

"Don't challenge me, boy. You know better."

His heart racing, Stephen slowly rose to his feet, fought the urge to run as the man approached him and slid a hand familiarly under his sweater, searching for a pocket. Fought harder not to close his eyes, to keep the room, the mountains outside the window, in focus, refusing the flashes to grassy hillsides and racing *obatsi*. Failing a shirt pocket, the hand slipped downward, eventually locating the concealed inner pocket on his tailored slacks, lingered a moment to deposit the vial, and caressed Stephen's hip as he readjusted the grey sweater.

"When he returns to Vandereaux, Shapoorian will see to it he learns all about you—"

"B–Bijan? Why—"

Herzog smiled and ran a finger along Stephen's jawline. Stephen jerked away from the touch and threw himself back into the chair, the vial a sharp-edged, unwanted presence at his waist.

"Did I say anything about Mialla's hellspawn?" The smile became a laugh. "You mean Smith hasn't told you that one of his oldest—and *dearest*—friends is Mialla Shapoorian's prime contact within the 'NetAT?"

"Doesn't make any difference. He—he doesn't want to go back."

"Ever? I doubt that. He's on a defiance kick right now. He'll get bored soon enough. When he does, he'll certainly look up this—friend. For old times' sake, you know."

Defeat sat like a lead weight in his belly. God help him, he didn't want Wesley to find out. Wesley *had* been a friend. No one had ever offered him what Wesley had, and even though he could never come back, would never be free to pursue that friendship, he didn't want Wesley to despise him.

And Herzog, damn him, knew it, and went for that weakness, no different than the adolescents he'd outlasted at the academy. Naghavian—

—At least she wasn't as openly aggressive.

Perhaps an answer existed, but at the moment, he needed time to think. Time away from this too-potent reminder of the past. "Wh–what do you want?"

"Your promise to return."

"I've no choice in that, and you know it. I mean for Wesley's freedom—*guaranteed*."

That appraising smile returned. "We'll think of something."

It was a sense-dep recording. One of those used for the most personal of messages, requiring a machine few people could afford. Wesley could. JP knew he had one, had been with him when he purchased it. Had refused the one Wesley had offered to buy him.

Evidently he could afford his own, now.

Wesley slipped in the contacts and adjusted the earplugs (leaving the other accessories in the drawer), threw himself on the bed, and inserted the memcube.

"*Hello, Jonni.*" The image might have been there in the room next to him. "*I wish I might be there to give this to you in person, but somehow I doubt that's what you'd want.*

"*Hope you enjoyed my little present. The moment I saw him, I knew Dr. Ridenour was our man—that he could get the truth out of you if anyone could. He's really quite talented . . . as I'm certain you've realized.*

"*It's really very important that you come clean, Jonni—with everything. We know what you've been doing, now we must know the how and the extent of the damage. I could have given the team carte blanche to arrest you—but I didn't. In fact, I've done all I can for you here—stuck my neck out. Your only chance is to tell Dr. Ridenour everything—give him what he needs to convince the 'NetAT your intent was benign, never mind what has actually happened.*

"*Above all, Jonni, don't allow Dr. Ridenour to stay there. I know he might be tempted—you're a very tempting fellow—but either he comes back . . . or you do. And much as I'd love to see you again, I don't want to see you destroyed. Ridenour, unfortunately, already has been. I'll do what I can to provide for whatever can be salvaged. For now, he's your ticket to freedom. Use him wisely.*

*"So, old friend, do me this one final favor—don't cause any
more problems."*

The image turned as if to leave him—silly affectation, and *so*
Jean-Phillippe—paused, and turned back.

*"By the way, Smith, if this is another of your practical jokes,
your ass is grass, whether you come back to Vandereaux or
not. Papa's lawyers won't buy you out of this one."*

Wesley reviewed the recording several times, generated a
hardcopy of the text, for all the good it would do.

'Jonni.' No one had called him that in years. To Jean-
Phillippe, the similarity of their names had always been a bond.

So he'd claimed.

He flipped the replay.

JP looked good. Had avoided the temptation to remake his
face—just kept it as it had been in his twenties.

Or maybe he'd programmed the image that way. Like the
name: man-i-pu-la-shun.

Damn him!

"Can't leave me alone, can you, JP?" Wesley asked that
too-real image.

He had to admit, Beaubien was getting smart in his old age,
playing all sides at once. Last thing he wanted was to remind
anyone of his past association with the 'phantom wormer of
Vandereaux,' but he was perfectly willing to *use* that association to get precisely what he wanted.

And what he wanted was Wesley Smith under his thumb
once and for all. That damned message was a challenge.

"Well, *old friend.*" He flipped the cube free and tossed it
across the room for a perfect bank-shot into the round file. "I
don't accept. *I* know my Stevie. *You* don't. And you, *old
friend*, are in for one hell of a surprise."

Wesley bypassed the *Do not disturb* phone lockout without a
qualm: Stephen couldn't possibly mean him, and even if he
did, Wesley had to warn him about Beaubien's message.

According to the SciCorps records, Stephen had checked out

of the offices hours ago. The 'NetAT flunkies sometime later. He'd expected Stephen to let him know how the meeting went. The fact he hadn't might mean the situation was under control and that *Do not disturb* was for some well-earned rest. In which case, they could get together for a late supper to discuss the matter.

Of course, Stephen's silence could also mean the flunkies were trying to use divide-and-conquer tactics.

Well, that wouldn't work with two *real* 'Netters with—

The call connected. The viewscreen lit up: monitor-eye view of the entire room.

"Oh-ho. Left the lights on, ki . . ."

The words died in his throat as the image cleared.

The bed was full. Long, blond hair streamed over the covers nearest the monitor, at least one other body's-worth of lumps elsewhere. The todes must have ousted the kid from the best room available.

So, where was Stephen? The lock out had his elegant programmer-prints all over it. Could be Stephen had bypassed a *secure* lock on the phone. This image was reading directly into some permanent file. Could be Stephen was spying on them. Perhaps even searching for a way out of his forced draft into their ranks.

Their arrogance really did surpass any he'd encountered before. The 'NetAT was getting too damned—

A caught breath, an almost-sob—like a child who'd cried himself to sleep.

Hardly an appropriate simile for such an obviously cozy situation. A long-fingered hand, tangled in the blond hair, stirred. A long-fingered hand attached to a familiar, slender wrist.

He swore, a flare of soul-deep jealousy blinding him, making his swipe at the cutoff miss. Always an explanation. Time after time after fucking time.

"*Good. You're awake.*" A deep male voice, as identifiable as the blond hair and generous curves beginning to creep from under the blanket, the polished nails on the hand reaching for the bedside table. *"No, no—my turn, Clarissa. And I want him clear-eyed, thank you."*

Well, there was no explanation for this.

The lumps stirred, covers fell away. Same frame—same musculature—same hair—same Stephen—until you got a good look at his eyes, their luminescence shaded now under sultry lids. The child Ridenour paraded out for Wesley Smith's gullible consumption was gone. In its place, a cool, controlled adult who accepted Herzog's possessive caress with barely a flinch.

Probably Herzog's hands were cold.

Only when those possessive hands ran up the undersides of Stephen's arms, stretching them, forcing them over his head, did a bulge of a well-shaped bicep indicate resistance, however silent. A momentary struggle and Stephen's arms thudded to the mattress.

"Even better," the deep voice approved, *"I like a bit of . . . opposition."*

Stephen's voice, low and steady, without a hint of stutter: *"Is that what you want?"*

The deep voice chuckled. *"Need you ask, Zivon Stefanovich?"* Herzog's hand touched Naghavian's arm, then gestured toward an out-of-view floor. *"Hand me my belt, will you?"*

Sickened, Wesley cut the connection, swearing long and hard. If this was the way Stephen Ridenour had 'dealt' with his Vandereaux 'inheritance,' he could fucking well deal with Jean-Phillippe Beaubien without Wesley Smith's help.

iv

Pillows.

A world made of pillows.

Pillows under his head, at his back, between his legs, clenched to his chest. . . .

"He's good, isn't he?"

Quiet voices discussed him, as though he wasn't there, or hadn't ears to hear. Stephen buried his hands deeper into the pillow, pretending not to notice the chuckled response.

"And he plays the part to the final round."

Or perhaps they considered their words complimentary.

Coolth on his upward side: sudden absence of covers. Hands tracing the marks their previous touches had left.

"Better than the SDCs." Naghavian, he thought, his mind beginning to separate and categorize sensation.

"I told you." The hand probed bruised flesh. He gasped and buried his head deeper into the pillow. Laughter: blood-chilling ghost from the past. "Pretty, pretty 'buster-boy." The probe became a mocking caress. "Wouldn't Stefan Ryevanishov be proud of his son now?"

His breath caught. He couldn't help it.

"Still—" Naghavian again. "—he's got a—sweetness—you never mentioned. —Or is that Smith's legacy? You're not indifferent to him, are you, boy?"

He told himself it didn't matter, to hold out five more minutes, and then they'd be gone.

"Or is it the 'buster-girl you mentioned—Anevai? We looked up her records, you know. Pretty little thing; you two would look lovely together. Perhaps we can arrange a little get-together."

Indifference vaporized. He glared at them, intercepted a smile from Herzog and buried his face again.

Herzog said, "She's got a point, boy. Tell your friends they should try again—perhaps you could talk Smith and the girl into joining you. 'The Princess, the Tycoon, and the...' —Whatever. The mind boggles. I hope you got a good deal on that first lot. Royalties should be pretty decent by now."

He turned slowly. "Royalties?"

"You mean you didn't know about SDCs?" An exchanged look that didn't include him, which mocked his growing horror. "I fear you've been had, boy. In more ways than one. But I wouldn't worry. You're in demand. When the full-body tanks hit the open market, you'll be able to write your own ticket.''

The horror was short-lived. Neither did the revelation particularly surprise him; Bijan and his mother's crowd were capable of most anything. But then, so was he—now.

The 'NetATs finished dressing and collected their belongings, paying no attention to him whatsoever. Ignoring a painful twinge in his lower back, Stephen pulled himself upright and reached for the notepad he'd 'borrowed' from the SciCorps legal department and left casually on the side table.

Herzog hadn't noticed that, either. The man was decidedly careless—or overconfident—where Stephen Ridenour was concerned.

Naghavian turned at the door and smiled. ''I guess it's goodbye, for now, Dr. Ridenour. We'll be heading back soon—possibly before you're finished with Dr. Smith. Planets make us—uncomfortable. I wish you joy with him—not my type at all. But we'll see you aboard *Cetacean* tomorrow. —Don't make us come back after you.''

She tapped the door release, prepared to effect a sleek exit, to match all her sleek moves. Grim satisfaction absorbed at least part of the humiliation filling him when the door failed to open.

''Not quite yet,'' he said quietly. ''There's still our—business transaction.'' He opened a special file on the notepad while the reps watched in tight-lipped silence. The notepad could connect, like all keyboards, to the local network—and so, if you knew how, to the 'Net itself—but unlike other notepads, this one had very special abilities. He pulled up the prepared statement, requested bioscan authorization, and held the pad out to them in silence.

Naghavian took a step back. ''You must be joking.''

''We had a deal,'' Stephen answered calmly.

Herzog laughed. ''You don't really think—''

Stephen windowed the file he'd retrieved from his vidfone tap, leaned back, and let them watch until they turned away.

"I thought you said the room was clear," Herzog hissed.

Naghavian lifted a brow at him. "Look at the angle, Dick. He used the monitor scan. Do *you* know how he did it?"

Stephen smiled, surprised—and somewhat repulsed—by his own enjoyment of the moment. However achieved, however fleeting, power and control were intoxicating.

A judgement-warping headiness he'd gladly exchange for Wesley's freedom—and personal anonymity—guaranteed. He raised the 'pad.

"Doesn't matter," Herzog said at last. "We'll just wipe it, boy."

"You're welcome to try."

"You can't hope to match our clearance."

Stephen laughed outright, and with some real delight, tempted to challenge them to even find the file. One thing he was absolutely certain of since that meeting yesterday morning, neither of these two could begin to understand the scope of Wesley's system.

His sense of power swelled as they exchanged another glance. Worried, this time. Sincerely worried. He blanked his face and held out the stylus.

They signed, the bio-stylus and retinal scans registering their biological identity beyond reasonable doubt. He closed the file with a SecOne seal he'd no right to use, all desire for control vanishing with the security that seal provided.

"Thank you," he said quietly. "I'm certain Dr. Smith thanks you as well."

Herzog threw the stylus down on the desk. It skidded to the floor. "You really think that means shit?"

A two-key touch activated the macro that opened a direct 'Link to *Cetacean* security files and designated the deposition to automatic transfer to the 'NetAT, Councillor Eckersley and Central Security PrioOne Files upon *Cetacean's* return to Vandereaux.

That done, he drew a deep breath and stated grimly: "I do now."

"What the hell did you just do?"

"You'll find out—once we're all back in Vandereaux. Might I suggest you don't try to go back on your agreement, however? I'm no longer quite so naive as I was five years ago. I control this distribution. Unless I cancel it, the video goes to all councillors automatically—the amnesty goes mainline. And once the GP knows the score, not even Shapoorian will dare threaten one Jonathan Wesley Smith."

Herzog's expression went cold, blank; Naghavian's mouth twitched in an enigmatic half-smile.

"May we go now?" she asked.

He released the lock. Gladly.

When they were gone, he forced shaking fingers to relock the door—a hard-lock only he could release—and let the keyboard drop as the shakes set in.

He'd thought it wouldn't matter. It wasn't as if it were the first time. But it had been years, and the lingering odor, the throbbing in his joints, wouldn't let him forget. He stripped the rancid sheets and stuffed them into the laundry tube, where they'd be cleaned and returned automatically, leaving no one to question the nature of the stains. He threw the curtains back and hauled at the window—wishing perversely that action had required more effort—and let the clean mountain breeze sweep over him, erasing the worst of the stench.

And freezing him. The shakes set in with a vengeance and he stumbled back to the bare mattress, clawing at the blankets with fingers gone numb, and wrapping himself in a cocoon—

—a cocoon like the Other, the gentle Cocheta presence who'd tried so hard to protect him from Nayati's mental assault. He wished the Other were here now. He could use a friend, and somehow he didn't think Wesley would want much to do with him once he found out. And he would find out. They'd make sure of it. No matter they promised otherwise.

He'd self-indulgently forgotten, for a time, what he'd been trained for more effectively than the gym or the 'Net. Eventually, Wesley would know everything. How then would he understand the endless denials of the person he'd befriended and asked so little of in return?

Tempting, to leave with Herzog and Naghavian—to jilt Wesley's dinner invitation with people he'd never see again. But for Wesley's sake, it would be best if the truth came from him—along with what excuse he had. And tonight, after the dinner party, if Wesley still wanted—that—from him, Wesley would get the best he had to give.

His left hand, tucked around a pillow, trembled in front of him. Lonely. Another hand appeared, steady and warm, and wrapped around it, brushing the knuckles gently with a soft-balled thumb, comforting, warming.

He tightened his grip, felt the pressure, and hugged his clasped hands closer, pulling the pillow over his face, shutting out the light, the cold, and the emptiness, letting the memory of the Other and its mountain surround him.

V

Stephen turned his head slowly, judging the line from all angles, paused and without taking his eyes from the mirror, dipped the brush and blended blue into green a millimeter higher, disguising bruise and swelling in the same stroke.

He glanced down, met gold eyes reflected in the mirror. "What do you think?"

The *pii'chum* sneezed and leapt down from the bathroom counter, disgust in every liquid move, and slithered out the door to inaugurate the newly made bed with blue fur.

Obviously, no appreciation for the fine art of camouflage.

Careless of Herzog to have marked his face that way. He wondered indifferently what excuse the 'NetAT had expected him to give. Indifferently, because he didn't intend to let it become an issue.

He plucked the dinner invitation free of the mirror and

perched on the counter, shifting his weight to ease a newly discovered tenderness.

Gilt writing on heavy paper and hand delivered that afternoon:

> *Jonathan Wesley Smith*
> *requests the honor of your presence*
> *for an evening of dinner and conversation.*
> *Cocktails at sunset.*
> *Miakoda Moon*
> *Formal*

Knowing Wesley, 'formal' was likely to mean this year's sweater, so he went him one better. Full face paint. Very rev. Not something he'd seen here, for all he'd had the paints delivered from the SciCorps novelty shop. Not the first time he'd worn them, nor likely to be the last.

Besides, it hid the bruises.

It was a pattern he'd used before, though the suit he'd worn was still aboard *Cetacean*. For personal aesthetics, he continued that pattern down over the chest and arms, up the legs to cover other bruises so he could pretend they didn't exist, even under the cover of clothes.

And if—that—was on Wesley's agenda tonight, following the patterns would heighten the effect. . . .

He closed his eyes and sprayed the sealant, waited for the cool of evaporation, before exiting the bathroom to finish dressing.

Tunic, slacks and gilt-rope belt laid out on the freshly made bed. . . .

(Arms closing around him. Pressing the warmth, remotely grateful for the quiet refuge. The unusual lack of demand.

(Laughter, rude, loud. Sudden, sharp pain.)

(''Hold him still, Rissa.'')

Ancient memory and new in a confused montage . . .

(''Hang in there, Ridenour. Almost over. . . .'')

(Gentle, reassuring words. He choked on swallowed protests and buried his face in soft flesh. . . .)

(A hand lifting his chin. A mouth. A probing tongue that left bitterness in its wake. . . .)

(And always, ultimately, the Need of the other overriding his disgust and fear.)

Stephen shuddered, pulled the clothes on without looking again at a bed populated with grinning faces and ancient ghouls. He'd always made a point not to use his own room— now he knew his instincts had been right.

The *pii' chum* unwound from the pillow, crossed the mattress to rub against his hand, silent demand for attention. He rubbed the Spot behind the ears, and the creature's gentle purr chased the ghouls away.

Tonight, they'd use Wesley's room.

Ridenour showed up all right, five minutes early, and dressed Spacer to the max: sea-foam green shadowing teal blue draped gracefully above—tailored—forest-green slacks. Gold rope, twisted several times around his narrow waist, glinted among the folds as he moved.

He'd affected the face paint that was the current fad among the elite punks in Vandereaux: peacock-colored designs that would make a less exotic face look ridiculous.

He should be laughing.

Instead, Wesley settled his lapels, pulled a draped ruffle into place around the opal pins, and stepped into Ridenour's path. "So, you showed up."

Ridenour looked him up and down, smiled delightedly as he took in the pins, the suit he probably thought he didn't own. His smile, though hesitant, gave no hint of hidden guilt. "You say formal, you mean formal. —Wasn't I supposed to?"

He shrugged. "You've been unavailable all day."

"Sorry." A wave of genteel confusion wrinkled a blue triangle between green-tinted brows. "I—slept late, then I had another meeting. . . ."

"What'd the 'NetTodes want this time?"

"To return to the ship." Stephen grinned. "The Outside is getting to them—no one will close their drapes. They wanted me to go today, but I refused on the grounds of prior engagements. As it is, either I'm on tomorrow's shuttle, or they're coming after me."

"You going?"

"It's my job, Wes," he said, blatantly skirting the issue. "Anyway, I worked out in the gym, showered, took a few last-minute notes, dressed, and came here. Thought I'd be late." He craned his head to look past Wesley's shoulder. "Are the others—"

"Just us."

"Just us?" Another search of the shadows. Disbelief. A hint of anxiety. Opal eyes settled on him, openly dismayed. "You mean I went through all this for nothing?"

Bitterness twisted his attempted grin. "Nothing? Thanks, Ridenour."

Musical laughter, easy and apologetic. "I didn't mean it like that. It's just—" He gestured vaguely toward his painted face. "For you, I'd rather not play the clown. I thought to amuse—"

"Consider me amused and go wash your face. —I'll wait."

"I . . ." The unreadable mass of color ducked. "It would take forever. Takes special solvent . . ."

"So, I'll laugh. Just tell me when." He jerked his head toward the stone path. "Let's eat."

A light touch to his elbow delayed him. Not even the exotic paint-job could hide Ridenour's quite credible confusion. "Wes, are you mad at me? Whatever I've done, I'm sorry. Is it because I didn't call to confirm? On the way from Acoma, you made it *sound* as if you had a busy schedule and preferred not to be interrupted, so I—"

Mad at him? He didn't know if he wanted to laugh or swear or punch the bastard out.

So he shrugged. "Forget it. Let's go eat."

Ridenour bit his lip and followed him to the table without any further comment.

The *Miakoda* was empty, of furniture as well as people—all but their own table set out in the central tier: the one spot in the restaurant where the view included the star-speckled firepit at the room's center as well as the rift outside the clear dome.

The sight and sound of water surrounded them: open rippling streams, an occasional surprise glimpse through a hole in the rock. He'd planned this a week ago. Planned to make a lasting impression—one Ridenour would carry back with him—constant temptation to return once his duty with the 'NetAT was fulfilled.

Now—he could care less.

He wished to God he felt the same indifference when Stephen's eyes flickered toward every hint of light—holographic fireflies and the very real stars overhead reflecting equally in their pearlescent irises—or when the gentle breeze he'd ordered stirred the curls on Stephen's forehead.

All through a mostly silent dinner, Wesley watched that childlike appreciation of his carefully planned ambience, his anger growing with each oh-so-innocent blink. He played the part so well, and little Zivon was irresistible—until you remembered that Zivon Ryevanishov was Stephen Ridenour's major offensive line.

Wesley picked at his food, drank too much and too fast—the wine deserved more respect. But he didn't care about that either, finished the second bottle and popped the champagne before Ridenour had started his berries and cream.

He pushed the flute across...

Stephen chuckled lightly, eyeing him through the bubbles. "You're trying to seduce me."

...raised his own in careless salute. "Did I succeed?"

Long, dark lashes dropped, camouflaging opal eyes. A pink tongue (He wondered Was it painted, too?) paused in its tour of the bubbles. Placing the flute back on the table, the clone studied the golden liquid, deliberately tracing the rim with a crystylic-painted fingertip. Wesley's gut tightened as the tongue brushed alcoholic dampness from the glittering fingertip and traveled slowly across peacock-blue lips. "All you ever had to do was ask."

"So," he said shortly. "Here?"

A blink. "Floor's a bit hard." Hesitantly, but not implying that option totally ruled out—likely one of the more comfortable locales Ridenour had tested. "Table's full . . ."

"No, then."

"I didn't say that." With a laugh hinting uncertainty, he stood up and melted into the shadows between two stony outcrops. A moment later, from the next level down: "You coming?"

Wesley swore, restraining the obvious rejoinder, drained his glass—and Stephen's—grabbed the bottle and followed the trail of elusive, soft-spoken taunts.

At the fireside, Stephen was waiting, the fur throws piled together and himself planted dead center, stark, staring, bare-assed naked.

Except for the paint. Exotic purple-blue shapes flickered an iridescent pathway down sleek, elegant lines that seemed no longer quite human—certainly bearing no relation to the modest pretender—but rather some creature exuding sensuality, a 'changeling' in the most ancient, most fey, sense of the word. In the shadows, the gold rope coiled like a glittering snake atop neatly stacked clothes. The effect was—fascinating, and despite his coldly determined preparations, for a moment Wesley's mind went on hold.

But a single cynical neuron noted those painted designs in no way reflected the tailoring of the carefully folded clothing, and that realization fractured his entrancement.

Like hell it had been intended for his 'friends.' Unless he'd planned to entertain the lot. . . .

Another of those inviting chuckles. "You going to stand there all night?"

. . . Maybe he had.

He treats it like currency. . . .

The clone's arms reached for him, but he ignored them, seeing in his mind's eye the man-child he'd held against soul-deep tremors, remembering in his heart a one-time desperation offer: *You want me to make love to you, Wes? I will . . . I can . . . just please, don't hate me. . . .*

He could never hate the man-child, no more than he'd been able to accept that offer, but for the clone who destroyed that sweet memory . . .

He dropped to his knees in the fur nest, staring openly. Stephen's head cocked in his patentable quizzical-bird posture, his hands dropping to fold demurely in his lap.

Wesley made no move, offered no opening. An inviting smile banished the quizzical bird, and Stephen reached again, this time for Wesley's shirt buttons.

Something shattered at this final mockery of the friendship he'd so carefully protected, and Wesley launched himself past Ridenour's hands, forcing him to the furs, spitting into his startled face: "I'll fucking well strip when I'm fucking well ready."

"I— Okay, Wes." Stephen tried to free himself, evinced quite believable startlement when he failed. "I'm—I'm s–sorry. I thought—"

"Well, *stop* thinking! That's what always fucks you up!"

"I—" Another futile attempt to wiggle free.

"Hold the fuck still." He leaned one forearm across Ridenour's chest, used the other to work his coat off, flinging it into the shifting fireshadows before starting on his shirt.

"Please, Wes, let me—" Hands brushed his chest. Hands he didn't *want* to feel on his body.

"Dammit!" He struck the hands away, gathered them over Ridenour's head and—bitter memory of last night—reached for his belt . . .

. . . and swore. He wasn't wearing one.

Gold-glint in the shadow: Ridenour, on the other hand, had come prepared. Wesley grabbed the belt, scattering the clothes. A splash of water: something taking an unscheduled dive. He took a wrap around one high-tendoned wrist and reached for the other.

Eyes wide and blank, Ridenour let him proceed without protest, without making the slightest move toward escape, awareness dawning in opal eyes meeting his across bound wrists.

"Yeah, Ridenour," he sneered, pulling the loop-knot snug with a snap, releasing all the pent-up anger, all the betrayal, at last. "Herzog isn't the only one who likes—opposition."

Opal glistened wetly in the firelight—no question Ridenour understood then—and dropped. A shiver rippled through the body trapped beneath him, a quiver of soft lower lip, an undeniable aura of growing fear.

Damned if the clone didn't have each move down pat.

A sudden, supple twist; Ridenour snaked away. Wesley grabbed the tasselled cord and jerked him back, ramming the tassel between two floor slates, swearing as his hand hit rocks and the cold stream beneath. He hooked Ridenour's ankle, jerking him flat. Forcing bound wrists upward, he buried his face in the pounding throat-pulse and thrust his hand under fire-heated skin to warm it.

Ridenour arched up, gasping.

An oddly detached segment of his mind registered how accurately various Ridenour body parts brushed and prodded, rousing a rather less detached something in him to fevered pitch.

Panic edged the anger. This fiasco had been intended to put Ridenour in his place, to call his bluff once and for all. He hadn't anticipated his own response. Had never intended the lesson to go this far. Did not *want* to feel—what he was feeling—under such hate-filled conditions.

And in the midst of blinding heat and anger, an ice-drenched neuron mocked that purism, reminded him mercilessly... *even then, if you'd been well-trained...*

A handhold slipped; he regained it easily. Too damned easily, considering another wrestling match, the iron strength that had once saved his life. Stephen had been a top-seeded gymnast. If he'd *wanted* free, he'd be free. It was all—

A sudden jerk. Chest muscles contracted and stretched arms descended, knocking him away. A slither, a twist, and Ridenour was scrambling away. Wesley rolled and grabbed an ankle, hauled him back facedown in the fur, and collapsed on top, fighting for breath, holding him flat via the simple expedient of superior mass.

"Dammit!" he gasped into the curls brushing his mouth. "What are you, a mind reader?"

From Stephen, there was no sound at all, only breathless gasps and a renewal of the struggle when Wesley eased away to let him breathe.

Wesley cursed, pressed them together with one hand to slow the action, adjusting his own clothes with the other. Finesse was not an issue; he just cleared what was necessary and wrapped both arms around Ridenour's waist for simple courtesy . . .

. . . and his own blinding need evaporated in a mental chill more effective than any cold shower.

He swore and thrust himself away.

"Get the hell out of here," he hissed, blindly pulling his clothes to rights, and waited for the telltale sounds of retreat. When neither objection nor audible evidence of compliance occurred, he spun around. "I *said*—"

Homicidal anger imploded.

Ridenour was crouched against the stone, gnawing wrists and ties like some animal ready to sacrifice a limb for freedom.

"Shit!" Before he thought, he was on his knees, forcing Ridenour's hands down, slapping him to a semblance of sanity, until Ridenour collapsed to the slate floor, face buried in his forearms, his back heaving.

Freeing the water-soaked tassel from the slates, Wesley jerked the madman's bound hands out of the shadows. The loop was hopelessly snarled, the gilt cord swollen with blood and spit. He forced Ridenour's chin up and spat into his face: "Touch that—move—and die. You understand me, clone?"

Comprehension of the threat, if not rationality, glowed between purple-tinted lashes, and when he returned with a steak knife, Wesley found Ridenour in *exactly* the same position, even to the awkward, painful twist of head and neck. A position he didn't break, even when wide, panicked eyes took in that knife. Wesley ignored the look, jerked the hands up by the cord, and worked the knife between the bloodied wrists.

He peeled the pieces of cord free ("Damnfool—think you'd never seen a quick release...") and jerked away, flinging the scraps into the fire.

Stephen huddled on the fur, shivering, arms wrapped ineffectually around his hunched shoulders.

"For God's sake, clone, you're free." Wesley sank to the stone floor, exhausted, propping his back against fire-warmed stone. He flourished the steak knife toward the exit. "Move. Get out of here."

And still, he didn't leave. Purple-tinted lashes blinked; eyes cleared, focused on him; blue lips asked:

"Wh–why didn't you—" A pause for breath—or perhaps a search for polite terminology.

Feeling no such etiquette restrictions, Wesley snarled, "Because I'm not into jerking off in public."

"N–no one else...here—"

"*You* are, clone." He flipped the knife into the firepit before he gave in to the temptation to finish Nayati's self-appointed task. "Fucking waste of time and energy."

Firegold flickered on iridescent face-paint. "I—I thought you w–wanted—"

"Well, you thought wrong, didn't you?" He hooked the scattered clothes with a toe and kicked them in Ridenour's general direction. "Get dressed."

Shaking hands managed to shrug the soft fabric over his shoulders, but swollen fingers slipped hopelessly from the buttons.

"Get over here," Wesley snarled.

Ridenour obeyed, standing quietly while he fastened the

front, pointedly touching only buttons and fabric. He reached for a cuff, detected dampness, and, grabbing Ridenour's hand, pushed the sleeve back. Blood stained newly healed skin. Ugly, but hardly life-threatening.

And not a mark from . . .

"Herzog's technique better than mine, was it?" he asked, deliberately crude. The hand shook in his clasp, a silent, honest response more eloquent than any verbal excuse. He felt his anger falter.

Excuses, he could have ignored.

He sighed. "Let's get you to your room. I'll find something to put on these."

"I'll manage." The low, hoarse voice held a spark of defiance, relief in the midst of heretofore witless compliance.

Defiance he challenged—along with his own softening mood: "I doubt it."

He raised the tunic, following a bloody souvenir of their struggle, found a darkness on the upper thigh: bruising older than the scratch, visible beneath the blue paint at this range. Herzog's legacy. He traced the bruise with a finger and poked with calculated cruelty. Ridenour's breath caught, but he stood his ground, blatantly prepared for—or anticipating—further abuse.

Made a body feel like puking. Made a mind wonder what in the name of all Anevai's multitudinous deities created such a creature.

But if rough was all that turned Stephen Ridenour on, he'd have to look for it elsewhere.

He let the tunic drop, caught Stephen's far hand and pulled him around to search his face—a move which nearly proved his resolve's undoing. Behind the paint, it was all Zivon Ryevanishov: sweet, sad—aching for . . . something.

"Why, Stephen? What did you think to accomplish?"

A long pause, during which Zivon faded, leaving only a very weary Stephen Ridenour in his wake. The captured hand twitched in a helpless little gesture. "Only coin I have, Wesley."

He treats it like currency. . . .

And this wasn't the first payment he'd made today.

"How *dare* you?" The question exploded out of some deep, painful bitterness, which increased at Ridenour's startled step backward. "How *dare* you equate me with those bastards!"

Another step, hands dropping free. "I d–don't—"

"You owe me nothing! Do you hear me? *Nothing!* Damn you!" His voice broke on that same nameless agony.

Stephen pulled his sleeves closed, painted brows tightening as he forced swollen fingers into compliance and worked the buttons through bloodstained holes.

"So my sanity—" Once again, defiance edged the low voice. "—my very *life*—are nothing. Even to you. —Thanks, Smith. Glad to finally know exactly where we stand."

Speechless, he watched Stephen pull on his slacks and slip a scraped foot into the one shoe he could locate, each movement increasingly less coordinated.

With a dispassionate glance at visibly shaking hands, Ridenour said, as if to himself, "I'd better leave while I still can." A calm, straight look froze the retort rising in Wesley's throat. "I don't suppose we'll have occasion to meet again, Dr. Smith, at least not in private. Since you were—obviously—watching last night, you are undoubtedly aware of the . . . arrangement I've made with the 'NetAT. I trust you'll have the sense to abide by it and the power to enforce control over—your friends."

Arrangement? Stephen was up the first handful of stairs before Wesley comprehended. He jumped to his feet and demanded, "Is *that* why you were with them last night?"

Slow, careful turn, a bloodstained hand to the stone for balance.

"What did you think?"

He could only gape wordlessly, thinking what a bloody useless waste . . .

"So," Stephen continued softly, expressionlessly, "you didn't bother staying to the end."

. . . uncertain himself precisely what had been wasted.

"No wonder..." Stephen's head bowed slowly, he shrugged and started up the stairs, staggered and missed a step.

Wesley was at his side in an instant, but Stephen thrust him away.

"Don't *touch* me!" And as if that explosion had destroyed some barrier: "Dammit, Smith, you bring me down here—I try to do what you want—*be* what you want—" Desperate eyes met his, and the explosion faded to a whisper. "Where'd I go wrong?"

"You really don't know, do you?"

A helpless sweep of a hand set him swaying. Wesley steadied him, immediately let go when Stephen shrank openly from his touch.

"Shit. Look, clone, I was trying to seduce you—*yes:* into staying here. That's *all* I wanted, until— You *didn't* owe me a damn thing. Whatever I've done to help you was totally selfishly motivated. —Dammit, boy." He reached out and brushed that painted cheek, seeing only the beauty beneath the outrageous colors, trying to ignore the Zivon-esque head-tilt toward his hand. "You'd given me a son—a son of my mind and soul—so much more, so infinitely more special, than some chemical continuity—and you took that away. You're nothing but a lie—Shapoorian's plant. Can you blame me for accepting what you offered?"

"Sh–Sha*poori*..." Stephen seemed to gasp after air; and this time, accepted Wesley's supporting hold without objection. "But I'm *not*..." He stopped, staring at his palms. "...am I?"

Anger deflated. "If you don't know, boy, how can I?" Wesley wrapped his arm around Stephen's shaking shoulders. "Fuck it. We're neither of us real coherent tonight. Let's get you to your room. I'll fix your wrists; you can get some rest; we'll sort it all out in the morning."

Amazingly, Ridenour did the sensible thing and nodded wearily.

vi

There was something incredibly surreal about sitting on a toilet seat, dressed in silk pajamas, with the person you'd just invited to rape you winding antiseptic dressing around the very wounds inflicted as a result of that invitation.

Wesley pressed the end of the self-adhering bandage flat on his right arm and silently reached for the left. Rolling the sleeve out of the way, he sprayed antiseptic coating on a dully aching elbow, then examined the wrist, silent until he turned it palm-up, exposing the only significant damage.

"I'll get it," Stephen said, and tried to draw his hand away.

But Wesley's grip tightened, and he growled around his own string of curses, "Hold *still*."

Stephen shrugged, feigning indifference. In truth, Wesley's presence was not something he wanted. He'd far rather go to bed and worry about the whole thing in the morning. Forget where he was. Forget he'd ever met Wesley Smith. Forget he'd ever read *Harmonies of the 'Net*.

But he couldn't forget. Not *Harmonies'* theories, not its author.

And if Wesley left, it would leave him alone with the specters haunting the bedroom beyond the bathroom door.

Reflections in the mirror: the gaunt, dark-haired man he could never quite reconcile as himself, soft fabric ruthlessly defining a bony shoulder—too much time in hospital, not enough in the gym—pale face, bruises showing clearly now the paint was off, features he personally found vaguely repulsive, the damp countertop filled with the detritus of first aid: spray caps, bits of paper, a roll of adhesive, the bottle of paint solvent and skin creams; and just visible over the reflected countertop, Wesley's head, sun-bleached and ruffled, long hair getting in his eyes, and him with both hands occupied.

The air was filled with the scent of antibiotics, the hiss of the fan and Wesley's cursing mutters and tirades about fools who ignored quick releases—

"Wh—what do you m—mean, quick release?" Stephen asked, hoping to halt the stream.

A quick stab of pain as Wesley's hands jerked. Long hair brushed his hand as Wesley flung his head back to stare up at him. "The knot, CodeHead. You don't like the game, you pull the end with your teeth. If you're going to play, learn the fucking rules."

Rules Wesley Smith obviously knew. Effectively silenced, Stephen closed his eyes on the mirror and its images. Virtual images, but real virtual reality, not simulated. Real light, reflecting real counters and real hair with real faces and real pain.

It was hardly logical. Laughter might have happened, had he had the energy.

"What the hell do you think you're doing?"

He opened his eyes to find his free hand entangled in Wesley's wayward hair, smoothing it back. He pulled both hands free—of Wesley's hair and Wesley's grip—muttering, "Good enough."

Wesley jerked to his feet. "You're welcome, clone."

Some final iota of pride kept him silent in the face of that cold sarcasm, and with far more passion, Wesley spat:

"Damn you, Ridenour."

"Whatever. —Look, just leave, will you? I really need to get some rest." He pulled his robe up over his shoulders, and to clarify his own official stance on the evening's events: "I'm sorry I spoiled your dinner tonight, Dr. Smith. It was a . . . nice gesture to a departing colleague, and I apologize for . . . misinterpreting your intentions."

"Yeah, right." Wesley worked his sleeves down in short, abrupt tugs, and fastened the buttons. "Chalk it up to experience."

Chalk it up to experience. Appropriate final advice from this individual he'd come so far to meet: one more reference he could only understand from context, delivered in a bitter and utterly impersonal tone of voice.

Stephen dropped his attention to the floor tiles, the plush rug beneath his feet, the hiss of the fan, anything but that retreating figure, the footsteps that—

—never came. A furtive glance revealed Wesley still standing in the doorway, back propped against the jamb, a scowl line deep between his black brows.

"Listen, Ridenour, we've got to talk."

He dug his toes into the soft rug. "Nothing to talk about. Said it yourself—I'm as prepared as I'll ever—"

"Dammitall! I didn't mean that, and you know it."

He tucked his shaking hands against his sides and met Wesley's anger with what he fondly hoped was controlled calm. "That's all there is *to* talk about—for us."

Anger faded. "Stephen, just—just don't do anything stupid before tomorrow, okay? This is nothing but another misunderstanding, and—"

"Not another, Wesley. The last." He pulled himself to his feet and held out his hand. "Consider the matter forgotten, Dr. Smith. I'll do all I can for you, believe me. If—" He felt himself cracking as the specters haunting the room beyond Wesley were suddenly more real than Wesley himself. "If you c–could somehow bring yourself to . . . edit your memories of me, I—I'd like to think you were s–still m–my. . ."

But Wesley was ignoring the hand trembling violently between them, and in the face of that indifference, he discovered he couldn't say it, it sounded too much like begging.

He wanted out, more desperate for escape now than he had been during their fireside struggle—Wesley's slouching presence in the doorway far more effective a deterrent than the rope belt had ever been.

"Shit," Wesley said, and brushed past Stephen's hand to pull him close, wrapping his arms around his shoulders, rocking gently and pressing Stephen's head into his neck. "You *are* my friend, Stevie-lad. I don't pretend to understand why you did—what you did—with me or with the 'NetAT slime, but I'll not let you leave like this, do you understand me?''

The tense body failed to relax. Wesley hugged harder, and whispered into the curls, "I'm not letting go till you promise me, brat."

A sigh brushed his neck and Stephen was holding him back, subtly conforming to his embrace, one vertebrae at a time. But the adjustments felt controlled rather than responsive, and instead of the requested promise, a cryptic murmur: "I—I wish you'd told me."

He stopped the gentle sway, fearing the boy's meaning. "Told you what, kid?"

"You said you wanted . . . like Herzog. If—if I'd known you wanted me to—"

His arms spasmed. Stephen gasped and pressed closer, burrowing his face into his chest, a completely natural response that undermined Wesley's growing revulsion.

"You'd have what? Obliged me? You think *that* would have been any better?"

"It's just . . . I—I thought . . ." Stephen's clasp eased as if he intended to withdraw, but Wesley refused to let go, and eventually Stephen's arms returned, along with a barely audible: "I thought I loved you, don't you see? And I—I thought that when that happened, you were supposed to want to . . . to . . ."

"To make love?"

An extremely hesitant nod.

"And you don't."

A longer pause before the curly head turned slowly side to side.

"I'm not surprised, considering." He released Stephen and stepped back. "Stephen, look at me."

With a return of that appalling submission, he raised his head. Wesley bit back a reprimand—as much his fault for making the request a demand—and concentrated on one issue at a time:

"A lot of people confuse love, lust, and exercise, all of which are, as far as yours truly is concerned, legitimate excuses for sex between consenting adults. But sex isn't an automatic consequence of any of them—including love. I have no way of knowing what you feel for me, but I'll be honest with you, lust attracted me to you, although—'' Sequential time going existential on him: "—I can't say if that was really before or after your understanding of *Harmonies* already had me intrigued. Either way, the fact you don't want to *doesn't* mean I have to feel any differently about you. Doesn't mean I won't dream about jumping your bones. But I'm not interested—not really and truly—unless it's a two-way. Got it?''

"Then that's why you . . .'' Stephen whispered.

"Why I stopped? —That and because I never really got into the S and M scene.''

"But you said—''

"I lied.''

"But–but the —'' Stephen glanced at a bandaged wrist, then deliberately hid it in his robe.

"Doesn't mean I haven't tried. Safer to know the tricks. Main trick is not to do anything *stupid* after a damned communications foul-up. Got it?''

Stephen's head cocked confusedly before he said, with a decidedly forced grin: "Okay, Wesley, okay. I promise: nothing stupid.''

"And you'll talk to me tomorrow?''

The vestige of humor died. *Anything! Just leave!* the eyes said, but Stephen just nodded and led the way to the apartment door. Wesley, pausing in the opening to check him over one last time, intercepted a nervous opal flicker toward the bed. He shook his head and reached a finger to brush the bruised cheekbone, wished Herzog a fast trip to hell for that mark.

"Not to be frightened, child. No need to ever let anyone hurt you like that again. Believe it or not, what's in your head is far more valuable than anything below it. Learn to barter that instead.''

Stephen's head shook a slow negative. "You barter for the

best deal. Besides . . ." His finger traced a bandaged wrist. "It wasn't Herzog who hurt me."

"Stephen, I'm—"

Zivon's gentle, sad smile stopped him; somehow, Wesley knew it wasn't the bloody wrist he meant.

"Good night, Wesley."

The door slid shut between them. Wesley stared at it a moment, half expecting it to open, not certain what he'd do if it did, then headed reluctantly down the hall toward the atrium and his own rooms on the next floor.

A moment later, quick footsteps and a whisper, full of barely contained terror:

"Wesley? —God, Wesley, please, wait—"

He turned; Stephen skidded to a halt, just out of reach, and stood there, shaking.

He leaned a shoulder against the wall, arms akimbo. "Why?"

"I—" Stephen bit his lip. "Please, Wesley, s–stay with m—me tonight."

He frowned. "Why?"

"I just—I just—"

The kid was stark white and shaking, his eyes flickering spasmodically toward the open door to his rooms. What the hell was the matter with him?

"P–please, Wes. I—I'll sleep on the floor, or—or not at all, as you like. I—I just don't want to be alone tonight." His eyes flickered again. "N–not in there."

Dammit. This AC kid was sincerely beginning to spook him. But even as that thought crossed his mind, he knew he was going to say:

"Sure, kid. Why not."

vii

Nigan Wakiza was sitting on the floor beside the auditorium door when Cantrell rounded the rimcurve.

He was yawning.

She grinned at him. "Forget your BioRegs, Nigan?"

"Naw..." His head drooped and he rolled sideways into a credibly lifeless lump on the floor.

"Not bad, kid. Not bad at all. —But time to go to work, now. Hononomii's waiting."

A limp hand lifted. She laughed, and grabbed it, and pulled him to his feet.

"Why aren't you inside with the others?"

"Wanted to ask you something."

"So?"

"Say this works with Hononomii, what happens when Ridenour snaps? And he will snap, admiral. Nayati will have made sure of that. We know what he said, but we don't know what all he did. Maybe we just *think* we understand what his suggestion meant to Ridenour. Have you *anything* to relate to Stephen on a gut level?"

Nigan Wakiza was one of the odder young persons Cantrell had dealt with over the years. He worked very hard at his jokester image, yet Stephen Ridenour was alive at least twice over thanks to his defiance of Nayati Hatawa's leadership, and since he'd come aboard, he'd denied much of his obvious personal fascination for his surroundings to devote his time to his friend. Now...

She nodded toward the door. "Let's go inside where we can sit down."

The engineers had finally finished converting the auditorium, and Chet was in the process of reprogramming the HoloImager. Not a moment too soon, what with the 'NetAT agents' imminent return looming over them.

Naturally, the instant she showed her face at the entrance, three people demanded her attention. But she raised a hand, said firmly, "Can it wait?" and they all left her alone, albeit reluctantly. She slipped into a seat on the uppermost tier, nodded to the one beside her. When Nigan had settled: "I'm curious. Why do you care what will happen to Dr. Ridenour?"

"I—" Nigan frowned, and slumped down in his seat, sliding the flute back and forth between his fingers. "For one thing, I respect him—I think I could like him a great deal. He's shown personal bravery, wisdom, and integrity. But it's more than that. My people owe him, admiral. He could have behaved very differently. Could have condemned us all. And he never has. Has even tried to understand why we did—what we did."

"You mean what Nayati did."

"What Nayati did, we did. What Nayati is, we made him. He doesn't exist on his own. He's a part of us." His head lifted, the long black hair a ragged frame for gawky, large-boned features, his one truly elegant feature the mouth years of playing that flute had created. "How can I *not* feel responsible for what happened, and grateful to Ridenour? How can I *not* care that a man who has shown such greatness of spirit could be destroyed because one part of myself acted impulsively and without all the facts and another part of me failed to prevent the damage? If I can heal what Nayati began, how can I not?"

"That's very eloquent. But you are an artist. A musician. Perhaps even a poet. Is it rhetoric? or personal conviction?"

Nigan simply looked at her, blank-faced as ever his chief was, and Cantrell smiled faintly.

"You're a better friend than Nayati deserves, Nigan Wakiza."

"That's impossible, ma'am."

"I stand corrected."

McKenna arrived with the patient and his parents.

"For now, you've got a job to do. For the other, let's worry about that later. —And, Nigan—" As he rose to join the Tyeewapis, he faced her politely. "I'd appreciate any suggestions you have on the matter. —And thank you for asking."

He smiled, warm and very real. "You're welcome, admiral."

"What's this?"

Cold air swept across his back; a finger traced a line down his spine and over his left gluteus maximus, down the gluteal fascia to the iliotibial tract. He booted up the Mentor's sport's med diagram, used that mental image to force specific muscle group relaxation as the finger approached.

"Someone has done some body work on you." Five fingers now, and a palm. 'Appropriate. New life. New set of rules. New brands." The hand splayed, dug fingernails into sensitive flesh. "Where shall we set the first?"

The kid's long, even breaths grew into ragged, muttered denials; searching fingers found the cover, pulled it tight, leaving half of Wesley exposed to the night air.

A most important half.

If he had any sense, he'd rouse himself and pull the quilt from the foot of the bed. . . .

"R for Rostov."
Stab of pain.
"R for Recon."
A second stab. The unforgettable burn of KwikHeal.
"R for Ryevanishov, —Ridenour, —and R for—'
He buried his face in soft flesh, feeling her hands in his hair, silently begging her soothing words to drown out:
"Rich. —You'd like to be rich, wouldn't you, pretty, pretty 'buster boy?"

Stephen stirred again, fumbling after covers, obviously cold, obviously in the grip of one hell of a nightmare.

A soft cry, a protest to 'Rich.'

Didn't take a genius to figure who 'Rich' was. I *thought you were dead. . . .*

If he had no sense whatsoever, he'd say to hell with Stephen Ridenour's veracity and call his bluff; warm them both up in a hurry, eliminate any vestige of nightmares.

"God does it!" Laughter. Loud and nasty. Zivon frowned and backed away from the researchers.
"You're lying," he whispered. And louder, louder than their

laughter, louder than the embarrassment pounding in his ears:
"It's not nice to lie. God—God won't like you!"

"Oo-oo-oo, I'm scared. —Go home, 'buster boy. Someone
like you will never understand. You're too damn stupid—fact,
boy, proven fact."

"N–not s–s–s–s—" He choked on the stutter and ran from
their laughter.

Wesley crushed the pillow over his head, shutting out the
chatter of Stephen's teeth, the breathless mutters, too soft to
make any real sense, but loud enough to keep a man from
sleeping.

He should never have come back. For all he knew, Stephen
Ridenour was wide awake and fully aware of the effect he was
having. But if he wasn't . . .

Their relationship had grown too tangled to ever sort out—
certainly for any real trust to every play a part in it—and he
was doing neither of them any favor being here. He was getting
no sleep. Stephen was still having nightmares . . .

. . . or whatever.

The road home stretched endlessly. His knees shook. His
eyes blurred.

He was going to be late. He wasn't supposed to go down to
SciComp. Mama would be mad. . . .

A loud honk. He stumbled up the rutted bank and slumped
onto a rock to let the car pass, except it didn't. It slowed and
stopped. One of the fancy SciComp hover cars.

He'd never seen one up close.

A man leaned out and said, "Why if it isn't a little lost
'buster. Who let you out alone, little man?"

He stood up, tired as he was, and answered politely, "I'm on
my way home, sir."

"You look very tired. What's your name?"

"Zivon Stefano—" He had to pause for breath. "—vich
Ryevanishov, sir."

The man turned to the others in the car. Laughter. Zivon frowned and dug his heel into the soft dirt behind him, wishing they would leave.

"You're a long way from home, Zivon Stefanovich. Would you like a ride?"

Maybe they weren't laughing at him. He thought of the long walk, of the fact he wasn't supposed to be here, of the fact that Mama would be very mad, and of that wonderful floating car. . . .

"P–please, sir."

The door opened wider and he climbed into the back seat beside the man. A man and a woman in the front seat said Hi, and in the back, in a big flat space filled with pillows, another man and a woman he thought he knew. One of Mama's friends, he thought, so they must be all right.

He smiled and said Hello, then the car took off down the road and he bit his lip on a squeal of excitement. The man beside him laughed—a nice laugh—and he was smiling. Zivon smiled back and ducked his head, turning back to the window as they left the road and whooshed across the field.

They began chasing obatsi, which he knew they shouldn't do, but he laughed anyway, feeling very grown up and wicked with his new grown-up friends.

The laughter from the back took on a different note, and he rose to his knees and balanced against the seatback as the car tilted, dipped and swerved beneath him. In the pillows in the back—

He gasped and dropped back into his seat, hugging his knees to his chest and staring out the window, feeling his face grow hot. The man beside him said something to the one driving and the car stopped. Outside were bushes and tall grass. He didn't know where they were, but he knew it wasn't home.

"What's the matter, Zivon Stefanovich?"

Hot breath on his neck. A hand touching his knee, moving up his leg.

"I want to go home," he said to the window.

"What do you say?"

"P–please, s–sir, t–take m–me—"

"Not 'sir', Zivon Stefanovich. 'Rich.' You'd like to be rich, wouldn't you, pretty, pretty, 'buster boy?"

Stephen was awake now. The mutters had faded, buried in a pillow, and a steady shivering had taken their place. His knees, drawing slowly up to a fetal position, pulled at the blankets. Again.

Grabbing his remaining corner, Wesley complained blearily, "Gad, boy, *park* it, will you?"

"S–sorry." A heavy-lidded, over-the-shoulder glance, a careful measure of blanket, which left a neatly pleated pile between them. Wesley stifled laughter, as Stephen curled into a tight ball around a pillow and pulled his careful share of the blanket up over his head, staying as close to the edge as possible, evidently reckoning his falling out of bed would be less disruptive than his taking six more inches of mattress.

"C'mere." Wesley put a hand on the silk-clad shoulder and pulled gently, but insistently. "I know a better solution."

With a surprising lack of resistance, Stephen rolled over and burrowed in against him. Wesley arranged the blankets, then wrapped his arms around shivering shoulders and settled his chin into soft curls. As their combined body heat drove the worst of the shivers away, the flesh and bone lump between them unwound and slipped comfortably around his waist; Stephen's cheek snugged in against his neck, flicking lashes fanning damp drops to tingling evaporation: remnants of silent, intensely private tears.

"About time, kid," he whispered, and ran a gentle, soothing hand over his shoulders, wishing some miracle would erase twenty years of nightmares—not the least of which had come from the past three weeks of horrendously missed signals. Zivon Ryevanishov should have had a lifetime full of—what had he called them?

He tightened his hold, and grinned down into the sleepy face that blinked confusion at him. "Just because, Stevie-lad." And kissed his forehead, before relaxing the hug. "Just because."

His amazing eyes, luminous even in the faint glow from the window, widened and filled, then clamped shut as the boy fought humanity's most natural pressure valve. Wesley chuckled and kissed each damp eyelid. "Go ahead, brat. I'm waterproof."

Laughter exploded, Stephen's pressure releasing through an alternate natural valve, and no-longer-waterlogged opal glittered up at him. "Wicked, Smith."

The ball of his thumb brushed the remaining liquid from Stephen's cheeks. "You only just noticed?"

A snaky strike; Wesley yelped and froze. "Hey, I *need* that." Stephen's grin stretched around his captive thumb. "Dammit, brat, I'm losing—" Stephen opened his mouth and Wesley jerked his hand to safety.

Stephen laughed and hugged him close, settling quietly, as if nothing had happened. Wesley eyed the shadowy curls suspiciously, and gingerly worked his arms around Stephen's accommodating body.

When all fingers were safely deposited on Stephen's back, he asked, "Why?"

Stephen shifted slightly, and murmured, "Just because."

"I meant, Why'd you bite me, bit-brain."

He could hear the smile in Stephen's voice when he repeated, "Just because."

"Just—? You changed the rules!"

"Did I?" Stephen's head tilted back. "Maybe you just didn't understand them."

He stared down into that relaxed, happy face, wondering what other rules he'd misunderstood, decided it didn't matter. . . . "Maybe I didn't."

. . . Not tonight.

Stephen smiled, yawned, and tucked down again.

Tonight was for little Zivon, wherever he was within the man-child's body. But what about tomorrow? And the next night? Richard Herzog was accompanying the boy back. Had already lured him into a renewal of whatever power he'd once held over him. Would likely be in the 'NetAT council chamber when the boy made his report.

And where would Wesley Smith be? Soaking his ass in a HuteNamid hot spring.

He shifted, settling Stephen a bit higher on his shoulder. The boy murmured contentedly, did some shifting of his own, his flexible body molding itself to his.

Changeling, for sure. One face for Cantrell, another for Herzog. For him ... He supposed he'd seen them all, none more real than another. But this one—this sweetly accommodating armful—was a memory worth keeping around.

At least for a while.

Wesley let his hand drift gently over Stephen's silk-clad shoulder, listening to the long even breaths for signs of disturbance which never came, eventually drifting with them, letting his mind and body float apart, as sleep closed over him like a warm, soft—

—cold, hard fingers running races down his spine. His whole body contracted, his knee hit something soft that yelped and skittered away.

Unless—equally possible—that yelp was his. He sat up, rubbing his face vigorously with both hands.

"For the love of all that's holy." He blinked several times, shaking his head and running a hand through his hair. *"Warn* a body, will you? Kid, trust me, *your hands are freezing!* You want to cuddle a bit, I'm all yours, just let me in on the secret first, okay?"

Startled, soundless gapes trickled into smothered laughter, then exploded into something akin to hysteria.

Wesley grabbed a pillow and attacked, eliminating the hysteria, if not the laughter. The kid hadn't a chance—impossible to laugh and defend yourself at the same time—and in very short order, Wesley had him pinned on his back, his no longer cold hands held captive on either side of his head. The laughter faded, and for a time they just stared at one another, panting. Finally, Wesley asked:

"Are you sure this is what you want, kid?"

Those luminous-in-the-moonlight eyes gazed soberly up at him, careful consideration of his question in their bottomless depths. "I'm not a kid, Wes. I haven't been for a long time now."

"I don't—shit, how can I say this?—I don't love you, you know. —I *like* you just fine, but I don't—" Stephen just stared calmly at him. "Dammitall, say something!"

Another of his solemn, processing silences later; Stephen turned his head to stare past his shoulder. "Never mind, Wes. It's hardly fair after..."

Wesley dropped his forehead to Stephen's chest, hiding his laughter. "Sometimes I wonder how many people you've driven insane before me, brat. Then I wonder if I'm only the first."

The chest heaved up against him, a sigh that ruffled his hair. "I don't expect you to love me, Wes." Stephen's voice drifted over him. "It would be...pointless. But—I wonder if you can possibly understand. I..."

A gentle pull: a request for freedom he immediately granted, rolling aside to rest, propped on his elbow, where he could meet Stephen's gaze. But Stephen had his own ideas. He snuggled back under Wesley's shoulder, and captured Wesley's hand.

"I'm—amused by small things—"

He jerked at the light hold. "Well, if you're going to get personal..."

Stephen chuckled and tightened his grip, held on until he relented, then began tracing his fingers one by one with a fingertip, sending an insidious tingle up his arm and down his spine. "Most of my life, I'd be content just to be able to do this without...embarrassment. The handful of times in my life, I've tried to offer...more...the offer has been...rejected. People evidently preferring to take—"

"Now, wait a minute. You're overreacting."

"How else would you explain their actions?"

"Maybe they just weren't interested—"

"Like you weren't?"

"Good God, Ridenour, what you don't know about people—"

Stephen's fingers tightened around his. "I was trying to learn, Wes. —But in this, trust me, they were interested."

"They. Like who?"

"You don't know? Haven't guessed?"

"You can't mean *Herzog!*"

That seemed to surprise him. "No, not Richard. Funny, though, that you should think of him. No, Richard was a long time ago—a *long* time . . ."

Then, somehow, because it was Stephen Ridenour, he did know. "My God. Bijan?" Stephen's silence was evidence enough. *"Why?* What could ever prompt you—"

Stephen's shrug brushed his chest. "Bijan's rooms were the safest place in the academy."

"Safe? From *what,* for God's sake?"

"Cold. Fear. Loneliness. God, Wes." His low voice caught. "I was so lonely. I was willing to fill that void any way possible. Bijan—for whatever reason—would . . . touch me. Look at me and not laugh, or flinch, or . . ."

Stephen's hands fell away, his head dropped back into the pillow and turned away.

"Or what, Stephen?"

"Maybe it was the fact they didn't *dare* tap his room. Maybe it was the fact I knew exactly what to expect from him—"

"Yes, but—"

"Knowing eliminates the fear, Wesley. Pain can be dealt with. Fear . . . fear haunts you with what might happen. I thought I knew last night. But somehow . . . Naghavian was nothing. What I expected, no more. Herzog—he . . . He got to me, Wesley." His eyes dropped to their laced fingers. "I wonder if it's fair . . . but then, I never really expected anyone to understand. I'd just gotten it figured—had spent nearly two years free of them all—Bijan, Dev, even the memories of Rostov. I was playing the game and succeeding—at least in a minor way—content with the loneliness, because I *was* succeeding. But then..." He coughed. His fingers tightened, but he seemed disinclined to continue.

"Then what, Stephen?"

"I—"

He sensed the tension in Stephen's fingers and hugged the boy's shoulders, whispered against his hair: "Finish the story, brat," deliberately adding that most dreaded of childhood threats: "or else."

A broken chuckle, then: "It was *Harmonies*."

"Huh?"

"*Harmonies of the 'Net*." Stephen squirmed free and sat upright, catching Wesley's arm in a bruising hold. "My God, Wes, have you *any* concept...I wasn't alone anymore. I wasn't crazy—or if I was, *someone* was in that madhouse with me. I *had* to find you, Wes. Can't you see that? And once I'd found you—" That painful grip eased, became a gentle caress that traveled up his arm and to his face. "If anything happens to you, I lose that. I'm—alone again. Absolutely. Utterly. And there's *no* one else out there, Wes. I know that. *You* do. Whatever it took—I didn't care. I *couldn't* let anything or any*one* threaten you. And Herzog—"

"I'll kill him. So help me, kid, I'll go up to *Cetacean* and—"

But Stephen's light laughter, his quick hug, shut him up. "I don't want that, Wes." He snuggled back in underneath Wesley's arm. "—And I doubt I'll ever again want what I want right now."

"Want, Stephen? Are you finally admitting to *wanting* something?"

And out of the shadows beneath him: "Absolutely."

"And what is it you *want?*" He propped up, positioning himself so moonlight illuminated Stephen's face, considering the ramifications to the kid—and to himself—of one more disastrous encounter. "No euphemisms, Stephen. No more mistakes."

"I want memories to take back with me. No one can take memories away—I know that now. And knowing you're here, safe and happy, I won't *be* alone anymore. Ever." Stephen's eyes dropped. "It's not...I don't want you to love me. I want you to make love *with* me. I want—I want something to permanently overwrite Richard Herzog's files. I want to know what it's like when—when it's a two-way. I want—I want a just because, Wesley."

A just because. And for Stephen, that was no euphemism.

He took a breath—

"Wouldn't be fair not to let you have it, then, would it?" —and plunged. "Since you have not yet..." Thinking of those cold fingers on his spine. "...gotten the technique quite figured out, why don't you let the old master here do a little warm-up." He stretched, cracking his knuckles. "You just relax and take notes for a while."

"If that's the way you want it." Stephen sat up too, began unbuttoning his shirt.

He grabbed those presumptuous hands. "Don't try to second-guess the artiste, son. I said relax." He pointed to the pillows. "Facedown, pillow under the chest—no, not that one, it's too thick. That one's fine—now let your chin hang over the edge—"

"Wesley, what—"

"No questions. Trust me."

"I *do*. But—"

"*Stephen!*"

"Okay...okay..."

viii

The flute's delicate tones floated through the star-flecked darkness, echoed off the moonlit riftside.

Nigan had been right to insist on this change of venue: the newly dubbed HoloRoom acoustics were infinitely superior to sickbay's—particularly when a carefully programmed sim was available to provide those realistic echoes.

McKenna had fought the room change—the portable LSU they'd brought to the auditorium hadn't anything like the emergency facilities they'd need if Hononomii pulled one of his freakouts; but even McKenna proclaimed she was glad now she'd been out-stubborned: never argue with a magician, she'd said.

And magic it was. A magic the delicate breeze he'd requested unquestionably enhanced. Nigan had played tirelessly for what seemed like hours with no visible change. Then suddenly, Hononomii Tyeewapi began drifting on that sound, swaying with it, even chanting with it.

Suddenly: "Nigan? Nigan Wakiza, it is you, isn't it? Nigan, where are you?"

"I'm here, Hononomii. Feel my hand?"

"Nigan, where are we?"

"It's all right, Hono. You can trust what you've seen, *and* what you've heard. You're aboard the *Cetacean*, but this is me. You *know* how long I've wanted to get into space. I'm here, Hono. And it's wonderful."

"That's what the music was saying, isn't it?"

"Yes, Hono, but it's time to go home now."

Their prearranged signal to TJ to bring the lights up. Soft actinic light slowly touched the two young men. Caught Hononomii's eyes alight with awareness and focussed intently on Nigan's face.

Nigan grinned and said softly, "Hi, there. Concert's over, old man, Paul said to tell you it's time to go back to work."

It was almost fun, adding to the kid's confusion in this way; Stephen was so thoroughly ignorant, a moron could appear an expert—

—and J. Wesley Smith was no moron.

Steady, relentless massage made Stephen's neck and shoulders more pliable with each pass. Once properly limpified, the slightest tug rolled him off the pillows and onto his back, exposing the much-disputed buttons. Wesley slipped those buttons, one by one.

Beautifully contoured muscle. Not an ounce of excess fat. He traced the smooth skin with a fingertip, judging pressure to a nicety: just enough not to tickle. Stephen's breathing deepened; the contours responded with involuntary quivers.

Other buttons had stood between them once upon a time. Crystal buttons, now in Anevai's possession. Buttons which had graced a Designer of the sort he himself used to squander his money on, in his Highly Stupid academy years. A jacket which had skewed so many early impressions of the young man lying relaxed and trusting under his hands.

Somebody should have warned you, kid, he thought, and slid his hands up Stephen's sides.

A gasp. A startled stretch. He had the shirt off before the kid knew what hit him. A little shiver as a stray breeze from the window drifted over them.

His whispered Too cold, kid? gained a barely audible *HmmMmm*, and he quit worrying about anything other than introducing the elegant body to its various nerve endings. Some things required total concentration to do right. And if Stephen thought the Cocheta suit was talented...

That slight breeze caught the lightweight fabric, billowed the shirt over bare skin and of a sudden, Stephen was no longer quite so relaxed. His whole body arched to meet the silky touch, the moonlight making ridges of his ribs, a hollow cave of the contracted diaphragm. He lowered the shirt; the tail slithered over and around the cave, rippling as the muscle beneath began quick, gasping contractions.

"Oh, God. Wesley..."

A whisper so low, he wasn't certain he heard it at all. He pulled the shirt away. "You want me to stop, Stephen? Just say the word and I will."

Stephen's eyes glittered, his tongue flicked across his mouth, and he said with some difficulty, "You want to see tomorrow, Smith?"

He grinned. "You've got it, sport."

Stephen stopped thinking, stopped wondering, and let himself flow with and respond to the sensations Wesley raised. Where his hands went, he didn't know: somehow they knew better than any rational consideration what Wesley wanted.

But as his hands slipped over and around Wesley's responsive body, he became aware of a driving rhythm, a heartbeat not his own, a throb that reached in and captured his own, forcing synchronicity.

Just as the mountain had done.

And as he'd sensed the course of the mountain streams, he felt the blood surge through Wesley's veins—or was it his own? He was no longer certain. He couldn't tell what was Wesley, what himself—who was touching, who was touched.

He felt Wesley's gasp, knew it to be one of exquisite pleasure and revelled in his power, then wondered whose the gasp and whose the power, decided it didn't matter, and laughed in sheer joy.

Or perhaps it was Wesley laughing, which likewise made no difference. The carefree ecstasy was mutual; *that,* he knew without question.

Then they were three.

He screamed objection. He didn't want or need the Other's cocoon of safety. When Nayati's tape had forced reaction from him—as Richard had, as Bijan had—the Other's intervention had been profoundly appreciated. But then was not now. *Wesley* was not—

The sensation clarified; it *wasn't* the Other. It was the Cocheta Nayati had chosen for him. The first. The source of Nayati's power over him. The one he thought dead—or at least...disconnected...was back, and this time, the alien responses fed on his own desires—fed and grew more powerful, and fed again—until darkness began to settle in and around that which was, or had been, Stephen Ridenour.

"Wes? Wesley, please! Stop . . . you've got to—" He thought he screamed the words, but the sensations did not stop, and Wesley had promised—

Anevai jerked awake and stared into the darkness.

"Hell of a dream, bozo," she told the little freeloader in her belly. "If that's one of your side benefits, I might keep you around after all."

She yawned and stretched, thoroughly awake now, and realizing the probable source of both dream and awakening. She rolled out of bed, tossed a robe over her head, and staggered down the hall to the bathroom.

Voices: downstairs and barely audible above the sound of running water. Strange. It was late. Her grandparents had gone to bed before she, and they no longer handled the late-night emergencies in the clinic.

Anevai dried her hands and went to eavesdrop at the top of the stairs.

". . . got to wake her up. It's an emergency. Cantrell's waiting—"

"Dr. Paul?" she called, and ran down the stairs and into the living room where Paul Corlaney stood, in fur-lined coat and gloves, facing her equally inappropriately clad grandparents. Behind him, *Cetacean* crew members with atmospheric flight crew insignia on their uniforms. "You flew here? What's wrong? Is it Stephen? Did something—"

"Whoa, missy, slow down," Paul said. "As far as I know, Ridenour's fine. I just got a call from Loren, and she wanted me to get you online to *Cetacean*."

Emergency. That meant it was— "Gods. It's Hono, isn't it, Dr. Paul?"

Suddenly light-headed, she groped for a chair and sat down. Her grandparents and Paul rushed to her, but she waved aside their concerns for her.

"For the gods' sake, Dr. Paul," she said, irritation and worry equally mixed in her emotions. "Just get that connection made, will you?"

Paul cupped her face, made her look at him, grinned and patted her cheek. "Okay, sweet-stuff."

He didn't look worried. Maybe it wasn't Hono. Maybe—

He handed her the phone.

"Admiral? What is it? What's wrong?" Anevai couldn't control the shake in her voice.

"Please hold."

Not Cantrell. She glanced at Dr. Paul in confusion. His blank face told her nothing. Bad enough to get dragged out of bed in the middle of the night; when the dragger was Paul Corlaney and the reason given was an emergency call from *Cetacean* . . .

"Anevai? Annie-love, are you there?"

"Oh, gods . . ." she whispered. Looked to Paul, whose grin threatened to split his face. "Oh, gods, is that really you, Hono?"

"It's me, sis. Break out the drums, we're coming home."

"Stephen?"

Wesley? What . . .

"Stephen! Wake up, for God's sake, man, wake up!" Hands he'd come to trust struck his face, causing pain enough to make him cry out, after which those same hands hugged him close and Wesley's voice whispered *Oh, God. Oh, my God* in his ear.

"Dr. Smith? Are you there? The team—"

Wesley leaned over, pulling him with him, and said to the speakerphone, "It's all right, guys. Cancel the emergency. Sorry to pull you out of bed."

"You owe us one, Smith."

"Hell if. That's what you're paid for. Get the hell off my line."

"Watch it, or I'll tell the squad to break the door down."

"All right! I owe you! Now fuck off!"

"Tell Ridenour to wash your mouth ou—"

Wesley surged against him. A crash. A startled cry; and the strange voice stopped.

"Shit. —Are you all right?"

It took a moment to realize Wesley was speaking to him; that the cry had been his. He shuddered. Felt that minor convulsion in every joint in his aching body. Thank God he'd been with Wesley and not someone else. Wesley would understand, Wesley could help him figure:

"What happened?" he whispered, all the voice that seemed available to him.

"What *happened?* You tell me! Shit, I've seen some fast responses in my time, but that one takes the prize. And not a single damn sound after you told me to stop—*which I did*—not that it did much good. What the hell is going on here?"

Wesley was perturbed.

"Listen, Wes, I'm—"

"Sorry doesn't cut it, boy. Not this time. I want to know what happened."

He laid a hand on Wesley's chest, felt the thumping heart, felt—with that not-quite-dissipated inner awareness—the blood coursing too rapidly through his veins, the anger, the terror—as if— But why? How? He felt his eyes drifting shut and his body swaying in time to that rhythm. Sensed the danger in that course and severed contact with an almost painful wrench.

He rolled out of bed. "I've got to take a shower."

"God, Stephen. Is it because of what I . . ."

The question made no sense. He blinked at Wesley's image, trying to make it or the words clear, shook his head and wandered into the bathroom.

The shower was cursory—more to clear his head and for time away from Wesley and those senses that threatened to absorb him. He wrapped a bath sheet around himself and returned to the bedroom, half hoping Wesley would be gone.

He wasn't.

He was standing beside the bedtable's open drawer. He looked up, an expression of pure unadulterated hatred on his face.

Stephen stopped short.

A flip of the wrist. A crystal vial skidded across the sheet. "Guess that answers my question."

He turned for the door, and as it slid open: "Least you could have done, Doxie, is warn Anevai. That shit is why she's pregnant, and she deserves to know what kind of monster she's due to give birth to."

He was gone before Stephen could ask what the hell he was talking about.

IV

i

Hononomii looked wonderful—if you didn't know him. His step, though firm, lacked the bounce Anevai had always associated with her elder brother. His face, though he smiled when he saw his mountains, hazy shadows through the persistent fog, lacked the glow of beloved recognition, and Anevai cursed the cold front that had moved in during the night, creating that fog and forcing this inside-the-terminal reunion.

But Hono knew her. His hug was enthusiastic and lifted her feet from the terrazzo floor. He asked about Bogatu, seemed sincerely regretful for the colt's death, but asked no further regarding the events of the past weeks, said nothing about their meeting aboard *Cetacean*. It was as if Bogatu's birth, that final shared event before his arrest, was his only real association with the sister he'd grown up with.

It was as if Hononomii was home, but part of him remained

in space—some ... VirtualSpace of his own, or Nayati's, making. But her mother and grandparents and Dr. McKenna had conferred, and decided he was well enough to come home and Cantrell hadn't argued. Dr. Paul said she wanted them safely off the ship. But seeing him, Anevai feared it would take Nayati to call Hononomii back, if even Nayati could manage after all this time, and if Nayati would condescend to return, once *Cetacean* left the system.

"Hononomii?" Dr. Paul's voice held a strangely wistful hesitancy. "Welcome home, —son."

Hono looked past her shoulder, his brow puckering in confusion, to where Paul stood, slightly removed from her family, as if he didn't belong anymore. He and her father were eyeing one another like rivals—one of the dumber fallouts from the past weeks' events, to her way of thinking—and Anevai wanted nothing more than to hit them both, to knock sense into these two, who were playing power games at the expense of a sick man.

But Hononomii, with all his old charm, and innocent defiance of rules unfathomable to him, reached out to Paul, who received his handclasp with visible relief, pulling him into a warm embrace, which Hononomii returned in full measure, then, turning, held out a hand to his father.

Her father and Dr. Paul closed in on either side of Hononomii, leading him off toward the 'Tube, leaving her to greet the admiral and her mother.

Cholena hugged her and said, "Nothing much has changed, has it, child?"

She looked at the trio of male backs walking obliviously down the terminal corridor. "I don't mind, Mom. Not this time. Hono is Dad's hope and Dr. Paul's best aide. They came terribly close to losing him."

"And are you really going to let the matter rest there, girl?"

Anevai caught the disappointment in the admiral's voice and grinned up at her before linking arms with them both and heading them in the men's wake. "Of course not. But I'll wait until Nayati's back, then kick their behinds collectively."

That was another promise Cantrell had made: Nayati had become the *Dineh's* problem. Her way, so Cantrell said, of protecting the entire subject from the 'NetAT investigation.

Cantrell chuckled. "Good girl. They just need time. Paul's a proud man. Your father, for all his intentions were good, pulled a very nonethical trick on him, taking him into the Library and using the Cocheta machine on him." She shrugged. "At the moment, Hononomii is a convenient weapon."

"Was," Anevai corrected. "He sheathed himself in a hurry."

"Perhaps," her mother said, but Cholena obviously wasn't satisfied, and excused herself to go play referee, declining Anevai's offer of help.

Maybe the grandparents *should* have come to the airport rather than wait for them in her parents' home. Her mother looked tired. Probably she could have used their moral support.

But Anevai wasn't worried. Paul and her father were friends, and friends worked things out.

She had friends, too—neither of whom had shown up, though she'd invited them. Neither of whom had bothered to call her after their meeting with the 'NetATs, though they'd both promised faithfully. "I wonder where Stephen is? I thought he and Wesley would be here. We flew straight in from Acoma, but I left messages for them everywhere I could think of."

"Smith, I wouldn't hazard a guess. Stephen's probably packing," Cantrell said. "I talked to him this morning from *Cetacean*. He's supposed to meet the 'NetAT shuttle here soon. He's to debrief this afternoon with Chet and Herzog, then leave for Vandereaux on the 'NetAT ship tomorrow—possibly even tonight."

Anevai stopped short, shook herself free. "You mean he's leaving without saying goodbye?"

Cantrell shrugged.

Anevai looked at the backs disappearing down the escalator. "You say he's coming here to meet this other shuttle?"

Cantrell nodded.

"I want to stay here—wait for him."

"He could have had constraints put on him by the 'NetAT. They have something major going down. You might not be able to speak to him at all."

"Doesn't matter. I can wave. At least he'll know I tried."

Cantrell smiled, and rested a hand briefly on her shoulder. "You're a good friend to have, Anevai Tyeewapi. I'll explain to your family."

"Hey, wait up!" a voice called, followed by rapid footsteps.

"Nigan? Where have you been?"

He ran down the corridor, a duffel, sprouting socks from a half-zipped pocket, banging at his heels. He caught up with them, held up three aces, grinning ear to ear.

"I *won!*"

9:15. Anevai's brother should be back, the happy reunion in progress.

Another fifteen minutes, Stephen reckoned, and they should be well on their way to the Tyeewapi house. Safe, then, to head for the airport and the 'NetAT police, who were to meet him there.

Coward, he chided himself, but the critical self-evaluation didn't make him rise from the chair, nor pick up his luggage, nor start for the lift down the hall.

The huge bed was stripped, of sheets as well as ghosts. His mind was—numb. He should have contacted Anevai. Should have told her what Wesley had said, but he couldn't. Couldn't ruin this moment for her. Couldn't explain what Wesley seemed to think he should know.

Something to do with Eudoxin and her pregnancy, but he simply didn't know, and nothing in local files could tell him. He'd tried to call Wesley this morning, which had, not surprisingly, gotten him nowhere. But Wesley was so damned smart. And Wesley was her friend. Wesley could damnwell tell her.

He was an outsider. A 'NetAT Del d'Bugger with universe-consequent matters to deal with. He had other things to worry about.

Coward.

The room was growing chilly, external temperatures slowly invading since he'd cancelled the environmental regulators. He pulled his 'prezzie' from Wesley tight and buttoned it up, carefully straightening the fringe. He should leave it here.

Somehow, he couldn't.

Of course, he reasoned, maybe he *wasn't* the father. Maybe Anevai was just saying that. Herzog confirmed the missing scars, so his memories weren't totally suspect.

Maybe it *wasn't* him.

And maybe that—*thing*—which had taken over his mind last night was a figment of his imagination. And maybe he wasn't worried about what would happen back at Vandereaux, with people asking him questions he'd been programmed to resist and that—*thing*—ready to envelop him the minute he broke that programming.

And maybe—

He leapt from the chair, grabbed his suitcase and duffel from the bed, and ran down the hall for the lift.

The underground transport tube was slower, and used primarily for cargo, the environment-loving onworlders preferring the surface tracks—which meant that much less chance of encountering the party from *Cetacean*.

Stephen gripped his duffel on his lap, shifting forward on the hard seat, searching for a position that didn't hurt, padding it finally with the fur-lined jacket. Stupid thing was too warm for the heated compartment anyway.

Keep it, Stephen . . . Looks better on you . . . Say Thank you, Uncle Wesser . . .

He crossed his arms over the duffel, hugging it to his chest, rubbed his hand absently over the bandage hidden beneath his shirt's wide cuff. Little pain remained this morning. By tomorrow, the bandages could go altogether. In the meanwhile, the cuffs would ward off embarrassing questions.

Damn Wesley. Damn Herzog. And damn that *thing* in his head.

A watch-ward glance. Five minutes. Five more minutes. He clutched the duffel and rocked forward and back on the seat, focussing into the middle-ground of nothingness within the compartment.

He wanted back at Vandereaux, the report given and whatever was going to happen, over and done with. Cantrell had offered to drop her search for the Cocheta and take him back. To protect him from the 'NetAT. He didn't want that. It wasn't part of the deal he'd made with Herzog, and any change he willingly took part in risked negation of that contract.

By the time he reached the airport, oblivion was beginning to sound quite attractive. Fanning the cynical flames, he charged the ride to Wesley's account—*Go ahead, Smith, argue the ten credits*—heaved the duffel over his shoulder, and touched the floater button on the suitcase.

Damned if he'd strain one more muscle for the sake of this—

Mountains.

There were mountains outside the door, not the spaceport terminal.

This wasn't where he meant to be.

But there was tarmac outside, and shadows—he looked carefully around the edge of the door—from a large building behind, and a roboporter waiting to load cargo.

The 'Tube had surfaced at the airport service entrance. Had he programmed it properly, the far door would have opened, he'd have stepped out into the terminal storage and never thought twice. But out this side...

Stephen stepped out onto the tarmac, unable to keep his eyes off those peaks floating in the mist.

He didn't want to hate this place. Didn't want to resent his time here. If he had one molecule of truth left in him, he'd admit, at least to himself, that he didn't want to leave at all. And if he had to leave, why couldn't it be aboard the huge *Cetacean* shuttle parked outside the loading dock?

And as Truth crystallized in his mind and soul, the Other's sense of homecoming reached into his gut, as it had that first day, making him ache with longing to be a part of—

A whine of dissipation shields. A dark shape, rapidly descending through the mist. 'NetAT. He knew it. In the way he *knew* those mountains.

'NetAT. Herzog. The ache became panic. Panic that made his heart race and his hands sweat, that roused memories of awareness and safe, insulating cocoons, and then enveloped him in blackness.

The younger Tyeewapis' home was an elegant piece of architecture. Made of wood and stone from the surrounding woodland, it matched every square foot enclosed for modesty or practicality with open-air or minimally protected patio or garden, full of running water, growing plants, and live animals.

Leaving the Tyeewapis to conduct their multigenerational reunion in private, Paul, TJ, and Cantrell settled in one of those patios, reinforced with lemonade, coffee, and cookies.

"I could grow to like this." TJ sighed, drained his second glass of lemonade, and shoved another cookie in his mouth.

Cantrell watched this performance in disgusted amazement. "Someday, TJ Briggs, if there is *any* justice in this universe, your metabolism is going to change."

"Never." He grinned around the cookie. "God loves me."

"Which one?"

The grin widened. "All of them."

"Scum," she said, and turned back to: "Paul, would you even consider returning with us to Vandereaux?"

"For what? Just to testify about the Cocheta? What's your hurry? Stick around. We'll find those Libraries, then you won't *need* me."

"What about Stephen? Because of the reckless use *your* friends have made of Smith's system, these 'NetATs are hauling him back—probably tonight—to face what will very likely turn into a Combined Council investigation committee alone, because he doesn't want *his* problems to disrupt *our* investigation of the Cocheta.''

''It's his job, Cantrell. It's what he signed up for. No more, no less. Wesley says his paper's got it covered; he'll be fine. He's right in one other thing: you should be concentrating on the Cocheta.''

''And if he tells them *all* about the Cocheta before we get back? They could have handpicked investigation teams here before we even get back to Vandereaux.''

''He won't tell them.''

''Because of Nayati? That suggestion wasn't worth spit, and you know it, not if they go after the boy with all the mind-sifting techniques available to them.''

''No. Because he'll never get the chance. You know that. I know that. We're talking chance of a lifetime here, Loren. Danislav—unless the 'NetATs get to it first—will claim little Stevie's investigation for his own. Smith can complain all he wants, but if the 'NetDB is in trouble, they won't ask permission. They'll just swallow your Del d'Bugger whole. If he tries to buy his way into attention with the Cocheta, they'll hush him up faster. Label him crazy and lock him away.''

''And his very real knowledge about Rostov? About what happened there?'' Cantrell pressed, searching for something of the man she once knew in the individual coldly dismissing Stephen Ridenour's future. ''He's not the innocent in those areas he was when he came here. He won't have the immunity of a child's innocence.''

''Not everyone can *be* winners, Loren.''

She leaned back in her chair and eyed him over her coffee-cup rim. ''You're a cold-blooded bastard, Paul, do you know that? I thought I was bad.''

''There's nothing wrong with you—or me. This is a damn tough situation. There may have to be a few sacrifices.''

''And heaven forbid Paul Corlaney should come out of hiding long enough to help save one boy's heart—maybe his life.''

''Getting melodramatic in your old age, aren't you, Cantrell?''

"Is that what you call it?" TJ drawled from behind his third glass of lemonade.

"Excuse me, Loren." Cholena's head popped out through a door. "There's a call for you."

Strange: any of her crew would have channelled through security communications who would have signalled her on her personal beeper.

She exchanged a glance with TJ; he grabbed another cookie and followed her into the house.

To Paul, she said nothing.

It was the 'NetAT police. They were at the airport, looking for Stephen, and . . . irate. Her security, forewarned about their arrival, had confined them to their small ship.

"As far as I know, he was meeting you there. Did you try his room at the SciCorps condos?"

"Of course we did, Admiral Cantrell. There was no answer."

"Then obviously he's on his way. Perhaps he's met a friend en route—"

"Admiral, our superiors warned us that you might interfere in Dr. Ridenour's departure. Please, don't make this interdepartmental warfare. What have you done with him?"

"I have no more interest in—warfare, as you call it, than you do, lieutenant. I promise you, this is none of my doing. But if you will remain calm, I'll see what I can find out. As for my security, believe me, the situation here is such that you *want* my people interfacing for you. I'll call my SecCom and have them tap you in as Chet deems appropriate." And before they could object: "—Cantrell, out."

Turning to TJ: "He's done it again."

ii

The message light blinked in the lower right-hand corner of the monitor. Wesley ignored it. On the third blink, it turned fluorescent orange.

He swore and jabbed *Esc*—

—not soon enough. The patented J. W. Smith 3D fireworks display announcing the blessed event disrupted the medical report displayed on the screen, slowly blowing it to pieces.

J.W. Smith kicked away from his desk, spun his chair, and stalked to the brewer for a fresh cup, splashed drops hissing over the warmer as he slammed the pot down.

The damned thing was supposed to get *other* people, not him!

He hooked his chair with his foot, pulled it farther from the Machine that was still spewing sparkles (persistent PitA), and slumped down, tucking one foot under him, spinning the chair slowly with the other, waiting for the display to end. If it was Stephen Ridenour, he could go to hell. If it was anyone else—at the moment, no one else mattered.

Wesley Smith was pissed. Wesley Smith was *severely* pissed. He'd spent the last—he glanced at the clock—ten hours busting his butt, illegally invading every file in the known universe looking for—anything. *Any* evidence to substantiate Stephen Ridenour's claims. But there was nothing. . . .

Other than a hell of a lot he *hadn't* mentioned.

For every black eye he'd taken to the infirmary, there were a dozen others with the same complaint. He had an unforgivably perfect attendance record—give or take a few unexcused late arrivals, he'd never missed a class. And not a single reprimand filed against his so-called persecutor. Of course, Ridenour could *claim* he never made those accusations. That *J. Wesley Smith* had made assumptions based on Stephen NMI Ridenour's battered-puppy behavior.

Admittedly, in between those sessions of perfect attendance, Stephen Ridenour had spent an inordinate amount of time in the hospital. Generally, while others were on vacation, he studied from a hospital bed. Admittance listed everything from generic 'respiratory viruses' to highly specific injuries, the dislocated shoulder accident being the most notorious. But injuries were unavoidable to an Olympic-quality gymnast who got sidelined because of an 'Attitude problem: high danger potential, low yield' report from his *coach* because of his insistence on working out solo.

Stephen NMI Ridenour's tax records had been another revelation. Damn right, he'd gotten gifts. All of which had been properly recorded. All of which had been properly taxed. All of which had been properly signed for—by Victor Danislav's accountant. Who also just happened to be Mialla Shapoorian's personal accountant.

All except those opal pins. Made J. Wesley Smith wonder.

Also made J. Wesley Smith curious when, following the Shapoorian connection, one found pictures of the Family. Pictures with a curiously familiar Look about their tailoring.

J. Wesley Smith had been led around by the nose for the past two weeks by the most convincing bastard he'd ever come across, and J. Wesley Smith didn't appreciate the experience. Not one damn bit. Stephen Ridenour was going to be severely sorry he'd ever tried.

He'd been inordinately attracted to the creature from the start. Stephen Ridenour oozed sexuality from his pores—by his own admission, had been trained by one of the best. Mialla Shapoorian, by all accounts, played hardball politics in bed as well as in the Council Chamber. Her son was evidently likewise molded. As far as J. Wesley Smith could tell, Stephen NMI Ridenour didn't know the meaning of the word morality.

But as the sparks faded and >BYE BYE, SUCKER! appeared on the screen, he saw luminescent eyes, heard a soft voice asking *Do you want to see tomorrow?* . . .

. . . and swept a hand across the desk, sending his keyboard and stacks of loose papers flying around the room.

>I BEG YOUR PARDON?

He stared at his shaking hands, horrified and disgusted as he'd been last night. Yes, Ridenour had infuriated him, but he *shouldn't* have reacted that way. He had *never*—not in all his years of experimentation—allowed sex and anger into the same bed. But *dammit!* —he looked at the screen, thinking of those damned torturously resurrected medical records—the Clone took Eudoxin, another experimentation he'd never been tempted to try. Ridenour could have slipped him some during that meal. Wasn't, as he understood, the chosen way for Doxies to imbibe the shit, but Stephen didn't do anything *normally.*

Do you want—

He shot the memory to hell.

If tomorrow contained Stephen NMI Ridenour, the answer was most definitely No.

"No answer there either," Cantrell said, and cut the connection. "What are those two up to this time, do you suppose?"

"What about Ridenour?" Paul had followed them to Sakiimagan's office and was leaning against the doorframe. "Any chance he did anything so sensible as send a message to the people he was *supposed* to meet?"

Cantrell frowned. "I'm hardly in a mood to be charitable, Paul. —As a matter of fact, he did. That's why they expected him to be there."

"Easy answer, Boss-lady," TJ said from the couch.

"So?"

"Have Chet check his beeper."

She laughed shortly. "From the mouths of—"

"I *resent* that, rug-rat!"

Extending the barest tip of her tongue, Cantrell signalled *Cetacean* on her personal beeper. With luck, Chet would be—

"Hear you, Boss-lady. What's up?"

Thank God.

"Had a bit of a mix-up with the 'NetAT cops. Check out the kid's beeper-loc, will you?"

'Already checked. Tyeewapi girl called through the base crew ten minutes ago, give or take, and asked.'

Cantrell chuckled. "The little so-and-so. Where was he?"

TJ looked a question and she held up a belaying hand, mouthed *in a minute.*

"On the tube to the 'port. Almost there."

She frowned. "Check again, will you?"

"You got it. Have to disconnect you for a minute."

"I'll wait."

While Chet ran a search for Stephen's beeper signal, she explained the situation to TJ and Paul.

TJ said, "Looks ominous."

Which, she suspected, was only half joke.

Paul said, "Forget him. He's a damned troublemaker."

Which made her want to do him severe bodily injury. But since she still might godforbid need him, she hissed, "Get out, Paul."

"Loren—"

"I said—"

"I'm here, admiral. Got an answer for you."

"Yeah?"

"The good news is, I found him."

"And the bad?"

"Looks like he's en route to Acoma."

"Again? Can we intercept?"

"Plenty of time. He seems to be on the underground freight line. Hard to get at, but no scheduled stops before Acoma."

"Did you try to signal him?"

"No. Will if you want. Thought you might not want him to know you're onto him."

"Good thinking. Keep your eye on him. Dispatch a team to pick him up, will you?"

"What about the AT police?"

"Suggestions?"

"Keep them contained. My judgement call."

Which meant, he assumed responsibility to the 'NetAT.

"You sure?"

"Damn right. This is a bolt, Cantrell. He knows we can track him. Knows we'll pick him up. I want to hear what he has to say, and we don't need them sending him into VSpace."

"I agree. You want me to place the order?"

"I can do it."

"Brave soul."

"Ha! I'll let you explain to Ms. Tyeewapi."

She laughed. *"Deal."*

"They're leaving from here?" Anevai tried to keep her voice matter-of-fact, tried not to let Cantrell know how desperate the news made her. "Let me go with them. *Please,* admiral."

There was a long pause on the other end. Conference, or just thought? She wished this hall phone had a vid, caught herself biting her lip, and decided maybe she was glad it didn't.

Finally: *"Let him go, Anevai. Your home is here. Your family is here."*

"Stephen is family, too, admiral. Can't you understand that?"

"Can't you understand that it's precisely that attitude of yours that is making it so difficult for him to do what he must? Trust me, girl, you can help him most by going to the celebration for your brother. Show him, however harsh it seems, that Hononomii means more to you than he does."

"I'm not sure he does, admiral." The truth was out before she thought.

"You don't mean that."

Anevai, thinking about Hononomii, and a cloud of well-wishers meeting him here, taking him home to a safe bed, in a safe world . . . Hononomii, who had done nothing but shoot his mouth off and get arrested and start the whole damned mess—who had let Nayati fuck up his head in the first place because he was too damned cowardly to tell his cousin to go to hell—

—and thinking about Stephen, who had nobody, who had been en route to the airport alone to meet people he didn't know, to be taken off to who knew what, who had offered his own life to Nayati for the sake of herself and Wesley—

Thinking about all that, she said, "Damn right I meant it."

A long pause. *"No matter, Anevai."*

"In other words, your people won't let me aboard."

"You've got it."

She gritted her teeth. "See you at lunch."

* * *

"Newsflash, Loren."

Cantrell jumped, half-turned in the bubblecar seat before she realized:

"Chet Hamilton, one of these days you're going to die."

"Tell me one I don't know, Boss-lady."

"I'm going to pull the trigger. *What* newsflash?"

"How's the view? Can you see the condos from there?"

"TJ," she said to her chief of security, sitting patiently at her side, "contact Chet, will you? Tell him to go to—"

"You win, Boss. Sorry about the surprise. Ridenour's jumped the train."

"Not again. Got him in view?"

"Yeah. I've already directed the team in his direction. They should have him in about ten minutes."

"Listen, don't tell the 'NetATs we've found him yet. Let's talk to him first."

"Gotcha."

"And remind me when I get back to tell Lexi I blew it. I wish to God she were down here right now."

"I'll remind you."

"And if he doesn't," TJ said as she signed off, "I will."

iii

How he had stopped the vehicle, why and how he had reached the surface, he wasn't at all certain. He remembered recording and sending a message to Cantrell's onworld security communications, but beyond that . . .

It was the Other. He was certain of it. Could fight the truth no longer. Whatever had happened last night, had opened the door. Whoever the Other was, it didn't want him leaving.

Or—his rational self insisted—it could be his subconscious taking over—putting his wishes into reality. Cantrell's people would know he was bound for Acoma. Would simply pick him up. Stop him from learning—what he had to know. What he had to find out for certain . . .

Stephen flattened himself against the stone, willing the Cocheta to him, grateful for the rocky nook's protection from the wind whipping down the gorge, grateful for the sun breaking through at last and beating on his bare shoulders. But he drove gratitude from his mind, reached for that *awareness*, sensing a need to accept that cold, the wind currents, and the sun as a part of the whole. Then trying not to think at all—thinking interfered with the Cocheta. He remembered that from the mountain.

Nothing.

But *something* had happened last night—and this morning at the airport. A horrifyingly familiar something.

(Sound of engines in the air—he pressed tighter to the stone, unwilling to relinquish this vantage, hoping no one would see him.)

Unless blaming his overwhelming reaction on the Cocheta Other was simply his own sick way of bypassing responsibility. Logic dictated it couldn't have been the Other; there'd been no preliminary tape, no—training program, such as Nayati had given him, no sense-dep helmet, not even the alien suit he'd worn when he followed the *awareness* through the mountain to Cantrell.

Maybe Wesley was right. Maybe Nayati had planted the tunnel layout in his head with the Cocheta machine. Maybe his sense of 'homecoming' was less the Other than a perfectly natural feeling for the people who'd befriended him in those mountains. Maybe his sense of 'whereness' was nothing but a hyperactive imagination.

(Once again, engines disrupted the air. He squeezed his eyes shut, refusing to acknowledge the mechanical existence, *listening* for the mountain.)

And it wasn't as if this had been his first experience with the alien machines. He'd worn the hats as a child, had the alien thoughts running through him, and remained himself in the years since. Granted the suits made a difference in the intensity of the experience, but that much?

On the other hand, he knew from equally personal experience that there were other means of . . . expanding one's body consciousness. Certainly it had *felt* as if another awareness had controlled him last night, but the human mind could simulate that all by itself.

(Engines: loud and hovering. VTOLs. *Cetacean* search vehicles, he'd lay odds. But then, the engines retreated, fading into the distance.)

He gave up trying to concentrate on not thinking, pushed himself shivering from the rock and pulled his damp shirt back on, tucking it in, positioning the cuffs, draping the fabric precisely—as if it made a difference.

Yet, somehow, it did—ultimately—make a difference. Wesley couldn't know how devastating his fashion critique had been. Stephen Ridenour had had few real triumphs in his academic career. That had been one. A search for individuality in a station full of egos had led him to one of Vandereaux's exclusive tailors, an elusive memory had led him to suggest designs that made him *feel* good when he wore them. And when those designs—'significantly altered', of course—showed up on *other* clients of that same tailor, clients who denounced *everything* Recon, his triumph, however silently enjoyed, had been complete.

And when Wesley, who epitomized everything he wished he could be, had blamed those clothes for . . .

But Wesley was right. Part of the elusive triumph of those clothes was the control it had given him over his own fate. Because by that time, Bijan had lost his power over him—the sentence had been served, the 'confession' recorded, and his own room safely under constant observation. That 'Look', whatever it was, had assured Bijan's continued interest; the security in his room had assured *him* power over when and where Bijan could express that interest.

Wesley had seemed amazed that he should seek Bijan's attention. He hadn't sought it—he'd already had it—but he'd used it. He'd used Bijan as much as Bijan had used him. Bijan had been a known, controllable quantity in his life. He'd also been—

He stared down at his hands, remembering Wesley's touch, the *feeling* of his response.

—human contact. He'd needed that. Maybe that made him weak, he didn't know. But he'd *needed* to feel the touch of a human hand, no matter how distasteful the memory of that touch was.

But only the memory. The touches, the blows, the deliberately cruel acts, had all been—pleasurable—in RealTime . . . thanks to the Eudoxin. Thanks to a chemical that put him more in touch with his partner's feelings than his own. For the first time, he wondered what *Bijan* had felt during those encounters; whether the awareness had been reciprocal.

(*"Why don't you cry, Ridenour?"*)

He remembered Bijan's thumb, brushing his cheek much as Wesley's had done last night. Remembered saying:

(*"Maybe there's nothing left to cry about."*)

The unusually delicate (for Bijan) touch had traced a path around his face. And Bijan had said:

(*"Maybe if you did, I'd stop."*)

He remembered smiling faintly—and an answer that had driven Bijan crazy:

(*"Maybe I'll keep that in mind."*)

Stupid, asinine challenge; he'd always wondered who Bijan thought he was punishing. Of course, if one hadn't had to live with the aftermath . . .

He shuddered. The very thought made him sick at his stomach.

Until Wesley, he'd never questioned alternatives. Until Wesley had told him, *When the time and person are right* . . .

Why last night? Why Wesley? Wesley made him feel awkward and stupid—at best like a foolish child. He felt more relaxed and comfortable—more normal—around Anevai.

He shoved his hands deep into his pockets and continued

down the trail, aimless, now he'd tried—and failed—to contact the Other.

Who did he think he was kidding? *Comfortable* had nothing to do with the feelings he'd been exploring with Wesley last night. He'd had no right even to try. But once into the situation . . . it had *almost* felt like . . . But Wesley would never use—and *he* certainly hadn't . . .

Besides, he *knew* that taste, in a way *nothing* could disguise. Whatever had happened, Eudoxin hadn't been a part of it.

Or had it? They said the stuff never really cleared your system. That it laid a film along your insides that eventually turned toxic. Perhaps he'd reached that point. Perhaps he was incapable of tapping those emotions without resurrecting a drug *designed* to play games with perception.

Could he trust *any* thought, any sensation, any decision, for the rest of his life?

A life that, if his suspicions were correct, if the Eudoxin was . . . *toxisifying* . . . inside him, wasn't going to last much longer.

He topped a small rise in the trail. Ahead: a deep narrow cut with the remains of a fallen bridge on the far side. Behind: a descending thrum of engines. Cantrell's people coming for him; no question this time. And a moment later:

"Time to head back, Dr. Ridenour."

He answered by lengthening his stride.

"Please, sir. Don't make us—"

He broke into a run, heard the exclamation behind him and ignored it as he leaped out over the gorge.

"Dammit, I knew something like this would happen." Lexi's blow to Chet Hamilton's desktop rattled magnetic paperweights designed to counter *Cetacean*'s best *v*-shifts.

She jerked to her feet and rattled bodily about his office.

"He spent last night with Smith, didn't he?" she asked sharply.

"Most of it," Chet admitted. "But calm down, Lexi. Done

is done. Question is, what do you suggest now? He could have killed himself—would have, if that leftover bridge hadn't been there.''

"I doubt that. He's many things, but suicidal isn't one of them.''

He frowned, thinking of records Lexi wasn't privy to. "You sure of that?''

She nodded. "He's a survivor, Chet, of the first water.''

"We've got to send someone after him.''

"And I'm stuck here babysitting. —How soon before I could get there?''

"Hours.''

"Not soon enough,'' she muttered, but not to him. "I should have been there. . . .'' She was thinking. Lexi Fonteccio was not one to waste crucial time on 'should haves'. Neither was she one to forget. She'd face the problem now (as her frowning concentration indicated) and make sure to remind Cantrell and everyone else—later.

"I think . . .'' She paused, still frowning. Then: "You have him on visual?''

He nodded.

"As long as he's in no danger, I'd recommend giving him a bit to come back on his own. If he doesn't, send Smith after him.''

"Smith? I thought you hated the man.''

"I don't hate him, Chet. I just don't trust him—not where Stephen's concerned. I don't think Stephen's timing is coincidental, and I don't think he's running away. My guess is *Smith* is jealous of Stephen and did everything he could last night to undermine Stephen's confidence. Hopefully, Stephen can work it out himself, but if he can't, I suspect it will take Smith to rectify the damage. Anyone else could well spark another such escape attempt—and the next might not be so successful. —Just tell Cantrell to threaten Smith's *cujones* if he comes back without Stephen.''

"Will do, Lex." He nodded toward the door to his office. "Better get back to Mr. Ali."

"Gee, thanks," she said sourly, and left.

Anevai had much to be proud of in her friends and family. Following their early-morning conversation, the girl had set the wheels in motion for a party celebrating her brother's safe return, and the HuteNamid Recons' enthusiastic response created an almost overwhelming assault on the senses.

Dancers in vividly colored costumes, fringes, beaded and not, flying with their movements, elaborate headdresses and complicated masks, drums, chants, flutes, and songs—

And food. A seemingly endless array of dishes.

Even the weather had conspired for them, the sun finally breaking through the morning fog to warm the outside dinner-theater-in-the-round just in time for the festivities.

Throughout the performance, Anevai kept up a constant monologue of explanation, responding as clearly as she could to the questions flung at her from all points along the table full of *Cetacean* personnel. Only Cantrell knew the reason for the occasional glance toward the entrance, and the empty seat at Anevai's side.

Smith arrived late, hollow-eyed and sullen, and imbibed a mostly liquid meal, but he added his post-performance kudos to the others' and seemed normal enough when he joined Cantrell's group for drinks and coffee.

An impromptu dance class started down on the stage, but rapidly deteriorated into a free-for-all round dance, which had the classic symptoms of an all-nighter.

Anevai brought her a cup of coffee and perched on the table beside her.

Cantrell said conversationally, "Hobbes got the GeoPhys in on those core samples, and the imaging readings were at least marginally accurate this time. The Library appears to have caved in. The tunnel maze has, for certain. It'll take months to clear a path through—perhaps years, depending on the stability of the post-cave-in superstructure. Especially since we'll want to protect and catalog anything we find.''

''Well, at least it will keep Nayati from performing too much mischief while you're gone,'' Anevai said, valiantly joining the topic of conversation.

Cantrell smiled, and winked approval.

''We should be so lucky.'' Wesley Smith, slumped in a chair on the table's far side, swirled the whiskey around and around in his glass, assiduously avoiding everyone's eyes.

''Take it easy, Wes,'' Anevai said. ''It's not Nayati's fault. A lot of it is the Cocheta influencing him. When he realizes Hono is home and the *Cetacean* has gone, he'll come back. As soon as we can get him home, we can help him.''

''Yeah, right. Everybody needs help, don't they?'' He drained his glass and sent it skidding across the table into a half-full wineglass, tipping them both over, the red wine spreading like blood across the polished wood. ''We'd all be better off if he'd been caught in his own trap and was a pile of squished juices inside that mountain.''

''What's wrong, Wes?'' Anevai asked, shifting position to Smith's back to rub his shoulders. ''You got a headache?''

He shrugged. And again, more vigorously. Finally he pulled away and growled, ''Keep your hands to yourself, girl, and keep the fuck out of my business.''

Anevai took a startled backward step as he lurched to his feet and headed for the exit where he met TJ Briggs coming in. He tried to brush past, but Briggs stopped him with a hand on his arm.

''If you please, doctor,'' he said calmly, ''I have a message for you and the admiral.''

''From whom?''

''Stephen Ridenour.''

Smith swore violently, and jerked free.

''Leave, Smith,'' Cantrell told his back calmly, ''and you're under arrest.''

He whirled. ''What the hell for?''

"Behaving like an ass in public. —Where is he, Teej?"

"Not him. Just a message. Came across the security line. SciCompCB-1 is reserved for your convenience." He raised a critical brow at Smith and added, "I would advise that your convenience be right now. The lad does not look well."

Smith muttered, "Surprise, surprise."

"We'll be right there, Teej."

"Speak for yourself, Cantrell."

Setting the coffee cup on the table, she stood up and approached Smith, who, for all his bravado, seemed frozen in place.

"Don't push me, mister," she said coldly. "You won't like the results, I assure you."

"You've got no right, Cantrell," he said through his teeth.

"You'd be amazed at what my rights are." She turned and said, "Anevai, my dear, if you will extend our excuses to the others . . ."

"Of course, admiral," Anevai answered, her voice more controlled than her face. "Wesley, please—listen as well as talk?"

He scowled, hard, without facing her. "I said, stay out of it."

Anevai looked stunned and hurt.

Cantrell said, "Smith, you—are an ass. —Let's go."

iv

"I don't know what more I can tell you, admiral—" While embarrassment reddened Stephen's face and clenched his hands on the duffel in his lap, it was a cool, steady voice that made the report, beginning to end. *"Except—"* His eyes, the only real indication of the strain he was under, seemed to seek out Smith, who simply stared obstinately out the window as he had since entering conference room B-1. As if Stephen could see him, the Academy Clone image faltered, the flush deepened.

"—Except that I never dreamed that without the suit I would feel . . . What—what happened last night was, to say the least, unexpected. However, now that I'm forewarned, I believe there is a simple enough solution."

A bark of laughter from the window. Cantrell hit the *pause* on the recording as Smith spun around, his face angry red. "Cocky little bastard, aren't—" He froze, staring back at the mechanically frozen image, meeting Ridenour's strained expression. "Dammit!" And about-faced to the window.

Stephen had said once he needed to make Wesley want him to leave—had used that as his reason for remaining planetside the first time. Somehow, she didn't think this was quite what he'd intended.

"I've got to find Nayati. None of you has ever understood— only he does. And only he has managed to control this—thing. If I can't, I'm no good to anyone anyway. Possibly even a danger. Certainly a liability to your mission, admiral."

"At this point, I believe I can safely say I've revealed nothing of significance to the 'NetATs. My memory of the time with them is . . . uninterrupted, and since they evinced no curiosity regarding your mission, I didn't even find it necessary to prevaricate. As for my mission: Chet Hamilton has my report. All I could do, he can and more. If—if I go . . . catatonic . . . in the midst of my debriefing, it will compromise everything—both my credibility with the 'NetAT and your control of the Cocheta Libraries."

His eyes seemed to search the room.

"Please, Wesley, believe me, I don't know what you meant last night. If—if there's s–something Anevai should know—tell her. I can't."

The control faltered again: wide-eyed terror that searched the spartan cabin surrounding him, a whispered: *They're watching . . .* and another fight for mastery.

"Admiral, I must go. Please don't try to stop me this time. —Wesley, I— Goodbye. Tell Anevai—" A helpless shrug, a touch of the control panel, and his image was gone.

"Copy that," Cantrell ordered into the empty room, then: "What the *hell* did you do to him last night?"

He glanced at her over his shoulder. "Cameras out of focus, were they?"

For a moment, he was certain she was going to hit him, and held his breath: unequivocal pain would come as a relief after the past week. But she didn't. She only said softly, "Sometimes, I truly regret my official status. —I happen to trust Stephen to let me know what's important for me to know. He's earned that trust and more. You, on the other hand, I don't trust in the least."

Damned self-controlled bitch. He pushed again: "Well, fuck you. Fuck you, fuck your trust, and most of all, fuck that damned phony little tight-ass."

"Did you?"

'*Ask him!* I guarantee, the answer will be—entertaining. Not true, but undoubtedly colorful."

"I'm asking you, mister." She rose slowly to her feet and walked around the end of the table to face him squarely. His heartbeat quickened, but he raised his chin and stood his ground. "I want to know, Smith, what you did that tore that kid's guts out in one night." He drew a ragged breath, felt his control break, and tried to dodge her at last, but she gripped his arm, preventing him turning away, and spat in his ear, "What he said gave me no clue at all. As far as the intimate details go: *yes*, if the details are what caused this regression. On the other hand, I don't think it was anything physical at all, except in that your ability to reach him that way is very likely what makes your rejection of him now so devastating."

"You seem to think it's easy on me."

"I really don't much care, Smith. Frankly, from where I stand, young Ridenour is worth ten of you, regardless of this Cocheta *contamination* you both seem so worried about."

"Now wait just a damned— *Stephen* thinks he's got a Cocheta in his head. *I* think he's loonier than—"

"So you've indicated. And he, poor sod, believes you, too.

I'd hoped to take him back, help him through this thing personally, and get him settled and safe for life. I doubt there's a chance in hell now. I'll be surprised if his mind survives long enough to sign the official 'NetAT report. —*What happened?*''

He stared at the screen, wondering what this latest move was for. Wondering what more Ridenour had to gain . . .

. . . or perhaps *not* Ridenour.

"Who suggested you use that approach on me?" he asked.

"You're avoiding me, Smith."

"When I want to avoid you, I'll let you know. I'm—formulating my answer. When you first contacted me about coming to the ship, you went to great pains to set me up. Poor, frightened young graduate—never been planetside—you know the routine. You performed it well enough."

"You're pushing, Smith. —But go ahead and push. Victor Danislav did."

"Danislav." Curious. He'd have thought Beaubien. Perhaps internal alliances had shifted in the years since he'd left. "And Stephen is his. Has been since he was litter-trained. Maybe they really did discover what the SmitTee.Sys is capable of and just sent Stephen, all primed and perfect, ready to impress the hell out of me, in more ways than one."

"You're paranoid."

"Am I? Somehow, I don't think so. I'm a veteran, Cantrell. I can *smell* a trap a galaxy away. I've had a lifetime of small people catering to my every whim hoping to become big, important people. Hoping to control *me*—without success, I might add. —It's stuck in Danislav's craw for years that I didn't conform to his ideal—didn't become the perfect little Vandereaux grad-u-ate. You should see the shit he flags my way: all the accomplishments of his other protégés. Stephen must thrill him no end. Stephen could well be designed to lure me back into Victor's disgusting little realm."

"That's ridiculous."

"Think so? Why'd the kid start his thesis so early? And who suggested the topic? And who put it into his head to go into the crazed heading of Philosophies of the 'Net?"

"You answered that yourself when you first met him."

"Oh, no I didn't. *He* did. He had *all* the right answers. Don't you see it, woman? He's a setup. Not just for me. For all of us. It's all an act, a goddamned sick act designed to manipulate us into doing what he wants—correction: what his puppeteers want. I don't *like* setups, Cantrell. And if you're part of this one, I promise you, you'll fry with Stephen Ridenour and all the rest."

"Now I know you're crazy."

"If I am, *he* drove me there." He slumped into a chair. *"You* didn't see him last night. I thought he was dying right there in front of me."

"So why didn't you call in an emergency team there?"

"Because frankly, ma'am, at first it had all the appearances of a very natural, if somewhat energetic, biological function. I thought my techniques were just unusually effective—if you get my meaning. When it turned into convulsions, I somehow suspected something might just be wrong and believe it or not, had put in the alarm when he came out of it—*voilà*. So I cancelled the emergency." He was shaking, and he damnwell couldn't stop it, couldn't keep the horror from his voice, couldn't keep from living those moments all over again. "God, I've never been so terrified in my life." He rubbed his eyes, nearly blinding himself, the hand shook so badly. "You may not believe this, admiral, but I loved that boy—" And God help him, he still might. "—or thought I did. Now, I'm not sure what I feel. He's been feeding me a line since we met, and playing it like a master."

"You've known for a long time why he's here, Smith."

"I'm not talking about that. What the hell do you take me for? I was *waiting* for a Del d'Bug man. It's the misrepresentation. He *never* told me—not even after he was down here."

"Never had much of a chance, did he? My impression was your brief time together was quite lively—more than enough to make a bright, lonely boy lose track of protocol. And you were never alone—until after you knew. How can you blame him for that?"

He shook his head. "I don't think I ever did—not really. But with all the rest . . . You know that—problem—he has?"

"I think the lad has a number of them: one of which is sitting in front of me. To which are you referring?"

"That's a damned low blow, and one I don't deserve, admiral."

She raised an eyebrow. "Prove it."

"I'm referring to sex, admiral. You're familiar with the term?"

"Enough to know you're jerking me around, Smith. Just because the boy wanted to make love with a man he admired—"

"*Make love?* It was pure and simple sex, admiral. This . . . child . . . who was so terrified of being touched, was immersed in it—Hell, he was out in the goddam ozone with it!"

"A Universal address with which you, of course, are totally unfamiliar. *You,* of course, never intended any such experience for yourself."

He slammed his fist on the table. "*Damned* if I'll take that kind of crap from you or anyone else, Cantrell. I'd passed beyond that, long since; I *thought* in respect to him and his wishes. I allowed myself to love that creature as I swore I'd never love anyone." He leaned both hands on the table—not trusting his own balance. "And damned if I can figure how he managed it. He's scenic, but I've seen prettier. He's bright—but whether his true talents lie in 'NetTech, PsychTech, or between the sheets, damned if I can tell. He's a fucking chameleon. I thought I'd seen everything, but when he turns on that Zivon Look—you know the one—"

"Actually, no, I don't, Smith. And I spent a great deal of time and effort on the voyage here trying to draw Zivon Ryevanishov out."

"Maybe your bank account wasn't deep enough for him to waste it on you."

"And maybe you're the only one Zivon trusts enough to talk to."

"Well, I'll trade you the distinction anytime. That little child looks out of those opal eyes and all I want is to hold him and protect him against the universe—and the instant he's on the inside, he stabs you in the heart—'' He paused on a sudden thought and laughed bitterly. ''Or perhaps I should say 'Kicks you in the balls'—I spent all morning searching his files, and you know what I found? What he *knows* I found? *Why* he was so upset when he left? The *boy* is a bona fide whore, admiral. Vandereaux Academy's full of them. The boy has a problem with sex, all right. He's a damned sick animal, considering the crowd he's been—servicing. Well matched, I'd say.''

''You would.''

''You disagree? Check his records, admiral. Hospital claims the *boy* attempted suicide. Mind, they didn't put it on his official record. *That* might put a slur on Vandereaux—not to mention undermine Ridenour's . . . market value. I had to go through all the hospital write-ups, bed by bed, to find it.''

''How? What method did he use?''

''Have a morbid streak, do you? Suicide, hell. The boy's a junkie of the first order—a 'Doxie. I know those readings—saw no few of my contemporaries taken out with the stuff—it was brand new and exotic when I was there. Your boy OD'd on Eudoxin, not difficult to do when you eat like a flipping bird. Stuff rots your gut out.''

''Ever think there might be another explanation for that— report?''

''Give me a— The *boy* pops pills, Cantrell. *Expensive* pills. He got carried away with it. You know what those pills do? You want to know what *really* happened in his room last night? Have your Dr. McKenna check the *boy's* blood.''

''And endorse your fantasies?''

''It's not *my* fantasies in question. What if all that *bullshit* he threw out about Rostov and the Cocheta is nothing but a cover-up for an out-of-control libido? Do you really want the Council to trust a 'Doxie? Do you really want the 'NetAT to?''

''So warn them. Let *them* make the decision. Don't destroy the boy if you don't—''

''—have to? Maybe destroying him is the only real answer,

considering the magnitude of political favors—or blackmail—he has to draw on.''

''Now wait a minute. You're stretching—''

''Am I? Ever consider what he paid to whom to support that little habit?''

''You're the one with all the answers. —You tell me.''

''Goddam ignorant— Shapoorian, who else?''

''Not the only possibility.''

''Like hell. Open your eyes, woman. Look at his goddam clothes.''

That stopped her. ''His *what?* —What do his—''

He interrupted with a bark of laughter. ''Learn your own damn culture, SpecOp. —Where's a Recon-brat get money to dress like that? Top of the line all the way. And I can name you his tailor—*and* who else that tailor serves.''

''Such an accomplishment. The man can ID a—''

''Don't mock me, woman, you won't get anywhere. —The Look. Shapoorian all the way. No one would *dare* without sanction. I'm only disgusted it took me so long to figure—that damned blue coat—if he hadn't looked so much better in it than Mialla's current . . .''

''He wouldn't be the first person to—''

''It's the lies, admiral. The boy—'' He choked on the word. ''God, listen to us. 'Boy.' 'Child.' Damned, manipulative snake is no more a child than Nicolo Machiavelli was. —Shapoorian has been his meal ticket for years—why should we believe any of his accusations? I'm beginning to feel sorry for old Bijan.''

He paused to lower his blood pressure and Cantrell just sat. The bitch was more disturbing than Stephen's spook-eyes.

Finally, she stood up and said, ''You should have checked into rather more recent files, while you were snooping. Next time you want to remind yourself just how clever you are, check into McKenna's report on the boy's health. Do it this evening—I'll call Chet and tell him not to worry if he gets an alarm or two. It's my considered opinion that you've been a thorough-going ass and you owe that boy an explanation. Unfortunately, mister, words won't cure the damage you've done. Damage only you *could* have done. You say Stephen manipulates everyone around him. I agree. Absolutely. You say that proves we are wrong to perceive him as a child. You're wrong, Smith. Children don't know love or hate, but they damnwell recognize fear and pain and they manipulate everyone around them from the day they're born to eliminate that fear and pain. Eventually, they *learn* to love. But Stephen never got that chance. Not from his parents, not from Vandereaux, certainly not here.'' She made her way around the table to the door, tacit invitation for him to get the hell out. "One more thing, Smith. Would you call yourself a sensual person?''

"Not that it's any of your business, but, yes—quite.''

"And what about Stephen? Would you call *him* a—''

He snorted derisively.

"Very well, Smith. Think how you would act if you had held your instincts in check all your life, especially—'' She eyed him, a deliberately rude scan of his person. "—through puberty. All of a sudden, you are given— Let me rephrase that: you give yourself the right to feel good. Not only that, you're with someone you trust, who is something of a self-proclaimed expert in making people feel—good. —Wouldn't you have been flying a bit into the *ozone* yourself, Dr. Smith?''

He bit back a protest and hissed: "What the *hell* do you want of me, woman?''

An ever-so-faint smile touched her mouth. "I want you to go after him.''

A setup. "Hell if!'' It was a goddam *setup*. "You've got his signal. Go fetch.''

"I can't. None of my people can, and you know it. This is not the act of a rational man. If I force him back, he'll fry—total burnout—if he doesn't kill himself trying to get away.''

"So what?'' he said, out of his bitterness.

"Then you'll fry, too. I promise you that. Not all your daddy's money and influence will protect you."

"You can try."

"I can do more than that. *No* one's too big to disappear, Smith. The 'NetAT wants a body. Yours will do perfectly fine. If that boy's head is screwed, so are you. You go and find him. You make up with him and settle your differences or your ass is—"

"—pushing up daisies," he finished sourly, trapped and damned sick of the same old threats and promises. He'd heard them all before; no one ever succeeded.

"That, too."

Except it wasn't her threats that trapped him. It was himself. His gut-level conviction that she was right. That *only* he could get the boy back safely—crazy as he was now.

"We can track him—" Cantrell was saying. "—he's still got his beeper. We'll wire you—"

"Hell if." Nobody was shoving one of those things into *his* skull.

"Not permanently. I don't want *that* responsibility. Communications. So we can tell you where to go."

"Within limits."

"If I tell you to go to hell after that boy, you'd better do it or you'll damnwell wish you had."

V

"We're leaving as soon as Capt. Wilson finishes her preflight."

"Fine." Chet, with a blitheness he in no wise felt, smiled and sat back in his chair. Rissa frowned and said:

"You've no objection?"

"None I can voice officially. Unofficially, I can say I think you're overreacting."

"Overreacting? If half what Dr. Ridenour indicated is the truth, the local situation is entirely out of control. He claims he has the answers, now he's gone missing—and *your* commanding officer has prevented my people from tracking him down. Pardon me if we want our autonomy back."

"No need for apologies, Ris. If that's what you want—why, *go* back to ZG and sleeping in each other's armpit. Not *my* idea of a good time, but if that's what turns you on these days . . ."

She frowned and dropped her once-unshakeable gaze.

"Ris?" he asked carefully. "Are you all right? Herzog's not forcing this move on you, is he?"

"Of course not." Her grey eyes hardened. "He asked me to speak with you because of just such misapprehensions. You've made it quite obvious you don't care for him."

"I never said that."

"You wouldn't. I can tell, Chet. But you don't have to like him—or me, for that matter. You simply need to do your job."

"And that is?"

"We need a copy of Ridenour's report."

"Thought you might."

He reached into his desk and pulled out the memcube, tossed it casually across to her. She stared at it, a look of outrage crossing her face.

"You *dare*—"

"I don't dare not. Truth, Ris, —it's that dangerous."

The seal on the cube was a Combined Council hardlock it would require three Council members, the Head of Security, and the Head of the 'NetAT to unlock.

"And the person who wrote it is down there? Vulnerable to these—Recons?"

"Careful, Ris. You're background's showing. But, yes, he is. And safer there than at Vandereaux."

"Cantrell *is* holding him."

"Actually, no. I could almost wish she were. He's bolted, Ris. I don't know why, but I suspect your associate is behind it."

"We did our job, Ham."

"I'm sure you did."

She pocketed the cube, then sat tapping her fingers on the chair arm.

"We want Smith."

"Sorry. He's—unavailable."

"You're treading thin, Ham. I don't want to see this Cantrell's obsession destroy you."

He smiled. "I believe that, thanks. But it won't. The 'Net will be all right—*if* the Big Three use their heads. If they don't . . . if they don't, we'll all be looking for new jobs."

Her lips pursed. She seemed to be testing his statement from all angles, then: "If Ridenour is not released to us by tomorrow, we're leaving the system."

"Fair enough."

"We'll leave Daoud here for the time being. He's—adversely affected by the ZG."

He grinned. "I can identify with that."

Glowcubes, emergency rations, first-aid kit, fur-lined jacket . . . and a dozen king-size candy bars?

Anevai held up one of the bars, opened her mouth—

—and caught Wesley's silent appeal over the BioTech's head. Obviously, his personal addition to the emergency supplies. She swallowed laughter and tucked the bar back into its hideyhole in the pack.

From the evidence lying about the small airport lounge, Cantrell was taking no chances of losing Wesley in the trees. Bits of packaging littered the floor, their previous contents scattered about Wesley's person, the emergency pack, the fancy suit and helmet laid out on the bed . . .

"Why take the jacket, Wes? Isn't that suit you're wearing insulated?"

His lip lifted in a half-sneer. "It's the 'NetHead's. Bit-brain bolted without it. Probably freezing his skinny ass off even as we speak."

Stephen's? She frowned and pulled the jacket out for closer examination.

The tech patted a patch into place on Wesley's back, then glanced at her, a hint of blush in his cheeks. "If you please, miss . . ."

"Doing his lesser half?" Anevai grinned. "Go ahead. I'm immune."

The young man looked uncertainly at Wesley, who glowered at them both and demanded: "What the hell for?"

"B—Bios, sir."

"I know that! *Which fucking Bios?*"

"I—" The poor sod stepped backward. Out of range, Anevai suspected. "Cantrell's orders, s–sir."

Anevai laughed. "Trying to keep you in line, Smith."

"Hell if! Tell Cantrell she can stick her patch—"

"Please, sir, it's the primary transmitter. It will allow us to locate you regardless what happens to the rest of the equipment. Can't risk you losing it, and the buttock is the easiest location to insert and remove, and—"

"*All right.* All fucking right." Wesley glared and, without so much as turning his back them, calmly shucked his pants.

The tech, bright red now, took an arcane instrument from his bag. "If you'll kindly lean over, sir."

"Yeah, yeah." Wesley propped his elbows on the couch armrest and fingered the coat lying in her lap, smoothing the fur collar.

She asked idly: "Isn't this the coat Tanika just finished for—"

"*Ouch!*" He glared over his shoulder at the tech, who shrugged an apology. And back to her. "Yeah." His tone did not invite further investigation, which attitude made her next question obligatory.

"The one you've had on order for nine months . . ."

His hand tightened in the fur. "Let it ride, Anevai."

"You can stand up now, sir. Thank you, sir," the tech said softly, and a second tech began backup check of his partner's handiwork.

"Wesley," she asked, "what's wrong? What *happened* between you two last night?"

"I told you before, Anevai—" Wesley scowled at her over the tech's head. "—stay out of it. This is between Ridenour and me."

"I want to go with you." Anevai drew her feet up and propped crossed arms on her knees.

"We can't always have what we want," Wesley answered shortly, and swore roundly as the tech got a little too personal with the tape.

"Sorry, sir," the tech said sweetly, "but we don't want to lose you," and ripped the tape loose to reset it.

"Dammit!" he yelled, and chased the techs out. "You can finish *later*."

He pulled his pants up and buttoned his shirt. "Damned, cold-fingered—what the *hell* do they need all this shit for, anyway?"

"You weren't listening, Wesley. They're to monitor your bodily functions. Tommy explained it all." Anevai unfolded from the couch and straightened his collar, tapping the various hidden patches. "These are for mental activity, this heartrate, this—"

"Yeah, yeah—they want to know every time I take a leak. Why the hell are you here?"

"You asked me."

"Oh. Right."

He settled into a chair, squirming uneasily; either the patches were itching, or what he wanted to say wasn't cooperating. "Listen, Anevai. This is no good. You've got to forget Ridenour. Let him *go*."

"I don't want to. He's—"

"A goddam nut case! Get it through your head, girl, *that's* what you're dealing with. Remember that stuff he took?"

"Stuff?"

"Yeah. You know. That—time—in the cave."

"You mean before we made love?"

"Yeah, right. You ever hear of Eudoxin?"

From the way he said it, he expected her to say no. He at least expected to shock her.

Well, she had and he hadn't.

"So what?"

He made her sit down. "Anevai, *that's* what he took. *That's* why you're pregnant, and it's hell on the fetus. Causes premature ovulation, and goes haywire from there."

She shrugged. "McKenna already warned us, but we'd been monitoring it anyway." She patted her stomach. "The little parasite's been rather more irritating than normal—not exactly surprising, considering what its host has been through—but so far, it appears perfectly all right, genetically speaking. We'll keep an eye on it, and if it's not, we'll take care of it."

"Why take the risk? Why the *hell* would you want it?"

"Because he's got good bone structure," she said flippantly, resentful of Wesley's attitude.

He swore and inhaled.

"And because I respect him, Wesley," she continued, obstructing his diatribe. "I respect his intelligence, his gentleness, his bravery and his honesty, as well as his obvious physical attributes. I hope to see some of that in his child." She lowered her chin, narrowed her eyes. "Correction: our child." And to his openmouthed silence: "You get him back safe, Smith, or don't bother coming back at all."

Chew on that awhile, Smith, she thought, and waltzed out the door.

Before the door closed on Anevai's retreat, two women in *Cetacean* teal stepped inside.

"Dr. Smith?" The smaller one held out her hand. "Lt. Phillips. I'll be your comTech in MobilCom III. This is Lt. Gravin. She's the pilot."

"Yeah, whaddaya want?" He refused the hand, not in the least inclined toward chatty at the moment.

The hand dropped. "We're here to review the hounder suit with you. —Put it on, please."

He glared.

"If you require help, please say so now. —We're on a tight schedule."

Swearing under his breath, he picked up the heavy pants.

"Forgive me, *sir*, but the suit goes over bare skin. That's how it monitors your body temperature."

He pressed his lips together and, staring her defiantly in the face, stripped down and pulled the bloody things on.

"Thank you, sir," she said, poker-faced. "The suit will automatically regulate your body temperature to 310.15K. You can reset the baseline temperature to personal preference and control most other suit functions—" She tapped a slim, flexible box on the wide cuff. "—here. This also contains a variety of useful time-passers—vid games, relaxation programs, and the like. Not something you're likely to need."

"Damnwell better not," he muttered.

"The fabric wicks moisture. Perspiration should not be a problem. If it is, adjust the temperature setting."

"And other...bodily fluids?" he asked, ostentatiously delicate.

"Dr. Smith, you can piss in your pants, if you're so inclined. Otherwise, I'd suggest you drop 'em. —Helmet." She handed it to him, settled it properly, and took a remote out of her pocket. "Admiral Cantrell wants us to approach Dr. Ridenour carefully—which means you'll have to approach him on foot. We'll be able to direct you from the MoblCom. However, if Dr. Ridenour passes from *Cetacean* visual, we can still track him using the suit's hounder. —Hand."

"Yes, —*sir!*" He snapped his hand out, at arm's length, palm up.

"Thank you." She held her own in front of it and adjusted something on the remote. "All right. Look around the room, then slowly turn toward me."

He swung around on his heel;a bright green light flared on the visor.

"Shit!"

"I told you: slowly. Adjust the intensity of the HUD on the wrist control to whatever you prefer."

"You could have said something," he grumbled.

"Do you hear anything?"

"Stupid question, Phillips. If I couldn't hear, I wouldn't answer, now would I?"

"I think you know enough. That HUD will lead you to him, once the unit is adjusted to his scent."

Wesley was busily punching buttons on the wrist control. "What are all these graphics? —Look like Bios."

"They probably are, then. Yours are red. Your quarry's, such as the hounder can read, will be green."

He punched another button. "What's—"

"Never mind, doctor. You know what you'll need. —Except, this suit is more valuable than a luxury condo on Vandereaux CapStat. I suggest you treat it accordingly."

"Golly gee, teach, I'll take half a dozen. What colors do they come in?"

"Five minutes to liftoff, Dr. Smith."

"Why are you here, Zivon Stefanovitch?"

Stephen spun on his heels, lost his balance and fell, half in and half out of the stream, the shaking handful of water he'd laboriously raised to his lips spattering his face.

"Nayati." He identified the shadow in the woods from voice alone, as the world spun around him. He'd not eaten since last night's disastrous dinner, a physical state not, in his experience, conducive to clear thinking. Closing his eyes, he waited for the buzz in his ears to end, then picked himself out of the stream and brushed at water-soaked slacks, swearing softly through chattering teeth.

"So. We know one another." Nayati stepped into the single shaft of sunlight. Fading bruises, arm in a sling, hint of unevenness in his step: Nayati had not escaped from the Library caves unscathed. "I ask again: why are you here?"

Stephen answered without a moment's hesitation. "To find out who—and what—I am."

"Why come to me?"

"Who else is there? What you did to me—what Stefan Ryevanishov did—that's *what* I am. He's—unavailable. You are not. Will you help me?"

"To do what?"

"Understand what I am."

"Is that all?"

"And control it."

"Surely you realize, I *wanted* you out of control?"

"Did you?"

"What makes you think otherwise?"

He didn't think. He knew. "Anevai said you were curious about my reactions. That you were testing me. I—I want to complete that test."

"The Library is gone. The machine is buried. I can't change that."

"That machine isn't necessary—not once contact has been established. You know that as well as I."

"Do I?"

"Dammit! *Yes!*"

"No longer." There was a bitterness, a longing, and a monumental resentment in the man's voice.

"Nayati? What's wrong? Are you—"

"Dead, Zivon Stefanovich. And you are my executioner."

The annoying lightness in his head increased, and Stephen sank to the ground before he fell.

"Nayati, I don't understand. Are you a ghost, then?"

"I'm not amused."

"I—I didn't mean it h–humorously. I think I could believe in ghosts—today." He squinted up at him. "But I don't think a ghost would limp, so I think, maybe, you're real."

Nayati's bitter laugh held a touch of amusement, which gave Stephen some hope, but:

"Go home, Zivon Stefanovich. You're not wanted here."

"I can't," Stephen answered simply. "I'm not Zivon Stefanovich—any more than I'm Stephen Ridenour. I want to know *who* I am, and *you've* got to help me."

"Why?"

"There's no one else."

"There's not me, either. One more chance, Ridenour." Nayati took a threatening step forward, his good hand reaching for the knife at his belt. "Go home."

Stephen didn't move, which seemingly flabbergasted Nayati.

"I could kill you, you know," Nayati said belligerently.

"Yes, you could."

"Cantrell's hounds have deserted you."

"Some time ago. Were you following that long? Or did your Cocheta tell—"

"The Cocheta have died—and taken me with them."

"Have they?" Stephen challenged his morbidity. "I don't think so."

"They speak no longer. Their—tongue has been cut out."

"They spoke for me—last night."

"You're lying, Ridenour."

Stephen felt like laughing. "I wish to God I were. Don't you see, Nayati? The 'Net is going mad—possibly unravelling from the changes *you* made, when you took the researchers off the 'Net. I know that danger exists, and somehow, I've got to go back to convince the 'NetAT. But I can't convince *anyone* of *anything* until this—*thing* is under control. *Will you help me?*"

"I cannot."

Nayati's cold dismissal washed through him, easing his growing panic. "Why not?"

"I'm blind, deaf, and dumb, and it's all your fault. They're gone. Dead." Nayati's remote composure wavered. His voice grew more human, more like the defiant—and bitter—young man Stephen had seen in the Cocheta Library just before the cave-in. "If they still spoke, do you think I'd be here? Do you think I'd be *anywhere* but with them? You challenged them, denied their voice, and when you—you, who Sakiimagan called *the one*—brought the spacer to the Library, you profaned their home.''

Bitterness Stephen understood—as he understood the hurt and aloneness it masked. ''I'm not any *one*. I have no idea what Sakiimagan referred to, but the Cocheta *is* alive, Nayati. It's in me. As yours is in you. *You* learned—teach me the same way. *Help* me. Help us both.''

Nayati stared at him, narrow-eyed, not yet trusting, not running away, either. ''How did you find me, Zivon Stefanovich?''

''I—I don't know. I was on the way to Acoma. Blacked out. Then there was a trail, a broken bridge...*I don't know, Nayati.*''

''You still got the beeper in your skull?''

''I—'' This could make or break his chances with Nayati. But to lie would destroy them for certain. ''As far as I know.''

Nayati scowled, and disappeared into the woods.

vi

''I've lost the signal.''

The pilot of the small craft ignored him. So did the comTech. Wesley hated being ignored. ''Dammit, I said—''

''I heard you, Dr. Smith. Please, be patient.''

Wesley hated 'just because' civility almost as much as being ignored. He grabbed the commer's arm. ''Have *you* got him?''

An iron grip closed on his wrist, forcing him to let go: the pilot.

The commer retrieved her arm with a firm: ''I said, be patient,'' and turned back to her instruments.

Translation: she'd lost him, too.

''Leave me here.''

''I can't do that.''

''Dammit, I've got tracks here. All you've got is a fix on where he *maybe* is. If they've ducked into a Cocheta tunnel or cave, we've got *nothing*. I *know* he was here. Let me the fuck out."

"Gladly," the pilot said, speaking for the first time. She set the hovering craft down in a clearing, pushed a button that unsealed the side door. "Shove him out, Phil."

'Phil' raised a brow. "At least she landed first." She pointed to a monitor display: trees, bushes, a distinctive rock or two. "There's your pickup point. Be careful, Smith. We'll keep in touch from here."

Wesley growled an answer and crawled out, shaking feeling into cramped muscle, and settling the incredibly fashionable helmet they'd forced onto his head more comfortably.

Phil's voice asked into his ear: *"Can you see his tracks?"*

"Hold your fucking—" He went to the spot she'd indicated and knelt down, holding a gloved hand near a single, clear-edged track. "Here you go. Get your fix, and hurry it up."

Moments later, a green light flashed on the HUD—

—and a shrill whine deafened him.

"God damn it!" Wesley clamped a hand ineffectually to where his ear should be, encountering the helmet's pad instead.

"So sorry, Dr. Smith."

The whine relaxed to a relatively pleasant *ping*.

"Asshole," he muttered, and headed down the trail, rechecking the fix with every few steps. He couldn't believe he'd let himself get talked into this farce. If Ridenour would ever stay put—

"Message received from the ship."

"Do I care?"

"Ask me when you do."

God damned, smart-mouthed . . . "What's the fucking message?"

"I'm sorry. I didn't quite copy that."

"If you please, kind lady, *what's the fucking message?*"

"That's better. Ridenour was in visual a few minutes ago. In the company of a second individual. Recon, by appearance."

Shit. Suddenly, the farce assumed decidedly tragic overtones.

He asked, far more seriously, "ID?"

"None yet."

Double shit.

"Altercation?"

"None reported."

"Thank God for small favors. —Tell your info-jockeys to try a match with Nayati Hatawa. Vid file in my personals—password—" Shit, what was it this week? —P. —Q. —R. "—Sybaris, I hope."

"I'll do that, sir."

"Sir. I like that, Phil-baby. But I'll settle for Wes."

A low chuckle in his ear. *"Want a lift to the sighting, Wes?"*

Tempting, but he was dealing with at least one crazy—maybe two. "How far is it?"

"Ten minutes at your present pace."

He sighed. "I'll pick it up."

Holes hid in the blackness underfoot, lying in wait for an unwary foot.

"Nayati!" Stephen gasped and picked himself off the ground. Again. "Nayati, please wait."

He stumbled after the only light in the tunnel—Nayati's tiny flashlight—relieved when it stopped and waited for him to catch up.

"No, wait." When Nayati started immediately. "P–please."

He leaned against the tunnel wall, panting, one hand braced on his knee, the other rubbing the whirling lights from his vision.

"What's wrong, spacer?" Nayati asked, his voice heavy with scorn.

"Soft. Out of shape, is that what you want to hear?" Stephen said on a gasp, and stared as straightly as possible through the watery haze covering his eyes. "Well, I won't deny it. There are also the small matters of sleep and food and the water your arrival cheated me out of. —But I'll manage. Just give me a damn minute to catch my breath.''

Nayati grinned, drew a deep breath of his own. "You didn't mention one other small matter: I've been pushing." And he sank down onto a stony seat, light from the small flashlight scanning Stephen from head to foot. "You're okay, Ridenour."

"I've been trying to tell you that," he said, a touch sourly, and sank to the floor, propping his back against the wall. "I thought you said the Cocheta tunnels were lost."

"What makes you think this is Cocheta-made?"

Stephen just raised an eyebrow at Nayati, who knew damned well the *feel* of a Cocheta tunnel.

Nayati's mouth twitched. "Fair enough. They *are* lost. Or inert. This is a minor tributary. I'm hoping it's silenced your beeper."

"Where are we going?"

"*We* aren't. I'm going to leave you here—"

Stephen tried to hide his involuntary shudder, but not soon enough to keep Nayati from noticing.

"Don't worry, spacer-man. Not here, precisely. Near the— exit, if you will. If you want them to pick you up, step outside. They'll hear your beeper and come. If you don't, wait for me to return."

"Why must you go? Where?"

"You said you wanted my help. To learn the way I did. I'm going to give you the only kind I know. The kind my father gave me."

"Your father? I thought he was gone. . . ."

"Gone. Not dead. Before he left, when I was a child, he taught me about the old ways. The Ways of the Sun Dance and Medicine Wheel—the Way of the Vision Quest and Reflections in the World. I'm going to help you See. At least—" His head dropped, long black hair a curtain on his expression. "—I'm going to try."

That had an ominous ring to it. Stephen fought the instinct to run. "Nayati, your father—"

"Don't say it." Nayati stood up. "My father *knows* the answers. Has found them. I still search. I will give you what I know. The rest—to follow or not—is up to you. Only you can find the courage to see yourself as you truly are. This is the only Answer I know to give, Stephen Ridenour. Until you can do that, you can't control yourself. And if you can't control yourself, you certainly can't control your Cocheta."

Stephen stared up at him. "And what about you, Nayati? Do you—control your Cocheta?"

Nayati frowned, and turned on his heel, heading into the darkness, taking the only light with him.

Rocks. Lots of very large rocks and budding, tangled bushes. And Stevie's little green light disappeared right into them.

Wesley pushed through, came to the blackness of a small opening into the mountainside itself.

"I'm at a tunnel, Phil." Wesley tapped a button on his helmet light, and a halo of light surrounded him. "Glory be," he muttered, "I'm an angel."

"Not bloody likely, Smith," Phil's voice whispered in his ear. *"You're sure that's where they went?"*

"So my little green friend claims."

"I don't like the way his signal just quit."

"Way of the Cocheta, woman. What'er my odds you lose my lovely heartbeat the instant I walk inside?"

"That why it's double-timing?"

"See right through me, don't you?"

"At the moment. Listen. Step inside. If we don't copy, get the hell back out."

"I can tell you right now, I'm gone, missy. Any last sweet-nothings?"

"Smith, you don't have to do this. Cantrell—".

"Will have my ass for dinner if I come back without the brat." And Anevai would flambé whatever was left. "Hang in there, Phil-baby. I'll buzz when I can. TTFN."

* * *

Nayati had not, as Stephen had feared he might, left him alone in these blacker-than-space tunnels. He was fully capable of doing so, had, in fact, once before. They'd walked in silence for a time, when:

"We're being followed," Stephen whispered, for all their shadow was nowhere near them—

—Yet.

"How do you know?"

"I feel it."

Nayati frowned. "Damn you, Ridenour, if you're lying to me . . ."

Stephen just looked at him. Nothing he could say would convince Nayati. He either believed, or he did not.

"Let's move it," Nayati said, and ran.

Stephen followed close on Nayati's heels, focussing down on those fringed moccasins, denying his own exhaustion, intent on avoiding pursuit, registering nothing but that fringe.

His senses dimmed . . .

Awareness.

He skidded to a halt.

Dim registration of Nayati's protest as he headed back the way they'd come, stopped, and groped into a rocky crevice.

A glow; not from Nayati's direction, but back the way they'd come.

Nayati's protest faded and died.

Stephen slumped to the ground; his arm trailing across sharp-edged stone.

A warmth of blood along his palm.

Nayati's hand on his shoulder.

"Let me see it."

He held out his arm mutely. The light fabric was torn and bloodied. Nayati ran the light over it. Probed silently at a long, shallow scratch running the length of his arm, cut off at Wesley's bandage.

"Not bad. —Hold this." Nayati thrust the flashlight into his hand.

A piece of his own sleeve ripped free and pressed to the arm covered the wound; a wide length of soft leather from Nayati's waist held the edges together and the piece of shirt in place. Complex process, deftly performed.

A process he saw quite clearly.

Light—beyond Nayati's pocket flash. Cocheta glow from the surrounding rock formations, ghostly presences in the diffuse light.

"Looks like you were right, Ridenour," Nayati said quietly. "They still live. —For you."

He rubbed a hand across his eyes, shaking, and he didn't know why, except that he was cold, hungry, and had no idea what his hands had just done.

Nayati helped him silently to his feet. In the light of that spirit-glow, what had been tunnel, was now solid stone, and they could proceed at a more sedate pace, pursuit, at least momentarily, thwarted.

Dead end. Deader than dead. Angel-glow bounced off nothing but stone—except behind him, thank God.

"Goddamitalltohell," Wesley muttered into his unresponsive helmet com.

He ran his hand along the solid stone face, searching for optically hidden crevices, hoping against hope for one of the Cocheta control panels, wondering what he'd do with it if he found it. Anevai had always accompanied him into the tunnels. She had handled the Doors.

Nothing.

He stepped back, scanning the area again, receiving green only in the direction of the blank stone face. The hounder figured Stephen had walked through that wall. Not impossible in a Cocheta tunnel.

On the other hand, what if they'd turned around? Would that register on the little green light? Damned gizmo should include a help screen.

He'd been so damned certain he heard voices—but by the

time he figured how to augment the audio pickup, there'd been nothing.

"Where are you when I need you, Phil?" he asked into the ozone and headed back down the tunnel, looking for alternate branches, looking for other green lights. Looking for any sign at all that Stephen Ridenour had taken another route.

"So help me, clone," he muttered, "when I find you, you'd better be alive . . ." He stumbled on an unseen rock, twisting his knee. ". . . because when I do—and that is a *when*, I promise you—*I'm* going to take you apart, bit by bit, byte by . . ."

"Admiral?"

Cantrell set the GeoPhys report on a sidetable and forced herself out of the comfortable couch to the security com on the far side of the room. She tapped the release:

"Cantrell, here."

"Have a relay from MoblCom III. Will you accept?"

"Go ahead."

A slight delay while they set up the relay codes. Cantrell pulled the drape back from the window to look out at the rift. Strange. It was dark outside. Not black, but—

"Admiral? Lt. Phillips. We've lost contact with Smith."

Their worst fears realized. "Go into a tunnel, did he?" she asked.

"Yessir." The lieutenant's voice sounded decidedly relieved. Likely figured she'd be blamed for the loss.

"How long?"

"An hour, sir. —I cleared with Mr. Hamilton before letting him proceed. —That's not the problem."

"Please be brief, lieutenant."

"Aye, sir. —We've weather coming in—bad weather. In another hour, we'll be grounded. I don't like the position we're in, should gusts reach the predicted levels. Dr. Smith expects us to be here. If he should find Dr. Ridenour—"

"Just a moment, lieutenant."

Cantrell tapped a rem-finger key, called up a schematic on the monitor across the room, got the relative positions of the lieutenant's vehicle and Smith's last transmission.

"Has Smith got an emergency pack?"

"Yessir."

"Weather comes in, he's not going anywhere anyway, lieutenant. He's got nature's own climate control in those caves—he won't freeze. Find a safety and batten down for a blow."

"Yessir. Thank you, sir. —Sir?"

"Yes, lieutenant?"

"Sure wish I knew where this came from."

"Planetary weather, free style, lieutenant. Keeps you on your toes."

"Yessir. I understand, sir. I was raised on Vandereaux, sir."

"Sorry."

"Thank you, sir. But this—there was no warning. Should have been some *indication of a front this size building. I don't like it, sir."*

And this wasn't the first strange effect they'd registered on this planet. Signals disappearing, or dancing around the planet like ghosts, rock disappearing and reforming on command, now inexplicable weather patterns. Nayati Hatawa's gods? Or the Cocheta's mechanical safeguards Paul Corlaney once mentioned?

In either case, *she'd* call it aliens with an attitude, or a damned dangerous sense of humor.

"Good point, lieutenant. —If you can't find a haven you're absolutely certain of, get the hell back to the field. Smith's not stupid. As soon as he's out, we can contact him, explain what's coming down on his head and he can wait it out in the tunnel. We know where he is. We'll get him out."

"Yessir. He won't like it, sir."

"I didn't ask him to like it. —Cantrell, out."

"Yessir. MoblComIII out."

vii

Snow swirled outside the window. Anevai pulled the blanket higher under her chin, thinking of that jacket left flattened on the transport seat, now stored in Wesley's pack.

Stephen must be freezing.

Unless Wesley had found him.

Or if he wasn't already dead.

It wasn't fair. Stuck here in her mother's home, refused any link to Wesley, Stephen or Cantrell . . .

Cantrell wasn't speaking to her. The admiral had been furious when she'd found her in Wesley's makeshift dressing room at the airport, had insisted she go home and insisted it was for her own good. Her mother sided with Cantrell, saying her hormones had her head in an uproar, what with the baby and all, and given her a mild sedative. Her father was too busy with Hononomii to care one way or the other, Paul Corlaney had returned to SciComp, and her grandparents, her usual source of sanity when parents went parental on her, were on their way home to Acoma in case Stephen tried to go there.

Which he might. He liked Mom's folks—everybody did. They were wise, and calm, and even *they* had left a message for her claiming the kindest thing she could do for Stephen Ridenour was taking care of the little piece of him growing in her belly.

Maybe they were right, but it *couldn't* be psychologically healthy, for her *or* the little parasite, to sit here wondering. If Wesley had found Stephen, there was no telling what he'd do. Wesley's 'reality' tended toward—mercurial—and highly contingent upon his current perception of salient (and sometimes irrelevant) 'facts.' Considering his attitude just before he'd left, Cantrell's sending him out there unchaperoned to deal with an innocent bit-brain like Stephen could have disastrous results.

And not necessarily to Stephen.

Something Major had happened between the morning Wesley

had given Stephen a favored coat and the next. Something that made Stephen leave a message and bolt.

He'd arrived here. Met with the 'NetAT agents. Had dinner with Wesley. . . .

She yawned.

But he'd *wanted* to make that 'NetAT report. He wouldn't arbitrarily sacrifice that. He must have covered *Harmonies* and Wesley somehow. . . .

Another jaw-cracking yawn: Mom's blasted sedative.

The flurry of snowflakes thickened. Strange, looked like a real blow building up. *Very* strange for this time of year. Especially for a front reportedly on its way through this afternoon. . . .

"Nayati?" Stephen clamped his jaw to keep his teeth from chattering.

Nayati paused immediately.

"You need a rest?"

"N—no. I just— Is it m—my imagin—nation, or is it g—getting c—colder?"

Nayati nodded. "We're nearing the other side. From the feel, the weather's changing. Time to decide, Ridenour. You want Cantrell's goons to come after you?"

Stephen shook his head, wrapping his arms around himself, trying to preserve the last spark of body heat, relieved it *was* temperature and not some delayed shock. Inclined, after recent events, to mistrust all sensory input. "I s—stay here, right?"

"Gods." Nayati pulled off his fringed jacket and threw it around his shoulders.

"Th—thanks," Stephen muttered, burrowing into the fur-lined warmth while he had the chance.

"Don't get used to it. You only get it long enough to stop the chill," Nayati said sourly. "If you were going to make a run for it, the least you could have done is worn a coat."

Stephen shrugged, thinking of the coat much like this one on its way to Acoma and beyond. "Sorry."

Nayati stared at him, then started to laugh. But it wasn't a cruel laugh. It sounded more like honest amusement.

"You're crazy, Ridenour, do you know that?"

"So I've been told."

Another bark of laughter faded abruptly, and as if on a second thought, Nayati asked curiously, "And do you believe it?"

Stephen shrugged again. "My opinion is—marginally relevant. Since most people treat me as if I am, I suppose I am. . . . At least as far as they are concerned."

"Interesting." Nayati answered slowly, and with greater energy: "All right, listen up. I'm going to go to—a special place. That's why I don't want you there. It's *my* place, my—holy place, if you will—and I don't want Cantrell's hounds knowing where it is. You either, for that matter."

"All right." Stephen could understand that. He'd had his places, too. Places of refuge for the body—and the spirit, though his tended to gymnasium storage closets, academy station having little in the way of privacy. "And I wait here?" He verified again, his weary brain's RealTime stability counting on that one given.

"That's right. —I need to pick up some—things. Things that will help you on your journey."

Stephen bit his lip. Not certain if it was his head or his hearing that was fuzzy. "Journey? Where am I going?"

"Dammit." Nayati rubbed his head as if his thinking, too, needed clearing. "Look, Ridenour, I'm no Teacher—not even a good Storyteller. I don't—"

Nayati scanned the floor around them, brushed an area clear with his foot, and began selecting stones and setting them in a pattern on the stone floor, muttering all the while about colors and directions and power, none of which made any sense at all. Then: "Sit."

"Why—"

"*Sit!*" And when Stephen had settled with his back pressed into cold stone: "Remember your answer to my question?"

"Which?"

"Damn you, *think*. We're not playing twenty questions. Your sanity."

"S–sorry." He rubbed his aching temples, trying to cooperate. "Yes, I remember."

"Well, you were more right than you could possibly have realized. We are what people think we— Shit, no, that's not— People are mirrors—"

"M–mirrors?"

Nayati scowled. "Yes, dammit, mirrors! *All* things in nature are Mirrors. People, flowers—*any* object, for that matter. Places, animals, stories. Every Mirror sees something different in every other Mirror. *What* the Mirror is, is the sum total of all its reflections."

"Then what I am is what everyone else *sees* in me?"

"That's only part of you. You are also how you see them and how you see yourself— And not just people. —Look at the stones. What do you see?"

"Rocks. All about the same size, in concentric circles."

"It's a *wheel*, fool." Nayati jerked to his feet, paced the claustrophobic cave. "This isn't going to work. You *can't* understand. Not in five minutes, not in five *years*."

"I can try, Nayati. I'd do better if you'd—*see* me as I am, not as you would like me to be."

Nayati frowned over his shoulder. "What's that supposed to mean?"

"I'm no fool, Nayati. And I'm not stupid. And I *want* to understand. *Need* to. Now. Doesn't that count for something? Will you please just try to explain?"

For a moment, all he could see was Nayati's back, his black hair hanging free below his leather-covered shoulder blades. Then, in a surly voice, Nayati repeated his earlier question:

"How *did* you find me?"

"I don't—" Stephen began, frustrated.

"Dammit, *tell* me."

"I'm *trying*. I . . . phased out. I wanted to find you. I did. That's *all* I know."

"Why did you want to find me? For a cure?"

"I don't want to go crazy. I want to know what happened to me."

"Perhaps nothing happened."

"Perhaps you are trying to drive me over the edge—finish the job you started. In either case, I want to finish the journey, once and for all."

Nayati's shoulders heaved, and he was a face again, crouching on the far side of the 'wheel.'

"I don't like it, Ridenour. I don't like you, I don't want to work with you. But the Cocheta meant you to find me; otherwise, you would not have. They *want* you to know the Way, at least for you to try. They may even, possibly, want to guide you. It's just as likely they'll drive you over the edge. But you want to know, they want you to know, therefore you listen, and you listen well. —This—" He indicated the ground with his chin. "—is the key to your journey, the vehicle upon which you will travel. It's called a Medicine Wheel."

"And each of those stones represents a Mirror?" Stephen asked, focussing on the concepts, ignoring the tone and the attitude as years at the academy had taught him he must if he was to learn.

Nayati nodded, an abrupt dip of his chin. "Or another Wheel."

"We're talking like . . ." Stephen searched for a common referent. ". . . an infinite regression of Wheels?"

A moment's consideration. A reluctant nod. "Close enough—I hope. The point is, you can't understand yourself until you understand your Place within the Whole which is the Dance of the Sun, which is the universal Medicine Wheel. Making that personal Wheel whole, and learning that Place, is what the Vision Quest is all about."

"A–and that Vision Quest—that's the journey you were talking about?"

"In part. —HuteNamid." Nayati said the name almost reverently. "SunDancer. I've always wondered if the first Council realized the importance of the Name. I doubt it. So much of what they did was without conscious wisdom. —But it was predestined. That's what you must understand, Zivon Stefanovich."

"Don't call me that, Nayati. I'm not—"

"But you are and you must be that person again. It was Zivon Stefanovich the Rostov Cocheta first Touched. He became the person you are now, which is the person the HuteNamid Cocheta chose for the Touching."

Stephen interrupted, chancing Nayati was more sane now than he'd seemed before. "Are you *sure* the Rostov aliens and yours are not one and the same?"

"Can a god desert its *raison d'être?*"

"I don't understand."

"Its reason for being, 'Nethead."

"But the Cocheta aren't gods. They made RealSpace machines."

"They are the spirits within the earth, with power to control the planet, and they refrain from using that power save in instances of perceived threat. To me, that makes them gods."

"But—" Stephen bit his lip. "Okay. I—I can accept that. Then the Rostov invisibles . . . primed me, so to speak, for what you did?"

"The Cocheta, the academy professors, your parents, Anevai and Smith—they all went into making you what you are now, which is the seed of the person you will be, the person the Cocheta will—or will not—speak to again. And you are simply reflections of the World around you. It's those *reflections* you seek—as well as your reflection within your personal Mirror."

"Nayati, please." It was making no sense—and it must. If Nayati was insane, there could be no hope for him. "I don't understand."

"Then *leave*." Nayati jerked to his feet and pointed down the tunnel. "Go out there and call Cantrell's people. They will take you and protect your body. But they will *never* welcome you as the Cocheta have chosen to, never protect your spirit. *That*," he pointed back into the heart of the tunnel, "is proof of their generosity."

"What proof? Cantrell's posse? or the Cocheta blockade? Whose generosity?"

"Take your pick." Nayati dropped back down, studying him intently across the stone pattern, excitement and reverence growing in his voice and expression. "Don't you understand, Ridenour? The Old Ones were right, just without all the facts. Within the Universal Wheel, most mirrors are whole—complete. Animals, clouds, rocks: they all know their natures and reflect pure Truth. Like all Things, each Cocheta is a unique Medicine Wheel, a creature of pure energy, alive and aware, infinite in power and knowledge, but like a Human Being, incomplete. Unlike a Human Being, that lack is specific: Body and Heart, without which they cannot touch the Real World, and without touching there cannot be Total Understanding. Only knowledge without wisdom, and both of those without feeling. And they're *lonely*, Ridenour. As we are lonely. That's *why* they choose us. We are their touch. That's *why* we can't desert them."

"I—" Stephen chewed his lip, afraid to voice a comprehension he might not have. Too much depended on it, and Nayati's words echoed too closely those he'd said to Wesley just last night for complete objectivity. "So the Cocheta are—incomplete mirrors, and humans provide the missing pieces."

Nayati lifted his chin in a quick acknowledgement.

"You also say, they need bodies—that we provide the touching."

"Not just a physical touch, Ridenour. It's more—and less."

"But if the Cocheta talk only to your People, and not to researchers, not just any human can . . . accept just any Cocheta. Right?"

"You must be right for each other."

"Like missing psychological pieces?"

"You're trying to analyze the process, Ridenour, and you can't. You do or you do not understand. You will or you will not, once you begin your journey. Last chance, Ridenour. If you cannot accept that, go back to Cantrell now."

"I . . . I don't want to go back to Cantrell, Nayati. I *want* to understand."

"Then look into the Wheel." Nayati pointed to the ground and the circles-within-circles of stones. "There lies Truth."

His gaze riveted Stephen's, and Stephen fell into those golden eyes, into an infinite regression of Stephens seeing Nayatis seeing Stephens, until Nayati, with a gasp, broke that link to stare reverently at the 'wheel'.

A wheel which, to Stephen's exhaustion-hazed eyes, began to rotate, setting a rhythm in motion until the stones began a similar regression, inward—and outward—to infinity.

"Wesley's *Harmonies* . . ." Stephen whispered.

Nayati froze. "Smith has no sense of the Universal Harmony."

"Are you certain, Nayati?" Stephen asked quietly, out of some inner awareness. Not the awareness he shared with the Other, but that simpler kind, which came of being human. "Wesley is a Mirror, too. Could he not be the—receptacle of some awareness you have not yet perceived? You said the Cocheta have chosen your people. How can you be certain the Harmonies are only for you? Have you—seen all your reflections? Have you—made your personal Wheel whole? You, who have so much of your life left to live? You, who struck Anevai when she tried to tell you how you've changed? Is she not one of your mirrors?"

"I didn't claim I was any good at this, Ridenour." His hands, high-tendoned and large-knuckled, clenched spasmodically, controlling a temper Stephen well remembered. "But at least I've tried. You've no idea the hours I've spent seeking the Way. And now—" Golden eyes glared at him. "—now, damn you, they've deserted me. —Evidently for you." But a more restrained temper. One that found outlet in surly jealousy, but not murder.

"Not an attention I sought, Nayati. But I need to control it. I'd *like* to release it, give it back to you—whatever 'it' is." He leaned across the Wheel and grasped Nayati's wrist. "You've got to show me how."

"It's not for me to show. That is for your guides."

"Guides? What guides? Who are they?"

"I can't know that. Perhaps I'm one. And perhaps I'm not. Perhaps I advise you well. Perhaps I lie. That's for you to discover."

"How will I recognize them?"

"You will. If you follow them, if you use their advice wisely and make wise choices, you will find your Place within the Wheel. If not, you will remain ignorant."

"Who were *your* guides?"

"Irrelevant." Nayati tried to shake him loose. Stephen tightened his grip.

"What was your journey like?"

"Dammit, fool, *listen* to me." That cool detachment vanished. "They're all different. This is no one-shot. I've travelled my wheel many times, in many ways, each time learning a little more. There *is* no quick solution. Done right, it requires personal sacrifice: deprivation of food and water to cleanse the body, sweat lodges to cleanse the pores and baths to cleanse the exterior, sleep deprivation to cleanse the spirit. For some, mutilation and pain play a major part in releasing their inner selves."

Stephen controlled the half-hysterical laughter that threatened, wondering if Nayati thought to scare him. He'd done all that, and more, though perhaps HuteNamid's Cocheta wouldn't recognize sacrifices made in space. "I'm halfway there, Nayati. I'm starving, and seeing ghosts in the stones as we sit. —I haven't *got* time, Nayati. I've only got *now*. They talked to me before; isn't it possible they'll talk to me again?"

Nayati stared at him, a deep, searching stare, then dipped his chin briefly, as though some decision had been reached. His hand twisted to return Stephen's grip, then released him. "Wait for me here, —Brother."

"Phil? Phil! *Dammit, Phil, where are you?*"

The wind howling through the rocks threatened to throw Wesley to the ground. Tiny white flecks pelted his visor.

After an uncomfortably long delay, Phil's voice said faintly in his ear:

"*Wes? Hey, fella, you all right?*"

"No thanks to you. How 'bout a pickup? Gettin' a mite freezacious out here."

Another measurable delay later:

"*Sorry, old man. We're grounded. Helluva storm brewing. Relaying to you through the ship.*"

Which explained the delay. Damned inconvenient RealSpace limitations.

"You mean I'm stuck here?"

"*Sorry. —You still got your emergency pack?*"

"Shit. You ever eaten that garbage? Healthier to starve."

"*If that's what you want. Just get back in the tunnel and keep your feet dry. We'll see you when the sun comes out.*"

"Hey, darlin', I love you, too."

"*Cantrell says to tell you Sweet dreams.*"

"Tell her to Go to hell."

"*She said you'd say that. Said to tell you you could do that, too.*"

"Shit."

"*If you have to. Just don't freeze the equipment off.*"

"Ha. Ha." He ducked back into the tunnel, thinking of that green trail leading into solid rock. "Hah." All he needed now was somebody to close the *front* door . . . on . . . him . . .

He ran back out. "Phil? Phil! Talk to me, sweetheart."

But where Phil should be, was only static.

Nayati left him, reclaiming his coat against the storm rising outside, but leaving Stephen with the tiny glowlight and a packet he said would help keep the cold away.

Nayati said he didn't know how long it would take him, with the increasingly fierce storm, that sleet was certain and snow a distinct possibility. In the meantime, he said, Study the Wheel and reflect upon what I have said.

Which sounded to Stephen like, Keep your mind busy and off the fact you're freezing to death.

The glowlight should have several days' charge at low intensity, so Nayati said, so he left it on, not wanting to relive the hours alone in the darkness any sooner then he must, and, following Nayati's instructions, sprinkled some of the contents of the packet on the lamp. When that got him a pleasant herbal smell and some relief from the chill, he tried a bit more.

And more.

Until a cloud grew in the small chamber-within-the-tunnel, some quirk of natural architecture keeping the wind, howling beyond the tunnel, from touching the air within.

Stephen inhaled the damp, scent-laden air, feeling the warmth grow within him. On the floor, the design of stones began to shimmer and dance. SunDancer, Nayati had called the planet. What a beautiful image. Planet, moons, and star in an endless, gravitationally determined minuet.

Or perhaps it was a waltz. He remembered a party seen through a window, Mama and Papa and all their friends. Around and around and around. An elegant swooping interplay of RealSpace elemental bodies and NSpace gravity wells in mathematically perfect balance, incorporating ships and spacestations and even people into their perfect harmonics, the balance of the whole such that new masses only added to the beauty, a simple, natural shift of gravitational center of mass.

Sharp intrusion of negativity. Bitterness. A taste that disrupted the Harmony. But the disruption lasted only a moment.

Wheels upon Wheels, each stone a separate but interwoven system. Moons circling planets circling stars circling galaxies circling the center of all that was. And within—or without—them all, the Wheel. Nayati's vision of true space. The Truth

that determined them all, from interstellar dust mote to super-
nova, from mitochondria to dinosaur.

Except, Nayati had said, Humanity. Humanity—and the
Cocheta—were the only determining spirits. Nayati had said,
make the Universal Wheel your Mirror. Make decisions wisely
that your Wheel within The Wheel might grow to Completeness.

Nayati had also said, *Perhaps I lie.*

But the Universal Wheel was before him, complete and
balanced, perfect Wheels within Wheels within Wheels, therefore, Nayati, at least in that respect, was one of the 'guides'
of which he spoke.

Nayati had also said, many Wheels were incomplete, and
closer inspection revealed reflective surfaces reflecting incomplete Wheels. And as he looked, more and more proved
incomplete.

But how, a part of him asked, can you find the answer, when
so many of the pieces are missing? How can you solve for the
unknowns when the number of equations, the number of
unknowns, is so large?

Another part said—don't ask. You are a fool, who asks such
questions. Formulate your equation. Create your own image.
Make them see that. Use the power that is yours.

And another, that looked in his Mirror with dark brown eyes
and black braids, said, The fool is he who fails to ask such
questions. Perhaps, Zivon Stefanovich, that is why the search
never ends. As we grow and learn, so do others, which
encourages us to change and learn and grow, as the trees
bending with the wind, rising to the sun's warmth, and growing
deep, ever-extending roots, and intertwining branches.

Yet that with which we begin, that which we learn along the
way, is forever a part of us as is the plant which dies, becomes
one with the soil and nourishes the next season's growth. It is
that Truth you must seek to understand.

So ask, Zivon Stefanovich. What is your next question?

Where is the Other?

Look into the Mirror.

Which? There are so many!

But the answer is obvious, Zivon Stefanovich.

And the answer was. He looked into the Wheel that was his . . .

. . . and suddenly he was falling, stars and galaxies spinning around and through the Wheel that was him. . . .

viii

"They've *left* me?"

Lexi laughed at the mixture of indignation and delight on Daoud's homely face.

"Not permanently," she explained, jumped and grabbed the bar, letting her own weight stretch arm and back muscles. "According to Chet, they'll send for you as soon as they have Stephen aboard. Taking pity on your stomach, so they said."

"I should thank them for that." He sighed, and pulled listlessly on the hand-loops. Hanging by one arm, Lexi reached and dialed an extra ten on Daoud's resistance. The loops whipped up and out of his hands.

"Dammit, Lex—" he turned and glared up at her. She pretended not to notice.

"Fifteen, sixteen . . ." Continuing the pull-up count silently, she said, "I've told you before, Do it right or—"

"—forget it. Yeah, yeah, I know. I'm just—depressed." He adjusted the resistance (splitting the difference, she noted with silent amusement) and restarted the count.

"About what?"

"You'll laugh."

"No I won't."

He finished the count and slumped on the slant board, watching three ensigns showing off with a shadow *jiu jitsu* warm-up. "It's this second desertion. I'm supposed to be here to gain experience, and all they've done is avoid me."

Arms burning, Lexi managed a final pull-up and dropped to

the floor. "Maybe they just found matters more sensitive than they expected and—" Lexi broke off, realizing, of a sudden, she should be telling herself the same. "And they don't want to involve you in something which could compromise your standing."

Daoud's smile hinted silent empathy. "Hasn't been much fun for you, has it?"

"What's that?"

"Babysitting me."

That unconscious echo of her original assessment made her laugh. "Actually, you're wrong. It *has* been—fun."

"I'm glad."

"It's just . . ." She hesitated. She had no business confiding in this person, but he seemed stuck in the same security limbo as herself, and he'd already shown discretion regarding the Tyeewapis . . . and *dammitall*, Stephen would need every friend he could get inside the 'NetAT, especially someone of Daoud's lowly status, at least in the early years. "It's just that I've been used to being consulted. Knowing it's probably gone beyond my security level is minor conciliation. It's Stephen I'm worried about—and he *is* my legitimate concern—regardless of the security ramifications."

A glance around the crowded workout room, a tip of his head toward the door. "I'm not much in the mood at the moment. Want to grab a cuppa?"

She gave him a halfhearted grin. "Are you ever? —But, honestly, neither am I today. My room or yours?"

He started. "I didn't mean . . ."

"Neither did I."

"Yours, then." He grinned broadly. "Fewer parasites."

It was a *pii'chum*. Not just any *pii'chum*. A blue *pii'chum*. Anevai's *pii'chum*, father of the kits in Acoma.

Stephen paused on a silvered sliver, the mirror reflecting a normal view of feet, legs and so on, as all the slivers on this plain of silver through a starry black landscape thus far had shown.

"Hello, Fuzzybutt," he said politely, addressing the creature as Anevai had. "Why are you here?"

The creature leapt toward him, a single high-arching bound.

Stephen dodged, involuntary reflex, but the creature landed on a neighboring shard, next to his mirrored stepping-stones, and stopped, its reflection not a *pii'chum* at all, but a creature of human shape, though the features shifted with each blink. And it was that reflected Pii'chum who said:

"I've come to show you the Way, Zivon Stefanovich."

The Guide of which Nayati had warned.

"Thank you," he said, as he'd been taught.

But that courtesy was a lie. He didn't want a guide. Mentor, his computer-generated instructor within the academy Program, had been a 'guide,' and it had lied—over and over and over again. The VRT Controller had been a 'guide,' and all that human operator had fouled his understanding of all that was important. Nayati had been a guide and had sought only to confuse him on a subject wondrously simple.

Thank the nice man for the ride ... be grateful for the opportunity to study at the Alliance's most prestigious facility....

And his reflection in the mirror changed. Became scarred and angry, and whispered *Anything you want ...*

Stephen recoiled, stepped to another shard, and a third, but the scarred image relentlessly pursued him.

"Gratitude for something you do not want is no gratitude at all." Pii'chum's reflection followed him as well. "You cannot seek Truth because others wish it. Neither can you run from Truth, Zivon Stefanovich, you can only refuse to accept it."

"Accept that?" he echoed, and gestured to the scarred and angry reflection. "That anger isn't Zivon's."

"And is Zivon all of you?"

Which was, of course, defiance of his own prevarication. He dropped to his knees, facing that anger squarely, the scars that belonged to the Ridenour. The one who said anything—*did* anything—to avoid the Loneliness, to succeed where there had been such absolute failure, then excused those actions with *I had no choice*...

And that was a lie. The ultimate lie. There had always been a choice.

"Was there, Zivon Stefanovich?" Pii'chum asked. "Does the human spirit have a choice in such matters?"

"There's *always* choice." Reflected anger faded to reflected pain. "I *should* have realized it wasn't right, should have had the strength of character to end it."

"Why wasn't it—right?"

"Because..." Lacking words of his own, he borrowed Wesley's. "Because it was never a—a two-way."

"Wasn't it?"

Horror joined the pain. "It *hurt*!"

"And did you want it to hurt?"

Horror increased as he realized:

"Yes," he whispered, and wanted to close his eyes on his reflection...

"Why?"

...and to run from the relentless interrogation. But there was nowhere to run to in this sea of intersecting mirrors. Here, Truth would follow. *If you listen to your guides, and choose wisely*... He chose to admit Truth. "Because," he whispered, and reflected scars began to fade, "because if touching hurt, then it wouldn't matter."

"What wouldn't matter, Zivon Stefanovich?"

Tears came. He blinked them away, fracturing images of fractured mirrors. "That Mama stopped touching me. That she sent me away."

"And did it stop mattering?"

More tears filling his eyes, flowing hotly down his cheeks. Cheeks that, in the mirrors, were smooth and rounded. Eyes filled with an innocence he'd never had.

So: even the Mirrors lied.

He shut out the lying image and forced the tears to oblivion.

"The Mirrors don't lie, Zivon Stefanovich. They can't lie."

"But their Truth is—relative."

"All Truth is."

The tears puddled on the Innocence he denied. He wiped it clear, traced the round sweetness with a fingertip. If that had *ever* been true, what had happened? What kind of mother wouldn't fight to protect it?

But he knew the answer. And it didn't lie within that face. The True Face had glowing, demon eyes and pale bones for cheeks. That sort, a mother had to get rid of, before the Truth destroyed everything she loved.

"Are you certain of that Truth, Zivon Stefanovich?"

"I—don't know."

"You are wise in that. You perceive the event from only one wheel. Others perceive it differently."

Others. Mama?

"Do you seek Truth of your mother, Zivon Stefanovich?"

"Sh–she's gone," he whispered through the ache in his throat.

"But not lost. Reflections in Mirrors, Zivon Stefanovich."

"Where . . . ?"

The *pii' chum* smiled—

—and bounded away across the shards.

Honey dripped from the end of the spoon, became a liquified swirl in the tea below. Lexi tested the result and pursed her lips, pronounced it: "Perfect." And handed the mug to Daoud. He sniffed suspiciously, raised an eyebrow and sipped cautiously.

"Good," he said.

"You sound surprised. Think I was going to poison you?"

"Would you?"

She shook her head. "No percentage in it."

"That's a relief. Now, what was this about Ridenour being *your* problem? You mean because he's Recon?"

"I said, my concern," she corrected. She put the finishing touches on her own tea and sat down on the bed. Daoud, as her 'guest' got the single hydachair. Cramped, but at least her special on-call status gave her private quarters. "Thanks, by the way, for not playing coy with me regarding Stephen. It's technically well beyond my fifth-level security clearance."

He shrugged. "Like I said before, common sense you'd be brought in on that bit, Lexi. That's why Cantrell hired you, isn't it?"

"Damn right," she muttered, at which he grinned widely. Slowly sounding him out, she gave him what of her concerns she could without compromising Cantrell's operations.

"And now you're worried because of this most recent disappearance," Daoud finished for her.

She nodded. "I want to know what drove him to it. He's bright, *very* bright, and he *wants* this chance with the 'NetAT. He'd not arbitrarily compromise the opportunity. I can't figure what he's up to, unless it's just time to think. He knows he's beeped; knows we can find him any time we want. Usually, I'd be down with Cantrell and in the middle of everything. I can't help wondering if I might have prevented this situation. —Maybe if I'd been down there, he'd have come to me first. —Worse, what if something I did precipitated it, and that's why I'm— forgive me—stuck here with you."

Daoud sat quietly sipping his tea for several moments, then: "This Ridenour...How well do you know him?"

"I don't believe it's possible really to know Stephen well, but I've observed him closely for weeks, talked with him, been something of a confidant at times."

A slight smile happened behind the mug. "I can believe that."

"What do you mean?"

"You're easy to talk to," he said cryptically, and: "What's your assessment of his character?"

"Desperate."

"That was succinct."

"It's Stephen. He's desperate to please. Desperate to succeed. Desperate to find some purpose so he can *be* somewhere."

"You mean 'belong' somewhere?"

"Not really. I don't think he had ever hoped for that. He's been scammed too often. I think he's desperate for some form of security in a life that's never provided any. He's also desperately shy, afraid of offending and pathologically modest."

"Shy?" His contiguous eyebrow puckered in the middle. "That doesn't sound like his file. I had a fair chance to review it on the way here. He was a top-seeded gymnast—handled the limelight better than most politicians. That was one thing Clarissa really noticed—thought he'd be a good front man."

"Front man?"

" 'NetAt PR; like her."

"He'd die. —Oh, he'd do it, but it *would* kill him. The gym...Have you ever seen him work out?"

"Only the vids."

"He—plays. He's in his own little world, gaining ... actualization ... from the movement within the room. It's—breathtakingly poignant. Personally, I doubt his competing had much to do with winning. He—" Lexi found herself at a complete loss for words. Finally: "The only time I ever heard him laugh—*really* laugh—was in the middle of the most amazing five-bar routine I've ever seen."

Frowning, Daoud went to her set-in terminal and punched up one of Stephen's competition records, watched in silence, with an occasional glance in her direction. The magic was hinted at, but nothing to what he exuded in person. Daoud looked puzzled, especially when, at the end of the broadcast, the camera caught Stephen leaving the gymnasium, dressed for the return home.

Daoud paused the recording and looked at her. "Modest?"

"He'll *wear* anything. But you won't catch him with his shirt off. —Unless..." She paused, recalling one instance where he'd exposed everything in the middle of a crowded parking lot.

"Unless?" he prompted.

"If he's trying to make a point, he becomes very—focussed. Liable to pull anything—"

Daoud was shaking his head. "This is all very interesting, but why do *you* feel any sense of responsibility?"

"I'm Cantrell's Recon advisor—it was my job to keep an eye on him. I've—made some decisions, advised him and the admiral in certain ways which may have influenced him to run. Or perhaps I failed to impress Cantrell with the seriousness of the situation."

"Situation?"

"I told you, he went back downworld for R&R while Cantrell finished her insystem business. I didn't want him to go. He avidly admires Smith. Is a bit irrational where he's concerned. Tries, among other things, to emulate him. If your superiors threatened Smith—"

"Then this bolt could be Ridenour's way of diverting their attention from Smith to himself?"

"Possible. I just don't know. As I said, they've quit confiding in me."

"From what I'm getting, you might have been out of the infoflow anyway."

"Not completely. Not where Stephen's concerned. If I'd only known—this whole scenario doesn't ring true. He'd never fly off and leave Smith vulnerable to the 'NetATs. I tried to tell you, Stephen has this notion that Smith represents everything good in his own life. To leave Smith open to prosecution and possible incarceration simply is not within his character parameters. He's either been forced into compliance, or has somehow covered Smith's tail."

Another consideration over a third cup of tea, then: "Let's go find Chet."

"It's off-hours for him."

Daoud cast her a quizzical glance. "He won't object."

"Wait!" Stephen cried, as knees buckled, sprawling him headlong on the shattered mirror. Fighting dizziness and fatigue, as tired as if he'd been running this endless distance for real, he sat up, noting, with some relief, Pii'chum sitting near his bare feet.

"Why am I so tired?" he asked, drawing his legs up and propping his forehead against his knees.

But this time the *pii'chum* remained a mute Creature, even in reflection, leaving the question unanswered.

Lousy sort of dream, as dream it must be. It was as if he'd entered it as exhausted and hungry as he'd been in the cave. He should ask Nayati for a refund on that fairy dust—

With that thought, he was back in the cave, only the remnants of sweet-scented fog to remind him of the Dream.

Dry lips. He licked them, carried the bitter taste into his mouth. The powder. The steam. A vaguely familiar taste. Like, yet not, Eudoxin.

He had a choice, as the chill set in with a vengeance. Sit here freezing his ass off, or return to that dream.

A drug-induced dream, he realized, now he was free of it. But a dream of some significance. An unfinished dream.

Without hesitation, he threw more of the powder on the lamp, his real arm aching with cold, sore muscles, his legs and back similarly affected, as if he'd been running after the *pii'chum* in this world, too. But he erased those feelings from his mind, concentrating instead on the Mirrors and Pii'chum. He didn't know what was happening, but he wasn't inclined to argue now—not when the fragments were growing fewer.

The mist thickened. . . .

ix

Pii'chum was gone. The mirrors . . . even the stars had deserted him.

In their stead, a misty landscape, constantly shifting: a world of greys and shadows, not the starkness of stars in space. A world of uncertainty.

A world containing a creature like Anevai's Bego, but large.

Grown, as the mother had been grown, but with the pointed ears of the off-spring, and taller, more massive than the female had been. About it was a Sense of Power...

On that thought, the creature fissioned, became Bego and his mother, the shifting mists became walls and a roof, enclosing him in a world of sparkling dust motes, and Anevai atop a wooden rail, chanting softly....

I sing for Be'yotcidi...

It had been a moment of change, a moment of empathy. Certainly a turning point in his relationship with Anevai. The creature standing reunified before him might have been Anevai's poem incarnate; or it might be what the tiny creature might have become. Perhaps the magic within the barn which had brought himself and Anevai together had imbued the young creature with the Power of the Song.

Stephen didn't know where the thought had originated, but of a sudden, the Bego-creature wavered and flowed into human-oid form, much as had the Pii'chum's reflection.

And Bego was smiling.

"You Sense the Harmony, do you not, Zivon Stefanovich?"

"I—" He hesitated, mistrusting this change in the Dream. "Where is Pii'chum?"

The smile broadened. "I came to fetch you."

"Did Pii'chum send you?"

"I came to fetch you, because you want to find the Truth and the way is long, and sometimes hard, and you begin your journey already weary. Do you trust me to take you there safely?"

"But how do I *know* you are a guide and not something sent to trick me?"

"You don't."

Would you like a ride, little man?

"...No..." he whispered. Then louder: "No!" And he ran blindly through the mist. But he soon fell, exhausted as he was, and wept for the Trust betrayed.

"Zivon Stefanovich?" Soft paw patting his face. "I'm here, Zivon Stefanovich. Will you accept my advice?"

He blinked up at golden eyes and blue fluff. "How can I? You deserted me when I needed you most."

"Because, someday, you must trust again, Zivon Stefanovich. Sometimes that means you get hurt, but if you do not run the risk, you simply run. —Will you trust me?"

"—Yes—"

"What you're saying," Lexi said, choosing the words carefully, holding temper in check, obviously aware her career might hang in the balance . . . "is that I've been had."

. . . and obviously not giving a damn, speaking directly to him, Chet Hamilton, rather than the Central Security agent sent to check her credentials for a security upgrade.

"D'you think I enjoyed it?" Daoud asked defensively.

"Frankly, Ali," she said bluntly, "I don't care. I want to know why my superiors—crewmates I thought friends—knew and failed to warn me."

Daoud said: "Wouldn't have been much of a test, then, would it?"

But Chet stared down at his note-strewn desk, aware of how justified that accusation must seem to her. Everyone aboard ship knew how unique her job was—that standard rules simply were not applicable to her position, but how could an outsider, in only a handful of days under unusual circumstances, be expected to evaluate that uniqueness?

He'd had no way to anticipate this revelation. Ali was supposed to come and go and make his report to his superiors without Lexi ever knowing she'd been tested. Now he was in a most uncomfortable situation, and he didn't even know why.

Lexi, scowling at them both, evidently shared his curiosity. "So why come clean now?"

"It's this business about Ridenour. I can't ignore it, even though it's technically outside my province."

"What about him?" Chet asked.

"Lexi's evaluation of him doesn't fit the official profile brief I was given. His recent actions don't."

"Different how?"

"He's listed as a cool customer. No intimates. And a rep for promiscuity. I'm beginning to wonder if it's the same person."

Chet said, "Nothing about promiscuity in his academy records."

"Wouldn't be. Not information they necessarily want spread. I had it out of Central Security records."

"Maybe I just read him wrong." Lexi challenged him, ready to take offense at the slightest hint, now her integrity had been questioned.

But Daoud was shaking his head. "No, I don't think that for a minute, Lex."

Chet's mouth twitched. Lexi had this one hooked, unless he missed his guess. "Why not, Ali?"

"She doesn't make arbitrary observations. And she's a hell of an instinctive psychtech."

"Translated, she's a people-person."

"I'd say that about covers it."

"Well, she's right about the kid, and I can vouch that the person we call Stephen Ridenour is the one who wrote that paper. I haven't studied his personal history much—was too busy on the academic side—and I don't know who evaluated your information, but Stephen Ridenour's a sincerely nice kid." He grinned. "And he didn't hit on me once."

"If you'd told me that yesterday," Ali said, his face somber, "I wouldn't have believed you."

"I was kidding!"

"I realize that. I'm not." Ali's jaw worked, like an animal worrying a bone. Then: "I don't like this. I wish now I *had* gone downstairs with those two. Have they—tried anything?"

"What do you mean?"

"Did you record the meeting? Did they—Lord, I don't know—did they pressure him in any way?"

"C'mon, Daoud," Lexi said sternly, "out with it. What are you trying to suggest?"

"I'm just wondering if maybe it's not *Smith's* fault Dr. Ridenour's gone. Maybe he just doesn't want to go back with . . . them."

Chet's mouth turned sour, a taste not even coffee relieved. "Why? What about them?"

Ali shrugged, patently embarrassed. "I told you: Ridenour has a—rep. These two were—interested."

"Oh . . . my . . . God," Lexi whispered, looking as ill as he felt.

"I'll get into the downstairs files," Chet said. "See if I can discover anything—where they were, what they did—you know. In the meantime," he keyed up Mo's file on Stephen, cleared it for copy to his office, "I want you both to take a look at this."

Pii'chum was waiting, sitting on a wispy rock, its tail folded over its front feet. The movement between his legs halted. Pii'chum flowed to his side, stretched a paw and hooked his bare foot.

No pain. Only an insistence to dismount. To follow on foot.

As he passed Bego's head, the soft nose shoved him in the back, demanded attention. He turned to face—

—not Bego, but Meesha, his childhood pet *obatsi*. Small and woolly, when she transformed, rising to human stance, her soft pelt covered her head, curling down her arms and torso, like a woman made of clouds.

"Caution, my Zivon. Truth is not always as we would have it. Do not trust too easily."

And that was all. She resumed her beloved, familiar form and he dropped to his knees beside her, hugging her about the neck as he had as a child, burying his nose in the warm fur, glad the Dream retained their relative size, then realized, looking inward at his own reflection, the change was not in Meesha, but in himself, and the reflection was . . .

"*Zivon?*"

Soft voice from the mist.

His heart stopped, then burst in his throat.

"Mama?" he whispered, and turned to what seemed the source. "Oh, God, Mama, is that you?"

And again, stronger, more directional: "Zivon?"

Two stumbling steps through the mist and there she was, blond hair floating about her beautiful face, blue gown drifting massless around her slender frame, making him aware for the first time of his own nakedness.

He avoided her gaze, embarrassed and humiliated, yet unable to believe it was she. Mama was gone, on faraway Rostov. But when the entity drifted to the misty ground and held out its arms, without hesitation, without conscious consideration, he was in them, and the warmth, the softness, the heartbeat that was and always would be Mama enfolded him, filled him.

"Zivon," she murmured into his hair. "Oh, my sweet, sweet child, I've missed you so."

He blinked up at her, unable to speak, the block of ice his heart had become unable to share that regret honestly. But then she smiled, and her smile warmed the ice within, and the melt dripped from his eyes. She kissed the tears away without a hint of scolding, which only made them flow faster. And still she didn't scold, but held him with gentle hands—the touching he'd sought for so very long—that traced patterns of easement across his skin. He revelled in that bittersweet security, wanting nothing else from her.

But eventually the tears waned, and from the corner of his eye: Pii'chum and Meesha, waiting for him to seek the answer he'd come here to find. Mama had held him once, loved him once. But that love had gone away. It did no good to regress to the before-time. He knew that, and knew the after. It was the between-piece he was missing.

"Why, Mama?" he whispered the Question, fearful of the Answer, fearful it might drive this dream away, but unable not to ask. "Why did you stop holding me?"

"I hurt you with that, didn't I, darling?" Wistful regret in the words caressing the air above his head. Pain. He didn't want Mama to hurt, but in this world of Truth, he dared not lie, not even to ease that pain. So he hugged her tighter and nodded.

Her gentle hand stroked his hair, her warm breath brushed his skin, surrounded him, filled him with trust and security.

"I was afraid, darling."

Even the mist was a Mirror here. He shut his eyes on reflected features: gaunt cheekbones, ill-suited to the young face, and demon eyes. Eyes that had betrayed his bastardy to the world, eyes that had made other children run in fear. He withdrew his arms, and asked fearfully:

"Of me?"

Her arms tightened. "No, darling. Of myself. Of the feelings I was having. I was trying to protect you from what I didn't understand—from what I was becoming. What I expected of you."

And of a sudden, he thought he understood. He took his own balance, cupped her face—he was taller than she now, no longer the Zivon-child, but the Ridenour-man—and brushed her lips with his own. "Was this what you wanted, Mama?" And took the kiss deeper, thinking that a choice between that and the loss of her touch was no choice at all. But:

"No, sweetheart." She gently disengaged him, and he pressed his Zivon-face into her soft breast, welcoming the reprieve. "I *didn't* know. Now, I do. We were delving too deeply into the alien tapes, living their senses too fully. We were warping the interfaces in our impatience to comprehend." Her lips brushed his forehead. "Your papa was worst of all. He tried to turn a child into a man overnight." Her arms tightened around him. "I almost killed him for that."

Suddenly, suspicion. A part of him drifted away, viewing the reunion with less involvement. A mother and her child. That was all. A wish-fulfillment Dream, the Ridenour-within categorized cynically, nothing more.

But Curiosity was not so easily assuaged. Perhaps not a

dream. His mind would not conjure those words for his mother. Perhaps this was all more—and less—than he believed.

>*Ya' at' eeh, Zivon Ridenour.*< A voice said from the mists—or perhaps simply within his head. A voice that had once told him, *We will not corrupt the interface.*

The voice of the Other.

Blackness in the mist. Dimensionless shadow-shape, and within that black silhouette, an intricate network of silver exploding at each intersection into sparks of color. The shade held out an almost human hand.

>*Come with me, Zivon Ridenour. We've work to do.*<

He evaded that Touch.

"I think not."

>*Truth, Zivon Ridenour. Bijan was a Lie you accepted. A Lie which affected only you. Bijan was not the only Lie you accepted. And that other Lie affects many, many others. You cannot ignore this Truth.*<

The hand touched him, and he, too, became a shade of rippling networks. He looked beyond the Shade to Zivon and Mama.

>*We don't need him for what we must do.*<

"He's part of me. I can't leave him. . . ."

>*An old part, Zivon Ridenour. One who has found what he needs. Now, you must discover the rest.*<

Virtual fingers entwined in his and they were elsewhere.

Stars. An endless sea of stars glowing in the blackness of space: on another level, points of energy floating in a liquid of opalescent energies. Clouds of colors, rippling sparks of suddenly there lightning—red, gold, blue, and colors for which he had no names.

Himself: dimensionless blot, shadow-body against the opal, like the Other's.

Energy radiated from his virtual head, disrupting the image.

>*Then eliminate it,*< said the whisper inside his head.

How? he thought, and:

>*Make it part of the Whole.*<

He sought the source of the radiation within him, and imagined it into opalescent glow. The Image stabilized, momentarily.

A second disruption: distress of the RealWorld Body pulling him back.

>*Ignore it.*<

Will the Body die? he wondered, with minimal perturbation.

>*Does it matter?*<

And of a sudden, he knew that it did not.

Because this was the core of all knowledge, the essence of the universe as he'd known it *must* be. The Reality that Rasmussen's equations had stolen from him. This was NSpace.

This was home.

X

Waiting was the hardest, according to the Rule Book.

And for once, the rule book was right.

Cantrell paced her temporary quarters, wearing the carpet evenly among the various rooms, too prudent to seek distraction in the well-stocked (and complimentary) liquor cabinet, no matter the temptation. Her stalking brought her to the balcony door, face to swirling snowflake with the weather that held them all hostage.

For years she'd maintained (on a philosophical basis) that planetary living, and its associated contact with Nature at her most elemental and unpredictable, was psychologically healthy for humanity. That forces beyond their control kept humanity humble.

She hated humility—almost as much as being helpless.

She also hated being pushed, but that was increasingly the case.

For whatever reason, Stephen Ridenour had snapped. Unless

she wanted him on her conscience for the rest of her life, she was going to have to pull rank on the 'NetATs, defy Stephen's express wishes, and take him back to Vandereaux personally. If they got him back alive.

Also, while he claimed he'd said nothing to the 'NetATs regarding the Cocheta—and for the moment, she believed that—she could in no way count on his further discretion.

Either way, Paul was going to have to—

"*Admiral?*"

Chet: coming through on her personal beeper. She acknowledged with a tap behind her ear.

"*You alone?*"

A second tap.

"*Got a confirmation and location on the kid's signal.*"

"Visual?" she asked, aloud this time.

"*You kidding? He's in the middle of a blizzard. Spark of heat is all, but it was him.*"

"Was?" She didn't like the past tense.

"*His beeper signal—exploded.*"

"Ex–ploded."

"*Definite nova-esque flare. Spooky, I call it.*"

"You're sure he didn't just walk into another Cave? Maybe it's just a different Cocheta defense system."

"*Not certain of anything. But it was very different. Got a continued heat reading for a few minutes, but it's disappeared, too.*"

"Could he have stepped off a cliff? Maybe hit his head and taken out the beeper?"

"*Wouldn't rule it out, but surface topology doesn't put a cliff anywhere close to the signal's demise and nothing I've seen personally or in the records accounts for the flare phenomenon.*"

"One more mystery?"

"*For now. God, admiral, I hope this mess clears out in a hurry. Kid's in trouble. No way not.*"

"Reading my mind, Chet."

"*What about our neighbors-in-orbit? They said they were*"

clearing whether the kid showed or not. Personally, I don't want them going back and ruining Stephen before he gets a chance to prove himself.''

"If he's going crazy, maybe they should get the warning in."

"At least let the boy give his side of the story before you crucify him."

"You know something I don't?"

"Maybe. Maybe not."

"Don't get cryptic on me, Chet. I'm not in the mood."

"Sorry, sir. Didn't mean to be. Had some excitement up here with Ali. He decided to bring Lex in on everything. Seems it's possible we have our neighbors-in-orbit to thank for Stephen's sudden departure. I'm looking into it now."

Curiouser and curiouser, as Lexi would say.

"How do you suggest we stop them?"

"I'll see what I can do. Maybe I can get them to delay another day. Pull some double talk on them. —They might buy the idea we have the power to put a hold on them."

"Go ahead and—" A sudden gust of wind pelted ice crystals against the window. Cantrell grinned to the empty room. The 'NetAT's police were sitting warm and comfy—and out of communication with their mother ship—at the Tunica airport. Their little asteroid hopper was parked in an airport hangar. This blow wouldn't stop *Cetacean's* shuttle, but any lesser machine . . .

"Admiral? I didn't copy that."

"Got a better excuse for you, Chet. Oldest and best in the book."

"What's that?"

"Serendipity. Nature at her finest. They're grounded."

The flickering lights' tempo increased, echoing the staccato *thrum* in his ears.

Here it comes—Wesley thought, sensing the program's climax approaching. And the following instant: blackness. *Well, that was boring.*

He pulled the helmet off and shook his hair loose, half-expecting crawly things to fall out. Damned thing made him sweat.

Stupid headgamers. *Theta waves*, indeed. The stone walls around him were no different than they'd been three hours and four equally useless mindbending routines ago. He felt no more relaxed and certainly no less claustrophobic. Might do some good for the miniheads these suits were designed for, but a 'Netter with time on his hands needed RealTime diversions. These ridiculous little lights weren't *connected* to anything, had no underlying logic.

A real 'Netter knew the true beauty of light and color. Knew the multidimensional energies and resonances they represented on holographic NSpace mappings. Sensed the order within the chaotic randomness of color and used it to communicate with the universe.

They didn't just sit there and watch colored lights.

Heaving himself off the floor, he clipped the helmet to his belt by the chin strap and wandered down the tunnel. To the edge of the lamplight and beyond, until he stood in that void of sight and sound only hundreds of meters of earth could provide, not touching the walls, only the pressure of gravity providing any awareness of direction, and that only *up* and *down*.

Hard to imagine what it must have been like, hours spent all alone with no rational hope of getting out alive. Maybe that had snapped the kid's mind. Maybe that was the origin of the crazed message to Cantrell, the crazier bolt after Nayati.

He stood there in the dark until his senses began providing input suspiciously like that bloody mindbender, then retreated to the light, shiveringly grateful for his faculties.

He understood that once people born deaf or blind, or who lost sight or sound, had simply had to live with it. He understood there were places even in Alliance where this state of deprivation existed once again, and for a moment empathized in a very real way with the Recons who complained of their government's neglect.

But it was an empathy which faded in the glow of the light, other concerns superseding it.

He searched the pack for his stash, and peeled the paper off a third candy bar. This time, he nibbled a nut off the side and chewed slowly, deliberately savoring each roll of nuttified chocolate around his mouth.

Phil had insisted the temperature in the cave would remain constant and that he wouldn't freeze. That the inbuilt mindbender and HUD vid-games were designed to belay boredom. All the comforts of home. He could even piss in his suit, if he wanted to.

Which was all well and good, but evidently his concept of freezing and Phil's were quite dissimilar. He wanted a good book and a fire, thank you, not mental fireworks and an insulated suit. Better yet, a warm bed and a warmer, accommodating body.

He shivered—

—and took another, larger bite of chocolate and nuts.

. . . become one with the Wheel . . . dance with the Sun.

It was so simple, now he knew. He swung, leapt from one intricate webwork to the next, absorbing one quantum of energy, releasing a different color before arcing to the next, each absorption a Byte of the Whole, each release a newly formed connection. Like flying in the gym, each touch predicted the angle and goal of the next leap.

Some energy was new; intriguing; tapping infoflows he'd skipped in his quest for understanding of the 'Net. Others were old friends, and others . . .

A touch—brush of a virtual fingertip across a sparking blue thread:

Harmonies.

The word echoed in his Awareness. He grabbed the spark with his hand and propelled himself into a cloud of blueness, diving, soaring through the familiar currents, revelling in the sense of Right, sensing the Other's amusement at his admittedly childish antics, the Other's approval as he sensed a Wrong, extended a finger and adjusted the Color of the energy flow.

>*A good beginning, Zivon Ridenour.*<

Beginning? Of what?

>*What do you see, Zivon Ridenour?*<

See? He saw Color. Beauty. Knowledge. . . . The 'Net as he'd always known it would be.

>*Remember the lesson of the Mirrors, and look with more than your desires.*<

Hearing, he understood, recognized the energies for the DataBase. An infoflow he knew flawed and inefficient, not the elegant perfection he chose to believe in.

And as he acknowledged absolute Truth, flaws shattered the opal. Dark strands with frayed ends, unraveling with increasing rapidity. Reality? or embodiment of his simile for the chaos rupturing the ComNet?

>*Does it matter?*<

And he knew then, the appearance was merely the artistry of the interpreter. Whether Rasmussen's, or Smith's, the Quintessence the equations interpreted was the only significance. Reality was, that quintessence was damaged and must be repaired.

Stephen grasped one frayed end, recognized it for Data, sensed its Rasmussen-determined match in another frayed end, reached an infinite arm to connect them, and sealed the equation with a caress and gentle release of personal energy.

Another frayed end brushed his virtual hand: gift from the Other. Stephen sensed its match and sealed the tear.

Satisfaction from the Other as he placed a third end in Stephen's virtual hand.

>*Now do you understand, Zivon Ridenour? Do you understand why you had to exist?*<

But he didn't understand. The Other saw the same flaws. Could he not—

>*No, Zivon Ridenour. We are similar but not identical. The BaseLine differs. We, as part of this Space, could sense the Chaos, but could not access until the process of disruption initiated, and by then, the corruption was already too large, the choices too many, where a wrong choice could potentially destroy the whole.*<

Balance. Harmony. Order and chaos.

'Why he had to exist.' Why did the Other call him Zivon Ridenour? Or was the Other 'speaking' to him at all? Was that simply how he perceived himself? He was, after all, some odd amalgam of Zivon Stefanovich Ryevanishov who first encountered the Cocheta, and Stephen NMI Ridenour, who was . . . reunited?

>Are you Zivon Ridenour's 'invisible' or the Other?<

>*Both, and neither.*<

>Did you . . . create me?<

>*Excellent, Zivon Ridenour. What answer do you perceive?*<

Consideration. Comparison of Possibilities. Result:

>That it doesn't matter. I am here. The damage exists and must be repaired. You say you cannot. I can.<

>*And is that Truth?*<

He swept his free hand toward the restored sections.

>There lies the proof. Unless I deceive myself and only believe I have repaired. And whose reality matters, if not my own?<

Satisfaction from the Other, and the next frayed end.

xi

Lexi took another pass through the photos, then wished she hadn't: throwing up all over the office might not go over well with Chet.

"Why the hell didn't someone tell me?" she said, letting

emotion out in a less messy form. She threw the photos into her abandoned seat and paced the cluttered room.

"Cool down, Lex," Daoud said. "They couldn't. You were under active investigation—"

"I know that, but why *now?* Of all times—"

"That's the whole point, there never is a good time. Sit down, Lex. That door's open, in case you've forgotten, and I think Mr. Hamilton wants it left that way."

She swept McKenna's report onto the floor and threw herself onto the couch beside Daoud. "But it's Stephen's life at stake."

"If not Stephen Ridenour's, then someone else's. That's *why* Cantrell's so determined to get you that upgrade. My investigation was the only way Old Man Morley could consider it. You haven't been around that long, you know."

"Not to mention my unfortunate choice of parents."

"Your being Recon has nothing to do with it, Lexi. Not where Morley's concerned, and he's the ultimate say in the matter."

"So, do I pass?" she asked sourly, not really caring.

Daoud shrugged. "Hell if I know. I just report to Morley." He half-grinned. "If it were my say, you could have anything you asked for."

Lexi shook her head. "No offense intended, Daoud, but I'd give that personal beeper up in a second if it would get me back down there with Cantrell and TJ."

He smiled rather wryly. "Yeah, I know."

"Can you blame me? I mean—look at these!" She swept her foot through the stack of photos. "I'd never have believed—no wonder you never caught him with his shirt off in the gym. And this—" She tapped one with a toe. "—it looks like they used dull scissors!"

"They probably did," Daoud said expressionlessly. "They frown on giving students sharp objects."

"How can you say it so calmly? *Someone* did this to him. *I'd* like to return the favor. Maybe clip a little deeper."

"But you can't, Lexi. *I* can't. You know that. I do. Dr. McKenna says she fixed it. Says he'll be able to sire all the little Ridenours he wants. Let it rest."

"If he survives at all."

"He will, Lex. Trust your own evaluation. He won't risk Smith, and he won't let Herzog and Naghavian win."

"He's already seen to that, Ali," Chet said from his office doorway. He entered and shut the door behind him. "Sorry, guys, didn't mean to eavesdrop, but I thought you might just be interested in a file I found." He handed them the printout. "It's amnesty for Smith. Signed. Bio-Sealed. And ready to be delivered the minute *Cetacean* enters Vandereaux System. —Along with some video neither of you are old enough to view."

Lexi felt no inclination to laugh. On the other hand, as she read through the surprisingly comprehensive legalese, her desire to kill faded, a vague satisfaction replacing it. "Not Ridenours, Daoud."

"What do you mean?"

"Stephen's name is Ryevanishov—child of revenge." She met his eyes and smiled grimly. "Appropriate, don't you think?"

Frayed ends grew fewer; Patterns began to form. Complex Patterns which should be simple. Efficient. Smith's way, not Rasmussen's.

Not waiting for the next strand from the Other, He severed a nearby strand, reconnecting as the pattern dictated, the superfluous segment shimmering and fading into the background color.

The Other registered horror. He laughed and severed a second.

>*You defy Wisdom.*<
>You cannot See. How can you evaluate?<

>*You waste Energy.*<

>On the contrary: I conserve. Witness.<

And the severed strand shimmered, became the sealant for the restruct, and the next, and the next, each leaving residual energy, color to immerse in the ozone-glow.

>Efficiency. Harmo*nics*. Cause and effect. Repair requires Energy. Harmonics generate it.<

>*You are crazy.*<

>Crazy? Here?<

>*Unbalanced. Lacking harmony.*<

>So I've been informed. Sanity is a judgement call. I exist. I perform a function. I perform it efficiently. Is that insane?<

The Other's presence vanished for a time. He continued the improvements to the Pattern. Finally:

>*Such actions could endanger the Totality. One mistake—*<

>I won't make one.<

>*And if the damage spreads to the interface you've corrupted before you effect repair?*<

The Other was trying to psych Him. He knew the tactic. But the advice was sound. Time, the universal Determiner. Rather than waste time arguing, He accepted the next damaged end and sought its match, sapping Energy from his Source to effect repair.

The tunnel's end was no longer dead.

Wesley retraced the last half-dozen meters and scanned the tunnel carefully, found the strange flowerlike stalactite which had caught his eye the first time through. The wall had vanished. The green dot that indicated Stephen's passage, while fainter now, definitely continued down the tunnel.

Closer investigation of the previously blocked tunnel segment revealed further evidence of Stephen's presence: blood. No more than a drop or two smeared on stone, but enough for the whiz-suit to recognize and analyze. And extrapolating the trail, he discovered the control pad for the 'door'.

He didn't touch it. For all he knew, he could form a door right around himself.

Life would have been so much simpler if they'd made that damned mindbender in the least accessible—he hated permachips. He could have programmed it into something interesting. As it was, he had to get bored. Had to go exploring.

Had to find the damned hole, and the blood, and now, dammitall, he was going to have to go after the little bastard, because, dammitall, he was *worried* about the little bastard.

Returning to his campsite—such as it was—he tried one last time to raise Phil, the ship or the local pop radio station. But either the equipment had failed, or they were all hibernating, or he was too close to the mountain to reach anyone, and he finally decided Screw them all. It was black outside, and he'd had to break through waist-high drifts to clear the tunnel mouth at all. If Stephen was still alive, he'd lay odds it was at the other end of this tunnel, and he didn't need anyone's damn permission to go fetch him.

"Nothing more we can accomplish here," Lexi said, rising from the couch and stretching until her joints popped. "We'd best get out from underfoot and let you finish up and get to bed."

Chet leaned his elbow on his desk and propped his chin in his hand and sighed. "I'm here for the duration—doubt I *could* sleep til I find out what happened with the kid. —Besides, with Cantrell and Briggs downstairs, I'm supposedly in charge."

Another piece of information she'd never realized. Always part of Cantrell's entourage, she'd never considered who handled the ship while the admiral was gone. Every section, from the navigation bridge to the kitchens, seemed so utterly self-sufficient, one forgot that, ultimately, someone had to be responsible.

"We're for a late supper. Want to join us?"

"Now that—" The message light on his desk monitor lit. He

held up a hand. "Scuze." And touched the key that would relay the message through his personal beeper.

Lexi touched Daoud's arm, and mouthed exaggeratedly *Let's go*. But Daoud shook his head and nodded toward Chet, who was frowning intently and busily pulling up something on his screen.

"Thank you," Chet said into the air, and looked up. "Good. You're still here. —Well, Ali, looks like your ride's leaving without you."

"Wonderful," Daoud said, surprisingly calm for someone who'd just been stranded. "Not even waiting for their own police?"

"Evidently not." Chet's light tone vanished. "They've already broken orbit. I suppose we should thank them for not revving those engines beside us. —Damn, I wish we could stop them. They were *not* happy when Cantrell curtailed their police action. They must figure to get back to Vandereaux and work their own version of the story with the 'NetAT before we can be there to deliver Stephen's little bombshells."

"Won't do them much good, will it?" Lexi asked. "They've blown their mission here any way you slice it, haven't they?"

"Depends on what they've got on whom," Daoud said. "My guess is, they're in Shapoorian's pay."

"Proof?" Chet asked.

"None I could swear to. But if they've got enough dirt on Ridenour, she might extend protection. . . ."

"I just hope they've sense enough to deliver that report on *Harmonies* while they're at it, 'Net security being somewhat more important than their reputations. —But *dammitall*, I hate to see them have a chance at the Council before Stephen's there to defend himself."

Daoud chuckled wryly. "It's too bad, actually, that I made an issue of staying here."

Which helped even Chet grin. "Don't worry. Cantrell will let you bum a ride home. We can clear out a corner in the laundry room."

"Thanks." Daoud smiled obligingly, but didn't really seem to be listening. He was staring at the departure pattern charted on the screen. "But if I were aboard, I might be able to stop them. I'm no pilot and I'm certainly no 'NetHead, but my security level is higher than theirs, and if I were aboard, I might have been able to bypass their control—abort the run."

Chet's grin vanished. "How?"

"I've got the navigation codes and crossover keys. —Morley demanded I have them—for safety sake, so he said."

"Where?" Chet asked.

"Probably would have blown up the ship instead, but I could have tried."

"*Where are those codes?*"

Daoud jumped. "I–in my briefcase."

Lexi said: "If Stephen—or even Smith—were here, he could use the Smith's tap to reach the systems from here."

"Stephen, hell," Chet said with a certain indignation, "you've got me. —Ali, get me those keys."

Daoud positively flew out the door. Lexi stayed where she was. Something in Chet's almost gleeful face, the flair with which he punched a code into his com, the excitement in his voice making her decidedly uneasy when he told Dora Partain: You want a chance to fly that hummer, get your behind down to SecCom, stat.

"Is this legal, Chet?" she asked into the first breathing space.

He shrugged.

"Shouldn't you ask Cantrell first? She's got a whole lot more at stake here."

"Don't worry. If we do this right, they'll never know what hit them, and if they can't trace it, they can't throw accusations at anyone, can they?"

"How can you know . . ."

"I've read that paper of Stephen's. No one else has, and for damned good reason. The biggest danger is *anybody* could do it: that damn tap is a natural security buster. As for Cantrell, she, TJ, and I have already agreed to stand behind each other in a three-way decision.''

"I just wish you didn't seem to be so—happy about it.''

His grin widened. "Can you blame me, Lex? Isn't often a program peddler has a chance to play God.'' And looking beyond her shoulder: "Hi there, Dora. How do you feel about a remote hijacking?''

Vandereaux.

The Sense identified a Place that was almost a directory apart—a unification of information with very few branches extending into the Totality, one of which fluxed with impending dissolution.

The Ridenour Self supplied Hypothesis: connection of gradu ates to the outside world occurred in a single annual transmis sion. All further connections to those individuals happened subsequent to their Vandereaux years, hence the connecting ports would be topologically Elsewhere.

>Sounds good to me.< He replied to the partial Self and dived into the infostream, sweeping deeper and deeper, following the disruption until He found Himself out of opalescent space and into far more recognizable logic structures.

RealSpace. Vandereaux Academy files. His files. Wesley's files. Separate emanations inexorably linked through *Harmonies of the 'Net.* A Harmonic in danger. He healed the fray, strengthened it with costly redundancy.

Another linkage: infiltration from the 'NetAT Source files.

Curiosity bordering on need-to-know. That Linkage was the threat to the Ridenour/Smith Harmonic. He followed the linkage to the source. Sensed awareness of the breakdown within the DataBase. Sensed a need-to-know, and fear of the consequences of not knowing. But their knowledge was limited. They still grasped at possibilities, hence the envoy to investigate the Ridenour/Smith Harmonic.

But He was repairing the DB—eliminating the fear, and hence, the threat. And He knew the key: modify without deleting. Elimination of the chaff, the Smith Harmonic had said. Data was not chaff. Only superfluous, energy-hungry linkages were.

He sensed concern from the Other at his absence and followed that concern back to a strangely less stable Opalescent Totality.

A frayed end brushed his hand. He found its match with some difficulty, the Totality phasing in and out of focus; he joined the ends, exuded energy to effect repair—

—Energy depletion. Sensory chaos. Dissolution of the Totality. . . .

Dim glow in the tunnel ahead. Long shadow momentarily eclipsing it. Wesley pressed up against the tunnel wall and increased the audio sensitivity in the helmet.

A faint curse: definitely not Stephen. HuteNamid Recon and he'd bet he knew the source.

He eased toward the light, wishing like hell he had some sort of weapon—preferably with a range of about 10k and the ability to shoot around corners. He could pick up a rock, but if Nayati had his knife—not much of a hypothetical: Nayati slept with the damn thing—a boulder wouldn't do him much good. Besides . . .

He paused.

. . . he had an image to uphold. Wesley Smith, as everyone knew, was a lover, not a fighter.

Retreating a handful of steps, he fumbled in the pack for the glowlamp, clipped it to his belt, peeled another candy bar, slung the funky helmet with its lowE imager on his belt, and sauntered back to Nayati's lair . . .

. . . whistling.

Rounding the final corner, he stopped in his tracks, his gasp of startlement only partially feigned.

Exhaustion in every line, covered in snow, crouched beside a tiny glowlight, a leather pouch at his feet, a blanket hanging from one hand, and a bloodied silk shirt from the other, Nayati looked up with sunken, haunted eyes, and murmured, "I'm sorry, Wesley. I never meant for him to die."

xii

Darkness. But the ordinary darkness you found behind closed eyelids, not the darkness of an underground tunnel, or the dissolution of the Totality.

"Zivon? Are you awake, darling?"

Soft voice from above, not the Voice in his head, as the touch in his hair was not the brush of virtual fingers.

He opened his eyes to the world of mists and mirrors. Of:

"Mama?" he whispered.

"Hello there, handsome." Which she used to say when he was tiny. "How are you feeling?"

He thought about that. Remembered the Opalescence . . .

(Strand after strand. As he successfully sealed one frayed end, the Other located the next. The Other knew the whole, but couldn't recognize the specific, couldn't mend. That made sense. He was the comprehension—he knew the logic there and here. They worked together to halt impending Chaos. He was (and the Other registered satisfaction) the one—created for the job.)

And earlier . . .

(Running to match pace with the pii'chum: Why am I so tired . . . ?)

And part of him registered a physical self, the Body, seeping energy, but that Self didn't matter. The True Self belonged here—where he had Purpose.

"Tired, Mama," he murmured at last. "Very tired."

"Then rest, darling." And her hand stroked his head. "Close your eyes and sleep. . . ."

But with sleep came dreams. . . .

(Cold. Lonely. Arms to warm him and drive the loneliness away . . .)

("It's no good if it's not a two-way....")
But it was a two-way—it was good.
("C'mere, I know a better way....")
So very, very...
And within the Totality, a rich nova of color that drew him in, held him, filled him with all he needed and more...

"Th–there!" Nayati cried through teeth that chattered and above the rising wind, extending an arm from the blanket to point into the wind-swirled snow-fog. "Sh–should be in easy range—"

Expanding the radius of the helmet's imager to maximum, Wesley received a linear HUD display of a small, unnaturally regular mound, and an associated structure of more houselike dimensions beyond the generic whiteness surrounding them. Nayati's cabin and sweat lodge, just like he'd promised, which augured well for other promises of real food and real warmth—and a real bathroom.

None too soon, by his way of thinking. The wind flinging vision-obscuring snow airborne felt like another storm brewing; Nayati was already leaning heavily on him and *his* knees were buckling; and the damned chime warning of the suit's dangerously low energy reserve refused to shut up.

Phil had said guys lived off these suits for days.
She lied.
"Cut the lamp," he shouted to Nayati, which eliminated the increasing whiteout around them and allowed him to cut the HUD to minimum intensity, conserving what power remained. He followed the lowE schematic, fighting the wind every step of the way, beating a path through the snow for Nayati and himself, until the building came into visual range.

He stumbled, fell to his knees, pulling Nayati down with him. "Sorry," he gasped. "Give me—minute."

Nayati said nothing, just huddled under his blanket. Wesley

closed his eyes, snapped them open as he began to sway.

That's it, bit-brain, he said to himself, *fall asleep ten meters from food.*

His stomach grumbled. He made it a silent promise and searched for his legs which from the feeling—or lack thereof—had disappeared. No wonder Nayati was dead on his feet. He'd done this twice already today.

Of a sudden, against the visor protecting his eyes from the wind, the little green light, in his ear, the gentle *ping* that advised of Stephen Ridenour's presence, both vanishing in the next breath.

Startled, he almost dropped Nayati back in the snow; saved him with a jerk to which Nayati took very vocal exception.

Imagination. Stephen was dead. Had to be, out unprotected in this stuff.

Why in hell he hadn't stayed in the Cave . . . *It should have just relaxed him* . . . Nayati had insisted regarding the powder he'd left with Stephen . . . *kept him oblivious to the cold* . . . Which it evidently had done with a vengeance. So oblivious, he'd shed what clothes he had and wandered out into a blizzard in the dark, leaving them with no damn way to find him.

Leave it to Stephen Ridenour to react uniquely to any given substance or situation, and add Nayati's guilt trip to the others he'd left in his wake.

Still, the helmet flashed and *pinged* with some regularity throughout those final meters to the cabin, which only made him tempted to fling the helmet over a cliff.

He didn't care, dammit. Stephen Ridenour was dead and gone. Good fucking riddance to a hell of a bad deal.

He held the cabin door open with his insulated body as he steered Nayati inside, then followed Nayati's abrupt floor-ward example, letting the door slam shut behind them, severing his connection to that elusive 'scent' without a single qualm.

* * *

The Body was weakening, and that weakness reflecting into this shadow self. The Self lay content, warm and safe in Mama's grasp; the Body was dying. He must return to the Body, see to the Body's needs.

>*The Body doesn't matter,* < the Other's voice echoed in his pounding head. >*Your work here matters.* <

>The pattern is forming, stabilizing.<

>*Severed ends remain. New ones form. Your function is incomplete. By its nature, it can never be complete.* <

But there was a flaw in that reasoning. A flaw he saw even if the Other didn't.

>Where does the Energy to repair the strands originate?<

>*Where do you think it originates?* <

>You'll not deflect me so easily. If it comes from the Body, I must see to the Body—rejuvenate it—or the Work cannot continue.<

>*There is always Energy. The Body ceases to function, becomes one with the soil, and creatures and their Energy become bonded to the Self. There is always Energy.* <

>And do *you* sap RealSpace as well?<

>*For us, there is no need.* <

But the Other's reflection in this world of mists—and Truth—wavered, and he remembered Nayati's explanation of incomplete Wheels and the need to Touch the World.

>Is that why the Libraries exist?< he persisted.

>*I said, there is no need. The Libraries provide the Hosts, that is all. The purpose is not to destroy the Host, but to trade Awareness Expansion for the chance to Touch Reality. You are not a Host. You are here. You perform your function. Is that not enough?* <

He thought of that blaze of Energy within the Totality. A blaze he'd consumed without compunction. A blaze that, in retrospect, *felt* familiar.

>If the Body dies, will I necessarily seek another in order to perform my function?<

>*I—don't know.* < And again the reflection wavered. >*You*

are—different. Your entrance into the Totality, unique. Your function, unique. If that unique function does require a new Energy source, is not elimination of Chaos sufficient justification?<

Breakdown within the 'Net meant at the least economic disaster for millions of people throughout the ComNet Alliance. At the most—people would die.

If he remained, continued the process, his body would die. Perhaps this virtual self would die with it. If not...

He'd leeched Energy without a moment's thought to its origin. If that Source was, as he feared, Wesley Smith, Wesley Smith could be dead. If not this time, then the next. If not Wesley, then perhaps another.

And he wondered, in a vague portion of his mind, as Mama's hand stroked his hair, whether that thought should concern him. . . .

The fire was virtually out, only a glowing coal or three evidencing its former glory. And he without the slightest talent at revivification.

Wesley dragged himself over to Nayati's still-as-death side and shook him.

"C'mon, man," he grumbled, deliberately callous. "Snap to it. You want us to freeze to death?"

"Go to hell." Nayati groaned and rolled over, leaving a trail of blanket and half-melted snow on the earthen floor. "Won't freeze."

The snow *was* melting rapidly, the dry, packed earth absorbing the moisture thirstily. The fire might be dying, but its job had been thoroughly accomplished.

"Good insulation."

Nayati opened one golden-brown eye. "The best."

The eye closed for a moment, then, with a sigh, Nayati heaved upright and began pulling off soaked clothes. Leaving them in a pile beside the dying fire, he disappeared behind a woven hanging, and moments later, the sound of running water betrayed his objective.

Wesley parked on the side of the firepit and pulled off the helmet and gloves. While a shower sounded theoretically wonderful, he wasn't about to give up the insulated suit until he knew the temperature of the water he'd be stepping into.

Nayati's compact cabin lacked very little. The dome-shape allowed the central firepit to draft naturally through a very modern-looking vent. Nested furs to sleep in, backrest, and a fair number of storage bins around the edges hinted at extended—or frequent—occupation.

The only conspicuous absence was a computer—of any sort. Human, Cocheta, not even a calculator.

No computer; no phone. Nayati's little hideaway, indeed.

An odd little radial ditch ran from the firepit to a pelt flap across from the door. Beyond the flap, a tunnel filled with very cold air leading to another pelt-covered door. Wesley let the flap fall and returned to the firepit, adding an arbitrarily chosen stick from a corner pile, and begging it to light. When it responded positively to his request, he gathered an armload from the pile and dropped it on as well.

The water stopped. Promising steam escaped into the central room.

Figuring his turn imminent, he began slowly unfastening the suit, cursing his inability to forget that elusive, just outside the cabin, warning. What if Stephen Ridenour *weren't* dead? What if, in some delusion-crazed inspiration, he'd endeavored to follow Nayati and gotten this far?

For that matter, what if Nayati Hatawa had turned ax murderer and planned to add Wesley Smith to the deep freeze?

Telling himself it was satisfying vulgar curiosity, Wesley slipped the helmet back over his head and stepped out into a night gone amazingly still—with his luck, the quiet before the storm. *The better to smother your screams with, my dear.*

Squeezing the last erg out of the power supply, he got a reading—and a heading.

His own curses echoing in the helmet, he went back inside, where Nayati, wrapped in a towel, his long hair dribbling hissing droplets into the coals, was reorganizing his pile of sticks. He scanned Wesley head to foot and asked dryly: "Lost your mind, too, 'NetHead?"

"Maybe."

Nayati's brow raised at his serious tone.

"I think, maybe, Ridenour's alive."

"You are crazy."

Wesley tapped his helmet. "Not according to this."

Nayati frowned. "I pray to the gods you're wrong."

"Why?"

"Nothing we can do."

"I can go after him."

"In this?"

"Not much choice, is there? But it's died down. Maybe it'll wait until I find whatever the helmet thinks it smelled."

"You said you were out of power. Maybe it's just a final power snit, and not Ridenour at all."

"Maybe."

"But you're still going to check."

"Have to, don't I?"

Nayati nodded. "Hang on. I'll get dressed—"

"I'll worry about Ridenour. I've got this suit—it'll keep me marginally comfortable. You worry about that fire—if the damn fool *is* alive, we're going to need it to thaw him out."

The little green light still thought it sensed something. Wesley cut all power systems except Stephen's hounder, trusting the material's insulation to protect him from frostbite, and the pointer rang true, if not intensely. He wished he dared try contacting *Cetacean*, but for all he knew, such an attempt would destroy even that faint potential link with Stephen.

So he went with the little green light.

At least the air was clear and still, and the moons provided light ample enough to avoid tripping over trees, but not, as happened, slim, bare forms mostly covered in snow—

—just short of a sheer cliff.

"Trying to make sure of it, weren't you, brat?" he muttered, dropping to his knees beside the body. He swept the snow from the profiled face, his gut sinking with the demise of his final hope: the suit's instruments gave no indication of life, only the little green light indicating this was, indeed, the biological entity it had been calibrated to detect. Nayati had been right all along. No one could survive thus exposed, least of all the thin-blooded Stephen Ridenour.

And maybe, he thought, brushing the ice-stiffened curls back from an oddly serene brow, this was what Stephen had really wanted all along, poor, unhappy clone that he was.

He wished he could say the sight didn't disturb him, but as he'd told Stephen, foolish human that he was, the sight of beauty brought him joy. And Stephen Ridenour had been beautiful.

Now, he was just dead.

And such a death. Poor sod was always cold. Almost made a person believe in premonitions.

Brushing the body free of snow, he wrapped it in Nayati's blanket. A limp arm fell free. He tucked it carefully back, his fingers encountering the bandage he, himself, had put there, the chill of fingers that seemed colder than the snow surrounding them. Unwanted thoughts of thin blood and cold hands and a thoroughly human search for a warm body to drive that cold away intruded, and he found himself rocking gently forward and back, clasping the blanket-cocooned corpse to his chest.

Liquid hazed his visor. He tried to wipe it clear, swept the thing into the snow when he couldn't, bent and pressed Stephen's cold face into his neck, trying fiercely to will warmth back into the lax body, free to be a fool, out here where there were no witnesses.

Snow pelted his cheek: the wind rising again. No time to waste. He shook the helmet free of snow and replaced it; then, unwilling to throw Stephen's body callously over his shoulder as common sense dictated, gathered it into his arms, appalled at the ease of the task. Either he was a lot stronger than he thought, or the kid had dropped twenty pounds.

Free to use the suit's final power, he tried to raise *Cetacean*, hoping the clear skies indicated open com lines, but got no response. Useless, except that when he failed to check in, Cantrell might actually follow up on it. Maybe even somehow locate them. She'd claimed Stephen's beeper would work even postmortem. Failing that, maybe that *thing* in his butt would guide her.

RealSpace comtech—

He tripped over a snow-covered rock. The bundle in his arms slipped. He hugged it tighter.

—God, he hated it.

"The Body is dying. Mama, I must go back."

"Not just yet, my darling. I've missed you so. It's been so very long."

He slumped against her, that being the easier course. "I'm tired, Mama."

"Then rest, my darling. And when you're ready, there's still much to be done here. You need never return. You're safe here. Wanted."

"I'm needed there, Mama. They don't understand—I need to explain."

"Your friend, Wesley, can tell them."

"Not even he understands." And not, he thought silently, if I leech his Energy to stay here.

>*There is your report. There is Hamilton. You are not the only one who can carry the message. You are the only one to rectify the damage.*<

>The report is incomplete. I must return and—<

>*No!*< The Other's objection pelted his mind: a naked infostream. The Other wanted him to stay and continue the repairs on the DB. They'd been waiting too long for him. Were fed up with the mess. Would destroy the 'Net if improvements didn't happen.

A surge of protest. >Clean it yourselves! Find a willing slave!<

>*Do you claim you were unwilling?*<

Flash of the joy, the sense of usefulness, of power. He buried his head in Mama's lap. Her hands soothed as though she were unaware of the struggle progressing in his head.

>I can return.<

>*The Body is the ultimate link. It must die. Return to it, and the link is strengthened, making the function more difficult. Once gone, the Function is the only Truth.*<

>And if you destroy the 'Net, as you threaten, what happens to you?<

Silence from the spot in his head reserved for the Other. He pursued his momentary advantage:

>I've stopped the deterioration—<

>*It will begin again!*<

>The 'Net is stable< he insisted, >at least for a while. I'll tell them the rupture is sealed. Don't panic. Don't destroy Wesley. Then I'll come back.<

>*Tell them through the 'Net.*<

"No," he said aloud, defying the Other, denying the Unity, and buried his head deeper into Mama until the Sense of the Unity told him the Other had gone.

The door opened before he reached it.

"Thanks," he said on a gasp, as Nayati took half Stephen's bulk one-handed, the other in a clean sling.

They lay the bundle beside the fire and peeled back the blanket. Nayati squatted on his heels beside the body and examined it without touching. Probably some damned Recon phobia.

Avoiding Stephen's corpse for altogether different reasons, Wesley turned his back and began peeling off the suit.

"Doesn't look too good, does he?" Nayati commented at last.

"For God's sake," Wesley snarled over his shoulder, "he's dead. Least you can be is civil."

"Dead?"

The puzzled note in Nayati's tone made him turn. Nayati had his hand in front of Stephen's face.

"Don't bother. Of course he's dead. Flash frozen to the marrow." And openly mocking Nayati's motions: "What d'you think we should do with it? Dump it back in the cooler outside?"

Nayati pressed his ear to Stephen's bare chest, then sat back, staring quizzically at the still body. "I—don't think so, Smith."

Wesley leaned over and held a hand under Stephen's nose. "Nothing. Dammitall, he's *dead*."

"Not like that," Nayati admonished. "Lick it fir—no, fool, the back. It's more sensitive."

Even that way: "Nothing. I tell you—"

"You're the one who's dead, Smith." Nayati adjusted the fur under the corpse's neck, tipping its head back. "He's not frozen stiff. If he's gone anywhere, he's not been there for long." He slipped his hand free of the sling, and pinching the corpse's nose, locked mouths.

"Into necrophilia, Hatawa?" Wesley asked, sourly.

Nayati switched his attention to Stephen's chest, but with the second thrust, he cried out and fell back, holding his arm, his dark-skinned face pinched with pain.

"Damn fool—" He dropped to his knees beside Nayati and reached for his arm. Dead was one thing, pain was another. But Nayati jerked away, for all it wrenched a cry out of him, and said:

"Curse you, this is *old*. Look to him!"

"Damned if I'll kiss a—"

Nayati's backhand sent him sprawling. Wesley rolled and wavered to his knees, ready to fend off further attack. An attack that never came. Nayati was back on Stephen's body, trying to do one-handed what had always seemed to Wesley to require at least three. He sighed and growled: "Move the fuck over."

* * *

Sense of urgency from the Body. So little time left with Mama, so much to tell her.

Stephen thought of the lies Danislav had told him. His belief that his parents had relocated and requested dissolution of their parental responsibility. He remembered the broadcasts, the Flight he'd made just for her. If she were here, if she Knew, as he now Knew so much more . . .

"Mama, did you see me? I tried, Mama. I tried to show you. I was good, Mama. Some said, the best ever. I flew—"

"I saw, darling. I know. And you can fly again."

He shook his head against her breast. "No, Mama. Never the same. I—I fell, Mama."

"That's the Body's limitations, not yours, darling. You're in the DB forever. . . ."

Her hand lightly covered his eyes. . . .

(The finals. ZG requireds. Fifth-level specialty. . . .)

For an instant, he gloried in the feeling, the return of his one-time power, the sense of floating and absolute control of his destiny, but it was *exactly* the same—and that was no good. The joy was in the serendipity, the challenge of the instant. The Adaptation to each new gym. If he stayed, he could probably program in an uncertainty factor, but with the Sense, he'd always know—would never miss, never experience even a remote thrill from the *possibility* of missing—unless he programmed that in as a random variable to the equation as well.

Calculated imperfection.

Not the same.

He fell from the infostream and back into Mama's arms.

"I must go back, Mama."

"We need you here, darling. We *want* you here."

. . . One with the Body. . . .

"Do you, Mama? Or is this just one more desire to control me? Wesley needs me. The Body is still functional. Maybe I'll be back. Maybe not."

. . . Desperate concern. . . .

"Maybe isn't good enough, Zivon."

...Begging awareness....

He stood up, his full Ridenour-stature, and thinking of that programmed flight: "Is it even really you, Ylaine Ryevanishov? or simply Zivon Stefanovich's reflection of you?"

...Pain....

Her beautiful flower-blue eyes softened. "Does it matter?"

His eyes filled; Mama reached for him. But the distance between them was too great—

...Pain he can't leave untreated.

—and growing greater.

"Yes, Mama," he whispered. "It matters."

A sudden gasp. An inhalation that sucked the air from his toes. A softening response of the mouth locked with his.

Wesley jerked free and rocked back on his heels, vaguely disgusted. Even nine-tenths dead, the creature had sex on what passed for his mind.

"I've got a pulse!" Nayati whispered excitedly from the creature's far side. And as the creature gasped a second time, murmured softly and stirred: "Looks like you did it, Smith."

"Yeah, right." He rubbed the back of his hand across his mouth. "Just call me God. —You got any decent alcohol in here?"

"No."

"Shit. Any *indecent* alcohol?"

"No! —What the hell's wrong with you?" Nayati frowned up at him, pulled a dry blanket over Stephen and stood to confront him squarely. "Did you want him dead?"

He was sorely tempted to answer in the affirmative, but looking down at Stephen's pinched face he reluctantly shook his head. "But I sure as hell don't understand *your* sudden concern. As I recall, you were noisy enough about wanting exactly that, not so long ago."

Nayati shrugged. "Maybe I wasn't as smart as I thought. Maybe I was wrong."

"And maybe you were smarter than all of us. Don't trust

anything you feel about him, Nayati. He's crazier than a VSpace miner, and the virus is contagious.''

"And maybe he's the sanest one among us.''

"He *has* got your number, hasn't he?''

Nayati just shook his head and dropped back beside Stephen. "Ridenour? Hey, man, wake up.''

Stephen muttered softly, stirred enough to dislodge the blanket from his shoulder, but nothing more.

"He's still freezing,'' Nayati said, verifying the obvious. "Let's get fur under him—better insulation than the blanket.''

None of their manhandling fazed Sleeping Beauty in the least, and the emaciation of his body was painfully evident as they pulled and resettled the blanket.

"Can someone lose that much weight that fast just shivering?'' Wesley asked rhetorically.

Nayati shrugged. "He's not getting any better—won't with anything I know to do. We've got to get him to real medical facilities.''

"I'm open to suggestions.''

"That helmet have a com?''

"Not that works. You got a phone hidden in the back room?''

Nayati shook his head. "I've got to go. Get help.''

"Go where? From whom?''

"Cantrell. Her people are the only ones who have a chance of getting through in this weather.''

"It's better out there. Maybe—''

"Cantrell,'' Nayati said firmly. "Time we met, wouldn't you say?''

"Doesn't seem right, Cantrell winning this way. Let me go.''

"You couldn't tell them where this place is.''

"Ridenour's got a beeper.''

"I doubt it's functional. They'd have picked him up by now, weather or no.''

"I've got one in my arse.''

"Won't do them any good if you're with them.''

"Dammit, she'll fry you, Nayati."

"I doubt it."

Wesley glanced at Stephen, lying oblivious on the floor. "He's not worth the risk, Nayati."

"Others might disagree."

"You'll never make it."

"If I can get to the Tunnels, I can make it."

Wesley finished stripping the suit off. "At least wear this. Its powerpack's virtually depleted, but the insulation's pretty effective." And over Nayati's protest: "It'll help substantiate your story—hell, for all I know, it's recorded everything."

Nayati frowned, appalled, likely, that anyone would doubt his word, but he slipped the suit on, as well as three or four additional layers. He took the gloves, but left the helmet lying.

Not that Wesley could blame him.

"I've got to go before I boil to death." Nayati glanced at Stephen, all but comatose beside the fire. "Take care of him, Smith. I'm not sure how or why, but we can't let him die. Not yet."

"Not yet?" From somewhere, he found a grin. "Big of you, Nayati."

Nayati shrugged. "Everybody dies, Smith."

"Yeah, right. Drive carefully. Don't pick up strangers. And we'll see you after the spring thaw."

Wesley was alive. That brush with Reality brought reassurance.

But Wesley had vanished again, leaving him adrift in sensory limbo. Directionless. Aware of the pain and distress of the Body. Aware of the mists that held the Mother. Aware of the Opalescence and the Other.

And without the slightest impulsion to achieve any of those Energy states.

Sense of triumph, not his.

>*You see: you were wrong. You are not wanted. Not needed. Not in that world.*<

And this time, his own doubts gave the attack leverage. The

Wesley harmonic had left him, leaving a taste of revulsion—the RealSpace resonance gone silent. The Mother was silent. Only the Other...

Sudden sensory assault: the Opalescence.

And this time, the Other was but one of a mass of massless, star-shot shadows, as the Voice was but one of a chorus:

>*We cannot let you leave, Zivon Ridenour.*<

And beyond the shadows, millions of fraying ends fractured the Opalescence.

V

i

No time to think. No time to consider. The 'NetDB was crashing, and for all he knew, for each rent he sealed, the Cocheta created ten more.

His virtual body no longer sparkled—it glowed and flared, simmering with energy awaiting release.

A frayed end brushed his hand, one among many.

Recognition.

Awareness.

Tranquillity: solution to a subdirectory progwuzzle.

He grasped the end, sensed the match and reached for it, creating the bridge, but not the seal, recognizing Potential.

And of a sudden, the Other was before him—along with his counterparts.

>*That was given you in error.*<

The Other extended a shadow-hand. A tacit order Stephen ignored.

Evaluation. Weakness of the Body; a handful of frayed ends

yet to be mended—the Cocheta had reckoned well: only enough damage to destroy the Body, no more.

But this one—he sent Awareness along it, found the Linkage. Like the Vandereaux Linkage, only this was confined to a single, high-energy extension into the 'Net.

... could not access until the process initiated ...

Nayati's original mistake: his deletion of Data that had linked Human space to Cocheta; Nayati's second error: destruction of the Library, the energy flux that had created the bridge and sent undirected disruptive power into NSpace.

The end pulsed; He Sensed it for the Source of the Cocheta themselves.

>No more.<

Collective protest.

>I say, no more, or I will seal the error and sever the Link.<

The Other separated from the collective shadow and gestured to the handful of severances left.

>*You cannot return, Zivon Ridenour, and leave these unattended.*<

Holding the ends in one neutralized hand, he extended the other to sample the Data affected. Only one was of significance. One-handed, he took it to its match and secured the connection.

Sensory input wavered; the Cocheta had calculated his remaining energy with distressing accuracy.

>You claim you don't sap Energy from the Hosts, yet Energy was needed to effect the damage. Whence came the Energy?<

>*We do not seek to damage the Hosts.*<

>Destroy the DB and we will survive. Will you?<

>—*Uncertain. Insufficient data*—<

>Fair enough. Without adequate warning from me, the 'NetAT will utilize the new ability to adjust Data indiscriminately. Chaos will proliferate beyond my ability to rectify. Leave me alone to deliver the message and renew my resources, and I shall return to complete the Function. Stand in my way again, and your Link is severed. Chaos will triumph.<

>*You couldn't.*<
>Couldn't I?<
>*It would destroy you. Not only your Body. The Self as well. You wouldn't do it.*<
>Wouldn't I?<
>*You can't return to this space without help. We won't help you.*<

The Totality wavered again. Energy fading. Desperate, he sought the Energy Source he'd tapped once before, discovering his own price, willing to risk even Wesley's life to control his own destiny—to complete the message.

But the glow was gone. The Totality fading. He was back in the Limbo between realities with the Other's cocoon weaving inexorably around him. . . .

Wesley left Stephen alone long enough for a brief shower and other necessities, discovering state of the recycling art plumbing and good cotton towels behind that traditional woven room divider. Evidently, Nayati adhered only to those traditions that did not compromise his personal comfort.

Made him far more likeable, to the Wesser's way of thinking.

And he had food. Good stuff: dried meats and fruits, instant hot chocolate—and peppermint liquor.

"Damned liar," Wesley muttered, and fixed a mug of generously laced chocolate, heaped a plate full, wrapped a towel around his waist—Nayati's wet clothes being the only other option left in the place—and returned to the fireside.

But Stephen was—gone. Like before, except this time he could see the infinitesimal movement of the chest, could detect a feeble pulse.

"Shit." He set plate and mug down, and pulling Stephen upright, slapped him hard. "C'mon, clone, snap out of it."

A technique that did wonders for him and nothing for Stephen, who continued deteriorating rapidly. Disintegrating before his eyes. Actively gasping now, like a fish too long out of water.

The scuz was going to die on him after all. And Cantrell

would manage to blame him for that, too, never mind no one ever told you what to do with someone who *had* a pulse, whose tongue seemed perfectly normal and who couldn't possibly be choking on food he hadn't had.

In desperation, since oxygen appeared to be the problem— and because he honestly didn't want Stephen Ridenour to die—he drew a deep breath and locked his mouth on the gasping fish's—

(Hands. Lips. Aching need. Pain.

(Desire.

(Disruption of the Unity. Fear of the Feeling from Zivon, escape from the Feeling from the Ridenour, insulation of the Unity from the Feeling from the Other.

(But the Need was Concern for the Body. The pain the Body's fight for continuance. The Desire the Body's response to the Need.

(He ran from that need—Danger, so the Other called it. He felt none of it himself. No fear. No need. Only a drive to change the error. To eliminate the confusion and heal the Body. But the Other's desire to escape was strong, and so he ran.

(But the need outraced him. Pulled him back. Isolated the Matrix and identified itself.

(The Harmonic. The Host.

(The Other protected from the Feeling. The Host invited him to join in the glory of it. One was safety, insulation. The other, his own Danger. Serendipity. That which made the Flight worth doing . . .

("It's not the same, Mama . . .")

—this time, he'd swear the resultant gasp sucked his toes inside out.

Stephen's trembling shook them both. Stephen's arms looped his neck, pulling him closer, Stephen's lips softened . . .

"What the—"

. . . and breathed into his mouth: "Anything you want,

Wesley..." Stephen's hands began a skillful, exciting trail down his spine and around the towel. "Anything... you..."

He *didn't* want this—had not come after Ridenour for this—but somehow, the younger man's urgency caught him up and he quit thinking at all, his world reduced to his own physical responses until, as excitement grew into fever, he realized:

"Stephen, you're—"

"Doesn't *matter*—" he gasped, his features unrecognizable in their need.

"Kid, I *can't*. I'll hurt—"

But Ridenour wasn't damnwell listening. Ridenour had his own ideas. There was nothing sweet or tender, loving or even refined about their coupling. They were two animals in rut seeking release, and Wesley was helpless to stop it, caught on a wave of sheer lust that engulfed him at Stephen's touch, a wave that shattered his self-control, at once terrifying and disgusting him, furious with the Doxie-clone for bringing them to this.

Yet despite the disgust and the fury, he discovered himself echoing Stephen's passions, mindlessly willing, until the only emotion left, as they collapsed into a tangle of sweating limbs, was exhaustion.

"I'm back." Stephen whispered enigmatically and on a gasp, but with absolute coherency; his arms and legs entwined Wesley like an octopus with no intention of letting go, his face pressed into the hollow of Wesley's neck; he was shuddering, exhausted, but breathing healthy, deep gasps of air, the near catatonia seemingly banished. "Oh God, Wesley, I'm back."

Sweaty, disgusting, and Wesley didn't dare try to remove him; neither, incredibly, did he want to.

That wanton single-mindedness, the oblivion to his own pain—classic 'Doxie, as he understood the type.

The reports never warned you the symptoms were contagious.

"Anevai?"

Blackness. Either predawn, or her eyelids were glued together. She yawned widely and buried her head in the pillow.

"Gods, Nayati, what do you—" *Nayati?* Of a sudden, she was no longer the least bit sleepy. "Nayati, *is* that you?"

"Anevai, . . . please . . ." Shadowy voice from a shadow propped in her bedroom door. ". . . help . . ."

She was at his side before the next gasp, pulling him inside and shutting the door silently behind him. He slipped out of her hold and collapsed to the floor. Biting her lip on an exclamation, she threw on the light and knelt beside him.

Sweaty and shaking, obviously at the limit of his endurance, at least he was conscious. She helped him sit up, propping him against the bed, and brushed fumbling fingers out of the way to strip him of the layers of stifling clothing.

"Nayati, what's wrong? Why are you here?"

"S—starving."

One soaked layer gone. She paused briefly, realizing:

"Me, too." She shook her head to clear it, and started on the next layer. "I'll find us something in a minute. What the hell are you doing in my room?"

He grabbed her hand, squeezed it, forcing her attention. "Ridenour. Must help." His eyelids drooped. He forced them open with obvious effort. "Cantrell."

His head fell back against the mattress; to all appearances, he was asleep.

The sweater, also soaked, joined the pile on the floor. The next layer—

Anevai's fingers froze.

—had the *Cetecean* logo on the breast pocket.

Every muscular contraction threatened cramp: electrolytes desperately out of balance.

Old skills frequently proved useful. Despite the impending cramps, Stephen worked himself free without waking Wesley up. Twice before he'd waked up to find someone staring in his face, and he didn't think he was up to the consequences this—

—morning?

When—*where* was he?

Faint ambient light revealed nowhere he knew, but the dim outline of a familiar logo on a dark just-out-of-reach lump suggested a *Cetacean* pack. Emergency supplies.

Food. Primal instincts screamed recognition.

Ignoring muscular objections, he wormed his way to the lump where a blind, fumbling search came up with what felt like a coat, emergency ration packets, and three (from the smell) candy bars.

He worked the coat on, huddled as much of him under its tent as would fit, and tore one of the ERats open with his teeth. Time to find out if McKenna's shot had done the trick. If it hadn't . . . well, he could hardly feel any worse than he did already.

By the time he started on the fourth packet, the ambient light was increasing rapidly, and he was altogether certain he had no idea where he was. Not that it mattered. Somehow, Wesley had found him. Somehow, Wesley had pulled him back from that—place. And somehow (Thank God it was Wesley and not Nayati who had managed the trick.) when he woke up, Wesley would understand what he'd done and why he'd done it, and help him decide what to do.

As if Stephen's thoughts had disturbed him, Wesley stirred, muttered something that sounded vaguely obscene, and patted the nest of furs and blankets surrounding him. The patting hand paused, began a second, slower search. Then:

"Dammit, Ridenour, where—"

Stephen met Wesley's outrage with a half-eaten (and the last) candy bar. "Breakfast?"

"So, how long before Cantrell gets here?" Nayati, showered and dressed in a towel, reached in front of her for another sandwich, and Anevai, licking her fingers clean of her third, said,

"You *are* hungry." And pretended not to hear his caustic rebuttal as she washed the crumbs down with her second glass of fruit juice. "I'd say—soon now—real soon."

"Close enough." He stood up and stretched, and asked around the last bite: "I'd better go filch something suitable from Hononomii's room."

"Be careful not to wake him up," she cautioned without thinking. When she did, she met his startled glance casually. "He's home, Nayati."

"How—" He swallowed visibly.

"—is he?" She finished for him, and shrugged. "He'll be better, now you're home." Home in all senses of the word. This was her friend, not the stranger who'd looked through Nayati's eyes at her the past several months.

"I wish I could be certain of that."

"I don't think I like the sound of that, cousin."

"The suggestion was made under the Cocheta machine's influence, Anevai." The pain in Nayati's voice was real. "The Library is gone and—"

A quiet knock on her door silenced him.

"*Anevai? What's all the racket up here? Are you all right?*" Sakiimagan.

A tap at Nayati's leg got his attention; he answered her tacit question with a shrug and a nod toward the door. "It's okay, Dad," she said, "you can come in."

The door opened. Sakiimagan took one look at Nayati, standing half-naked in his daughter's bedroom, his daughter, sitting on the floor beside her bed and the plates of mostly eaten food, and said, "Mind if I join you?"

"Listen to yourself, Ridenour! This is basic psych—classic MPD syndrome. Abused child splitting off individuals to absorb the pain—leave the essential you free to—"

"Stow it, Smith," Stephen retorted, his head aching from an overdose of ERat—and J. W. Smith. "The psychs have been in my head daily for the last ten years. I *know* that shit. If I was, I integrated all·by myself years ago—*I* remember, *I* know."

"You know now. Not so many days ago, I recall finding a kid, high on dope, absorbing a diary—*that's* where your integration came from. Nayati's little trip just—introduced you to the original holders of the memories.''

Stephen scowled, trying to ignore the voice of RealSpace Reason. He *knew* what had happened, whether Wesley Smith believed him or not. Somehow, he'd convince those who mattered.

He'd thought Wesley Smith ranked among those.

Now he wasn't so sure.

''I can't believe,'' Wesley persisted, ''that *you* believed this—thing—was inside you, that you perceived these risks and still kept it all to yourself. Lord, boy, how stupid can one person be?''

''Dammit, Wes, I don't consider withholding extraneous information stupid! I *thought* it was the damned suit!'' He jerked to his feet and went to the window flap they'd thrown open for ventilation, staring out into the morning's rapidly melting snow. ''I didn't tell her I used Positive Self-actuation Theory to free myself from Nayati's damned Cocheta machine either, but that's *how* I did it. Why should I feel compelled to tell her *how* I found the damned exit! —Or that I *felt* Anevai—'' *And you!* ''—the way I *feel* the mountain?''

He struck the frame with his clenched fist. What was it he'd thought before? Thank God it was Wesley? *He'd* understand? How wrong could he have been?

''It's embarrassing enough to explain this to you when we've—and you've—'' He choked. In angry desperation he cried, ''What do you want from me? My whole fucking life story? Well, now you've got it! Give you a thrill, does it?''

There was a loud silence from the room behind him. He swung around to find Wesley pulling Nayati's fringed-leather pants on. Stephen clenched his teeth around the plea he longed to make.

''I don't deserve that, Stephen,'' Wesley said, yanking a matching, stained tunic on over his head. ''And if you can't see the difference between the two examples you cited, you can damnwell go back to the Council and the Alliance and stay there—you can damnwell go to hell as far as I'm concerned.''

He took three quick strides to the door, jerked it open and said, over his shoulder, "One final piece of advice, Dr. Ridenour, which you can take or not—as you please. You tell your Admiral Cantrell about your little piece of withheld information, and you tell her fast. She deserves to know if she's carrying a time bomb back with her—a bomb that makes the situation she's counting on you to defuse look like an excited bottle of champagne. Goodbye, Dr. Ridenour. Have a safe journey home.''

"Wes . . . ?"

The flinch of Wesley's head might have been reflex or no more than Stephen's imagination. He did not turn back. "Fool me once, Ridenour—or in my case, being something of a trustful bastard, seven or eight times—I've no more trust in me, clone. Regardless of what you may or may not have been through at Vandereaux, you learned your lessons there, and you learned them well, considering the games you're playing and the stakes you're playing for. Remember what I said about the clothes you wear? Well you can add this to it: take care what you advertise—sometimes people are ready to pay the price. —Cantrell's goons will be coming for us. Until they get here, I'm just outside this door. Don't plan on going anywhere."

"This had better be good, girl.'' Cantrell strode into the foyer, jerking her gloves off. Behind her, TJ Briggs, and behind him—

"Sgt. Fonteccio!" Anevai grinned a greeting. "I didn't realize you'd returned. Welcome."

"This is no time for idle chatter. It's colder than hades out there, but we've got the air ambulance. Now, where's the person who found . . .''

"Admiral Cantrell?"

Déjà vu of Vandereaux Station dockside. Of a person she'd

been chasing all over two stations. A person who should have had the decency to look his truant part and instead had every long, black hair neatly in place, every fingernail on the extended hand neatly manicured and every stitch on his lean body tucked and tailored.

"How do you do. —My name's Nayati Hatawa."

ii

Lexi closed the conference room door behind Smith and the admiral and settled into the easy chair beside TJ's. He appeared to be asleep, slouched down, feet up on another chair, elbows propped comfortably on the armrests.

Lexi adopted a similar pose, but kept her eyes open, being too apt to fall asleep otherwise.

She'd arrived on this morning's shuttle at Cantrell's orders—Cantrell had *wanted* her downworld to deal with Stephen when they found him—only to have Cantrell herself waiting for her on the landing field. They'd gone straightaway to the Tyeewapis' and on to Stephen and Smith from there.

As happened, Cantrell hadn't needed her at all. Stephen, although grateful for his rescue—even more so for the warm clothing they'd taken along—had been quiet, distant, even when Cantrell announced he'd be returning to Vandereaux with *Cetacean* rather than the 'NetATs.

Calm. Collected. Even while the EMTs examined him head to foot. They'd pronounced him healthy enough, just dreadfully dehydrated and underweight, a state Stephen had been trying to make up for ever since. —Right up until this meeting.

Cantrell had barely spoken two words to her; TJ none at all.

Suddenly, from the slouched figure at her side: "Welcome home."

Articulate. Brief. Eminently TJ.

"Thanks." Alexis Fonteccio could also be brief.

"Missed you."

That's it, Teej? 'Missed you?'

"Ditto."

His thin lips stretched in a smile beneath closed eyes, his hand crept over the armrest, found and squeezed hers, then slipped back from whence it came.

The next sound out of him was a soft snore.

". . . I don't know *what* the Other is. My gut considers it an entity, perhaps one of the aliens existing on the 'Net as I was—perhaps his body had died and left him there—but for all I know it might just be an alien program which I perceive as an entity because that's how I'm able to comprehend it. Whatever it is, contact with it does tend to leave emotions a bit—on the surface. Nothing I can't handle well enough to make the report, but I think maybe that's why Nayati acted strangely. But the Cocheta didn't seem—malevolent. The main thing is, whether or not anyone believes me, the 'Net's safe now, stable . . . for a while."

"And so we should all kneel down and worship the great god Ridenour, right?" Smith snarled over his shoulder.

"I didn't say that, Dr. Smith," Stephen responded quietly.

Déjà vu of another meeting in this same room: Smith staring out the window avoiding the issue—*any* issue, Stephen making a difficult report. Only this time, the third party was real, not a video image. All too real, in the untempered backlash of Smith's wrath. And Loren Cantrell's only option was to sit and watch what developed. She could scarcely blame Smith's skepticism. Certainly Ridenour's story sounded—delusory.

She wondered if he realized what these revelations meant. Regardless what he may or may not have done in the past, the possibility Stephen had been contaminated with a potentially violent personality, combined with his demonstrated ability to use Smith's system, meant quite simply he'd never put his hands on a keyboard again.

Then she remembered that report sitting in the briefcase at her feet. —He *knew*.

Stephen's gaze left Smith and turned to her. "This morning we had a discussion—"

"Discussion—hell!"

"Shut up, Smith," she said.

Stephen's eyes flickered to Smith and back to his tightly clenched hands resting on the conference-room table. "This morning—before your arrival—Dr. Smith and I—we argued, a–and Dr. Smith felt compelled to leave before I'd had a chance to fully explain."

"Bull*shit*."

"If you insist, sir." No faltering this time. "Admiral, I'm fully aware of how this new information compromises my report—"

"So *that's* your game, you little bastard! You're afraid they'll kick you out of the nice cushy job they've got waiting because you've got a freeloader in your skull. If you're so fucking clever, why don't you *ask* the freeloader where to find more of these Cocheta? Afraid we'll check it out? Show up your scam?"

A valid enough point, but Cantrell was less interested in Smith's points than in Stephen's struggle to maintain that quiet exterior in the face of those points.

It does tend to leave your emotions a bit on the surface ... but nothing I can't handle.

On the other hand, sometimes emotions could use a helping hand.

"I don't think you've got it quite right, Dr. Smith. Stephen, do you care to tell him what you sent to Chet along with your last report?"

Stephen exclaimed softly, "You weren't supposed to get it until—"

"Until we were back at Vandereaux? Did you think something that significant would go unnoticed? Chet sent it to me—along with a note to stop you."

"What are you two talking about?" Smith snapped. "Ridenour, what have you done now?"

Stephen's unblinking stare followed the report from her briefcase to Smith's hands, then shifted to his water glass. Half the liquid spilled before he steadied the glass two-handed and set it down untasted.

Smith flipped through, reading at random till he reached the last page. He jerked that page from the binding, tossed the rest of the report to the table, and read again, his face cold. Finally: "Quite a gesture, Ridenour. But then, after yesterday—"

"Look again, Smith. Check out the file date."

Stephen winced and touched her arm. "Admiral, please. It's hardly . . . He has every right to—"

Paper crackled. Smith: watching them, Stephen's resignation crumpled in his fist. Stephen's hand drew away as Smith moved slowly over to drop into one of the plush chairs, raking a hand through his hair and across his face.

"Stephen, I don't know what to say."

"*Then for God's sake don't say anything!*" Stephen jerked to his feet, the hard, straight-backed chair he'd insisted on toppling to the floor. He leaned over to pick it up; it caught in the carpet and wrenched from his fingers. He swore and kicked at it, then let it lie, taking Smith's place at the window, nursing the hand and staring blank-faced and wide-eyed out the window, shoulders hunched under the bulky sweater.

Thin shoulders. Thin and exhausted. A vibrant young man turned wraith literally overnight, whose ghost-face betrayed everything the mind tried to hide.

It does tend to leave your emotions a bit close to the surface . . .

Smith shrugged and turned his attention elsewhere.

. . . but nothing I can't handle. . . .

Stephen gave a choked gasp and dropped to the window seat, eyes closed, fists pressed to his temples.

"*Stephen!*"

Her own cry echoed Smith's, and she joined him in his scramble to catch Stephen as he collapsed in a boneless drip to the floor.

* * *

He'd been so worried. He'd known this moment would come and feared the eventuality. But in the end, it was so simple: release the hold on RealSpace Wesley had provided him, and he was back in the Opalescence.

Wesley, whose touch had made him so thoroughly aware of the Body, he couldn't stay in the limbo Between. Wesley who had responded only because he'd asked, and then hated him for it after, unable to believe.

Wesley wanted proof, had put a quantification on that proof. An Equation with an Answer. Before crossing over, he had feared the process.

Now he simply sought the solution.

The Other was waiting—alone.

>*You're back.*<

>As promised.<

Keeping only the equation in his forebrain.

>*Your energy source is revitalized? Your message delivered?*<

>In part.<

>*Which?*<

>Both. Return is imperative.<

>*Why? RealSpace has nothing to offer one who sees the Totality.*<

>No? Possibly you're right. Probably you are. But the Function must be performed, and that requires my return.<

>*—Function?—*<

And in that instant of confusion, He thought of the Cocheta Linkage, reached for it, absorbed its infoflow, located its Source, severed the Link, and fused Nayati's enabling rent in a single command string.

He sensed the strain on the Body, but it survived. He checked the energy level, discovered sufficient to finish effecting repairs on the 'Net. Quiet, lonely work. The Cocheta driven out, isolated within their own Directory.

After that, he waited. Either Wesley would draw him back or he would not. The task might be—simpler this time without the

Cocheta to retain him. Less . . . energy-hungry. Likely Cantrell would appreciate that.

He sensed a presence: the Other, though he didn't see the dimensionless shadow.

>I thought you'd be gone.<

>*How can I? My Link is here.*<

>Me?<

Acknowledgement.

>*Your Function has isolated me—here.*<

>It had to be done.<

Acknowledgement.

>*Will you leave?*<

>If I can.<

>*A prudent individual would stay to guard me. I could still destroy the 'Net.*<

>But you won't.<

>*Are you willing to gamble a universe on that?*<

>You forget: I know you. —It's not a gamble.<

Amusement.

>*I shall miss you, Zivon Ridenour.*<

>I'll write.<

>*You begin to Feel like J. Wesley Smith.*<

>Does the fact surprise you?<

>*No. Your patterns are very similar.*<

>Yet you never spoke to him, except—<

Sudden realization.

>—Except through Anevai.<

Acknowledgement.

>*Of necessity. He is Similar, not Identical.*<

>Why didn't you simply—adjust him to your purposes, the way Nayati's Cocheta did?<

>*You cannot blame Nayati's actions on his counterpart. We cannot create that which does not already exist within the host. If we could, you would not have been necessary.*<

Sorrow. Regret for the pain he suffered. But no sense of apology.

>*It had to be, Zivon Ridenour. You had to exist, amalgam of Truth and Human misrepresentation, in order to effect repairs. You are still needed. What happens when new rents occur in the fabric? —What then, Zivon Ridenour?*<

>I don't know. Can't.<

>*You will know when they occur.*<

>Through you?<

Acknowledgement.

>I'm—glad.<

>*But perhaps we speak in hypotheticals. Your friends have not come.*<

He thought of Wesley then. Wondered *would* he care enough, possibly even to risk a repeat performance of this morning. *We cannot create that which does not already exist within the host*... Interesting. So it wasn't Nayati's chosen match that created the mindless ecstasy within him. . . .

>*I misread you, Stephen Ridenour, thought you were frightened of it.*<

Thoughts following the same path.

>I was frightened when I thought it came from outside myself. But it's a part of me. I can't be whole and deny it.<

>*But if that is what you really want, we can give it to you. Can give you everything you want.*<

>We?<

A virtual shrug.

>*I, then. —The transition comes hard.*<

"But it is 'we,' Zivon."

He was in the mists, and Mama was holding him. And behind her, Papa and Granther, Meesha and Pii'chum and—

"Nevya?" he whispered, and his cousin smiled. But they weren't real. *Couldn't* be real. He slipped free of Mama's touch and drifted away.

>*They are real. As real as you wish them to be.*<

>And nothing more than that.<

>*But they are. They touched the Totality, as you have. These are reflections of that Touch as much as of your heart. Many of*

your other friends had counterparts here. They would be again, if you repaired the Linkage.<

>And endanger all my friends? Your destructive actions on the 'Net took its toll on them.<

>*There is no danger. We don't seek to damage the Host. It is a bargain—a trade. An expansion of their awareness—our chance to Touch the World again.*<

>And the destruction of the Body?<

>*Necessary to effect change. We do not consider it lightly. Your presence here is—necessary to the balance. We sought to force that balance. We were wrong.*<

>Once—long ago—you promised me you would not foul the interface, that you *knew* me. You don't really know me at all. It's all guesswork for you, too. Experimentation, that's all I am for everyone. Everyone except Wesley.<

>*Because his needs are basic. His wants simple.*<

>That's right. But he wants it for me. Not for himself.<
>*That makes no sense.*<

"Doesn't it?" he said, defiantly aloud, defiantly Human. "Perhaps that's where you've misunderstood me all along."

Amusement.

>*Perhaps. But you are young, yet. —Goodbye, Zivon Ridenour. Do not worry, your—friends—will come for you.*<

"And should they reject you, darling . . ." A caress on his cheek, though he was far away from her. "We'll always be here . . ."

iii

(A moment of Limbo, then:)

Hands touched him. Through those hands he sensed fear and concern such as he could no longer achieve for himself. Difficult to be afraid when all death of the Body meant was an eternity free of pain, in a place he was wanted and needed.

Even if the wants and needs were simply his own wishes given form.

For a moment, he hated them all for that concern, his mist-world parents, Wesley and Cantrell, even the nameless Cocheta. He lurched to his feet and away from the humans. The Cocheta would never be gone.

He staggered up against a table, fumbling madly for RealWorld orientation, his muscles defying any suggestion made of them.

The SciComp conference room. Cantrell. Smith. The meeting. The Cocheta infodump he'd risked everything to retrieve.

"Get me a map." His voice was hoarse, as dysfunctional as his muscles.

"What the hell—"

"I don't know how long I can hold the image. *Get me a goddamn map!*"

"Map of what?"

"The whole fucking planet!" He gasped. Held his breath, and, behind closed eyelids, visualized the infoflow. "I know where they are."

"My God." He heard Cantrell's mutter. Ignored it as he could. "Get onLine, Smith." Ignored, as well, Wesley's protest. "Find that map! Detailed as you can get."

The following period was a blur of impressions and transformations. Impressions of maps and video correspondence. Transformations of that information into the Cocheta infoflow and back.

Transformations increasingly uncertain.

Finally, he had to admit: "I just don't know, admiral. I can't promise you anything. Maybe Wesley's right and it's all a delusion. My—professional opinion—as your—expert advisor— would be: listen to Smith. Ridenour's nothing but a doped-out Doxie with half a brain left, and that's stuck in VSpace. My personal advice—" He shrugged and collapsed into the soft chair, safe, now in its comfortable confines. Safe, now, to sleep, perhaps, even, to dream. "My personal advice would be: what have you got to lose? Try one out. If there's nothing there, Wesley's right. If there is—hell, does it even matter? —Call it a freak coincidence. Luck. At least you'd have your proof.''

''I've already ordered teams sent out to the locations, Stephen.''

A rather painful bubble found release in a wry chuckle, and he dropped his head into his hand, rubbing his forehead and eyes.

''Stephen, are you all right?'' Wesley touched his shoulder, a touch that moved to gently massage his neck, like it hadn't better sense.

''All right?'' Stephen shrugged out from under the touch and moved around the table to his former straight-backed chair, righted it, and sat down, folding his hands on the tabletop. ''Hell, I'm fucking wonderful.'' He caught Cantrell's startled glance and blushed hotly. ''I—I beg your pardon. —I've a damnable headache and could use an aspirin—maybe some fruit juice and a cracker. Electrolytes on the fritz, I suspect. I'll be fine.''

''Is that what really happened last night, Stephen?''

Smith's gentle tone confused him. Smith was angry. He'd betrayed Smith's trust and Smith hated him now. He was prepared to deal with an angry Smith. He wasn't ready for Wesley. He said calmly, deliberately misinterpreting: ''Last night, Dr. Smith, I didn't realize what the Cocheta could do. Now I know. *I* can control the interface now. Quite simple, really: strong emotions give them the advantage. I'll just recognize strong emotions for what they are and—ignore them.''

''Like you did last night?''

He shrugged.

''So what are you going to do? Go back to Vandereaux? Crawl back into that virtual bubble you existed in before you came here?''

He shrugged.

''Dammit, Stephen, you *can't!*''

''It's not a problem, really. I've survived quite well for years.''

"Survived, yes, but—"

"Lord, Wes, what difference does it make to you?" His voice cracked, but he fought it steady. "A few hours from now, I'm history here. You'll never have to *think* of me again!"

"How can you say that so cold-bloodedly?"

"That's almost funny coming from you." Bitterness flooded him. He examined it, decided it was his, and let it out. "What choice have I? Did I say I want to go back? To be barred from the 'Net for the rest of my life? —Barred, *hell*. I've *been* the 'Net, no matter you don't believe. They'll have to count on my ability to stay *off* the damn thing, because not even *you* believe me. And without you . . . —But there's no choice! I never have had. I didn't say anything, because I had no choice: my father took care of that—" The old disciplinary pain shot through his head. He controlled it furiously. "—and what free will he left me, Nayati and the Cocheta claimed. *That's* why I put in my resignation." He turned to Cantrell. "Mostly I fear why I actually avoided telling *you*. Once, I would have said the Cocheta was quiescent unless actively called upon. Now—" His hands started to shake. He hid them under the table, clamping them between his knees. "Admiral Cantrell, I recommend—as the 'Tech advisor on this mission—that my memory be—studied—for what I might have unwittingly with-held, and for—verification—of at least my *perceptions* of what took place last night. I—I would prefer to wait until after my report on *Harmonies* . . ." Please, God, let him remember that one accomplishment—if only for a few hours. ". . . but will fully understand if you deem it best otherwise."

"Stephen, —" Wesley again, sitting down beside him.

He ignored the interruption—Wesley's proximity was more difficult.

"I—I also believe my so-called resistance to Deprivil is more the result of my father's conditioning than any real physiological abnormality. Since I want to cooperate, I might manage those reactions. Any other possible complications are immaterial: the suggestion is of my own free will and on record. The only request I'd like to make is that you do the probe. I—I think it might make a difference having someone I trust do the—operating, so to speak.''

"I'll do what I can, Dr. Ridenour.'' Cool. Professional. Thank God.

"Dammit, Ridenour!'' Wesley's hand on his wrist forced his attention, but not, he suspected, in the way Wesley wanted. Through that touch, he sensed Wesley's heartbeat, the flow of the blood through his veins, the glow of sheer vital energy, and he disengaged, fled to the far side of the table before that glow began to flux the wrong way. He was too tired, too hungry, to fight the desire that made him want to wrap himself around that warm glow until he was no longer cold, no longer hungry.

Perhaps as the Other claimed, the Cocheta felt no such temptation to absorb their—Host—but Stephen Ridenour had no similar bargain to offer, no expansion of his host's Awareness. Only feeling. One-way and, without question, evil.

When he had that need controlled, he met Wesley's eyes. "As for the virtual bubble, as you termed it, it's not a problem.''

"Not a problem?'' Wesley challenged him. But all Wesley saw was a Doxie, out of control, and getting himself into a situation that could end him up exceedingly dead.

Stephen dropped his gaze to his clenched hands, forcing them to relax, and began tracing the grain in the table with a fingertip. "Somebody told me, once, I should start selling what lies above the neck rather than what's below it. Thought I might try that.''

"Money's not always the issue, Stephen.''

"*Money* never was, Wesley.''

"*What* then?''

Stephen shook his head. "And you call *me* young. . . .'' He managed a shaky grin. "Anything else—well, I'm leaving all my temptations behind, aren't I?''

"Lord, Stephen, there's so much I want to—''

"Well, you *can't*, can you?" He bit his lip on that protest, and said wearily, "Let it drop, Wes. It doesn't concern you."

Wesley looked far from convinced, certainly not willing to—let it drop.

Stephen choked on a half-laugh. "—Hell, Wes, I've had perfection. Why should I settle for anything less?"

"That's not funny, Stephen."

"Isn't it? Maybe I didn't mean it to be. But let it be, Wesley. Let it be funny. I've learned a lot here, but most of all, I've learned how to laugh. No one can take that away from me."

"I don't like this talk as though you're never coming back, Stephen."

"Neither do I," Cantrell said firmly. "I'm not going to put that resignation in, Stephen. No need to rush into things right now. If everything pans out, Council's going to owe you—Big Time. Name your price—*Cetacean* will back you. Even if, heaven forbid, that price means bringing you back here."

Stephen smiled. If Cantrell wasn't careful, her admiration of Wesley Smith would show. "That's—kind of you, admiral, but I've thought about it all week, and I could never, in good conscience, accept a position of trust. I could never be certain which thoughts were mine, and which . . ."

"Still, we'll wait. Who knows what Paul and the others will discover here while we're in transit? Perhaps the secret of your particular brand of lunacy will turn up. Don't burn your bridges too soon, son."

He felt his hard-won serenity waver, and cried desperately, "Will you both please stop? You've seen my transfer. Danislav calls the shots for my career—hell, for my whole damn life! That was part of the deal that got me into Vandereaux in the first place. No Councillor's whim can change that. They don't *want* me on my own. Danislav can't afford to have a ten-year investment yield no data. And if he can't have positive results, I've got to fail—openly. Visibly."

"Dammit, boy," Wesley said, "What's Danislav got on

you? Danislav owes *you!* He *owes* you! For this and a hell of a
lot else!''

''Wesley, for God's sake . . . What *else?*''

''You know what I'm talking about. It makes no difference
what you did. You were a child. Your record's clear now—has
been for years—and you're *still* carrying the—''

''You *bastard.*'' Rage surged. Stephen forced it back, but
only for an instant: the Unity of Zivon, the Ridenour, and the
Other was too strong, the issue too old, the injustice too much
a part of him to lie dormant. ''You fucking sonuvabitch. *You
had no right!*''

''The hell I didn't. Damn right I searched your records. I
wanted to know *what* I had in bed that night.''

He kicked the chair out of his way and went to the door.
Clasped the handle and took a single lung-filling breath, and
said quietly, ''Well, now you know and there's nothing more to
say, is there? —Admiral, what time tomorrow does the shuttle
leave?''

''Stephen, don't run out on this.'' Cantrell looked worriedly
from him to Wesley and back. ''If you've got something to
say . . .''

He shook his head. ''There are some things worth fighting
for and others that aren't. I won't jeopardize HuteNamid's
future . . .'' And to still the Other's arguments for the future to
which he was condemning the Self: >my *child's* future—< . . .
in some ultimately useless attempt to change my own. I'll survive. I always have. I'll even be content enough.'' His voice
cracked. He steadied it. ''When, admiral?''

''Tomorrow. Noonish, local. I'll call you. Are you going to
be all right, Stephen? Do you want someone to go with you?
Lexi's here.''

''I'm fine. Just—tired.''

From across the table, a coercive: ''Stephen . . . ?''

''*No!*'' The protest escaped before he could edit the tone. He
took a deep breath, settled his pulse, and continued: ''Good*bye*,
Dr. Smith. It's been—an experience.''

But objections still permeated the air. He paused at the door, and without looking back, said colorlessly, "You asked me what Danislav's got—what his hold over me is. It's not a hold over me, and it's not Danislav. You should have realized when you were—snooping. It's Shapoorian, and my significance to her cause, and, worse, what can happen to my investigation's credibility—and your amnesty—if my background becomes generally known." He looked back over his shoulder, met Wesley's frown. "She's got my confession."

The frown deepened into bewilderment: a somewhat empty triumph. Stephen shook his head and opened the door.

"Think about it."

Smith's tortured eyes followed Stephen's escape, then shifted to her. "My God, admiral, what have I done?"

Cantrell raised an eyebrow, signalled TJ, and said, without taking her eyes off Smith, "Ridenour just left here. Ostensibly for his room. Have Lexi keep an eye on him. Don't let him do anything stupid." Then to Smith: "I can't answer that, Smith, but whatever it was, I hope what you got out of it was worth the price."

He winced. Good. About time someone *else* hurt around here.

"Don't pull any punches, do you?" he said drily.

"I'm not feeling exactly charitable at the moment."

Smith went to the much-used window and stared out for a long time. Suddenly:

"*Dammit!*" He hit the wall with his fist and whirled around. "He's done it again!"

"What, in your so learned opinion, has Stephen done now, Smith?"

Smith strode over to the table and explained at point-blank range:

"Don't you see it?" He waved toward Stephen's chair. "Look how we're both reacting to that little performance! The clone sits there, innocence incarnate, and twists us both into thinking and feeling exactly what he wants us to. *Poor little Stevie*. God, how could I fall for it *again*?'' He slammed his fist on the table and turned his back on her.

''You pushed him into this confession, didn't you?''

''Well, dammit, you had to know!''

''What do you think I am, Smith? A fool? I knew there was a great deal Stephen hadn't explained yet. I'd have gotten it out of him eventually—and painlessly, damn you—leaving his pride, and a whole lot else, intact.''

He reached around her and picked up Stephen's resignation. ''This—'' He waved it in front of her face. ''Is a crock of shit, as I'd have realized if those damned opal eyes hadn't been staring at me. He knew you—and if not you, the 'NetAT— would refuse to accept it.''

''You could make that argument for anyone at any time.''

''Hell if I could. He *can't* resign, Cantrell. Danislav doesn't own him; hasn't since Stephen signed up for 'Net studies.''

''What do you mean?''

''Once you enter that program, you're 'NetAT. No way not, and Stephen knows it.''

''What makes you so sure?''

''Hell, he had to sign the same fucking contract I did— everyone does.''

''And is this—'' She tapped the scattered stack of notes and maps. ''—a 'crock of shit' as well?''

''He's probably known all along—at least since Nayati hooked him into the Cocheta VRT. He *knows* how and when to release information, Cantrell. Was probably saving this bit to sell to the highest Vandereaux bidder.''

''So why sell it to us so cheaply?''

''Cheaply? He's got *you* believing his fairy story, doesn't he? Is that cheap?''

''Why'd he run? Why almost kill himself?''

''The man's insane, Cantrell! He said it himself: a spaced-out Doxie. Just another of his damned manipulative—'' And with another of his lightning leaps of conversational logic:

"You notice his getup just now? Sexless as a kitten: big sweater, loose slacks. When, in all the time you've known him, have you seen him dress like that?"

"What difference—"

"A hell of a lot. I called him on his clothes last night—told him if he was going to advertise, he'd best be ready to sell."

"That might just make me change my clothes too, Smith."

"He wasn't taking my advice, woman, he realized he'd overplayed his hand and was throwing my words in my face— challenging me to disbelieve him. And it's not just the damn clothes. It's *him*. He knows precisely what he's transmitting— can go from whore to angel in a microsecond without a stitch on."

The man was a program on continuous loop with only one keyword. She went to the door and opened it. "Go to bed, doctor. Sleep content in your conviction that you've exposed the devious manipulator. Rest assured I'll keep a close eye on him and not let him destroy the Alliance single-handedly. Don't even trouble yourself that the offer he just made—which I shall undoubtedly be compelled to take him up on: it *is* on official record—will more than likely destroy one of the brightest, gentlest minds I've ever known.

"Personally, I choose to believe the person who wrote that resignation wrote it in all sincerity, and if you think he was unaware of the risks to himself, his career and his mind, then you truly don't know him at all. He had protection when he came here, Smith—the academy had taught him not to care, not to hope. You've stripped that protection from him. But don't worry, the last thing he'll ever do is blame you."

"Why the hell should I—"

"I haven't the ability to protect him—of necessity, my scope is larger. To concentrate on one troublesome and very troubled boy might well undermine what else I might accomplish. If I'm wrong and you're right, who's been hurt? Stephen will make his report, we'll scan him under Dep—thoroughly—and either the 'NetAT will absorb him or his 'Doxie friends can have him back. If you're wrong and I'm right, even if Stephen Ridenour's mind survives his 'NetAT report, I very much doubt his soul will survive Shapoorian's talons.''

His jaw tightened. ''Ask me if I give a shit. He should be put away—for his own sake as well as others. You heard him, Cantrell. He's burned out. Totally. Yet *look* how everyone reacts to him. Hell, for all I know, it's *all* Eudoxin—maybe the clone *exhales* the shit.''

Smith was making no effort to leave, for all she'd invited him out, was shaking with pent-up emotion.

''You know, Smith,'' she said cautiously, watching his pupils, ''you're a fake. Your problem isn't that you don't give a shit, it's that you care too God damn much. You *want* to believe it was Eudoxin that made you react to the boy, because, if it wasn't, you've got to admit that you care. That you care so deeply, you could no more refuse once he'd asked than you could crash the 'Net. You're a blowhard, Smith. You've isolated yourself here because if you were back in Vandereaux, you'd have to *do* something about all the things you despise. You're fighting what you *know* is true about Stephen, because if you've *seen* all there is, that boy is in deep trouble and *you* have to do something to help him.''

He was frowning. Hard.

Cantrell waited, suspecting where Smith's own delusions of knighthood were leading him. He was a scoundrel of the first water, but he was honest—as far as his own existential sense of reality allowed. And he *wasn't* one to hide behind a false sense of personal injustice.

In many ways (frightening thought) she and Smith were a lot alike.

''Danislav would know,'' he said, suddenly, and she stopped a grin just in time.

She'd had a bellyful of Victor Danislav's holier-than-thouism when she'd met him at Vandereaux. She'd love the chance to throw that purism in his face—

—And she and Smith were very much alike.

He made the door in two long strides, slammed it shut. "I have an idea."

She leaned her shoulder against the wall, arms crossed, making him the subject of a carefully calculating scan. He didn't flinch.

Finally, she pulled away from the wall, gestured toward the table with her chin. "Let's talk, Galahad."

Lexi found the boy tucked in among the rocks in the Researcher Condo's central atrium, a single fish nibbling at the lax hand drifting in the clear water. She'd had a brother once, about Stephen's age when she saw him last, and with almost as good a talent at disappearing when life grew complicated.

"Stephen?" She laid a hand on his knee, the only part that wouldn't fit conveniently into the niche he'd found. "Come, lad, time for bed."

He failed to respond; she gave the knee a shake. It tucked up, the hand trailed along the side of a blue and green spotted fish, pulled out of the water and joined the knee inside the shadow. "Go away, Lexi. I can put myself to bed, thank you."

"And lose my job? You'll fall asleep here and fall into the pool and drown. Then they'll have a search party out for you in the morning and it's Goodbye, Lexi."

An almost chuckle escaped from under the hanging vines and a hand reached up to her. She grasped it and pulled him to his feet.

They wandered toward the staircase, their progress delayed every few steps while Stephen stooped to examine some new stone or fish or plant, touching with gentle fingertips, inhaling deeply. Lexi recognized the symptoms—she'd done much the same thing the night before she left Venezia for good—and gave him as much time as he wanted.

As they headed up the winding staircase, she asked, "I understand there's an impromptu bash getting going at the *Watering Hole:* Ms. Tyeewapi and her brother, Mr. Hatawa, some of the other locals, a bunch of *Cetacean* personnel—"

Even the 'NetAT police had landed there, though she wasn't about to tell Stephen that. "Mostly just a friendly community drunk, I'd guess. We've all certainly earned it. Interested?"

Stephen smiled, but shook his head. "Thanks anyway. I'm—pretty tired. Didn't get much in the way of sleep last night. Think I'll just—pack it in."

He stopped and leaned on the balcony railing, staring out across the sparkling garden. His breath caught, and he lowered his head into his arms.

"O God, I'm tired. I'm so tired. I've ruined one world, don't let me make a mess of things for this one too."

Not meant for her—but she answered it anyway. Leaning on the rail beside him, she said, "You've done pretty well so far, Zivon Ryevanishov. Going to fall to pieces on us now? When we need you most?"

His head lifted. Tortured, swimming eyes turned to her. He struggled to respond, his mouth moving soundlessly.

"That's good, boy. Imitating the fish, are you? I doubt, however, the Council will be impressed."

A gulp, then: "Wh—what the hell are you talking about?"

She smiled. "Better, Zivon. Much better. For a long time, survival was the key: survive with enough of your heart to care, enough of your wit to stay sane, enough of your brain to know friend from foe and when and how to attack. Because you have survived, now is the time to fight back. To get the records straight, and to use what has been done to us—*us*, Zivon, not just you—to achieve justice. This particular round started with you. Spread it now to HuteNamid. Start with the specifics—the rest will follow."

"I—I wasn't about to run away, Lexi."

"I know that. But sometimes the fight gets to be very, very hard, and we have to be reminded there's good reason for the hurt. And sometimes we take responsibility for what isn't our fault at all. You didn't cause the downfall of Rostov, nor have you the sole responsibility to protect HuteNamid. But you can, and will, be spokesman for a lot of very fine people in a short time. What I'm asking you is much harder than not running away now. I'm asking you to come back. Try to survive—deserve to live.''

"That's what Nayati said."

"Well, for once, Nayati was right."

A reluctant smile— "Because he agreed with you?"

"Absolutely." She winked and looked back out over the garden.

"Lexi, why'd you let me go?"

"Let you go? Go where?"

"That night in the tunnel. You never did answer me. You let me get away, let me follow Cantrell. I *could* have been crazy. I *could* have killed someone—perhaps you. You certainly risked your whole career. Why?"

"Because, Zivon Stefanovich, the way I figured, you had a reason for wanting to go with the admiral into the mountain. If your reason was legit, for her sake, you should go. If you were Nayati's man . . . well, I figured I wanted to know that *before* you were back on *Cetacean*. Either way, for the admiral's sake, it was worth the risk."

A long stare ended in a cryptic: "I guess we all need someone worth the risk, don't we?" He scanned the atrium one more time, then turned and started down the hall to his room.

"Stephen?" she called softly as he reached his door.

He paused.

"I'm glad it worked out the way it did. You're a good man to have on our side."

His door slid open. "Good night, Lexi."

iv

Cool breeze across bare skin: the blanket had slipped.

Stephen released the pillow to pull the quilt back into place. Something warm and soft tapped his fingers, followed by something small, cold and wet.

In the instant of startled immobility, a low rumbling vibration near his ear halted his instinctive recoil. Only one thing he knew sounded like that.

He rolled carefully onto his back and met two very wise, very earnest gold eyes surrounded by sky-blue fluff. "Well, hello there, Fuzzybutt. How did you get in?"

The rumbling grew louder. Four feet crawled one at a careful time onto his chest and began massaging rhythmically, sharp claws halting just short of penetration. When the *pii'chum* determined his skin suitably prepared, he settled with a maximum of sinuosity into a fluffy lump and stared unblinking at him. Propping his elbow on the pillow at his side, he scratched it behind its small, rounded ears and then rubbed it gently under the chin. As it stretched its neck out, the better to accommodate him, Stephen felt last night's tranquillity settle over him once again.

One small part of him clung stubbornly to the future. That portion remembered his original reasons for agreeing to come here and cherished the hope that somewhere, still, there was a spot in the 'NetAT for him; he could still catalog and track with the best—a screwed-up mind shouldn't affect those lower functions.

Another, much larger portion, which should have been terrified, was merely curious. Curious about what would happen at the upcoming 'NetAT hearings, and the subsequent Council inquiry. He'd have answers for them. Perhaps not what they wanted to hear, but truths all the same. Following his meeting with the Combined Council, Cantrell would scan his mind, and then—

Then, he'd either be on the 'Net picking virtual petunias under the Philosophies of the 'Net flag, or scrubbing floors in the 'NetAT rest rooms.

Either way, he'd never be Lexi's spokesman: whether or not the 'NetAT believed him, he'd be under their security lock for as long as he lived. . . . Which, considering the bloody warnings of late, might not be all that long anyway.

The *pii' chum*'s low rumble increased; he pressed his head up hard against Stephen's hand, demanding attention.

Wesley didn't believe him; likely the Council wouldn't either—without proof. Bottom line, he *knew* what he'd done. By the time he got back to Vandereaux, the 'NetAT would be well aware of his repairwork on the 'Net. They'd try to figure out how he'd done it and there'd be no way to tell them. He'd have to reenter to prove his point, and once in, he very much doubted—without that physical touch of his Host to call him back—that he'd ever care enough to return to RealSpace.

There were worse deaths.

Might even be interesting, in the long run. Perhaps he could program a virtual Wesley into one of the academy's VRTs. Perhaps simulate Wesley's Touch.

Then he remembered the Awareness, the lesson of the Mirrors. It wouldn't work. It wasn't the physical Touch he picked up on, it was all the rest that made up Wesley Smith. Mostly, it was Wesley's caring—the sense of *just because*— that no part of him—not Zivon, not the Ridenour, not the Other—could ignore.

By leaving now, he ensured the safety of that Host. If he remained, one day the temptation would overwhelm him, and that vampiric leech he had become would destroy Wesley.

Not so bad an accomplishment for a lifetime. Save a star-spanning economy and the one individual vital to that economy in one act. Alliance needed Wesley now more than ever—they just needed the time to realize it. He'd given them the time. Given Wesley the time. Wesley would do the right thing—once he'd made his point, once the Combined Council came begging— and of the two of them, Wesley was by far the more useful. RealSpace was important to Wesley.

And Wesley's safety was vitally important—to himself and to the Alliance. Like Lexi, *he* needed someone worth the struggle. He didn't really care what happened to Alliance—that obscure entity had never really mattered—but Wesley did matter. His own sense of justice did. And he had to prove—if only to himself—that this time, he *was* in control.

With his own peculiar sense of immediacy, Fuzzybutt leapt from his chest to the foot of the bed and over the rail in a mist of floating blue fur, a half-dozen hairs settling on his still-raised hand. The *pii'chum* of his dreamworld had left no such calling card—possibly because he'd never before noticed. He wondered, if he reentered that place now, would its *pii'chum* shed?

A persistent scratching roused him from the bed. He opened the door and the *pii'chum* streaked its way down the hall, disappearing around the corner, white-tipped tail flicking impudently.

Turning back to the room, he leaned the door closed. 10:13. So why hadn't anyone called yet?

Then he remembered the party he'd purposely avoided. More than likely, everyone was still sleeping it off and the scheduled liftoff had been postponed.

He showered, dressed, and packed the duffel.

Past 11:00 and still no call.

He went to the terminal and tried calling TJ: better to wake him than the admiral. As the system tracked him down, Stephen noticed an envelope propped against the window with his name handwritten on it.

The script was typical Wesley—hurried and flamboyant:

Party time, brat. Up to my armpits in hot bubbling water. Pack up your birthday suit and hop the first train outta town...

Wesley's invitation to join him and Anevai in Acoma. It had been here all along. He hadn't forgotten. Hadn't meant to leave him...

He folded the note carefully and slipped it into a back pocket as the terminal alert sounded: the computer had located TJ.

>SecOp Tomas J. Briggs—location: Tunica Air&Space/ status of call: inaccessible.

The spaceport? Why? And with whom?

>*Call and search request: SpecOp Admiral Loren Cantrell.*

And moments later:

>**SpecOp Admiral Loren Cantrell—location: Tunica Air& Space/status of call: inaccessible.**

Oh God. *Oh my God!*

A slow panic set in on the heels of gut-level premonition. Stephen called up the scheduled shuttle flight plan:

>**STD: 1130LPT \ ETA: 1435LPT.**

And *Cetacean's*:

>**SYS \ ETD: 1500LPT.**

Snatching his duffel off the bed, Stephen ran for the lift.

Outside, on the airport tarmac, maintenance crew scurried about the shuttle, like chicks around a hen.

"Well, Paul," Loren said, standing at his side before the wall of windows watching the activity. "Last call. Want to change your mind and come along?"

Paul shook his head. "Not a chance."

"Going to miss out on a high-speed, deep-system pickup."

"I'll survive. —Any word yet on what happened?"

Loren looked at TJ. TJ looked at Lexi. Lexi looked—at the floor.

"What's that supposed to mean?"

"Well, Paul." TJ inhaled, blew it out in cheek-puffing bursts. "You know how it is with these prototypes. Ghosty problems. Never quite know when a . . . whigmaleery's going to go . . . kerwhacky."

"Ker—whacky." Paul raised an eyebrow. "Convenient timing, don't you think? Might have caused problems, their getting back first."

"Still could," TJ said seriously, "when the 'NetAT hears *their* side."

"At least, this way, you'll be there when it happens."

"Might actually be fun." Loren grinned wickedly. "They're such delightfully sanctimonious scoundrels, and if they really are Shapoorian's, we could have a real chance at her at last. So whaddaya say, Old Man?''

''Not even that tempts me anymore.'' He took her hand and squeezed it. ''It's been wonderful seeing you again, Loro, but we've changed. Besides, I've got some caves to look into.''

''Came through, didn't he?''

''Wish I could figure how he did it.''

''That's one reason you've got him. Just don't kill the patient to find the cure, promise?''

''Anevai'll wring my neck if I bend a hair on his head.''

''Speaking of—'' Loren turned to Lexi Fonteccio. ''Go give those two the high-sign, will you, Lexi? Five minutes, no more. I want to get out on schedule.''

Lexi nodded and disappeared into the hallway.

TJ eyed the two of them, and held out his hand. ''Paul, take care of yourself.''

Paul nodded, grasped the hand briefly but warmly. ''Not as if you won't be back.''

TJ nodded, and disappeared down the boarding tube, leaving Loren and him to a private farewell.

''Don't count on it, Paul,'' Loren said.

''You've got to come back. Council will want their own specialists involved in the excavations. Somebody's got to bring them back.''

Not to mention one crazed 'NetHead. He *still* wondered how Loren had talked Wesley into it.

Loren was shaking her head. ''Ferrying expert personnel's a bit too—mundane for *Cetacean*.''

''Mundane?'' He laughed. ''Seems to me, this particular little jaunt began as personnel transfer. You agreed to it.''

''Oh, no.'' She faced him and set her hands on his shoulders. ''Even Council had to come up with better bait than that to reconcile us to this job.''

''Oh, yeah?'' He wrapped his arms around her hips and swayed against her. ''And what might that have been?''

* * *

The shuttle's engines were warming, all her passengers, save a select few, long since boarded. The only people remaining in the lounge were Dr. Paul and the admiral. They were—saying goodbye. Sgt. Fonteccio, standing on Wesley's far side, coughed discreetly.

A slight flurry of hands, and Cantrell broke away, laughing. "Smith, you ready?"

"As I'll ever be," Wesley answered, and out of the side of his mouth, without even looking at her: "Looks like we're going to make a clean getaway after all. He's your problem now, girl."

"Still doesn't seem fair." Anevai looked from Wesley to Cantrell to Paul, hoping to find one who agreed with her.

Paul shrugged. He'd already refused any responsibility for the whole affair. Wesley set his jaw and avoided her. Cantrell said:

"It isn't, Anevai, but it's the only way. Trust me on this."

She raised her chin and stared straight at Cantrell, unwilling to accept the answer. Cantrell looked startled then thoughtful.

"Forgive me. You've earned a better answer than that."

Her backbone relaxed. "So?"

"Stephen could be in a lot of trouble if he goes back, Anevai. You ask him. Let him tell how much he wants you to know. He needs time. Time to heal. Time to decide what he wants to do. We're trying to give him that time."

She scowled at them all. "You could have asked him if *he* wanted it."

"I thought you were explaining to her," Cantrell said to Wesley.

Wesley shoved his hands in his pockets and glared at the floor.

Cantrell shook her head. "Not on this. He hasn't the perspective. And neither, my young friend, have you. Talk about it. Get him to. Perhaps, together, you can find that perspective." She tapped an acknowledgement on her beeper. "Last call. Let's go, Smith."

"Loro?" Paul said.

Cantrell looked him in the eyes, her serious look lightening. He held out his arms.

"Bait's always here."

The smile widened into a grin. "I'll remember that, Paul. —Anevai, we'll meet again."

"Admiral."

Cantrell nodded. "Let's go, Smith." And headed down the boarding tube.

Wesley glared up from under his brows. A glare that travelled from herself to Paul, and back to the floor. "Yeah, well, hahstee later, folks." And, turning on his heel, he strode for the tube.

"Wes?" Anevai called after him hesitantly.

Wesley's stride lengthened.

"Dammit, Smith!" Anevai chased after Wesley, grabbed his arm and set her heels.

He spun off balance and slammed into the wall, arms up as if to strike back.

She slipped in under the blow, grabbed him, and hugged him—tight. His arms closed briefly, before he shoved her away, pressing something into her hand.

And then he was gone.

Her fist closed. Paper crumpled.

A letter. Addressed to Stephen.

"Anevai?" Dr. Paul's voice. And it was Dr. Paul's hands that closed on her shoulders. "What's that?"

Dr. Paul, who had been willing to let Wesley leave without so much as a handshake. Who had let Cantrell and Wesley determine Stephen's future without so much as an argument.

"It's for Stephen." She eluded him and went to the window to wave, just in case Wesley could see her. The letter slipped free and fluttered to the floor. She stopped it with a toe and picked it up, half tempted to break the seal and check it out before deciding whether or not to give it to Stephen.

But if Wesley wanted her to know what was in that letter,

he'd have told her—maybe even shown it to her. Whatever it contained, it was between him and Stephen.

At least he hadn't left without giving Stephen some sort of explanation. Strange, though, that he hadn't simply given it to her to begin with. Maybe . . . a spark of hope, faith in her friend restored . . . . maybe he'd been hoping all along Stephen *would* get there before they left. That he'd have the chance to explain in person.

But Stephen hadn't, and he hadn't, so now it was up to her to play messenger. She folded the envelope in half and put it into her pocket for safe-keeping.

The shuttle paused for its final check.

Rapid staccato of running feet in the corridor.

The shuttle began its takeoff run.

Stephen burst around the corner and skidded to a halt by the window just as the great ship lifted majestically from the ground.

He reached a thin, shaking hand to the window, then let it fall, quietly watching the rapidly shrinking shuttle until it disappeared behind puffy white clouds.

Anevai exchanged a glance with Dr. Paul; he gestured toward Stephen with a minuscule nod of his head.

Sure, why not? She should have known he'd leave it to her to fix.

But then again, who else was there?

Her touch didn't surprise him. He knew she was there—had seen her as he stumbled into the waiting room—knew that sooner or later his privacy would be assaulted. But as he turned to Anevai, Stephen realized that he wanted her there. Wanted someone who could tell him . . .

"Why, Anevai? Why did they leave me?"

She pulled a letter from her pocket, handed it to him wordlessly.

"Wesley . . . ?" He looked at her for some explanation.

Confused. Her face gave him no clue. He slipped the seal:
"What has Wesley to do with..."

Dr. Ridenour:

I owe you an apology for my behavior of the past two
days. Whether my assessment of your actions was correct
or not is not the issue. My high-handed actions based on
those assumptions is. I had no right to accuse you as I did
and humbly beg your apology.

If I was correct, I trust you understand the reason for the
action I am taking now: HuteNamid does not need a
representative with questionable—perhaps purchasable—
motives.

On the other hand, if you are, as the admiral maintains,
innocent of the sort of exploitation I fear, I beg your
forgiveness with all my heart. If you are, indeed, the
Stephen Ridenour I thought I knew, then you may not
understand why we've made this decision without consult-
ing you, nor, possibly, what the true ramifications may be.

If the former is the case, as I still fear it is, then this
letter is at an end. I repeat myself: you can go to hell. You
have a sweeter prison than you deserve. Sakiimagan will
keep you under constant surveillance until the Combined
Council decision is made regarding both the fate of
HuteNamid's Cocheta and you.

If, as I hope to God is the case, you are indeed the rare
gem I believed I'd discovered, please believe that I said and
acted as I did because of what I thought you'd taken away
from me. That I could suspect such motives of you is
because they are far too real in this universe and I've seen
much more of them than I have honesty and innocence.

If you can't find it in you to forgive me, at least listen
to me one last time. I am *not* replacing you because of any
lack in your ability. I am going in your stead, my friend,
because of the non-Council non-'NetAT pressure which will
be part and parcel of this—inquisition. If we'd all used the
sense God gave us, we would have discussed this option long

before we all made fools of ourselves and hurt one another so profoundly.

Because of my meddling, you have been put in a position you are now ill-equipped to handle. You know damn well what a session under Deprivil would do to you, and I would never forgive myself for making you attempt it.

Your experiences at the academy should prove more than sufficient to free you of Danislav's representation. What happened to you here on HuteNamid is more than sufficient grounds to leave you here until I can see our way around those legalities. You see, I do have the connections—and the will—to do for you what you refuse to do for yourself.

So I leave you in the hands of the finest people I've met in the Alliance. If I have read you wrong and you can't be happy here, I ask you to forgive me in this as well. If you cannot be happy here, at least you will be alive and safe.

And that's important to me, Stephen. Somebody told me once he'd do anything to keep me safe, because he didn't want to be alone in the universe.

Well, son, neither do I.

Anevai stood helplessly at Stephen's side as he scanned the letter once, then flipped back and read it again, more slowly, and again until he had to stop to blink his eyes clear. Then he turned to the sky into which the shuttle had long since disappeared.

"Damn you, Smith," he whispered. "You've got a hell of a nerve. You make it back here or I'll—"

She slipped a hand around his waist, relieved to see the spark back in the spook-eyes. "You'll what, Ridenour?"

Long fingers clenched. Paper crumpled. He smoothed the letter deliberately, and returned it to the envelope. Folded it and stuck it back into his pocket.

Epilogue

Eagle's Beak Lookout: *her* place; no one else would *dare* invade it.

Anevai pulled herself up over the lip and reached to help Stephen. His hand clasped hers, strong and sure, and with a gasping *Thanks* he joined her on the ledge.

It wasn't an easy climb, but she'd brought Stephen here anyway, offering him the only escape she could think of from her friends' well-meaning inquisition. They quite understandably wanted to know why he was still there, why Wesley wasn't and why the station cargo shuttle had shown up with two big trunks and a suitcase destined for Stephen's room.

She flopped down and hung her feet over the rim, letting Stephen look his fill. She loved it here. There was no higher spot overlooking the rift and while the wind usually threatened to blow you away, it made you feel as if you'd fly instead. Stephen's expression, as he stood gazing out over the rift, breathing hard, the unseasonably warm wind whipping his hair and plastering his shirt to his body, was all the payment she needed for this violation of her secret sanctuary.

She grinned up at him.

He smiled back, looked beyond her into the valley, and swayed, his face turning whiter than ever. She grabbed his hand and said, "Sit!"

He eased down beside her, finding a spot that didn't hurt, he said, laughingly, which wasn't surprising, when you were skin hung on a skeleton. And that wasn't all that was bothering him. Given time and rest, perhaps they could even do something about that. Sometimes the old ways were best.

She brushed the hair out of his eyes and said, "Get that skin tanned a bit so you don't fry, grow your hair out to human length, and you'll be passably good-looking, Ridenour."

"Thank you, Ms. Tyeewapi." His soft voice held a note of real humor, as if he might be relaxing at last; it was real hard to stay tense when every muscle was exhausted. "Is it possible I might yet make some headway in your favors?"

She giggled, saying, "You sure do talk funny, Dr. Ridenour, sir. My favors, so to speak, is already spoken fer—"

His face fell. She put a hand on either side of his face, kissed him on the nose, then leaned her forehead on his, crossed eyes meeting crossed eyes.

"And a great big chunk of them already belongs to one funny-looking pale-skin with too-short hair. You might be able to claim a few of his."

She released him with another light kiss—not on the nose—and said, "I made something for you."

His head cocked to the side, puzzled. "Why?"

"Missed your birthday, didn't I?"

"My—*birthday?* What's my—"

She laughed outright. "Never mind, Ridenour, never mind. Here. Your first official item of gen-u-ine Re-con attire."

She pulled the small package from her pocket and handed it to him. He held it for a long moment, just looking at it, touching the rather crumpled folds with his fingertips, while the diffraction ribbon curls blew in the wind, throwing tiny rainbows across his hand.

His mouth quirked. "Prezzies?"

"Prezzies."

He took a long, shaky breath and worked the ribbon free, tying it carefully around her braid—so not to lose it, he said—and began turning the folds back. Slowly, deliberately easing the tape, smoothing the crumples.

Of a sudden, she realized how long it had probably been since he'd received a present—there'd been no one at the academy likely to throw him a birthday party—and here she was, casually tossing it at him like it meant nothing to her to give it or for him to receive it.

With the final fold still to go, she closed her hands over his.

"Before you look at it, I want you to know, there are only three like it in the entire universe. One here—" She caressed his hands. "One here—" She tapped her carefully covered throat. "And one someplace—" She waved her hand toward the sky. "—out there."

Stephen's sparkling spook-eyes followed that gesture.

"W–Wesley?" he whispered.

She nodded, and drew back the final fold for him. In his hands, silver and polished stone formed a pattern of blue, silver and red. An ancient pattern with her own unique touch: at its center, a bright, twinkling, crystal button.